W9-CJS-288

A NOVEL BY
HAROLD ROBBINS

Descent from Xanadu

SIMON AND SCHUSTER
New York

Copyright © 1984 by Harold Robbins
All rights reserved
including the right of reproduction
in whole or in part in any form
Published by Simon and Schuster and Pocket Books
Divisions of Simon & Schuster, Inc.
Rockefeller Center
1230 Avenue of the Americas
New York, New York 10020
SIMON AND SCHUSTER and colophon are registered trademarks of Simon & Schuster, Inc.
Manufactured in the United States of America

In Xanadu did Kubla Khan
  A stately pleasure-dome decree:
Where Alph, the sacred river, ran
Through caverns measureless to man
  Down to a sunless sea.
So twice five miles of fertile ground
With walls and towers were girdled round:
      . . . .

That sunny dome! those caves of ice!
And all who heard should see them there,
And all should cry, Beware! Beware!
His flashing eyes, his floating hair!
Weave a circle round him thrice,
  And close your eyes with holy dread,
  For he on honey-dew hath fed,
And drunk the milk of Paradise.

> "Kubla Khan"
> SAMUEL TAYLOR COLERIDGE

BOOK ONE

The Search

1976–1980

1

◆ THE TINY DOCTOR, hidden by tinted European eyeglasses, rose from her desk to face the windows. She gestured to him.

He towered above her, then followed her hand to a giant fountain in the expanse of green-blue grass.

"Do you know what that fountain is, Mr. Crane?" she asked in her mid-European accent.

He nodded. "Of course, Dr. Zabiski. The fountain of Ponce de Leon."

She looked up at him. "It's a legend, Mr. Crane. An allegory. It's not a reality. There has never been a reality like that."

He was silent for a moment. "I know that too, Dr. Zabiski," he said.

She went to her desk and sat in her chair and waited until he was seated opposite her. She held her tinted eyeglasses in her right hand, then placed them on the desk in front of her. "You have dark cobalt-blue eyes," she said.

A faint smile crossed his lips. "And yours are tawny yellow-brown, almost like a cat's."

She met his gaze directly. "If it's immortality you seek here, Mr. Crane," she said in a soft voice, "you've wasted your time."

His gaze had not changed. "That's not what I heard."

"Then you've heard incorrectly," she said.

His expression did not change. "Twenty million dollars incorrectly?"

The tinted glasses covered her eyes again. "I guess what I've heard is true," she said. "You are one of the richest men in the world."

"Now you have heard incorrectly," he said softly. "I am the richest man in the world."

She tilted her head. "More than the Saudi king, Getty, Ludwig, Hughes?"

"They're all like children playing games," he said. "With a snap of my fingers I can take away their marbles."

"Then there is only one game left for you to play," she said. "Immortality."

"It's the last game, Doctor. We've played the space game and we've won it. The ocean depth game—we've won that, too. Speed, height, depth, you name it, we've won them all. And I've played all the other games. Money, power, sex. I love them and I play them all the time, but those are children's games. I'm going for the big one. Immortality. I want to be the first man to live forever."

"You don't want much! Only something that no man has ever achieved." She watched his eyes carefully. They never changed focus or expression. "But do you believe me when I tell you I have not been able to achieve it either?"

"I believe you," he said.

She hesitated. "Then I don't understand," she said. "What do you expect of me?"

"Nothing," he said quietly. "Everything. You have come closer to what I want than anyone in the world."

"I've had success in some cases of geriatric retardation. Nothing in geriatric arrestation. That's not immortality."

"But you helped many important people," he said.

She allowed herself a small modest smile. "That's true. And I like to feel I've helped them. *Der Alte* who came here from Germany, the Pope from Rome, even Stalin from Moscow. But in time—they all died."

"But they came here. All of them. And they did get something."

She nodded slowly. "In each case, the quality of their lives got better whatever their age."

"Mentally and physically?" It was almost more a statement than a question.

"Yes," she said. "But finally they died."

He looked at her. "On average, how much time do you think you gave them?"

She held up her hands. "I don't know. There were many factors. Not only their ages, and the time they came to me for

4

treatment." Again she hesitated. "There are some who do not respond to my treatment at all. There are no guarantees."

"If I respond to your treatment, what might I expect?"

"On average?" She was thoughtful for a moment. "You're forty-two now?"

He nodded.

"In eight years, in 1984, at age fifty, geriatrically you would be forty-five; at sixty, geriatrically fifty-two; at seventy, perhaps sixty and at eighty, possibly sixty-four to sixty-six." She paused, then continued. "That, of course, assumes you continue the program to its conclusion."

"That's to the end of my life?" he said.

"This is a life program, Mr. Crane," she nodded. "To begin with, you'll require a two-month stay here while we determine whether you will respond to our treatment. Then if we determine there is a likelihood of a favorable response, you'll have to spend one week here every third month for the treatment itself."

He smiled, not unpleasantly. "Dr. Zabiski, say that I do continue for the whole term of treatment, what happens to you?"

She smiled in return. "I will have long been dead. But that is not important. The treatment will continue."

He was silent for a moment. "Adding to the treatment time, I'll have to manage two more weeks for travel to come here. That will come to almost two months a year of my time. I'd have no way to take care of my affairs."

"That has to be your decision, Mr. Crane."

"Is there some way the treatments can be brought to me?"

She shook her head. "I'm sorry, Mr. Crane. It has taken me thirty years to develop this complex and it's the only one in the world."

"Drs. Aslam, Filatov and Niehans export their treatments," he said. "And you include some of their methodology in your own."

She agreed. "That's right."

"Then what's the secret ingredient you so guard that it cannot go elsewhere in the world?"

She half-smiled. "The secret ingredient, Mr. Crane, as you say, is you."

"I don't understand."

"I think you do, Mr. Crane," she said.

"I know all the theories," he said frankly. "I know you incorporated the procaine, magnesium and minerals of Aslam, the fresh placenta implants of Filatov and the unborn ewe cells injected by Niehans. I sometimes even think you've made them into one formula. But that would be much too simple. That's why I think there is a secret ingredient."

"You have not listened to me, Mr. Crane," she said patiently. "I have already told you that the secret ingredient is you."

He stared intently at her.

She was silent.

His voice was hushed. "Cloning?"

She remained silent.

"Implantation of living cloned cells from the body's own reservoir." His cobalt-blue eyes seemed to turn into the color of a night sky. "That's never been successful with humans."

For the first time in her life she felt fear, as though a chill wind was blowing through her body. Her voice was almost trembling. "Mr. Crane, I have other patients I must attend to."

He remained silent.

"But perhaps we may make another appointment tomorrow," she said.

His voice was thoughtful. "Tomorrow I will be in Pekin."

"Another time then," she said.

He rose from his chair. "Twenty million dollars will not be enough; I see that now," he said. "Fifty million dollars? Would that be enough?"

She looked up at him. "You don't understand, Mr. Crane," she said. "Money is not important. This is a socialist country. Everything here belongs to the state."

"Then forget the word 'money' and put in its place the word, 'priorities'" he said. "Each country has its own priorities and its own order."

"Now, you've lost me, Mr. Crane," she said.

He smiled. "You're a doctor and a scientist, Dr. Zabiski, and you understand your profession. Please allow me, my profession is in the trading of priorities." He held his hand out to her. "Thank you for your time, Dr. Zabiski."

Her hand was firm and warm. "I will always be at your service,

6

Mr. Crane," she nodded, and smiled although he had not expected it. She escorted him to the door. "Good-bye, Mr. Crane."

He stood there in the open doorway. "You're a great lady," he said. *"Auf wiedersehen,* Dr. Zabiski."

THE PRIVATE DOOR to her office opened as soon as Judd had gone. The tall Russian, his face strong with authority, reached her almost before she went behind her desk. An attractive young woman wearing a white lab coat followed him and closed the door behind them.

Zabiski slipped into her chair. "What do you think of him?" she asked.

The tall Russian swore. "The egotistic pig! He thinks his money can buy everything."

The young woman looked down at the seated doctor. "I thought he was quite attractive," she said. "And I have a feeling that he is very intelligent."

Zabiski looked across her desk at the man. "Don't underestimate him, Comrade Nicolai," the little doctor said. "He is very smart. See how quickly he seized on parts of our methodology."

"That doesn't matter, Comrade Doctor," Nicolai said. "You must make sure that he doesn't get away from us."

"What makes him so important to us?" Zabiski asked. "To me, he is just another man that wants to extend his life span. Exactly like many others who pass through this clinic."

Nicolai stared at her. When he spoke, it was as if to a child. "Crane Industries is not only the largest industrial complex in the world, it is also the biggest supplier of a range of products to the U.S. government. From office supplies, to medical, to aerospace and heavy armament.

"For many years we have attempted to infiltrate the executive level of that company. But it has been impossible. Because Judd Crane himself owns and operates it alone. He makes all the decisions and his assistants only carry out his orders. Any person who can get next to him cannot help but learn more about the policies and plans of the United States than perhaps is known by the President of the United States himself."

Dr. Zabiski stared up at him. "If you expect me to be that person, you're making a big mistake. If he wants me to go with him and work with him, that's impossible. I'm too old and not able to keep up with him physically."

"We don't expect you to do the physical work. We want you to convince him that you will cooperate with him. You will then assign Sofia to act as your surrogate. She has the legitimate credentials, both as a doctor and assistant professor of gerontology and geriatrics, and is completely competent to undertake the tests and prepare him for the treatments that you will undertake personally." He paused for a moment. "I listened to your conversation through the microphones. He wants to believe so badly that he'll accept every suggestion you offer."

Sofia turned to him. "Nicolai, he might think I am too young."

Nicolai smiled. "Don't be stupid, Sofia. Thirty isn't young. Besides you are a beautiful woman and you know how to use that. You've done it before. Just grab him by his cock."

"He's not that stupid," Sofia said, annoyed.

"We have his apartment at the hotel completely bugged," he said. "There are three whores waiting downstairs in his secretary's room for him. Of course, they are all employees of ours, but he does not know that."

"Is that all you think of me?" Sofia asked coldly. "Just another professional whore?"

Nicolai turned away brusquely. "I suggest that you meet with Crane as soon as possible," he said to Dr. Zabiski.

"I will do that, Comrade Nicolai," Zabiski said.

Nicolai looked down at her. "That crazy idea of his about cloning. Do you think it could ever happen?"

The little doctor held out her hands, palms out in question. "Who knows? One thing I know: We have many things to learn from him. Certain of our colleagues who have been in the States have told me that the Crane DNA Engineering Corporation is light-years ahead of us in DNA clone-copying and manufacturing."

Nicolai turned to Sofia. "See," he said. "That makes it even more important that you get close to him."

Sofia glanced at him contemptuously and then, silently, left the doctor's office.

SOFIA CROSSED THE corridor and went upstairs to her room. She stood looking out the window, smoking a cigarette. She was staring at the sparkling fountain when the door opened behind her. She didn't turn around.

She felt his hands rest on her shoulders. She still didn't turn. "What the hell got into you?" he asked angrily.

"Eight years," Sofia said bitterly. "But you still stay married to Ekaterina."

"I've explained that many times, Sofia," he answered, trying to mollify her. "Her father is still in the Politburo. If I divorce her, my career goes down the drain. We have to wait until Andropov makes his move, then I'll be my own man and we can be together."

She dragged at her cigarette, still silent.

His hands moved quickly behind her. Holding one arm around her waist, he pulled her back against him, with his other hand hoisting up the back of her skirt. Her thighs and buttocks were naked above the stockings. He cupped his hand over her pubis. "You're dripping wet," he said huskily.

She still didn't move. "I'm always wet," she said.

She heard the buttons of his fly snap open, then with one hand in the center of her back, he bent her over the windowsill. A moment later she felt him large and hard inside her. She gasped, the cigarette fell out the window, her hands resting against the windowsill for support. She gasped again. A mewlike groan came from her throat.

His hands grasped like vises against her hips as he rammed himself like a triphammer behind, shoving back and forth inside her. His voice was strong with triumph. "You still love it!"

She didn't answer, gasping for breath and moaning.

His fingernails dug into the skin of her hips. "Damn you!" he growled. "Tell me. You still love it!"

"Yes, yes!" she was almost screaming with pain and pleasure. "I love it!"

2

◆ HE CAME FROM the elevator and walked to the wide double doors of the penthouse and pressed the button. The chimes echoed through the closed doors. A moment later, Fast Eddie opened the door, a blue-black Colt .45 automatic in his hand.

Judd looked at the little black man as he followed him into the apartment. "Someday you're going to get a hernia, lifting a piece like that."

Fast Eddie locked the safety and shoved the gun in his belt. "Yugoslavia is the asshole of the world," he said. "Even got cockroaches under the toilet seats."

Judd nodded. "That's life," he said. "Some people have no class." He walked into the living room and stopped in front of the attaché case lying on the desk. He turned the combination locks and opened it. The bronze plaque inside was covered with red and green diodes. "Looks like a Christmas tree."

Fast Eddie nodded.

Judd turned a switch on the plaque, then pressed three buttons. Suddenly all the diodes turned to yellow. Judd smiled. "I wonder if cockroaches have broken eardrums?"

Fast Eddie laughed. "That's not my department, boss. I'm just your valet, remember."

"Then get me a drink," Judd said.

"The usual?"

"Atlanta cherry Coca-Cola with a lot of ice," Judd said.

He watched the little man walk behind the bar. "What made you so nervous?" he asked, still wondering about the automatic.

"Too much service." The little man filled the glass with ice cubes. "Three maids, one man with the vacuum cleaner, two window-washing men, an electrician, two telephone men. It was beginning to seem like O'Hare Airport." He opened a bottle of

10

Coca-Cola and filled up the glass, then brought it over carefully. "Toot?" he asked.

"Not yet," Judd said. He sipped the drink thoughtfully. He glanced at Fast Eddie. "How many rooms in this suite?"

"Five."

"Been in all of them?"

"Yes."

"The closets too?"

"No."

Judd placed his drink on the desk and lifted a small transformerlike box from the attaché case. He pressed the button on its side and cupped it in his hand. "Get your piece," he said.

Fast Eddie pulled his gun from his belt. He followed Judd through the rooms. At each closet door, Judd held the box against the door.

"That's a new one," Fast Eddie said.

"Brand-new," Judd said. "It's a heat scanner tuned to body heat. Anybody in there, we'll know about it without opening the door."

"Gadgets," Fast Eddie said. "You're cuckoo about them. Just like a kid."

It was at the room farthest from the entrance to the suite. Judd looked at the tiny quivering needle. "In there," he said.

"What do we do now?" Fast Eddie asked.

"Wait a minute," Judd said. He watched the needle for a moment. "We do nothing. This guy is already 98.2. Stupid for them to place an agent in a confined area like a closet. And even more stupid to assign an agent with a heart problem where only the slightest sonar shock would kill him."

He turned back into the living room and put the heat scanner into the attaché case, then turned off the buttons and switched off the power. The yellow diodes turned back to a red and green Christmas tree. He closed the case and turned the combination locks. He looked at Fast Eddie. "Now."

Fast Eddie pulled the gold chain from his neck and out of his shirt. He opened the gold vial with the gold spoon and held it out carefully to Judd. Judd took two healthy snorts.

Fast Eddie looked at him. "I could use one too," he said. "I'm still shaking."

"Be my guest."

Fast Eddie lived up to his name. He looked better in a second. Quickly the vial and chain disappeared. "Thanks." He looked at his boss. "Another Coca-Cola?"

"I think so," Judd said. "I think this one got a little bit flat." The telephone rang as the little man went back to the bar. "I'll get it," Judd said, picking it up. "Crane here."

"Mr. Crane, this is Dr. Zabiski." Her voice sounded more accented on the telephone. "I have had some further thoughts about our conversation."

"Yes, Doctor," he said.

"I can meet you at your hotel at twenty-one hours if that's convenient for you." Her voice echoed in the phone.

He glanced at his watch. It was six o'clock. "That would be convenient, Doctor. Perhaps you could join me at dinner?"

"I'll have my assistant with me."

"That's okay with me."

"Fine, Mr. Crane. I'll see you then. Thank you."

"Thank *you*, Doctor." He put down the receiver and looked at Fast Eddie. "What room is Merlin in?"

"Ten-oh-nine. The floor below ours."

Judd called the room. His assistant answered. "Yes, Mr. Crane?"

"Could you come right up and bring the portophone with you," Judd said.

"I still have three secretaries waiting here to be interviewed."

"We won't have the time for them," Judd said. "Pay them off and get rid of them."

"Yes, Mr. Crane. I'll take care of it right away."

Fast Eddie brought the fresh drink. He shook his head. "Too bad, Mr. Crane. That Yugoslavian pussy looked like it was prime."

Judd sipped the cold drink and laughed. "Can't win 'em all."

The portophone was in an attaché case similar to the one on the desk in front of Judd. Merlin held it as Fast Eddie opened the door for him. The little black man closed the door behind him and gestured before he could speak. Fast Eddie held an index finger across his lips, then pointed to the ceiling lights and to the telephones. Merlin nodded his head in understanding, then crossed the room to Judd.

"I have your messages, Mr. Crane," he said.

"Thank you, Merlin." Judd placed the portophone on the desk and returned the other briefcase to Merlin. He took the sheaf of messages from his assistant. "Tell the captain that we should be ready to leave shortly after midnight."

"Yes, Mr. Crane." Merlin opened the attaché case and picked up the portophone while Judd read the messages. Merlin listened to the captain and then turned to Judd. "The captain says that we'll have to make a refuel stop on the way."

"See if he can arrange it in flight," Judd said. "If we stop we could lose two, maybe three hours."

Merlin relayed his message and put down the portophone. "The captain says he'll try to arrange it."

"Good," Judd said. He returned the messages to Merlin. "We'll go over these in flight tomorrow. I have a dinner appointment with Dr. Zabiski at nine. Would you book a table at the restaurant in the hotel for us? I'll try to get in a nap and a shower before then."

"You have a seven o'clock appointment here with the under-secretary of tourism," Merlin said.

Judd made a wry smile. "There goes my nap. Guess I'll have to settle for just a shower."

"Is there anything else, sir?" Merlin said.

"I think that should cover it all. You can go back to the plane with Fast Eddie when I go down to dinner."

"Shall I check out then, sir?"

"Good idea," Judd said. "Then I could leave right from the restaurant."

"White shirt, black tie and suit, Mr. Crane?" Fast Eddie asked.

"Do we have any others?" Judd smiled.

"No, sir. But I can dream, can't I?" Even Merlin smiled. Judd had called those clothes his battle uniform. There had to be over a hundred identical black suits in Judd's closets, wherever he lived, anywhere in the world.

It was ten minutes to nine as they waited in the lobby for Dr. Zabiski. Merlin and Fast Eddie watched the bellboy carry the valises out to the limousine. "I'll keep the portophone with me," Judd said. Merlin nodded, the other attaché case in his hand.

Fast Eddie looked at his boss. "I'm worried about the suite you left behind," he said. "I think you should come to the plane with us."

"Twelve million says there won't be any problems," Judd said. "The tourism department was very happy with the four Club Adriatics and the two new hotels."

"Maybe it's not their ball game at all," Fast Eddie said. "It's some other department."

"There is only one department," Judd said. "That's the government itself. They're calling all the shots. Why do you think Zabiski called so promptly? She's been given her orders to negotiate with me. I'm not worried." He watched the revolving door at the entrance. "She's coming in now," he said. "I'll see you both at the plane." He left them standing as he walked to meet the doctor at the entrance.

A tall young woman with blond-brown hair, wearing a bad copy of a Chanel suit, came through the revolving door after the doctor. Even the bad copy of the suit could not conceal the body under it. Fast Eddie's words flashed through Crane's mind—Yugoslavian prime.

3

◆ THE LITTLE DOCTOR came directly to the point the moment the maître d' had taken the dinner orders. "Dr. Ivancich has been my first assistant for the past two years," she said. "Before that she was two years an assistant professor of gerontology at the Georgian Academy of Sciences, two years before that Doctor of Geriatric Studies at the Soviet Academy of Sciences in Moscow, before that two years in special studies at the National Institute on Aging in Baltimore. She is a graduate of Columbia University Medical School in New York."

Judd looked at the young woman. "I'm impressed," he said sincerely. "Dr. Ivancich has accomplished a great deal for someone so young."

She spoke in an American-accented English. "I'm not quite that young, Mr. Crane," she said softly. "I'm thirty."

"That's young," Judd said.

The waiter served the consommé. Judd waited until the man left the table before he began again. He looked at Dr. Zabiski. "You mentioned you had some further thoughts after our conversation."

Dr. Zabiski nodded. "If you're interested in my treatments, perhaps we could shorten the first two months to two weeks."

"How?"

"I can arrange a leave of absence for Dr. Ivancich to travel with you. In that way she could undertake the preliminary examinations and tests and could find out whether or not you will respond to our treatment."

As she was speaking, she passed a tiny piece of paper to him. Judd read it unobtrusively. It was in small handwritten pencil letters. "Destroy after reading. Dr. I. is completely trustworthy. I am very interested in your proposition."

Judd looked at her without speaking. He crumpled the paper

in his palm then popped it in his mouth. Slowly he chewed it for a moment then added several spoonfuls of his consommé and swallowed it. He smiled. "I've always enjoyed croutons."

Dr. Zabiski smiled for the first time. She nodded approvingly.

"I'm leaving this evening," Judd said. "If you let me know when Dr. Ivancich is ready, I'll arrange for us to meet wherever I'll be."

"Tonight, if you like, Mr. Crane," the little doctor said. "Her valises are in my car. I've already made my arrangements."

Judd smiled. "I knew the moment we met you were my kind of doctor." He turned to Dr. Ivancich. "I hope you enjoy travel, Doctor."

"I love it, Mr. Crane."

"Good," he said. "We'll be doing a great deal of it." He paused a moment, then added, "Dr. Ivancich is a very imposing name. What is your first name?"

"Sofia," she said.

"I'm Judd," he said. "It's very American to call each other by our first names. Would you mind, Doctor?"

"Not at all, Judd," she said with a half-smile. "After all, my mother was an American and I obtained most of my schooling in the States."

The maître d' approached the table. "There is a telephone call for you, Dr. Zabiski," he bowed.

The little doctor turned to Judd. "Could you excuse me?"

Judd nodded and rose from his seat for a moment as she left the table, then turned back to Dr. Ivancich. "You have a curious background, Sofia," he said. "America and Russia."

"Not really," she answered. "The two countries were the only ones that could afford the research and facilities in which I decided to specialize. If it hadn't been for the fact that my father spent almost twenty-five years in the UN in New York where I was born, probably none of this would have happened. It wasn't until we returned to Yugoslavia that I lived in Russia. And then only until Dr. Zabiski's work was recognized by our government, at which time I was able to come to work with her."

"That was two years ago?" he asked. "Certainly as a doctor you could have earned more money elsewhere than here in Yugoslavia."

"Probably," she said. "But, then, I would not have had the experience of working with Dr. Zabiski, who is, in my opinion, one of the true geniuses in our field."

"That's quite a compliment," Judd said.

"I believe it," she said.

From the corner of his eye, Judd saw the little doctor returning. He got to his feet. She seemed slightly pale. "Is everything all right?" he asked, as he held the chair out for her.

She looked across the table as he returned to his own chair. "Nothing important," she said. Then she looked deeply into the dark cobalt-blue of his eyes and that strange chill she felt in her office came over her again. It was as if he had invaded her mind.

She looked down at the tablecloth and placed her napkin on her lap before looking at him again. "Wouldn't it be strange," she said softly, "if we discover that death and immortality are one and the same thing?"

Death and immortality. The words echoed in the recesses of his mind. It was more than twenty years since his father had expressed to him almost exactly the same thought.

IT WAS 1956. Exactly two days after President Eisenhower had been reelected for his second term. Judd had taken the 8:02 from Boston. The day was crisp and sunny in New York and he went up the back staircase from Grand Central and walked up Park Avenue. New York was exciting and alive, the people busy and hurried. It was very different from the almost lazy pace of the Harvard campus in Cambridge. He looked at his watch. It was not yet eleven o'clock. He had time. His father had asked him to meet at his office at noon.

He was still twenty minutes early when he stood in front of the new office building and looked up at the burnished stainless steel letters over the entrance: CRANE INDUSTRIES. He walked up the steps between the two fountains and through the glass doors. Since he was still early, he leaned against the marble walls and watched the people go in and out of the building.

A few minutes later a uniformed security guard approached him. He was a burly man, self-important in his army Sam Browne leather belt and his holstered gun. "No loitering here, sonny," he said in a gruff voice.

17

"I'm not loitering," Judd said politely. "I'm early for an appointment. So I thought I'd wait here."

"Sorry, sonny," the guard said. "If you're early, come back later."

Judd shrugged. "I might as well not be early then," he said and began walking to the elevator bank which indicated the fortieth-floor express.

The guard stopped him. "They're executive floors."

"I know that," Judd said.

"Who do you have an appointment with?" he asked.

"Mr. Crane," Judd said.

The guard looked at him skeptically. He gestured to another guard standing in front of the elevator bank, who came to them. "This kid says he's got an appointment with Mr. Crane."

The second guard looked at him. "Do you have any identification on you, sir?" he asked politely.

Judd opened his jacket, the maroon sweater with the "H" crew letter over his white shirt seemed almost black in the light between the elevator banks. He took a leather billfold from his inside pocket. "Driver's license, okay?"

"Fine," the second guard nodded. He opened the billfold, looked at it, then at Judd. He folded it and handed it back.

"Sorry, Mr. Crane," he said apologetically. "We have to be careful. In the last few weeks we've had some problems with people who had no reason to be here."

"I understand," said Judd, returning his billfold to his pocket.

The second guard turned a key to the elevator bank switchboard. One of the elevator doors opened. "Forty-fifth floor, Mr. Crane," he said, stepping back.

Judd walked in and pressed the button. The doors began to close and the second guard's voice came to Judd's ears. "Asshole," he said to the first guard. "That's the boss's son, you were—"

Judd smiled to himself as the voice became lost in the rush of air as the elevator moved up. He leaned back and watched the indicator lights climb. It was five minutes to noon when he came out of the elevator.

The receptionist was waiting at the door. "Good morning, Mr. Crane," she said. "Your father is expecting you." She opened the doors to the private elevator to his father's office, the only one on the penthouse floor.

His father's secretary met him as he came from the small elevator. "Judd," she smiled.

"Miss Barrett," he said, leaning to kiss her cheek. "You're looking younger and prettier than ever."

She laughed. "That's sweet," she said warmly. "But I've known you since you were born. You don't have to give me that standard Harvard line."

"Believe me," he laughed. "I mean it. This is not Harvard." He followed her through the outer secretaries' room to her office next to his father's. "How is he?" he asked. "It's been almost six months since I've seen him."

"You know your father," she said, a strangely noncommittal sound in her voice. "He always seems the same."

He paused and looked at her. "What kind of answer is that? Is something wrong?"

She didn't speak. Instead, she opened the door to his father's office. He thought he saw her eyes glisten with moisture as he went past. She closed the door behind him.

His father was standing at the windows looking out, his back toward him. "Judd?"

"Yes, Father," Judd called from the door.

"Come here," he said, still not turning to him.

Judd came to the window and stood next to his father. They hadn't faced each other yet.

"It's very clear. You can see the Battery, Staten Island beyond, and northeast to Long Island Sound and Connecticut."

"Yes," Judd said quietly. "It's very clear."

His father paused a moment, then turned to him. He held out his hand. "You're looking well, Judd," he said.

Judd took his father's hand and, still holding it, tried to keep a lightness in his voice. "Have I grown too old to kiss my father hello?"

Suddenly his father embraced him and kissed his cheek. "Never too old, I hope," he said.

Judd returned his father's kiss. "That's better," he smiled. "I was beginning to think you didn't like me anymore."

"That's silly," his father said. "I love you, my son."

"I love you, Father."

His father stepped back. "At first I thought we'd have lunch at '21,' but then I thought it might be better if we had lunch at the office. We haven't talked for a long time and we'll be more private here."

"The office sounds good to me."

"Hungry?"

Judd smiled. "I'm always hungry."

His father pressed a button on the desk. A set of sliding doors opened and a small dining room with a round table appeared, large enough for eight but at this time only set for two. He turned to the switch at the interphone. "We're ready for lunch," he spoke into it.

He turned to Judd. "I'm having a Scotch and water. How about you?"

"Make it two," Judd said, following his father into the dining room.

A small black man in black tie came through another door into the dining room. "Mr. Crane?"

"Two usuals, Fast Eddie," Judd's father said.

The thin little man lived up to his name. The two drinks were brought from the small bar almost before they had been requested. "Fast Eddie, this is my son, Judd," his father said, taking his drink.

Fast Eddie handed Judd his drink. "My pleasure, Mr. Crane."

"Thank you," Judd said. He watched Fast Eddie disappear through the dining room door. "Cheers."

"Cheers," his father said.

They sipped their drinks. "How long has Fast Eddie been working for you, Father?" Judd asked.

"About three months. He's old Roscoe's grandson. Roscoe has been training him for two years. The kid's very good. It's hard to believe that he just turned eighteen."

"He seems nice."

"He's like his grandfather," his father said. "He's always there." His father sat down at the table. He looked at Judd opposite him. "Surprised that I called?"

20

Judd nodded.

"We have a lot to talk about." His father hesitated a moment. "Like the man said, Which do we talk about first? The good news or the bad news?"

"Whatever you think best, Father."

"Then the good news first. I've been alone since your mother passed away fifteen years ago. Sure, there have been women, but that was something else. Now, I'm getting married. And I think you'll like her too."

Judd looked at him. "If you like her, Father, that's all that's important. I'll be happy for you."

His father smiled. "You haven't even asked her name." He paused for a moment, then added, "Barbara."

Judd's voice filled with astonishment. "Miss Barrett?"

His father laughed. "Is that such a surprise?"

"Yes," Judd said, smiling. "But a good one. In some ways I don't understand why you didn't marry her sooner. It's like she has always been a part of the family. May I go inside to tell her how happy I am for both of you?"

"She'll join us at lunch in just a minute," his father said.

"When are you getting married?"

"Six o'clock this afternoon," his father answered. "Judge Gitlin is performing the ceremony at our apartment."

"I know Uncle Paul," Judd laughed. "I'd better hurry to get a black tie."

"It's not that important. Just a few of our close friends." Then his father's smile turned serious. "Now the bad news."

Judd was silent.

"I have Hodgkin's disease," his father said.

"I don't know what that is," Judd said.

"It's a kind of cancer of the blood." His father waited a moment, then added, "It could be worse, however. The doctors tell me I can still have five or six years in reasonable comfort, and who knows what they may discover in that time? They may turn up a cure anytime."

Judd was silent. He took a deep breath, holding back his tears. "I hope so. No, I'm sure they'll find a cure."

21

"And if they don't," his father said, "I won't complain. I still would have had a good life."

Judd was silent, looking into his father's eyes.

"I'm not afraid of death," his father said softly. "Death and immortality have always been very much the same to me."

4

◆ THE JEEP WITH the customs officers led the limousine through the air-cargo gates to the field. They followed the road in front of a long row of warehouses past the commercial planes parked at the far end to where the field was reserved for military aircraft. The midnight blue B-747 seemed like a giant queen bee standing beside the cluster of tiny Yugoslavian fighter planes around it.

Judd stepped out of the limo and held his hand to Sofia. She looked up at the plane. The white insignia of the whooping crane —its wings outstretched as it lifted into the air, and followed by the words CRANE INDUSTRIES—was clear in the light from the airport windows. A painted American flag was under the pilot's window and an even larger one stretched across the giant rudder.

She looked at Judd. "I've never seen a jumbo plane except in a film," she said. "That one had a big staircase to it."

Judd smiled. "Usually it's rolled over to the plane if they aren't parked at airports that have moving ramps. But this one's special. It's been built to my specifications."

The customs officers came to them. "If you would be kind enough to give us your passports, we'll stamp them," one of them said.

Judd handed his passport from his jacket pocket and Sofia took her own from a purse. The customs officer walked back to the jeep and looked at the passports under a flashlight.

The chauffeur brought three valises from the car trunk. One was made of aluminum. He placed them beside her. At the same moment, an elevator supported by stainless steel rods descended from the wheel bay with two uniformed men on it who came toward them.

Judd introduced them. "Sofia, this is Captain Peters and Chief Steward Raoul. Gentlemen, Dr. Ivancich."

Captain Peters shook hands. "Welcome, Doctor."

Raoul tipped his hat in a sort of salute. "And I welcome also, Madame Doctor."

"Thank you, gentlemen," Sofia replied.

One of the customs officers returned. "The passports are in order. But we have to inspect Dr. Ivancich's baggage unless we receive a special export license for her medical equipment."

Her voice sounded annoyed as she spoke quickly in Serbian. The officer spoke apologetically, his hands expressive. She turned to Judd. "I'll have to go back to their office," she explained. "They're like all bureaucrats. The export license was supposed to be ready. But, as usual—"

Captain Peters turned to her. "I'll go back with you, Doctor. I have to get the flight plan approved anyway."

"Take the limo," Judd said. "I'll meet you on board."

"I'm sorry," she said.

"No problem," Judd said. "It's just the usual fuckup."

The customs officers took her valises to their jeep and the limo followed them away. Judd walked to the elevator as Raoul joined him and pressed the button. They went up past the wheel bay, then the galley floor, and up to the main cabin floor.

"Put the doctor in the first guest stateroom," Judd told the steward.

"Yes, Mr. Crane."

Judd walked to the flight deck staircase, behind which his personal cabin was located. He turned back to the steward. "Could you ask Merlin to see me?"

"Right away, sir."

Judd went up the steps and through the door that separated his cabin from the operating crew on the flight deck. Fast Eddie was waiting with an ice-cold Coca-Cola. Judd slipped off his jacket and picked up the drink. Merlin knocked at the door as Judd sipped his drink. Fast Eddie opened it.

"Yes, Mr. Crane," Merlin said, his notebook in his hand.

"Dr. Ivancich, Sofia," Judd said. Merlin was already making notes. "I want a security and computer check on her. Everything we can find out." He quickly added everything Dr. Zabiski and Sofia had told him. "I don't want any surprises."

"Anything else, sir?" Merlin asked.

"Yes," Judd added. "Ask Doc Sawyer at Medical Research if he's heard anything about work being done on human self-cell-cloning implantation."

"We'll get on it as soon as we take off, sir," Merlin said.

Judd looked at Fast Eddie as Merlin left the cabin. "Ice up a bottle of Cristale," he said, picking up the interphone and buzzing the chief steward. "When the doctor returns," he said into it, "ask her if she would like to join me on the flight deck for take-off."

Fast Eddie already had the bottle of Cristale in the bucket, as well as the two iced champagne glasses on the stand next to his seat. Judd walked to the rear of the cabin to his bedroom and began to take off his shirt. "Get me a terry-cloth jumpsuit," he said.

Fast Eddie opened one of the closets and took out the jumpsuit and laid it on the bed. Next to it he placed a pair of terry-cloth slippers and on the bed a French silk bikini. Judd went into the small shower stall in the bathroom, pressed the button that automatically mixed water and soap, then rinsed after the water cleared again. Steam lifted out of the stall automatically; he dried himself with an oversized towel. He dressed quickly and combed his hair. He looked at himself in the mirror. Okay, he thought, but only okay. He still felt tired. And he didn't like that. He had several things he had yet to do.

He pulled out a drawer and took out a gold vial and opened the cap, exposing a plastic bullet-type screw. He unscrewed the plastic top and a tiny opening appeared. He placed it in one nostril, squeezed the bottom of the vial, and the cocaine shot up as he snorted. He did it again with the other nostril. He felt the hit bring him up immediately. He threw the vial back in the drawer without closing it. He looked in the mirror again. He didn't look so tired now. He smiled to himself. That's one advantage of owning a chemical company of your own, he thought. You never have to worry about the street shit.

Fast Eddie was waiting in his cabin. He smiled. "Nothing like a hot shower and a snowstorm, boss," he said. "You look better already."

"You're too fucking smart," Judd smiled. "Are they on board yet?"

"Just coming on now, sir," Fast Eddie said.

Judd picked up the telephone and called the chief steward. "Suggest to the doctor that she would be comfortable in one of the jumpsuits. I think a size eight might be okay."

"I've already thought of it, sir," Raoul said quietly. "But I left a size seven on the bunk. That's more her fit."

"I defer to the French couture," Judd laughed, and put down the telephone.

THE CAPTAIN'S VOICE came over the address system. "All personnel secure. Takeoff in one minute."

Judd looked at Sofia in the next seat. She was peering through the window. He felt the slight shudder as the big plane began to move. He glanced at her hands. They gripped at the arms of the seat. He was silent as they moved quickly on the ground and then, suddenly, softly, slipped into the air.

Her voice was low. "It seems almost like a house on wings."

He laughed. "I guess it could be thought of as that."

She looked down at the lights of Dubrovnik below. "How high are we?"

He pressed a button and a light went on in the cabin bulkhead in front of them. "About two kilometers," he said. "We're climbing up to twelve kilometers, about 38,000 feet, for our cruising altitude. At that time we'll be flying at 580 miles per hour."

The no smoking and seat belt lights went off. He snapped off the seat belt that crossed his chest and leaned over to help her. She hesitated a moment. He smiled. "It's okay."

She nodded and let him open the seat belt.

Fast Eddie came to them and placed a tray of caviar and toast on the table in front of her, then quickly filled up their glasses with champagne and disappeared from the cabin.

He held his glass to her. "Welcome to the friendly skies of America."

"Down below that's still Yugoslavia," she said.

"But you're not down there, are you?" he laughed.

26

"That's right," she smiled. She sipped the champagne. "Delicious." She looked at the tray. "Is that really Russian caviar?"

He nodded.

"We can't even get that in Yugoslavia," she said.

He placed a spoonful of caviar on toast and handed it to her. "Détente," he said, "has certain advantages."

"I like that," she said.

"So do I," he said, helping himself.

"Do you have Russian vodka aboard too?" she asked.

"Of course."

"May I have a drink?" she asked almost shyly. "Down there all I ever could get was slivovitz and that makes me sick."

"You got it," he said.

Fast Eddie brought a bottle crusted with ice from the freezer. He filled two glasses and left them next to the bottle on the tray as he disappeared.

She picked up the vodka, looked at him for a moment, then threw it down her throat. He caught a faint flush in her cheeks. "Enjoying it?"

"It's been a long time." She glanced at him. "You're not drinking."

"I'm not into drinking that much," he said. "Wine and beer, a light Scotch and water before dinner are about my speed. Alcohol is a downer for me. I'm not into downers."

"Dope?" she asked.

"Some."

"Marijuana, cocaine, speed, mind-blowers?" She looked at him.

He smiled. "At times."

"That's very American," she said. "I remember when I was there at school." She picked up his vodka glass and emptied it and her breath seemed to come out as a soft sigh. "This is very European."

"Dif'rent strokes for dif'rent folks," he smiled.

She leaned against the back of her chair. "I feel warm," she said. "I think I'm getting a little drunk."

"If you feel tired, you can go to sleep."

"Oh, no, I'm enjoying it," she smiled. "This is as much fun as I've had in a long time. Down there everyone is very serious."

She closed her eyes for a moment, then looked at him. "Do you have any cocaine?"

He nodded.

"May I have a little?" She saw his hesitation. "It's okay. It will pick me up a bit. I don't want to fall asleep just yet."

He went into his bedroom and came back with the gold vial. He turned it over in his fingers and tapped its side; the white powder filled the plastic top. "This is an injector," he said. "Place it in one nostril, press the bottom and snort."

"It seems complicated," she said. "Could you do it for me?"

He held it to her nostril. "Snort," he said, pressing the plunger. She caught her breath. Quickly he placed it into her other nostril. "Again!"

She held still for a moment, then turned to him, her eyes wide and shining. "I felt it go right up to my brain."

He laughed. "It does that sometimes."

"Now I feel really warm," she said. "Even my nipples feel hot and hard."

He watched her silently.

"You don't believe me," she said.

"I believe you," he said, smiling.

"You're laughing at me," she said. She pulled the zipper of her jumpsuit to her breasts. "Now do you believe me?" she asked.

Her breasts were strong and full, her nipples plum colored and rock-hard, jutting. He looked at her face. "Beautiful."

"Touch me," she said harshly. "Touch me for God's sake or I'll orgasm alone just as I have by myself for the last five years!"

He drew her to his chest, holding her head against him, his other hand cupping and caressing her breasts. He felt the shuddering racking of her body against him. Softly he pressed her long hair. After a moment she was quiet. He didn't move.

Her voice was muffled against his chest. "Were you with the three girls they sent up to your suite?"

"No," he said. "I sent them away."

She was silent for a moment. "I'm glad. They had hidden cameras over the bed in your room."

"That's stupid," he said. "What could that gain them?"

"I don't know," she said. "They had the entire suite bugged."

"That's standard procedure," he said. "I expected it." He laughed. "Nothing but children's games."

"They weren't children's games," she said. "A man was killed and three men are in the hospital because something went wrong with their power source."

"Too bad," he said. "I knew nothing about it."

She sneezed suddenly. He raised her head and handed her a Kleenex. "It's the coke," he said. "Rinse your nose out with water." He showed her to the bathroom and then went to his chair.

He was sipping champagne as she returned. He looked at her. She had washed her face and brushed her hair. "You think I'm terrible?" she asked.

"No," he said. "You're just human. You might be a doctor but you're also a woman, a very beautiful woman, and both of them have needs that have to be satisfied to be whole."

She hesitated. "I think I'll return to my cabin."

He rose from his chair. "If that's what you want. If you're tired."

She looked into his eyes. "What do you desire?" she asked.

He smiled slowly. "You already know."

5

♦ A FAINT SOUND of the pitch of the jet engines brought him awake. He picked up the telephone beside the bed. "How are we doing?" he asked.

"Right on schedule, Mr. Crane," Captain Peters said from the flight deck. "We're ten and one-half hours into our flight, twenty thousand feet above Delhi, India, and taking on fuel. We expect to land in Pekin in eight hours and twenty minutes. All systems okay and go."

"Thank you," he said, and put down the telephone. He turned in the bed. She was lying on her side on the pillow, her eyes wide open to him. "Good morning," he said.

"Good morning."

"Have you slept well?"

"I don't know," she said. "I think I was dreaming all the time."

He laughed. "You were sleeping. I know that."

"Too bad," she said softly. "I kind of preferred the dreaming."

He bent across her face. "So did I," he said, kissing her. He sat up. "Would you like some coffee?"

"May I wash first? I smell so much of sex I'd be embarrassed to walk through the plane."

He laughed.

"I'm not being funny," she said seriously. "Sexual excitement brings me quickly to multiorgasmic responses."

He tried to match her seriousness. "I never quite heard it explained like that, Doctor."

"Yes," she said. "For example, while you were on the telephone a moment ago, just the sight of your penis even half erect with sleep caused my juices to begin to flow immediately."

"That's a problem," he nodded gravely. "I understand that now."

30

"It's a psychological one, I know," she said. "But I have to solve it myself."

He turned on his side to her. "Is that a problem you have to solve right now, Doctor?"

"I don't understand what you mean," she said, puzzled. "And why are you calling me 'doctor'? I thought you were going to call me Sofia."

He pulled her face down to his phallus. "Sofia, Sofia," he half-laughed. "Don't you know that half erect is never enough?"

She looked up at him. "Now you are making fun of me?"

"You stupid cunt!" he said, his fingers gripping her hair. With his other hand he pushed himself into her mouth. "Suck it hard if you want to fuck it."

She pushed away from him angrily. "You're talking to me as if I were a whore!" she said, tears filling her eyes.

He looked at her for a moment, then brought her face to his own. "No, Sofia," he said gently, kissing her mouth. "Not as a whore. But as a woman who has been denied too much too long."

SHE FOLLOWED HIM down the spiral staircase to the main deck. He turned when she paused behind him. "Forward of the steps is the business office," he said, holding the curtains apart so that she could see into it. Merlin was at his desk and there were two men, each at a desk with two data- and word-processor screens before them. Merlin turned to see Judd.

"Be with you in a moment," Judd said, dropping the curtain and leading her back from the staircase. "First is the guest lounge, then the guest staterooms. Behind them are staterooms for the personnel, then the personnel lounge. Both lounges double as dining rooms."

Her voice was hushed, but impressed. "How many people do you have on this plane?"

"Flight personnel, ten men plus the captain; cabin personnel, nine including the chef and the chief steward, five business personnel plus my assistant and my valet, you and myself making twenty-nine people on board. But we can sleep as many as fifty-one if we need to."

She shook her head. "It is like a house! Do you really need all that? Just for you?"

He smiled. "I think so. I spend almost thirty-five percent of my life on this plane, traveling because of business. With the kind of equipment we have on board I'm always in touch with my offices and business everywhere in the world."

"Do all you American businessmen have planes like this?"

"I don't know," he smiled. "But many of them have planes and some even more than two or three."

"Too much," she said.

"That's very American," he said.

"That's what we said when I went to college in the States." She smiled. "Too much."

"Lunch in a half hour, too much too?" he asked.

"No," she said. "I'm getting hungry."

He watched her walk through the lounge to her stateroom, then went through the curtains to the office. Merlin rose from his desk. Judd looked at him. "Is it morning or afternoon?" he asked.

"In India, it's four in the afternoon, about twelve hours into the flight. But this is the next day," Merlin answered.

"I'll never get it straight."

"We have today's report," Merlin said.

"Let's do it," Judd said, sitting down at the small conference table. Merlin placed a looseleaf binder on the table. Judd opened it for a moment and then snapped it closed. "Anything special?" He asked. "I'm wiped out."

"Not much really, it's the weekend, you know," Merlin replied. "Just one big one. Malaysia awarded the construction bid to us, fifty-five million dollars for the Pahang River bridge."

"Shit!" Judd said. "How did we fall into that one? I was sure we high-bid for it."

"We did," Merlin said. "But that's what you have to pay for a good reputation. They said even though we high-bid, they felt more secure with Crane Construction."

"Balls. We're going to blow twelve to fourteen million." He looked up at Merlin. "Check the Jap steel manufacturers. They're cutting the shit under us and shipping from there is less than from the U.S. or Europe. Maybe we can save four to five million out there."

"I'll work on it. I'll get Judson to go on it out of San Francisco."

"Any other good news?" Judd asked sourly.

"Doc Sawyer," Merlin replied. "He said he doesn't know what the hell you're talking about. All he knows about is the genetic engineering experiments and the DNA project out of the Defense Department. He needs more details from you."

"We'll talk personally in Miami at the end of the week," Judd said. "Any word from Security about the doctor?"

"Not yet," he said. "It should be coming in within a few hours though."

Judd got up. "Okay. Let's check after lunch." He paused for a moment, then looked at Merlin. "By the way, join me for lunch with the doctor if you have time. I'd like to know how you feel about her."

Lunch was simple. A cup of clear consommé, grilled French loin lamb chops medium rare, garnished with shoestring beans and carrots, finished with a small salad with oil and vinegar and a cheese tray. A '71 Château Margaux was served throughout the meal, and when the table was cleared, coffee was served in demitasse cups.

Sofia looked at him. "You seem to eat sensibly."

"Lightly," he said. "I found when traveling as I do, jet lag cuts me down. Too much food puts me away."

"Do you do the same, Mr. Merlin?" she asked.

"We all do, Doctor," he said. "Our meal program was devised by dieticians at the Research Institute for maximum energy development. In the meal program, each of us gets daily a personally prescribed package of vitamins and mineral supplements."

"Then Mr. Crane does not necessarily take the same vitamins and minerals, for example, as you do?"

"Each of us on the plane has his own formula."

"How was that decided upon?"

"We have an annual examination at the Crane Medical Center in Boca Raton, Florida. The complete physical usually takes three days."

"Mr. Crane, as well?"

"Yes."

She turned to Judd. "Would it be possible for me to be shown the results of your examination?"

Judd nodded, smiling. "Of course. It's all computerized. I'll have it aboard the plane by morning."

"Thank you," she said. "That should be of great help to me."

"You're the doctor," he said. "Anything you want, just ask."

"This should be a good beginning," she said, "before we go further." She put her demitasse down. "Do you mind if I get some rest, Judd? I'm feeling so tired."

"Go ahead," he said. "I think that's a good idea for me also. I'm scheduled for a banquet at midnight in Pekin."

He leaned over to Merlin after she had gone. "What do you think?"

"I don't know," Merlin said. "She seems straightforward. How good a doctor she is, I'm not qualified to say."

"The report should give us something on that," Judd said. "Wake me up the moment it comes in."

Merlin looked at him. "I know you. Something bothers you."

"Not about her medical experience," Judd said. "It's her cool. That's more than just her being a doctor. She has antennae. She is aware. She is something more."

Merlin followed him to the staircase. "I'll let you know the moment it comes in."

Judd's telephone buzzed him awake less than two hours later. "Can I come up?" Merlin asked into his ear.

"I'm awake." Judd got up from the bed and moved to his lounge as Merlin came through the door. Judd took the photofax from him.

"The medical stuff all checks out," Merlin said. "It's only the last few lines that are interesting."

Judd read quickly. "Security sources from CIA unverified, repeat, unverified rumor that subject recruited by KGB on order from Andropov. Will continue other sources for information."

Merlin looked at him. "If it's true, what does she want from us?"

Judd shook his head. "Nothing from us," he said. "It's only Zabiski that interests them."

"You lost me," Merlin said.

"Zabiski is the smartest bitch of all. She's not going to let on how or what she does. Even the Russians don't know. That's why she unloaded Sofia on me. That's going to screw up everything for a while."

"I don't see that's doing anything for us."

Judd smiled at him. "We'll just keep playing the game. I have a hunch that Zabiski will pass the ball to us when she's ready."

"You really believe that?" Merlin asked.

"Yes," Judd said. "I looked into the old lady's eyes and touched her hand. I felt her. We were together."

6

◆ "QUAALUDES AND INTERFERON," Judd said. "I don't get it. It's a crazy combination."

"It's not as crazy as it seems," Li Chuan said, leaning over the back of the jump seat in the limousine. "The bottom line is hard currency." Li Chuan was an American-born Chinese who was the Asian sales manager of Crane Pharmaceuticals in Hong Kong. "By 1980 the production of Quaaludes will be almost banned in the Western world. Europe and Latin America have stopped manufacture already. Pressure in the U.S. is mounting and Lemon is quietly making plans to stop. Already most of the ludes are counterfeit and poor quality, and sold by street dealers."

"In that case, how come the Chinese are so into it?"

"The Chinese seem to be more responsive to antidepressants than Americans and most Caucasians. The drug is more effective for them because they metabolize it more slowly so they don't get highs from it. So as far as they are concerned its a legitimate medical practice." He paused. "The Chinese government takes the view that if their people pop Quaaludes instead of smoking opium, so much the better. Opium and work don't mix."

"They know the attitude of the rest of the world," Judd said. Li Chuan nodded.

"So the bottom line is—they want Crane Pharmaceuticals to be their pushers around the world."

"Yes," Li Chuan agreed. "But they'll give you a plum. Maybe two hundred percent in the total world supply of interferon. And Crane Pharmaceuticals would be the sold distributor for that."

"Shit!" Judd stared out of the car. "We're fucked if we do and we're fucked if we don't."

"If I know our friends," Li Chuan said, "they are going to ship the Quaaludes anyway, whether we do or not. They smell a lot of money for them."

Judd said quietly. "Fuck 'em. Pass." He glanced from the limousine to the plane waiting on the airfield. "I wonder if Sofia is awake yet."

Merlin smiled. "She should be if you didn't slip her a mickey."

"I wouldn't do a thing like that," Judd smiled at him. He turned to Li Chuan. "Sofia is the Yugoslavian doctor I told you about."

Li Chuan nodded smoothly, though his expression had tightened when he heard Judd's decision about the Quaaludes. "I have a feeling that she will prove interesting."

SHE AWAKENED SLOWLY into the darkness of her stateroom. It took a moment before she realized that the plane was on the ground and that the power of the jet engines was not gently vibrating her bed. She turned to the digital clock beside her. The soft blue light read 0310.

She sat up in the bed, surprised that she had slept through the landing of the plane. She lifted a window shade and the electric floodlights on the ground around the plane came into her stateroom. Quickly she closed the shade and went into the small bathroom. In the corner of the room was a shower stall. She closed the Plexiglas shower door and took a telephone shower spray. The water was hot and soothing and she held its flow over her shoulders and down across her breasts. A small button on the wall was marked soap. She pressed it; the soap foamed, mixing with the water. Quickly she rinsed the water from herself, then aimed the nozzle of water across her hips. She climaxed almost instantly. She held her breath, afraid that some sound would escape her lips. Then she turned off the shower and pulled a towel around herself and stepped back into her stateroom.

A stewardess was turning down her bed, her back toward her. The shower door clicked and the girl turned to her. "Good morning, Doctor," the girl said. "I'm Ginny. I've just brought you orange juice and coffee."

Sofia looked at the tray on the night table. "Thank you." She hesitated a moment. "Are we in Pekin?"

"Yes, Doctor."

"Is Mr. Crane aboard?"

"No, Doctor," Ginny said. "He's expected back here at 0400 hours."

"Do you think I'll have time to look around?" she asked. "I've never been in Pekin."

The stewardess laughed. "That's one of the problems of this job. I've been in many places I haven't been to. We're expecting to depart for Hong Kong as soon as Mr. Crane is on board."

"Mr. Crane hadn't told me of that," Sofia said.

"He gave me the message for you. He asked you to go shopping with me and to give me your dress and shoe sizes so we could wire them to Hong Kong. He wants you to obtain a complete wardrobe before going on to San Francisco tomorrow."

Sofia was annoyed. "I have enough clothes."

Ginny smiled. "Mr. Crane has his own ideas. He says you have a Paris body so you should have a Paris wardrobe."

"Is he like that with everyone?"

"Only those he likes," Ginny said.

Sofia was silent for a moment. "I don't know my sizes in Western styles."

Ginny held out her hand. "Give me your towel," she said. "I have a good eye. I'll be able to tell."

Silently Sofia let go the towel. Ginny looked at her appraisingly. "You have a great body," the stewardess said matter-of-factly. "Five foot seven, bust thirty-seven, waist twenty-five, hips thirty-six. Shoe size about seven."

"You seem experienced," Sofia said.

"I like clothes," Ginny said. "And beautiful bodies."

Sofia looked at the girl but could see no expression on her face. She reached for the towel, feeling embarrassment. "Thank you."

Ginny walked to the stateroom door. "I'll be in the lounge. If there's anything you might want from me, press the button on the table next to the bed."

Sofia paused for a moment. "Would you call me the moment Mr. Crane comes aboard?"

"Of course, Doctor."

"Thank you." Sofia watched the door close behind the stewardess, then sat down on the bed and lifted the glass of orange juice to her lips.

"MR. CRANE IS aboard," the stewardess's voice came through the phone.

"May I talk to him?" Sofia asked.

"Press number eleven on the telephone," Ginny said. "He's upstairs in his lounge."

Sofia pressed the dial. Judd answered. "I would like to speak to you," she said. "Are you alone?"

"Yes," he said. "Come up."

Fast Eddie opened the door for her as she walked into his lounge. He was sipping a glass of Coca-Cola. "Sleep well?" he asked.

"Very well," she said, an annoyed tone in her voice. "Why do you continue to treat me as a whore?"

"I don't know what you're talking about."

"I don't need a stupid wardrobe," she said. "My clothes are good enough."

"Maybe for Eastern Europe, but not where you're going," he said. "And not when you're with me. You have to be the best."

She stared at him. "I'm a doctor. Not a fucking model."

"Then go back to Yugoslavia," he said. "If you don't want to look like the beautiful woman you are, I don't need you. I'm sure there are other doctors that can do what Zabiski wants you to do."

She was silent.

He picked up a gold vial and spoon. "Here, take a toot. You'll feel better for it."

She laughed suddenly. "Now, who's playing the doctor?"

"You're the doctor," he said, holding the gold spoon to her nose. "So forgive me if I see you only as a beautiful woman."

The cocaine brought her up. "I have forgotten so many things."

"Now we can get down to business. I have the medical charts you asked for." He turned and picked up a folder from the desk.

She looked down at it. Across the file folder was his name. JUDD MARION CRANE MEDICAL CHART AND HISTORY. Inside the folder were seven pages of computer printout.

BORN: 25 JUNE 34   N.Y.N.Y.   DOCTORS HOSP.   5:01 P.M.
GENEALOGY:
FATHER: SAMUEL TAYLOR CRANE   BORN:
                                 DIED: 18 FEB. 62

7

◆ BARBARA LOOKED OUT of the window at the white carpet of snow that blanketed Central Park. "Your father said this was the most beautiful scene in New York. White snow across Central Park with the gray and glass skyline of the buildings behind it."

Judd stood next to her. "My father was a strange man."

"Only to you," she said. "And only because he was your father. All children think their parents are strange."

"You loved him," Judd said, less a question than a statement.

"Yes." Her answer was simple.

"Why did you wait so long before you married?"

Her answer was just as simple. "He never asked me before."

"But you stayed with him?"

"If you mean were we sleeping together?" she asked, and answered herself, "No."

Judd looked at her. "Strange. I always thought you did."

"Everybody did," she said. "But your father had his own ideas. He never mixed business with personal emotions."

"He was a fool."

"Maybe," she said. "But it's over now. Somehow it doesn't matter anymore."

He was silent for a moment. "How are you feeling?"

"All right," she said. "But now that it's happened, numb."

"It's going to be a circus," he said. "The whole fucking world is going to be there. Except Kennedy. The President never liked him. Maybe he didn't like the idea that Father had more money than his own father. Anyway he's sending Vice President Johnson to the funeral. Johnson liked Father. He always likes people with money and power."

Barbara smiled wanly. "Your father didn't care then, and I'm sure he doesn't care now."

Judd nodded. "In a sort of way that's what I want to talk to you about. I know that after the services at St. Thomas's his body is being taken to a crematorium."

"That was his wish," Barbara said. "He never liked the idea of being buried in a cemetery."

"I have another idea," Judd said. "I don't want his body cremated. I want it sent to the research hospital in Boca Raton."

"What good would that do?" she asked. "They must have already prepared his body at the mortuary."

"No they haven't," he said. "Less than five minutes after he died I arranged to have him frozen cryogenically."

"You don't believe that bullshit," she said. "That he could be revived in another year when that disease is curable and that he can be brought back?"

"That's not what I'm trying to do." He took a deep breath. "We have the technology now that allows us to examine cells in his body genetically and with DNA methodology discover the causes of his disease."

"That sounds ghoulish," she said.

"It's not," he said earnestly.

"I don't know," she said. "Your father's wishes were explicit."

"His wishes are no longer binding. Dead, he doesn't own his own corpse. His corpse is your property and you can do with it whatever you wish. That's the law."

Barbara looked at him. "Is that why you asked me?"

He nodded. "As his wife you have the legal right. I do not."

"What right do you have?"

"None. Unless you predeceased him and I'd been the next blood survivor."

She sat silent for a moment. "I think I need a drink."

He crossed the room and filled two glasses with Scotch on the rocks. Silently they sipped their drinks. After a moment she looked at him. "Do you think it might do some good?"

"I don't know," he said. "But we're trying to learn more about living longer. That's why I built the research center in Boca Raton. Maybe if we'd started years before we could have prolonged his life."

"And you, Judd," she asked softly, "what do you want?"

"I want to live forever."

She stared at him, then finished her drink. "Okay, I'll go for it."

He took a folded document from his jacket pocket. "You'll have to sign this."

She looked down at the paper. "You knew I would agree, didn't you?"

"Yes."

"How did you know?"

"Because we all loved each other," he said, kissing her cheek.

She looked up at him. "You're very like your father, but very different from him too. You haven't the acquisitive desires that he had. He wanted to grab every business he could own. You're content just to hold the line."

"Father did it all," he said. "There was nothing more in that area I could do. He's built a machine that takes care of itself. If all of us were gone the business would remain on its own. In a way it's a kind of a perpetual motion machine."

"Is that why you did what you did three years ago?" she asked. "As a kind of experiment?"

He nodded.

"Your father was upset at first. Then I think he began to understand."

"I hope so," he said. "I remember the day he turned his office over to me. It was the week I graduated from M.I.T. and the first time I told him I would begin the research facility at Boca Raton."

"He couldn't see that at all," she said. "It wouldn't make any money."

"He was right," Judd said. "But he didn't stop me."

"He kept his word," she said. "He said it would be your business and that's what he meant."

HE HAD WALKED into the office that day in June. His father was at his desk. For a moment he felt shock at how thin his father appeared, then he looked into his eyes and the brightness was still there. He kissed his father, then Barbara, and shook hands with Judge Gitlin and the three assistant attorneys and accountants seated across the conference table behind a pile of documents.

A screen was standing against the far wall. The first picture projected was a company chart showing the Crane companies and their interlocking lines. Under each company was the managing director's name and his first assistant.

There were two chairs at the head of the conference table. His father rose and with the help of a cane walked to one chair and gestured Judd to the other. Barbara sat in the chair at his father's left; Judge Gitlin joined them at the table to Judd's right.

There was a silence around the table. They looked at his father solemnly. His father took a deep breath. "The king is not dead," he said quietly. "He has abdicated."

The room was still silent.

"All of you knew what I had planned," he continued. "Maybe you believed I would not really carry out that plan. I don't know. Now you know that I meant it to be true."

The people at the conference table were still silent.

"Judd kept his word to me also. He finished his last year at Harvard, completed his graduate studies at M.I.T., and in between his studies, he traveled and visited every company and factory we control around the world."

He paused a moment and sipped from a glass of water in front of him. "The transfer of power is always difficult. In companies as much as in governments.

"My father's ambition was to build the most effective and diversified company in the world. A company that encompassed all the strata of the American economy. That was my father's ambition.

"That was not mine. My ambition was to expand that business into a multinational corporation that would encompass the world. With the power and wealth that affect its influence throughout the governments of the world—in truth, the number one company in the Fortune 500.

"But my vision is not necessarily my son's. His vision will be his own. And all the wisdom I bequeath can be summed up in these words."

He sipped again from the glass of water. "Power is both evil and good. I have always been conscious of this. For myself, I like to think that I have tipped the scale toward good. But I admit that occasionally evil has held some sway. I hope that in the end good has prevailed."

44

Again he sipped from his glass. "I will not bore you with all the technical details involved in the transfer of power that will take place here. The foundations, all the measures necessary because of laws that protect inheritance, that's all been taken care of, but in the end, it will all be the same. My son will have the responsibility and the power and the wealth that was once mine, and my father's before me." He turned to Judge Gitlin. "It's up to you now, Paul."

Judge Gitlin rose from his chair. "I've simplified the agreements the best that I could, but there are still twenty documents to sign in sextuplicate. You, Barbara, and Judd have to sign them and they have to be notarized. It could take several hours. Samuel, do you feel up to it?"

"I can manage," Samuel said. "Let's begin."

Judd interfered. "Father, maybe you'd better listen to what I plan to propose."

His father looked at him. "I don't even want to hear it. I said it would be your baby. You take care of it."

"Okay, Father." Judd looked at Judge Gitlin. "I'm ready."

The lawyer began to place the documents in front of them. The signing took almost three hours. The old man was gray and tired at the end.

He looked at Judd as the last paper was turned over. Judd was silent. His father leaned over to him and kissed his cheek. "May God be with you, son."

Barbara came around the table and kissed Judd on the other cheek. And at the same time Judge Gitlin and the others met him with a chorus of congratulations.

Judd didn't speak until they had all finished. Then he stood at his chair. "Many of you will not like what I plan to do, but as my father said, it's now mine to do with as I please.

"I plan to retire the present managing director of every one of our companies and replace him with his successor in line. That's because I want the heads of all the companies loyal to me alone, and to no one else."

Judge Gitlin nodded. "That's good thinking, Judd."

Judd looked at him with a faint smile. "I'm glad you approve, Uncle Paul," he said, "because yours is the first name I placed on the list."

8

♦ "ONE MILLION DOLLARS a year," Judd said.

"What for?" Barbara asked. "I don't need it. Your father took care of everything with the trust fund he set up for me. I'm a rich woman. Besides, I have the apartment here, the homes in Connecticut and Palm Beach."

"Pin money," he said. "Your life will change now that you're a widow. All your social life was built around my father. People are shit. The moment they discover you cannot do anything for them they'll disappear."

"I don't need them," she said. "I'm used to living alone."

He looked at her. "You were nineteen when you went to work for Crane Industries, twenty-three when you became his personal assistant. Once you had that job you moved into another world. His. That was long before you married him."

"I still went home after work."

"That's not what I'm talking about," Judd said. "You were close to the center of action. Now—zero."

She was quiet for a moment. "What do you suggest I do?"

"Build a life of your own," he answered.

She stared into his cobalt-blue eyes. "I don't know how." She looked down at her hands. "From the very beginning I made my life for his convenience. When we were married I thought it would change. But it didn't really. The only change was that I moved into his home with another title. His wife, not his assistant. The duties were the same."

"But you loved him?"

"Yes," she said. "And I believe he loved me too. But nothing could be, then. He was sick and it was all over. There was no sex, no children, no fun times. Only plans for a future that did not include the two of us, because he was going to die."

46

Judd sat down across from her on the couch. "You're still a young woman," he said. "There is much happiness you can find."

"I'm forty-eight," she said wryly. "Look at me. The only attraction I can offer is my money. I'd run last against the competition of younger women and girls."

"You're wrong," he said. "Physically your face and body are still good. In two months we can turn back the clock fifteen years as if you were thirty again."

She laughed. "Cosmetic surgery?"

"Don't knock it," he said. "The techniques today are unbelievable."

"And even suppose I do it," she said. "What could I do with it? I know nothing of life. I think I've only had sex once in my life. As a girl in the backseat of a car, and I hated it."

"That too can be corrected," he said.

She shook her head. "Judd, Judd. You really don't understand, do you?"

"Maybe it's you who do not understand," he said.

"You sound like your father," she said. "That's what he used to say."

He smiled. "Do you remember when I was twelve years old and I fell out of the willow tree onto the lawn of my home in Connecticut?"

She nodded. "Yes, I also remember your father was very angry because you would never explain why you had climbed the tree knowing the willow branches were very weak."

"I couldn't tell him," Judd said.

"Why not?" she asked.

"I climbed that tree because I could look into your window and see you walking naked in the room. The minute I would see you I began to masturbate."

"I don't believe it," she said.

"It's true," he replied. "And one time I orgasmed and took my hands off the branch. That was when I fell."

She began to laugh. "Children."

"I never forgot it," he said. "I can still see it in my mind. Even now, sometimes between being awake and sleeping, I find myself stroking myself."

"I never thought about it, never saw it," she said.

"Too bad," he said. "I used to think that if you could see me and watch me, it would be even more exciting."

She was silent.

He looked at her. "Thinking about it even now makes me hard."

She rose from the couch. "It's been a long difficult day," she said. "I think we'd better go to sleep. The plane is leaving in the morning."

He grasped her arm and pressed her back to the couch opposite him. "Freud," he said.

"What about Freud?" she asked.

"He said that frustrations make for insanity."

"You made that up," she said. "I never heard that."

"I want you to sit there and watch me."

"No," she said. "That's really insanity. You're not the child you were then and I'm not the girl you were watching."

He shook his head. "You don't understand. Nothing has changed. You and I are still the same as we were."

"In your mind," she said.

"What else is there?" he asked. "Except what's in the mind. You're still beautiful." He unzipped his trousers and held himself. His voice was husky. "You don't have to do anything. Just watch me."

She felt his fingers gripping into her arm and stared at his phallus growing larger in his hand. She felt the choking in her throat as if she couldn't breathe. She saw the reddish purple glans pushing above his foreskin and his hand a blur holding himself. Then a growling sound came from his voice and semen began spurting crazily over his hands and trousers.

She turned away then to his face. The cloudiness of his eyes began turning to the usual cobalt blue. He watched her for a moment, then smiled slowly. "Fifteen years," he said.

She didn't answer.

"Get me some Kleenex," he said. "I'm a mess."

Silently she went behind the bar and came back with a box of Kleenex. He looked up at her. "Clean me up," he said.

Without speaking she took several tissues and swabbed him. He looked up at her. "You're beautiful," he said.

"I feel stupid."

"You're not stupid," he said. "You're free now. And so am I."

She carried the Kleenex box to the bar and mixed two Scotches on the rocks and brought one to him. She sipped hers slowly. "That cosmetic surgery, will it work as you say it will?"

"Yes," he said. "Even better."

She took a deep breath. "Okay. How do I go about it?"

"It's already arranged," he said. "The plane to take you to Boca Raton and the doctor there is waiting for you."

THE PILOT'S VOICE echoed through the aircraft. "This is your captain speaking. First, I would like to thank you for flying Pan American and trust you all have enjoyed a comfortable flight from London to San Francisco. We should be on the ground in approximately twelve minutes, and meanwhile you can see from the left side the famous Golden Gate Bridge and at the right side, Oakland Bay Bridge. Again, thank you for flying Pan-Am."

Barbara glanced from the window for a moment, then opened her compact. She still felt the surprise of looking in the mirror. It had been two years since Judd had taken her to Boca Raton for the cosmetic surgery. The face in the mirror seemed that of a woman in her early thirties. And Judd had also been correct in urging her to spend the next years in Europe. For the first time in her life she had felt herself to be a real woman. She touched up her makeup quickly and wondered about Judd. How much might he have changed in two years?

She had read stories in the newspapers and magazines about Crane Industries but there never was a picture of Judd in any of them. They had photographs of his father and many photographs of other executives of the company, none of whom she had known, but Judd's name would only be mentioned, never a photograph. The telegram had reached her at the Dorchester Hotel in London.

Love it if you would cut the ribbon that would open the new World Headquarters of Crane Industries in Crane City just outside of San Francisco, Sept. 14, '64. Anxious to see you.

Love, Judd.

The first person she saw as she stepped off the plane to the covered gangway was Fast Eddie. Next to him was a slim young man in a dark suit and tie, and a uniformed customs officer. Fast Eddie came to her with a large bouquet of red roses. "I'm happy to see you, Mrs. Crane."

"I'm pleased to see you, Fast Eddie," she smiled, opening the envelope with the flowers.

The card was in Judd's handwriting. "Welcome home, Barbara. Love, Judd."

She held the roses in her arms. Fast Eddie introduced the young man. "This is Marcus Merlin, Judd's personal assistant," he said.

"I'm honored, Mrs. Crane."

Barbara shook his hand. "My pleasure, Mr. Merlin."

"We have arranged courtesy of the port for you, Mrs. Crane," Merlin said. "If you'll give me your passport and baggage checks, I'll transfer you directly to the helicopter."

Barbara nodded, and Merlin led her to a side door down a staircase to the field where a limousine waited. The customs official took her passport and baggage checks and turned away. A chauffeur held the door open and she stepped into the car. Fast Eddie quickly opened a bottle of champagne and filled a glass for her.

"Your favorite," he said. "Cristale."

"Thank you for remembering."

"It was Mr. Crane who remembered," Fast Eddie smiled. "You're lookin' real good, Mrs. Crane."

She smiled back. "I feel real good, Fast Eddie." She sipped at the champagne. "And how is Judd?"

"He's also real good, ma'am," he said. "But he's like his father, always very busy."

Merlin came toward the open door. "Six Louis Vuitton bags?"

"That's right."

He waved to the customs official. The chauffeur and Fast Eddie placed the luggage in the trunk of the limousine. Fast Eddie got into the front seat with the chauffeur. Merlin looked in at her. "May I join you, Mrs. Crane?"

"Of course," she said.

The car began to move away. "The helicopter is at the far end of the airport," Merlin said. "I think you'll like it. It's our newest passenger model. Carries twenty-four passengers and crew. The newest Hughes model carries only fourteen."

Barbara nodded.

"The flight will take only twenty-five minutes," Merlin said. "That's less time than it takes to drive to downtown San Francisco."

"From what I hear, Judd has built a whole city," she said.

"That's right, Mrs. Crane," Merlin said. "Six hundred apartments, one hundred private homes and twelve office buildings. Of course, there are schools, malls, shopping centers and, needless to say, a hospital."

Barbara looked at him. "But why *here?*" she asked. "The company headquarters has always been in New York."

"Yes," Merlin answered. "But if you remember, ten years ago sixty percent of manufacturing was in the East and South. Now forty-five percent is in the West, and only fifteen percent East and South. Microchips and computers grow like weeds in Silicon Valley. We make more wine in Northern California than Italy and France. Aerospace manufacturers are all around the states of Washington, California, Nevada, and Colorado. Projections show us in another ten years our growth will be up five hundred percent."

"But a whole city?" she asked.

"That was an idea Mr. Crane lifted from the Japanese. He saw that all the big Japanese companies—Mitsubishi, Nissan, Asahi, National, Panasonic and Sony—weld their production to their labor by guaranteeing lifetime security from the cradle on."

"I wonder if Americans will feel the same way," she said.

"We'll see," Merlin replied. "But as Mr. Crane says, it's only an experiment."

The car stopped. Merlin stepped out and held out his hand to her. His other hand gestured to the helicopter. "There it is," he said. "Mr. Crane said that the first one should be named for you."

Barbara stood there for a moment. The tears sparkled at the sight of the silver-colored helicopter. The letters were bold across the side: BARBARA ONE.

9

◆ "IT SEEMS LIKE a college campus," she said. "They all look like children. I think not a one of them is over thirty."

Judd smiled. "Except me."

She laughed. "Excuse me." She took out the plastic card that served as the key to her suite. "Come in for a nightcap."

He nodded.

She opened the door and he followed her. The door closed automatically. She led him to the bar in the living room. "Scotch on the rocks?"

"No, thanks. I'd prefer a cherry Coke."

She looked at him. "That's something new."

"Yes. Alcohol doesn't do it for me."

"But Coca-Cola does?" she asked. "Caffeine and sugar?"

"Something more," he said.

She glanced at him.

"Cocaine," he said.

"Isn't that dangerous?"

"Living is dangerous for your health," he said. "But the combination keeps me on the *qui vive.*"

"I don't know," she said questioningly. "I've never done it."

"I don't recommend it," he said. "Just that it works for me. I checked it with my doctor and he said that it's no worse than alcohol abuse. The idea is to use it carefully."

"How do you know when you overdo it?" she asked.

He laughed. "Your nose falls off."

She grimaced. "That sounds terrible."

He laughed again. "Okay, then. I'll have the Scotch."

She put the ice cubes into the tumblers and splashed some Scotch over them. He took his glass. "Cheers," she said.

"Cheers." She looked at him. "You've taken other drugs?"

"Of course," he said. "You have to understand. This is the age of dope and chemicals. Just as my father's age was the age of beer and alcohol."

"You've been doing it long?"

"Since prep school and college."

"Funny," she said. "We never knew it."

"I was never at home very much."

He crossed to a chair and sank into it. "Tell me about yourself," he said. "It's been about two years."

"It's been different," she said. She sat opposite him. "I'm different."

"I can see that."

"Do you like what you see?"

He nodded. "Yes. I now feel you're yourself. Before, you were a satellite turning around Father."

"I didn't mind," she said quietly. "I loved him."

"I know that," he answered. He sipped at his drink. His dark-blue eyes looked into hers. "I suppose you're wondering why I called for you?"

She nodded silently.

"It's time you came back to work," he said. "I need you."

"Need me? Aren't I a little over age for you?"

He laughed. "Touché."

"Okay," she said. "Tell me what's on your mind?"

"The Vietnam War has Johnson in a box. It will escalate until it blows up in his face. In the meantime there's a lot of money being made."

"I still don't know what that has to do with me."

"General Connally," he said.

She was silent for a moment. "Willie?"

"Yes," he nodded. "I've heard they're bringing him back from NATO and putting him in charge of procuring all weaponry for the Defense Department."

"I still don't know what that has to do with me."

Suddenly there was no expression in his eyes. "You've been fucking him," he said. "Pillow talk has sold more weapons than bribery."

"He wants to divorce his wife and marry me," she said.

"Don't let him do it," he said quickly. "That would blow his career out of the box."

"And we'd get nothing out of it," she added.

"You learn fast," he said.

She went to the bar and refilled their glasses. "Just for your information," she said, returning his glass, "I hadn't planned to marry him."

Judd was silent.

"Exactly what kind of material are you interested in?" she asked.

"Armed carrier helicopters. Hughes and Bell are already preparing bids. Armored personnel land carriers. Chrysler and General Motors are working on them. Shallow-draft river craft powered by jet instead of propeller. Jacuzzi and Piaggio are both shipping a few under test conditions."

"And that can come to a lot of money?" she asked.

"Could be several billion dollars."

She was silent and had almost finished her drink. "Several billion dollars! That's good whore's wages."

He didn't answer.

"What happened to your ideals?" she asked. "The dreams about immortality?"

"I still have them," he said. "But I also have a business that I have inherited and still have to nourish."

She took a deep breath. "If your father had asked me I wouldn't have hesitated because I loved him. And I wouldn't feel like a whore."

"We're all whores in our own way for our own reasons," he said. "Power, money, sex, ideals. The commodities of life."

"You really believe that?" she asked.

He nodded.

"You're wrong," she said softly. "You forgot the most important thing of all."

"What's that?"

Tears began to spill from her eyes. "Love."

SOFIA GLANCED UP from the medical computer printout. "There's nothing in here about whether or not you have ever been married."

"I've never been married," Judd said.

54

She turned her head to one side. "That's unusual. Usually a man of your age, by forty-two—"

He interrupted her. "You said that you were thirty and you hadn't been married. Do you think that's also unusual?"

"Yes," she said. "But I had a reason. My profession is very demanding."

"Perhaps mine is too," he smiled. "But I don't feel denied. Do you?"

She paused for a moment. "Sometimes," she said honestly. "I would have married and had children, but it never worked out that way."

"You should have married," he said. "And not just because you love to fuck. You would have given a great deal to your children."

Her eyes fell to the computer printout. "According to this, you are in very good health."

"That's due to dissipation and lack of sleep," he smiled.

"That's in spite of it," she said seriously. She put down the papers. "We'll have to find time to bring you into a hospital for three days."

"The next weekend in Boca Raton," he said. "We're due there anyway."

"In the meantime there are several tests I have to perform. They won't take much time."

"You're the doctor," he said. The telephone beside his chair rang. He listened for a moment. "Send him up," he said.

He turned to Sofia. "That's Li Chuan, he's Asian sales manager for Crane Pharmaceuticals."

She rose from her chair. "I can return to my stateroom if you want to be alone with him."

"Meet him first," he said. "He gave Ginny a selection of shops to check out when we land in Hong Kong."

Li Chuan came into the cabin and Judd made the introductions. Sofia smiled. "Thank you for your courtesy."

"It's my pleasure." He bowed slightly.

She looked at Judd. "Will I see you ashore?"

"I'm sorry," Judd apologized. "I'll be very busy."

"I understand." She nodded to Li Chuan and left the cabin. The no smoking and the seat belt signs went on as she entered her stateroom. She slipped into her seat.

Ginny opened her door and came into the stateroom. She glanced at the seats around her. "Mind if I keep you company?" she asked.

"Not at all."

Ginny took the seat opposite and clipped the belt. "Li Chuan has given me a list of some very interesting shops."

"I really don't want to see any of them," Sofia said.

Ginny smiled. "Mr. Crane thinks you ought to collect a complete wardrobe."

"His ideas and mine are very different. Clothes are not that important to me."

Ginny laughed. "Get them anyway," she said. "He's the kind of man who wants his own way."

"Is he like that in everything?"

Ginny nodded.

Sofia looked out the window. The wheels were beginning to touch the ground. A moment later the big plane was running smoothly along the runway. "I don't know how the pilot does it," she said. "You don't even know it when the plane lands."

"That's one of Mr. Crane's rules. If he feels the wheels touch, the pilot had better have a damn good excuse or start looking for another job." Ginny rose from her chair. "Shall we be ready to go in fifteen minutes?"

"Fine," Sofia replied.

AS THE DOOR closed behind Sofia, Li Chuan asked, "Your Dr. Ivancich is Yugoslavian?"

"Yes," Judd said. "How did you know?"

"I've heard the name. She spent time with Mao Tse-tung until he died. There was also a rumor from his wife and others of the Gang of Four that she killed him."

Judd was silent. Then he looked out the window. "We had nothing on her computer checkout about that." He turned back to Li Chuan. "Think you can find something out about it for me?"

"I can't tell yet," the Asian said. Then he laughed. "In the meantime, don't let her give you any pills."

Judd also laughed. "I don't think I'll have any problems about that."

56

10

◆ JUDD LOOKED OUT the window. Below he saw Sofia and Ginny enter the limousine. The telephone rang again.

Merlin was on the receiver. "Judson is calling you from San Francisco."

"Put him through," Judd said. There was a click. "How are you, Judson?"

"Good, Mr. Crane. I have some information about the steel for the Malaysian bridge."

"Tell me."

"Mitsubishi Heavy Industries will give you the steel for six million less, but there's a kicker. They want you to use their shipping line. That will up the cost about eight hundred thousand."

"That's just from one pocket to another," Judd said. "Do you have any other ideas?"

"You're in Hong Kong," Judson said. "If you could arrange a meeting with S. Yuan Ling. He has the largest cargo shipping line in the world. And most of his ships have been built for him by Mitsubishi. He has the clout to save us a few bucks."

"Last I heard," Judd said, "he was in Mexico working his oil tanker deal with Pemex."

"He's back in Hong Kong now," Judson said.

"Okay, I'll try him," Judd said. "Anything else?"

"Nothing that can't hold," Judson said.

"I'll be in touch then," Judd said. He turned to Li Chuan. "You get to S. Yuan Ling and tell him I want to meet him this afternoon."

"He only works in the morning," Li Chuan said. "He takes his lunch on his yacht, swims for an hour and afterward sleeps until dinnertime."

"I don't care if he sits on the crapper for an hour. You tell him that I want to see him."

"Yes, sir," Li Chuan said. "Then I'd better get into town right away."

"Okay," Judd said.

"What about the pharmaceutical deal?" Li Chuan asked on the way out. Despite the impassive Oriental face, he seemed anxious.

"You heard my decision. If it's tied to their Quaaludes, I'm not interested."

"The Quaaludes are where the money is."

"It may be for them," Judd said. "But not for us. You can tell them I'll triple the offer for the interferon, though."

"I'll tell them," Li Chuan said. "I'll call you from town the minute I hear from S. Yuan Ling."

"Thank you," Judd said. He watched the Asian leave the lounge, then pressed for Merlin. Fast Eddie came in before Merlin arrived.

"Need a lift, boss?"

Judd nodded. "That's an idea."

"Cherry Coke an' all the fixin's?"

"You got it."

The glass of cherry Coke was on the table as Merlin came into the lounge. He waited until Judd spooned the cocaine into the cola drink. Judd emptied the glass. "That's the way it was made in Atlanta when they did it first."

Merlin nodded. He had heard it many times. Caffeine was substituted for the cocaine sometime in 1903—or was it 1912— by the Food and Drug Act.

Judd looked at him. "Telex Security for more on Dr. Ivancich. Ask them how come they had no information that the doctor spent a year with Mao Tse-tung before he died. Also have them put a blanket on Li Chuan. I have a feeling he may be trying to make the Quaalude deal for himself."

Merlin looked at him. "Yes, sir. Anything else?"

Judd shook his head. "I'm going to get a nap. Wake me up when Li Chuan sets up a meeting with Mr. Ling."

THE FRENCH SALESGIRL looked at them haughtily, spoke in snob accent. "We have the latest magazines—*L'Officiel*, French *Vogue* and others. We can make anything you select from any photograph in twelve hours."

Sofia replied to the girl in French. The salesgirl nodded for a moment, then gestured for two chairs for them and walked away.

"What did you ask her?" Ginny said.

"I told her that we were not interested in *haute couture*. Everything has to be *prêt à porter* and we've only three hours in Hong Kong."

The salesgirl returned with another woman who seemed to be the manager. "What exactly would madame be interested in?"

Sofia replied in English. "Two simple suits, one in wool, and one in lighter fabric. Three afternoon dresses, one cocktail dress, black, and one long dress, also black. Accessories to match and shoes also to match. Three skirts, one white, beige and black. Six silk shirts, all colors. Two pairs of slacks, one navy blue, one black. Three pairs of jeans."

"Yes, madame," the manager said respectfully. "Would you be kind enough to follow me to a dressing room?"

A moment later Sofia was in a large dressing room. Ginny sat in a chair while Sofia undressed. The manager made a face when she saw that Sofia's undergarments were cotton.

"Perhaps madame would like to see some of our lingerie?" she said. "We have the latest styles, French and American. Silk or nylon."

Sofia smiled. "Thank you, madame. Perhaps I can use a selection of both kinds."

The manager came with a tape measure and Sofia undid her brassiere and slipped from her panties. Professionally the saleswoman checked her measurements. A moment later she left the two women in the dressing room.

Ginny looked at Sofia. "I told you before, but no one would know from your clothing, what a fantastic body you have."

"Thank you," Sofia said.

"No wonder Mr. Crane wants you to get a new wardrobe."

Sofia smiled. "I thought he did this for all his girl friends."

Ginny laughed. "Not all of them. But this is the first time he's ever done it for his doctor."

Sofia looked at herself in the full-length mirror. She saw Ginny stand behind her.

"Did you ever have your breasts done?" Ginny asked.

She met the girl's eyes. "Never."

"I can't believe it," Ginny said. "They're absolutely perfect."

Sofia still watched her in the mirror. "You can check them if you don't believe me."

Ginny hesitated a moment, then put her arms around Sofia's back and cupped her breasts in her hands. Sofia looked at Ginny's eyes in the mirror. The stewardess's hands were almost hot; Sofia felt her nipples harden.

"Do you believe me now?" Sofia asked.

Reluctantly, slowly, Ginny withdrew her hands. Their eyes were still meeting in the mirror. Ginny's voice whispered harshly, "Yes."

After a moment, the door to the dressing room opened. Ginny returned to her chair as several girls entered with piles of clothing.

THE SUN WAS hot and the air humid above the water on the far side of the island. Li Chuan and Judd stood next to the sailor driving the mahogany Riva. Li Chuan pointed out a motor yacht half a mile in front. "That's his boat. It's always in Repulse Bay."

"Would he be on board?" Judd asked.

"No, according to his schedule he should be swimming," Li Chuan replied. "He said the earliest appointment he could give you is three days from now."

Judd's voice was flat. "We'll talk to him right now. Slow down to two knots and keep a sharp lookout for him."

The powerful motors softened to a whisper. Slowly the Riva began a wide circle. Ten minutes later they saw the yellow balloon bobbing in the water and three black heads before it.

Judd began to take off his clothes. "Head as close to them as you can with safety." He pulled off his shoes and socks when the Riva was twenty meters away from them. He stepped over the windscreen onto the prow of the Riva. He waved his arms over his head. The black heads in the water suddenly grew faces as they turned to him. "Cut the engines," Judd ordered.

Judd stood naked except for his bikini. He could see one of the men treading water lift an Uzi submachine gun in a waterproof plastic wrapper which he tore off expertly.

Judd dove into the water and came up close to the man. "Be careful with that toy," he said. "Use it and we all wind up blown apart in this water."

Another man next to the one with the Uzi spoke. There was no fear in his voice. "What do you want of us?"

"I'm Judd Crane," he said, treading water.

The man looked at him. "Didn't your man tell you that we gave you an appointment three days from now?"

"Yes," Judd said. "But I thought it better that we meet immediately."

"Here? In the river?"

"It's as good as any other place."

"Very irregular, I must say." The man's face creased into a faint smile. "Do you always hold your meetings like this?"

"Not usually," Judd said. "But then, business doesn't offer me many opportunities to meet such men as S. Yuan Ling."

Mr. Ling laughed. "You are younger than I thought, Mr. Crane."

"Thank you," Judd said. "Do I have your ear?"

"That is a Chinese proverb," Mr. Ling said. "A deaf ear doesn't listen to opportunity."

Judd moved closer to him and they tread water face to face. "My information tells me you have a twenty-million-dollar deposit on six ships that Mitsubishi is constructing for you. Also that the first three are going to make their trials next spring."

Mr. Ling nodded. "That's true."

"My information also has it that Mitsubishi plans to ship the steel to my bridge project in Malaysia on those ships' sea trials. After that the vessels will be turned over to you for the remainder of the cost you and they have already agreed on."

The Chinese was silent for a moment. "How much are they planning to charge you for shipping your steel?"

"Eight hundred thousand dollars."

S. Yuan Ling nodded. "Very clever, these Japanese."

Judd nodded back. "Very clever."

"Would you agree to four hundred thousand dollars?"

"Yes," Judd said.

"We have a deal." The Chinese held out his hand. "May I invite you to lunch aboard the yacht?"

"I apologize," Judd said. "I'm running a bit late for some other appointments. May I have the honor another time?"

"Of course," the Chinese replied. "Any time."

Judd swam to the Riva. A sailor held out a hand and helped him aboard. Judd turned to the Chinese still swimming and waved his hand. He turned to the sailor. "Let's go."

Slowly the Riva reversed engines and moved away from the swimmers, then swung on a wide circle. The helmsman opened the throttle full and the speedboat raced back to shore.

11

◆ THE LIMOUSINE PULLED up next to the plane. Sofia and Ginny stepped out. "I'll have everything brought to your cabin," Ginny said.

"Thank you." Sofia smiled. She touched her head, a tinge of nervousness came into her voice. "Do you think he'll like the way I look?"

Ginny laughed. "If he doesn't, he has to be crazy."

"That was the first time I've been in a beauty parlor in five years," Sofia said. "I didn't even recognize myself in the mirror."

"You look just fine," Ginny said. "Stop worrying."

"It cost a fortune."

"Not to him," Ginny said. "Now, go ahead. I'll bring up your clothes and you can put on one of the new things. He'll be knocked out."

Li Chuan was in the lounge when Sofia entered. He bowed slightly. "Was your shopping trip successful, Doctor?"

"Very much so, thank you," she said. "Is Mr. Crane aboard?"

"He's in his cabin, getting a massage," he said. He held out his hand to Sofia. "It has been a pleasure to meet you, Doctor."

"You're leaving?" she asked.

"Yes," he said. "I have to get back to the office and the plane is leaving for the States at eight o'clock."

She glanced at her watch. It was seven o'clock. "That's in one hour," she said in surprise.

He nodded. "Mr. Crane told the captain to hold until you return." He paused for a moment; when he spoke again it was in Chinese. "I did not mention to him that we have met before."

She looked at him. His eyes revealed nothing. "Thank you, Comrade," she replied, also in Chinese.

He spoke quickly. "I think he would be more confident about

you if you told him about your work with Mao, rather than if he has to discover it through his security check."

She nodded, without replying.

"Also, if he should mention anything about the pharmaceutical deal, I would be grateful if you could pass his comments along to me."

"Yes, Comrade."

He switched back to English. "I hope we will meet again, Doctor."

"I hope so, Mr. Li Chuan," she said, also in English. "And again, thank you for your help."

She watched him leave the lounge just as Ginny entered with two porters carrying the packages behind her.

THE TELEPHONE NEXT to her bed buzzed softly. She pressed the rheostat so the light dimmed. "Yes," she replied huskily.

"I'm sorry," Judd's voice came over softly. "I didn't want to awaken you."

"That's all right," she said. "I didn't realize that shopping was so exhausting."

"Was it fun?"

"Much to my surprise, yes," she said. "By the way, thank you for all the lovely things."

"I wanted to do it."

"Did you have a good massage?" she asked.

He seemed to hesitate. "Yes. Would you like one?"

She became aware of the hum of the jets and glanced out the window. The night stars were flickering. "Don't tell me you also have a masseur on board?"

He chuckled. "Not a masseur. Two masseuses. They're very good. They're going only as far as Honolulu, then they go back to Hong Kong."

She was silent.

"You can think about it later," he said. "I called you to ask if you'd join me for dinner."

She glanced at the blue light on the digital clock. "It's ten-thirty."

"No hurry," he said. "I'll wait."

She heard the phone click off in her ear before she could

answer. Slowly she sat up in bed, picked up the telephone again and pressed the service button.

Ginny answered. "Yes, Doctor?"

"May I please have a pot of strong coffee?" she asked.

"Of course, Doctor," Ginny said. "I'll be there in a minute."

Sofia got out of bed and went into the shower. A few minutes later she was back in the cabin wrapped in a towel. The stewardess was there waiting for her.

The coffee was hot, black and strong. "That's good," Sofia said. Ginny stood there.

Sofia looked at her. "Is there anything wrong?"

The girl's voice was tight, strained. "You're going up to him, aren't you?"

Sofia nodded. "Of course."

Tears flooded into Ginny's eyes. "Please. Don't go up there. Not tonight. After we had such a beautiful day together."

"Ginny," she said softly, understanding. "Child."

"Please." Ginny seemed almost begging. "I don't want him to use you the way he does all the others. I love you."

"Have you ever—?"

Ginny interrupted her. "We don't have any choice. He buys and owns all of us."

Sofia looked at her, then drew the girl to her. Ginny's voice was muffled against her shoulder. "But you don't have to jump through his hoop. He doesn't own you."

"Child, child," Sofia whispered. "You do not understand. Everyone, yes everyone, is owned by somebody or something."

Ginny looked up into her face. "Then you're not in love with him?"

"No," Sofia said. "I am not in love with him."

"But you will go with him?"

"Yes," Sofia nodded.

"I hate him!" Ginny said angrily.

Sofia was silent.

"Do you love me?" Ginny asked.

Sofia met her eyes. "Perhaps, in time."

THE SUN STREAMING through the window was burning her eyes. By shutting her eyelids she managed to close the shade. She rolled over in the bed. She had a splitting headache and opened her eyes again. She sat up. She was in her own cabin. She took a deep breath. It was strange. She did not remember coming down the stairs.

She rolled out of bed to the bathroom. Quickly popped two aspirin tablets and a five milligram Valium. She took a deep breath and stepped into the shower, turned on the water full blast. Ice cold first, then hot, then ice cold again. Her head began to clear a little.

She stepped from the shower and reached for the bath towel, then was shocked frozen by what she saw in the full-length mirror. Her naked body was almost wholly covered with tiny black-and-blue bruises all the way from her jutting breasts, across her belly, to her hips. She stared at herself in disbelief. Her pubis had been cleanly shaven, her mons veneris was swollen like Mount Vesuvius and her clitoris felt sore and was red, like lava from the volcano's lips.

She took a deep breath and turned to look over her shoulder at her back. Thin red lash stripes criss-crossed her back and buttocks. Tentatively she touched the bruises. There was no pain. Again she coursed her fingers over her buttocks, then cupped her breasts. Still no pain.

Slowly she wrapped the towel around herself and walked into the cabin. She sat on the bed and tried to remember what had happened last night. But it was all a blank.

She picked up the telephone and pressed the service button. Raoul, the chief steward, answered. "Yes, Doctor."

"What time do we expect to land in Honolulu?"

Raoul's voice was impassive. "We departed Honolulu three hours ago, Doctor."

She hesitated for a moment. "Could you ask Ginny to bring a pot of coffee for me?"

"I'm sorry, Doctor," the steward said without expression. "Ginny left the flight in Honolulu. I'll have a pot of coffee sent to you."

Then it all came back to her. Just as she put down the phone. It was almost as if it had been a nightmare. The little Chinese girls, like two peas in a pod. Identical twins. Naked and rolling the

66

small pill-like gum of opium in their fingers, lighting the pipe and holding the stem to her mouth with delicate little hands.

Then the lovely clouds and silver mist. Floating inside her body and then feeling outside the beauty of her body as the tiny girls touched her, feeling the love in all her nerves. Then the orgasm that had exploded her into a million tiny fragments, shattering her body in the blackness of night.

The blackness was exploded by pain. She fought the night to climb back up to consciousness. Then the pain began again. She opened her eyes and saw Ginny's face, snarling with rage and hatred, teeth tearing at her, then the thin lashes of the whip. She screamed and screamed and screamed.

Then the door had been pushed open. Suddenly, Ginny was gone. Judd was looking down at her. She tried to speak to him, but she heard no sound.

It was his voice that she finally heard. "Ice pack, procaine, and ACTH ointment. Lots of it. Two Syrettes of Demerol."

"Pain," she said. "Pain."

"It will be gone in a moment," he said. Then she fell back into blackness.

A knock came at the door. "Come in," she called.

Judd looked in. "May I?"

She nodded.

He stood to one side as a stewardess placed the tray with the pot of coffee on the small table next to her bed. He waited until the stewardess was gone.

"How do you feel?"

"I hurt," she said. She sipped at the coffee. "Maybe you are a better doctor than I am. I never knew what was happening."

"The opium put you away," Judd said. "You were asleep when we took you to your cabin."

"Thank you," she said. "I could have been killed."

"The girl was crazy," he said. "None of us could have known that. Not until we broke through the door and saw her there."

She looked at him. "I'm sorry. I didn't mean to make any trouble."

"It was not your fault," he said. "Anyway, I'm happy that you're okay."

She was silent for a moment. "Again, thank you."

"We'll be in San Francisco in about four hours," he said. "Why don't you sleep until then? I know a doctor there who will help your bruises disappear in less than a day."

12

♦ THE HELICOPTER THAT carried them from the San Francisco airport to Crane City set them down exactly at eleven in the morning. Two automobiles were awaiting them.

Several men were standing as they descended from the copter. One of them, a tall distinguished man with salt-and-pepper gray hair, held out his hand. "Judd."

Judd grasped his hand. "Jim. Thanks for meeting us so promptly." He turned to Sofia. "Sofia, this is Dr. Marlowe. Brigadier General Marlowe, retired, was formerly in charge of the burn and skin center at NASA hospital in Houston. Jim, this is Doctor Ivancich, Sofia."

The two doctors shook hands. "How do you feel, Doctor?" Jim asked.

"Sore," Sofia answered. "But I feel they are mostly surface contusions."

Jim smiled. "We'll take a look at it. I'll take you to the clinic."

Sofia turned to Judd questioningly.

Judd smiled reassuringly. "I'll be at my office. As soon as Jim takes care of you, he'll bring you over."

He watched as Dr. Marlowe's car rolled away. Fast Eddie and Merlin followed him to the other car. He raised the window that separated the chauffeur from the passengers and looked at Merlin. "How come Ginny's psychomedical report didn't uncover her latent psychosis?"

"Nobody knows," Merlin said. "They're reevaluating the tests now."

"I want a full review of it as well as the complete tests and procedures. All it would take is one nut like that to blow us all out of the sky."

Merlin knew better than to reply. Judd's anger was never

obvious on the surface, but it was deadly. He had no tolerance for mistakes.

Judd changed the subject. "Did you notify Judson at construction about S. Yuan Ling?"

"Yes. He was very pleased. Also he asked me to tell you that he is reworking the bridge construction labor method and thinks that he can bring that down by about another million dollars."

"Good," Judd nodded. "Is Barbara meeting me at the office?"

"Yes, sir."

Judd nodded and leaned back into the seat and lowered the chauffeur's window. He snapped his fingers. Fast Eddie looked back over his seat. He knew what was wanted.

The small gold vial and spoon passed in the palm of his hand. Judd covered his hand and turned to the corner of the car. He felt better as soon as the two snorts of cocaine hit him. He nodded and palmed the vial and spoon back to Fast Eddie.

HE KISSED BARBARA on the cheek. "You look beautiful."

She smiled. "Flatterer. I'm a sixty-year-old lady."

"I won't tell if you won't," he said. "You can fake out everybody with forty."

"Thanks," she said. "You look tired."

"I am," he said. "But I'll get over it. I'll get a long weekend's rest at Boca Raton."

"You ought to give me a corporate title," she said.

"You tell me, you got it."

She laughed. "Godmother." She turned serious. "I worry about you."

"I'll be okay," he said.

"I hope that doctor you brought from Yugoslavia will do you some good at least," she said. "And that she doesn't play around with any more rough-trade dikes."

He was surprised. "What do you know about it?"

"I told you. I'm the Godmother." She paused. "I saw the telex you sent to the clinic."

He shook his head ruefully. "Shit."

"Don't be angry," she said. "Don't forget you have a very close-knit family."

70

"I'm beginning to find that out," he said. "Was it the same with Father?"

"More," she said. "You are away more than he ever was."

He turned to face the windows. It was nearing lunchtime and the offices were beginning to empty out. He turned back to Barbara. "Jack Maloney tells me NASA is not giving us any cooperation at all. Hughes has the next six satellites locked up tight."

"That's right," she said. "I checked with General Stryker at Hughes. He was an old friend of mine. He told me that they're sitting tight also."

"All I want just now is two of the six."

"They won't budge."

He thought for a moment. "We supply the directional semiconductors for Hughes, is that right?"

"Yes," she nodded.

"Have they been shipped yet?"

"I don't know," she answered. "What are you thinking?"

"If Hughes doesn't have those semiconductors, the satellites don't go up. Right?"

"I'm not an engineer," she said.

He called Merlin into the office. "Call the procurement office at Hughes, notify them we're not shipping the semiconductors. Tell them they're not ready yet, and we don't know how long it will take."

"That's going to cost you a forty-million-dollar lawsuit," Merlin said.

"Fuck 'em!" he said.

"You're the boss," Merlin said and left the office.

Judd turned to Barbara. "Now you can do your godmother bit. Call your friend General Stryker, tell him that because of your relationship with me, you could expedite those semiconductors if they waive two of their satellite launches to me."

"That's blackmail," she said.

"That's right," he said.

She laughed. "I love it!" She began to leave his office, then turned to look back at him. "I know the Hughes organization. It might take some time. Everything goes through channels."

"I have the time," he said. "They're the ones in a hurry."

"Do I get a chance to meet your doctor?" she asked.

71

"Dinner," he said.

"Lovely," she said and left the office.

"I DIDN'T KNOW that your stepmother was married to Dr. Marlowe," Sofia said, as Fast Eddie opened the door to the penthouse Judd maintained at the Mark Hopkins.

"It's been six years now," Judd said, following her into the suite.

"She's a young woman," she said.

Judd nodded.

"And Dr. Marlowe is a genius. I never knew a technique like that. Some things about American medicine are light-years ahead of us."

"What did he do?"

"Subcutaneous dispersal injections with a combination of ACTH, procaine and nonallergenic collagen. His touch is so gentle and light I never felt it."

"He's good," Judd said. "NASA didn't want to lose him. But he is seventy and decided that enough is enough, so he retired."

"They have a beautiful home on Nob Hill, is that what you call it? Have they had it long?"

"It has been in his family for ages," he said. "He comes from here."

"Your mother must be a happy woman."

"She is," he said. He led her into the bedroom. At the far end of the room just in front of the curved ceiling-to-floor windows was an oval Jacuzzi whirlpool bathtub. He pressed a button turning on the water. He looked at her. "Is water okay for you?" he asked.

"If it's not too hot," she answered.

"88 Fahrenheit?"

"Should be all right."

"Let's have a bath then," he said.

He was in the tub before her. He turned as she came naked toward him. "He is good," he said. "The bruises seem almost gone."

"He said that by tomorrow they will be completely gone." She carefully put one foot on the step and checked the water. "It's fine."

He held his hand up to steady her. She saw a smile on his lips. "What are you thinking?" she asked.

"Your pussy," he said. "It's like a baby's."

"Does it look funny?"

He shook. "On the contrary. It's a great turn-on. The way your clit pushes out there."

She looked down into his eyes. "Would you like to eat it before I get any water and soap on it?"

"Crazy question," he replied.

She pulled her hands around his head, then straddled her legs so that she could ride his face.

13

♦ DR. LEE SAWYER, director of the Crane Medical Research Center in Boca Raton, Florida, was a man of medium height, fortyish, bald, with water-blue eyes and the lugubrious expression of a basset hound. He sat in a chair next to Judd's hospital bed. "I never believed you would really go through with this," he said. "How long has it been since you've stayed in one place for three days?"

Judd looked at him. "I don't know. Where's Sofia?"

"She wants to attend every one of your tests," Doc Sawyer said. "I've arranged a suite for her on the floor near yours."

"What do you think of her?"

Dr. Sawyer shrugged. "She's asking for a lot of information. And I honestly don't understand why she needs it all." He looked down at the sheet of paper. "According to this, the first day you have to have six sperm counts and studies, half of each to stay here and the other half to be frozen and sent back to Yugoslavia. On top of that, each has to be taken four hours apart."

"Does that mean I have to have an ejaculation?"

"I don't know any other way," Doc Sawyer said. "What's more, we have to express your prostate each time so that the testes are completely emptied."

Judd stared at him.

"I don't know what you've done to the lady," Doc Sawyer said. "But you must have convinced her that you're Tarzan."

"What else is on the list?" Judd asked.

"Complete CAT scan, sonar reading and x-rays of all the vital organs, surgical shaving of pieces of the same, blood twenty-four analysis, oxygen-retention, carbon monoxide and nitrogen level, shavings of skin, hair, nails, both fingers and toes. There's more, do you want me to read all of it?"

"I'm exhausted already," Judd said. "Didn't she give you an idea why she wanted all these tests?"

"Only that Dr. Zabiski ordered them."

"Have you done anything more about human self-cloning tests?" Judd asked.

"Not yet," Doc Sawyer answered.

Sofia came into the room. She looked different in doctor's white. "How do you feel?" she asked.

"Okay," he said. "Tell me, did you ever give these tests to anyone else?"

"Yes, one," she said. "Usually Dr. Zabiski supervises all of them at the clinic, but you were the second person she okayed for all of this. The first was Mao Tse-tung."

Judd looked at her. "You worked with him also?"

"Yes," she said. "Then I stayed another year with him until he died. He insisted on the whole procedure even though Dr. Zabiski told him he was not a suitable candidate for her treatment."

"What did you do for him then?"

"Dr. Zabiski would send a weekly supply by air. It was a serum that I injected intravenously twice a day morning and night."

"What kind of serum was it?" he asked.

"I don't know," she answered. "No one knew except Dr. Zabiski herself. There were even laboratory attempts to analyze and break down the components. The Chinese never found out."

"That seems hard to believe," Doc Sawyer said.

"Every kind of analysis was tried. Spectrum, electrical, radiological, chemical. None of them worked. Believe me, Dr. Zabiski's the only one who knows. She probably has a system of her own to defy any attempt to analyze the serum."

"I don't like it," Doc Sawyer said. He turned to Judd. "Who the hell knows what she could be shooting into you? For all we know, it might be something that could kill you."

Sofia looked at him. "I know Dr. Zabiski, Doctor. Her only purpose in life is its prolongation. That's her dream."

Judd looked at Doc Sawyer. "Right now, all I'm doing is undergoing a number of tests. There's nothing that can do any damage just now."

Doc Sawyer nodded.

"Then let's go with it," Judd said. "Later we'll see what we decide."

Sofia looked at him. "The first thing you must do is have a good night's sleep. We begin at six in the morning."

"But it's only seven in the evening," Judd said. "I haven't yet had dinner."

"I've ordered a light dinner for you," Sofia said. "You should be asleep at nine o'clock."

The telephone next to his bed rang. He picked it up. "Yes?"

Barbara was on the telephone. "I've just been talking to General Stryker. He said that he's been on the telephone for three days and he hasn't been able to get any answer to the offer you made for the satellites. He said we're running out of time. The first launch is scheduled for the fifth of April. Their legal department has already prepared the lawsuit against us if we don't deliver."

"Why can't he get an answer?" he asked.

"There are only two people who can approve the exchange. Bill Gay and Howard Hughes himself. Neither of them can be reached. Gay is out of the country and no one can find him. Hughes is in Acapulco but he won't answer the telephone."

"It's hard to believe that," Judd said.

"It's true," she said. "Stryker says that no one has spoken directly to Hughes in years. All the messages from him go through Gay or Gay's men, who are always with Hughes."

"Then we'll have to talk to Hughes himself," Judd said. "Thanks for calling. I'll be in touch with you."

"Good luck," Barbara said. "Kisses."

"Kisses," he said and put down the telephone. He sat up in the bed. "Get my clothes. Sorry, but we'll have to put off the tests for a few days."

Sofia looked at him. "But everything is already ordered."

"Sorry," he said again, getting down from the bed. He turned to Doc Sawyer. "Do me a favor and get me Merlin right away."

Merlin was in his room almost before Judd had his shirt buttoned. "Yes, sir?"

"Call the plane and tell them we're leaving for Acapulco as soon as I get to the airport. Then call General Martés in Mexico City and tell him that I need ten *Federales* secret police to meet the plane in Acapulco. Tell him there's a hundred thousand dollars for him and a thousand dollars for each man. Tell him I also want to know where Hughes is staying in Acapulco and a plan that could penetrate any security that surrounds Hughes." He slipped into his socks and shoes. "I'll meet you in ten minutes downstairs in the car."

Merlin left the room. He turned to Sofia. "Make yourself at home," he said. "I should be back in less than two days."

She looked at him. "I've never been to Acapulco."

"Come then," he said.

"But what should I wear?" she asked.

He laughed. "In Acapulco all you need is a bikini."

14

◆ A TALL YOUNG man in an army uniform came aboard when the plane landed in Acapulco. He saluted Judd sharply. "I'm Lieutenant Colonel Ayala," he said in English.

"I'm Judd Crane," he said, shaking the soldier's hand.

"I am adjutant to General Martés. I have all the information you requested." Colonel Ayala held out a file folder. "Perhaps it would be simpler if I explained it all to you since it is in Spanish?"

"Thank you, Colonel," Judd said. He brought the soldier to the small conference table in the main lounge.

The soldier spread the papers. "Señor Hughes has the entire penthouse floor of the Acapulco Princess Hotel. Here is the floor plan. As you see, the corner room, the largest, faces the sea and is Señor Hughes' personally. Next to it is a slightly smaller room. It contains several telephones, a telex, chairs and two cots. There is always a man stationed in that room. The door between Señor Hughes' and that room is always open. There are four other rooms on the floor which are shared by Señor Hughes' personnel. There are usually fifteen men in his party but the exact number is uncertain at this moment. We know that four of the men are not in Mexico, nor is Señor Hughes' personal doctor. As a matter of fact, several days ago, the hotel physician was summoned by one of the Hughes men to examine Señor Hughes and we have learned that *el Señor* is very ill and should be hospitalized. But we've also learned that nothing will be done until his personal doctor returns tomorrow."

Judd looked at the soldier. "Did the doctor have an opinion of the nature of Mr. Hughes' illness?"

"We do not know what his own doctor has ordered. We know that blood tests were ordered. But we don't even know if they've been done."

"Are Hughes' men armed?"

"Some of them," the soldier said. "They are not professional bodyguards, more like secretaries and personal assistants. There is a professional guard at the elevator doors on the penthouse floor, but he is a Mexican hotel security man and not a very competent one."

Judd studied the floor plan. "Do you think noise could be heard in the other rooms?"

"It depends on how much noise is made," the soldier said.

"No guns and low voices," Judd said.

"Should be okay," the soldier said. "If we come upstairs on the freight elevator, avoiding the lobby, we could take out the floor guard because he always faces the passenger elevators. Then the element of surprise could overcome any of the others who made it to his suite."

Judd stared down at the floor plan. "I don't want anyone hurt," he said. "I simply want to speak with Hughes, nothing else."

"I understand, Señor," the soldier said. "Will you be accompanying us alone?"

Judd thought for a moment. He turned to Sofia. "Could you come with me? If he's sick, he may need help."

"Yes, of course," she answered.

Judd turned to the soldier. "This lady is my doctor," he said. "She will join us."

The soldier looked at him skeptically, but his voice was respectful. "Whatever you say, Señor."

IT WAS EIGHT kilometers from the airport to the hotel, then one more kilometer on the hotel road past the golf course to the hotel entrance. Sitting in the backseat of the four-door car, Sofia looked at Judd. "It's beautiful," she said. "Someday I'd like to see more of it."

Judd smiled. "I have a friend who owns a villa near here. Maybe we can spend the weekend."

"Not this time," she said. "First, we go back for your tests."

Colonel Ayala, seated next to the driver, leaned over the seat toward them. "We will drive around to the service entrance."

Judd nodded. He looked out the rear window. The soldiers accompanying them were following in a black-sided panel van.

The cars went around the hotel to the service entrance. They pulled into the parking area and got out.

The colonel spoke briefly to the gateman, who silently signaled them to pass. They went through the basement corridor and stopped at the freight elevator. A cleaning woman was pushing a cart into it. The soldier spoke sharply and the woman nervously pulled back her laundry. They went into the elevator and the soldier pressed the floor button. The door closed.

Colonel Ayala looked at Judd and Sofia. "You will wait until I tell you to come out of the elevator."

Judd nodded. He looked up at the floor lights over the doors. The numbers flashed slowly. It seemed forever before the PH light went on.

Several of the soldiers rushed out of the elevator almost before the doors opened. A few seconds later others followed. Colonel Ayala gestured for the rest of them to come out. He pressed a button to lock the elevator door open.

The guard was on his stomach on the floor, hands handcuffed behind his back, in front of the passenger elevator he was supposed to protect. Colonel Ayala spoke quietly to him. The guard gestured with his head to one of the doors, his eyes moving nervously.

Colonel Ayala inched his way along carefully, his back against the wall until he reached the doorknob. The door opened easily. It was not locked. Quietly, the soldier stepped through the door, Judd behind him. A man, his head resting on crossed arms on the table before him, was fast asleep.

A soldier stepped lightly behind the sleeping figure and touched him gently on the shoulder. The man awoke, startled. His eyes opened wide, staring down the muzzle of the Colt .45 automatic. He began to open his mouth.

Judd spoke quickly. "Stay quiet. No one's going to hurt you." The man turned to him.

Judd was reassuring. "We're not here to hurt anyone." He paused a moment. "Where are the others?"

The man took a deep breath. "Three of them are in their rooms asleep. The others went into town. There's an English-language movie today."

Judd looked toward Hughes' room. "Is he in there?"

The man nodded.

"I'd like to talk with him," Judd said.

"You can't," the man said. "He's sick and he's asleep."

"Wake him up," Judd said.

"I can't," he said. "He's really out. I think he's taken some pills."

"You lead us in there," Judd said. "The lady with us is a doctor."

The man looked at Sofia for a moment, then looked down at the doctor's bag in her hand. He got to his feet. Slowly they followed him into the room.

The room was almost dark, the blackout drapes closely drawn. The only light in the room was a small night-light next to the bed table. The wall-to-wall carpet was carefully covered by Kleenexes neatly placed one next to the other. There was a stench in the air that even the air conditioning seemed unable to remove.

"Open the drapes and the windows," Judd said. "Let some of the stink out of here and get rid of the damn Kleenexes. They only add to the mess."

"Can't!" the man said. "Everything has been sealed. Closed tight! And we are not allowed to pick up the Kleenexes. He believes that they are the only thing that keep the germs from him. Those are Mr. Hughes' orders."

"Turn on some lights then," Judd said.

The man turned on a lamp near the door. Judd gazed at the man in the bed. He lay on his side, his face against a pillow. The eyes were closed, the breathing labored, through his open mouth. His face was unshaven; his hair lay in long gray strands, unkempt, reaching almost to his shoulders.

Judd felt shocked disbelief. "Mr. Hughes," he called gently.

Hughes did not move.

Judd called him again, more loudly.

"He won't answer," his man said. "I told you, he's sick. He's been like that almost all week. We haven't been able to give him anything to eat."

Judd gestured to Sofia. "Take a look at him."

Sofia went to the bed. She opened her bag and took out a stethoscope. She listened for a moment, then searched for his pulse. "He's very weak," she said.

Judd watched her silently.

She lifted the sheet and looked down at Hughes' whole figure; she let the cover fall over him again. She leaned close to his face, lifting up one of his eyelids for a moment. Finally she straightened up. "This man should be taken to a hospital immediately."

"What's the matter with him?" Judd asked.

"I'm guessing," she said, "but I think he's beginning to show signs of uremic poisoning."

"How does something like that happen?" Judd asked.

"Look," she said.

Judd followed beside her. She raised the cover. "Look," she said. "He's covered with needle marks. Also, look at his emaciated condition. He's dehydrated. His bones are almost through his skin and there's an unhealed scar on his head as if a tumor has accidentally been torn off."

"Is there anything you can do for him here and now?"

Sofia shook her head. "Not without all the equipment we'd have in a hospital."

"A shot that could at least lessen his pain?" Judd asked.

"I have the feeling that he's already shot himself with enough pain killers," she said. "Besides, looking at his eyes I'd say he's more than slightly comatose."

Judd nodded then turned to the Hughes man. He gestured to the next room. They followed the man out. "What the hell is going on here?" Judd asked.

"I just take orders," the man said. "And we've been ordered not to touch him until his own doctor comes back from the States tomorrow."

"Who gave those orders?"

"The old man himself. Last week, just as he began getting sick. And no one—no one—countermands his orders."

Judd stared at him. "Isn't there anyone who understands he's no longer responsible for himself? Who can order the treatment he needs?"

"Only his doctor," the man said.

"You have a telex," Judd said crisply. "Get in touch with Hughes' office. Someone there must have the responsibility."

"The telex is not connected."

"You have telephones."

"We have already called. That's why his doctor's coming back."

Judd looked at the man for a moment, then turned to the soldier. "Let's leave," he said.

Sofia turned to Judd. "If we don't help him—and quickly—he will die."

Judd looked at her. His eyes were cold blue ice. "That's not my responsibility."

"But he's a human being," she said.

"Fuck him! It's his own choice," Judd said coldly. "There's nothing he can do for me and nothing I can do for him."

"Is that your only rule of measurement?"

"Do you know any better?" he replied sarcastically. "If I hadn't paid for those fucking hotels in Yugoslavia, do you think they'd even allow you to go out of the country with me?"

She stared at him for a moment and walked from the room. He turned to Hughes' man and placed ten one-thousand-dollar bills on the table before him. "This is to help you to forget you saw us."

The man picked the money up and placed it in his pocket. "Forget who?"

THEY WERE IN the air two hours on the flight returning to Florida when Sofia came up the staircase to his lounge. "May I speak with you for a moment?"

"Of course," he said. He handed a telex to her. "The whole thing was an unnecessary exercise. We've just learned from Stryker that they've accepted our proposal."

She put down the telex without reading it. "I apologize," she said. "I know it's none of my business, but the man is going to die."

"I didn't need you to tell me. I have eyes."

"But why did a man who had everything in the world for the asking want to live like that?" she asked. "Alone. Sealed in a vacuum bubble out of all contact with reality?"

"Maybe he thought that that way he would live forever," Judd said, then he was silent for a moment. "Or maybe he really *wanted* to die—and didn't have the guts to do it . . ."

15

◆ THE BUILDING WAS of green mirrored glass, reflecting the bright Florida sunshine. Its one-storied flat roof was completely hidden by the giant Florida cypress trees from the Crane Medical Center one block away. Next to the glass emerald doors was a small brass plate:

CRANE RESEARCH
NUCLEAR MEDICINE
PRIVATE

Two armed and uniformed security guards stood outside the locked doors like robots, with identical green-mirrored sunglasses hiding their eyes.

Doc Sawyer parked his convertible in the driveway and ran up the steps to the building entrance. He nodded to the security guards as he pressed his palm to the photo-sensitive identity plate. His name in L.E.D. letters rose over the plate and the doors silently slid open for him.

The main floor was completely empty except for another security guard seated behind a desk between the two banks of elevators. The guard looked up at him. "Dr. Zabiski said she will meet you at the fourth level, sir," he said.

"Thank you," Doc answered, opening the elevator doors. They quickly closed behind him and he pressed for level 4. Slowly the elevator descended. He looked at the indicator lights. This time the numbers for the floor did not indicate floors ascending. They ran from M, for main floor top, to 9, for the bottom subterranean level. The entire building was constructed underground.

He came out of the elevator. He nodded again at the ever-present security guard and hurried down the corridor to Dr. Zabiski's office. He opened the door without knocking. Dr.

Zabiski was seated behind her desk. "I came as soon as I got your call," he said anxiously. "Is there anything wrong?"

"Nothing is wrong," the tiny woman said reassuringly. "We've moved him to an intensive care unit. I thought you'd like to be here when we wake him."

He let out a sigh of relief and sank into a chair opposite hers. "Jesus," he said, pulling a pack of cigarettes from his jacket. His hand still trembled as he lit the cigarette. "This is crazy," he said, pulling the smoke deep into his lungs. "I'm beginning to believe more than ever during the last three years that we've all become Frankensteins."

"All doctors are Frankenstein at heart." She smiled slowly. "Is there a one of us who doesn't dream of playing God?"

"I suppose," Sawyer said. He drew again from his cigarette. "But we all know who God is, don't we?"

She laughed. But there was no humor in the tawny, catlike eyes. "Judd Crane?"

He laughed, also without humor. "He has to be God. I don't know anyone else who can afford it."

She was silent for a moment, then nodded. "You're probably right," she said. "When he first told me twenty, then fifty million dollars, I didn't believe him. I didn't think there was that much money in the world. Then I looked into his eyes. And I believed. Not in the money, but the man. He means to bring all the knowledge in the world to bear upon his own dream: Immortality."

He put out the cigarette. "And your dream?" he asked, watching the cigarette smolder in the ashtray on her desk.

"I'd like to be a part of his dream," she said. But he caught a tinge of sadness in her voice. "I don't know. I *really* don't know. Is his dream within our power to achieve? Perhaps knowledge and science are not enough." Their eyes met across the desk. "We have to realize that like him, we are human, not Godlike."

He nodded slowly. "Dr. Zabiski, I'm beginning to think that I like you."

She smiled. "Thank you, Dr. Sawyer." She changed the mood between them deliberately. "Let's see how he's doing."

He rose from his chair and stood next to her as she pressed keys on the computer on her desk. Numbers began flashing across the screen, yellow, red, blue, green, purple and white. "You'll have to explain it all to me, Doctor," he said. "I haven't the coding."

"I'm sorry, I thought you'd been informed," she said. "I'll explain. It's a simple color code with white being optimum or what we hope to achieve. The rest is normal, the other colors being percentages of normal. All vital signs and pathology are constantly monitored. At the moment, we are most concerned with his body temperature. Our target for this procedure is to stabilize his normal body temperature at 95.0 Fahrenheit. We must remember this is the third procedure he's undergone in three years. The first two times we were able to bring down his temperature, first from 98.6 to 97.3, the second to 96.1. In each case we've maintained those temperatures steady for one whole year before the next procedure."

Sawyer looked down at her. "If I remember correctly, according to the survival tables you've shown me, maintaining body temperature at 95.0 should bring him a life expectancy of one hundred and fifty years."

"That's correct," she said. "But that's not the only factor. Cellular implantation as well as placenta and Rumania procainum procedures should strengthen the vitality of his whole body so that another aging factor is significantly decelerated." She looked up at him. "We have to understand that the body has to withstand the time factor placed on it."

He stood silent for a moment. "One hundred and fifty years," he said softly. "That should be enough for anyone."

"Not for him," she said. "He's said immortality. We have four more temperature procedures planned over almost a five-year span. That should bring his body temperature to a fixed 87.8, the survival prediction of which should reach to two hundred and eighty years. But as I said, I don't know. It's all computer guesswork as of this minute."

"Shit!" he said. "I'm frightened."

She turned off the computer. "So am I." She filled a glass with water from a thermos carafe on her desk. She sipped from her glass. "Playing with the hypothalamus, even with a nuclear laser to bring down his body temperature, gives us no guarantees. One microsecond can kill him."

He went back to his chair. "Maybe we can persuade him to stop after this."

"I've had that out with him before," she said. "And I'll try again, I assure you. But I know what he'll say."

He met her eyes. "What?"

" 'I can die in an accident anytime!' he says. 'I'd rather die going for broke.' " She pressed the computer keys again, then looked up at him. "We can go downstairs. We'll be waking him in about fifteen minutes."

The elevator brought them down to the eighth level. The security guard nodded at them from behind his desk as they passed through the panel of glass doors into another corridor. This corridor turned at a right angle, hiding them from the guard's eyes. Glass doors in front of them were lettered in silver glaze: MONITOR ROOM.

Dr. Zabiski pressed her palm to the identity plate. The doors opened and they passed into the room. Though he had seen it many times, the monitor room always seemed to Dr. Sawyer like a miniature of the NASA control room during space flights. They entered onto a small platform; three steps took them to the main floor, the walls of which were covered with computers, whirling tapes recording the information received on silver-gray screens. The far wall was all glass, beyond that wall was the intensive care unit in which Judd rested. In front of it sat three technicians, each with his own printout computer and screen, monitoring the patient's every vital movement inside and outside his body.

He followed the little woman to the glass wall and he looked with her into the room. Judd was sleeping, his completely nude body covered with wireless electrodes which sent information to the computers. The only tubes attached to him were on temple-spectacles bringing a flow of oxygen to his nostrils.

Dr. Zabiski turned to the monitors while Sawyer still watched Judd. He thought he detected a moment's stirring. The movement became more pronounced. Unconsciously Judd was experiencing an erection.

Sawyer turned to the little woman. "He must be having good dreams," he smiled. "He's getting himself a hard-on all by himself."

Zabiski straightened up and looked at Judd. A sudden shadow

of concern crossed her face. "I don't like it," she said. "This is much too soon." She bent to the first technician. "Give me a reading on the EEG and call the neurologist here immediately. Also call Dr. Ablon, the cardiologist."

The second technician called to her. "Dr. Zabiski, we have a reading that his temperature is going up. It's just gone up half a point to 95.5. No, it's 95.6 now," she amended quickly.

"I want a blood chemistry reading and a go-through reading of all the vital signs," Zabiski ordered quickly, her gaze going over the shoulder of the first technician. She watched lines wiggle across the computer screen. She looked up at Sawyer. "He's dreaming all right," she said. "There is definite but slight hyper-active movement in the alpha sector."

"What do you think is happening?" Sawyer asked.

Zabiski looked at him. "I don't know yet. But I can make a guess." She did not, however, offer it to him.

Sawyer gazed at her steadily, waiting.

"I have a feeling that the hypothalamus is rejecting all the procedures and returning to normal functioning," she said finally.

"Will that be of any danger to him?" Sawyer asked.

"I don't think so," she said, reading down the screen. "Vital signs are all okay. Blood chemistry shows no abnormality or infection." She picked up the telephone and called the anesthesiologist in another room. "Keep the patient under a little longer. We have a few things to check out before we bring him up."

"Where the hell is Sofia?" Sawyer asked. "Shouldn't she be here?"

"I gave her a few days off," Zabiski said. "After working almost three years without any time off, I thought she could use it. Especially since she volunteered to be the control. After the last group of experiments she was tired."

"Did the experiment succeed?" he asked.

Zabiski looked at him. "If you mean did she become pregnant?" She answered herself, "Yes."

"Where did she go?" he asked.

"Mexico," she answered. "Sofia has been curious about Mexico since that time she went to Acapulco."

Sawyer was silent, thinking. Mexico was a curious choice for Sofia. If it was sun she was looking for, there was enough here in Boca Raton. Maybe she had another reason. He decided to tell Merlin to have Security check into her trip.

16

♦ JUDD PRESSED THE button at the side of his bed, raised the head of it to a sitting position and picked up the telephone. Merlin answered at once. "What's happening?" he asked.

"We had two frantic telephone calls from the inauguration committee. Reagan wants to include us in his personal party."

"That's next week, isn't it?"

"Yes."

"Tell them I'll be honored to be there. Also that I will make my own arrangements for travel and lodging." He glanced up at the clock on the wall. "What else?"

"The Finance Secretary of Brazil wants to fix a meeting to discuss whether or not you're participating with them on Ludwig's project down there. There are presistent rumors that D.K. wants out."

Judd thought for a moment. "Let's find out more about it first. Tell them we'll arrange something with him as soon as I can schedule Brazil. But make sure that he understands we plan only a discussion. We're not yet interested in the project."

"Yes, sir," Merlin said. "The government's approved our proposed merger of the South and Western Savings and Loan Association into Crane Financial Services. That brings us one hundred and fifteen bank branches and a billion in assets that we can transfer to net worth. It means eight hundred million can be turned into cash within thirty days, if we want, sir."

"Good," Judd said. "Any answer yet from our proposal to the Mexican government? The peso is worth shit and unless they guarantee to build a laboratory and factory for thirty million dollars for Crane Pharmaceuticals, we will not begin production in Mexico."

"We haven't heard anything from them yet."

"Goose 'em a little. Tell 'em how much Brazil is interested in a discussion with us."

"Will do it," Merlin said. He changed the subject. "How are you feeling?"

"Like shit," Judd said. "But don't worry about it. I'll be out of here in a few days."

"I'm glad," Merlin said.

"Thank you," Judd said, putting down the phone. He pressed for a nurse. A new girl came into the room, one he hadn't seen before, red-haired like a flame over soft blue eyes. "What's your name?"

"Bridget O'Malley," she said with a hint of a brogue.

"Irish?" he said. "And right off the boat?"

"The airplane, Mr. Crane," she said. "I was recruited especially for this job."

"You must have fulfilled very special requirements for my people to bring you over here for this job," he said. "What are they?"

A faint blush swept across her face. "I'd rather not discuss them," she answered, her brogue thickening.

"I'm thirsty," he broke off without warning. "Bring me a Coca-Cola."

"Sorry, Mr. Crane, orange juice or water. That's all you are allowed."

"Orange juice, then," he said, looking at the faint blush still visible on her face. She began to turn away. "Bridget," he called.

She came back to the bed. "Yes, Mr. Crane?"

He looked up at her eyes. "Did they tell you that I've got a temporary problem of priapism?"

Her eyes fell and she looked at the sheet across his legs. "Yes, Mr. Crane."

"Was one of the special requirements you filled the taking care of priapistic patients?"

She nodded silently.

"Where did you get your experience?"

"I was four years at the Veterans Hospital in Devon."

"What treatments were prescribed there, Bridget?"

She looked down at his face. "Certain drugs, acupressure, electromyograph (EMG) recording of biofeedback muscle relaxation—"

"Very interesting," he said, interrupting her. "Thank you, Bridget, for the information. I'd like my orange juice now."

He waited until she returned with the glass of orange juice. His erection was rock-hard and throbbing painfully. He sipped at the juice. "I've heard there is an operation that can correct this."

"Yes, Mr. Crane," she said impersonally, "but you won't want that, because once it's done it cannot be reversed. You'd never have an erection again. That operation's performed only in case of a perpetual and painful priapistic erection."

He looked up at her face. "Right now, it is very damned painful, I assure you. What am I supposed to do, Bridget? Masturbate again? My penis is beginning to be sore and burning. By the time I orgasm I'm in agony." He kept his eyes fixed steadily on her.

She picked up the chart at the foot of the bed and made a notation on it. "Let me check with the doctor," she murmured.

"Why wait for the doctor?" he said. "I thought you were brought in especially for your experience, know-how and method."

"I'm just a nurse, Mr. Crane," she finessed. "I am not able to do anything without the doctor's specific orders, sir."

"Fuck the doctors!" he said angrily. "I own this goddamned hospital and everything in it, including the doctors. Now, if you can help me, you'd better damn well do it."

"The doctor will discharge me," she said.

"We won't tell them," he said.

She pointed to the television monitor on the wall behind the bed. "You're monitored on the screen and videotaped around the clock."

He threw a towel at the monitor. It caught across the monitor and covered the camera lens. "Now, no one will see," he snapped harshly. He pushed the sheet down across his knees. His phallus sprang free like a wild beast flushed from a cage, red and throbbing. "Now, goddamnit!"

She hesitated for a moment, then moved to the side of the bed. She placed one of her knees on the bed next to him, then clasped his phallus tightly in her left hand. With the fingers of her other hand, she began digging into the nerves located in his scrotum, just above his testes. She looked down at his eyes. "It might hurt a little," she said gently.

His cobalt-blue eyes were impassive. He nodded assent silently.

Slowly she began exerting pressure on the nerves with her fingers, at the same time opening and closing them against his phallus, forcing the blood to return to the base of the phallus toward the scrotum. After a moment, she seemed to pick up a rhythm. Her hand continued grasping downward, fingers digging deeper and deeper.

She looked down at him for a signal that the pain was more than he could bear, but he held his lips tightly clamped against the agony. "I'm sorry," she said. "But it will only be a moment more."

He nodded understanding, a faint perspiration like dew formed on his forehead. Suddenly a knifelike thrust seemed to tear through his groin. An involuntary groan escaped from his lips.

She stepped up quickly. "It's over now, Mr. Crane."

He caught his breath for a moment, then looked down at himself. His penis was shrunken to its normal, relaxed size. He turned to her. "You really did it," he said in faint disbelief.

"Yes, Mr. Crane," she said quietly.

"I'm grateful," he said, and drew a deep, contented breath. "However, I don't think it will replace sucking and fucking."

For the first time she smiled. "Neither do I, Mr. Crane," she added.

HE SAT UP in bed and looked at Dr. Zabiski. "What went wrong?" he asked.

"Nothing much," she said dryly. "Only that millions of years of evolution don't agree with our computers." She glanced down at the printout in her hands. "We do have one small success though. Your temperature is now fixed at 98.4. That's two tenths of a point less than normal."

"What would that give me?"

"Ten or fifteen survival years on normal. And according to the PerScan and SonarScan examinations, the implantations program has been successfully tolerated by your body. If we continue with that program that should add approximately another twenty-five more survival years. Based on the average life span of

93

a man in your social and economic class, which is eighty years, you've already extended the possible survival life span to one hundred and twenty-five years."

"That's not immortality," he said in a voice as dry as sand.

She was silent.

"Do you think we should try again with the nuclear laser procedure?" he went on.

"No," she said flatly. "We were lucky this time. The next time we may destroy the hypothalamus and you'd become cold forever."

His eyes were blue as night. "Genetic engineering then, that's where we look."

"It will take much time before we know enough about the genetic code to make any use of it, I'm afraid," she said with a sigh.

"I have time. After all, haven't you already told me I have one hundred and twenty-five years?" He looked at her and smiled. "Okay. Now when can I get out of here?"

"Tomorrow morning," she said. "Physically, you are in perfect health. Even better than when we met. If you want to measure this in terms of years, you have gone from forty-two years of age to forty instead of from forty-two to forty-six."

"That's better than we had expected, isn't it?"

"Yes," she said. "But you'll have to take better care of yourself. Food, drink, rest, drugs. You should try another life style."

"You didn't mention sex?"

"The priapism should be temporary," she said. "After that, don't overdo it."

"I don't know," he said with a smile. "Maybe I should keep it. I find the idea exciting of having it ready whenever I want it there."

She didn't smile. "If you do, you'll shoot your life away through your penis."

"Then how do you propose to control it?" he asked.

"I won't," she said. "You will master it yourself. EMG biofeedback and yoga. How's that sound to you?"

"Like witchcraft, Doctor," he said.

"Better than saltpeter." She stood up. "You know, Judd, I'm beginning to like you and I want you to take care of yourself. I dream your dream, too, and I don't want anything to hurt the man who has custody of it for both of us."

17

◆ THE SCRAMBLER TELEPHONE on Merlin's desk rang twice. He picked up the receiver. "Merlin here."

"John D., Security," the man's voice began.

"Yes, John?" Merlin said.

"Our agent followed her on the flight to Mexico City," John D. went on. "She transferred to Aeromexico to a flight to Havana, where he lost her because he wasn't visa'd for Cuba."

"We have agents in Havana?"

"Yes, sir. Six men."

"I want three of them waiting for her arrival in Havana. I want twenty-four-hour surveillance. Bugs all around her, inside and outside. Got that?"

"Yes, sir."

"I want reports every three hours," Merlin said.

"Will do," John D. said. "We have a report that Li Chuan is arriving in Havana via Air Canada. Chances are they'll rendezvous there."

"Put a cover on him, too," Merlin said.

"Okay," John D. said. "Have you already received the lude report from Hong Kong?"

"Yes," Merlin said. "Three million ludes a year. That's a lot of Quaaludes."

"Fifteen million dollars," John D. said. "Transferred from the Crane Pharmaceuticals account to banks in the Bahamas and Switzerland. We're working right now to discover who owns those accounts."

"I have a hunch that one account is Li Chuan's own, the other is probably held for the Red Chinese government," Merlin said. "Our interferon account with them is under a million dollars."

"We'll find out everything," John D. said. "Anything else, sir?"

"Not right now," Merlin said. "Thanks." He looked down at the computer printout on his desk. Everything registered completely normal. He took a deep breath. That alone seemed wrong to him. Usually he caught numerous small computer errors. This was the first time to his knowledge that the computer was perfect.

He picked up the telephone and called Computer Central in California. A moment later he was on the line to the director of the Computer Services. "I want a recheck of every transaction over the last three years. Also, check the computer for taps and see whether anyone might have tampered with it and been able to dip into our storage banks."

"We run a routine check every day," the director said.

"I know that," Merlin snapped. "This time I want you to develop another form of checkout other than the usual one. Put that one on the scrambler when you figure it out."

"Mother is not going to like that," the director said. "You know how annoyed she gets when her routine is changed."

Merlin fell into the director's jargon, speaking of the computer as he would a person. "Tell the lady to stop bitching or we'll switch some of her favorite microchips on her." He put down the telephone and lit a cigarette.

"Damn mothers!" he swore silently to himself. He picked up the telephone to call Judd, then put it down without using it. He was going to be in the office in one more day in any case, he thought. And by that time they might have more information for him to work on before laying the problem out for the boss. He put out his cigarette. Another day couldn't hurt. Whatever damage has been done has already been done, Merlin concluded.

HAVANA WAS HOT and humid despite the waning afternoon sun. By the time she arrived at the hotel from the airport her clothing was sticking to her skin. Her room was preregistered and the room clerk called a bellboy to bring her to it without delay. "The air conditioning is not working yet," the boy said as he put down her luggage. He crossed to the sliding windows to the terrace. "It will be cooler as it gets dark," he added, opening them to the day's furnace outside.

She gave him a five-dollar bill for which he thanked her too profusely as he left the room. She waited until the door closed before she went out on the terrace.

The wide boulevard between the hotel and the beach was empty of traffic. The hot air was already growing somewhat cooler from a breeze that was beginning to blow in from the ocean. Even as she stood there, the broad promenade beside the beach came alive with people taking a late afternoon stroll.

She went back into the room and opened her valise. Quickly she hung her linen suit and two dresses in the closet and tossed her lingerie into a drawer. She snapped the valise shut and dropped her dressing gown on the bed. She took her small cosmetic case into the bathroom and placed it beside the sink. She turned on the water into the tub and squeezed a tube of perfumed gel into the rushing flow. She waited a moment until the perfume reached her, then went into the bedroom and began to undress. Neatly she hung her dress next to the others and dropped her lingerie into another drawer of the dresser. Naked, she turned toward the dressing gown and began to pick it up when she heard a key clicking in the door. The door opened before she could put on the gown.

She saw Nicolai, tall, heavy-set, black hair now shot with gray. He looked at her silently as he closed the door behind him.

The dressing gown still in her hand, she made no effort to cover herself. "You're early," she said in Russian.

"Four years, Sofia, was too long," he said. "I saw you when you came through the lobby and decided I could wait no longer."

"I didn't want to meet you sticky and smelling of sweat," she said. "I was running a tub with perfume."

He put his arms around her and kissed her mouth. "All I need is any smell of you," he whispered. She remained silent, unresponsive. He looked down into her eyes. "Is there something wrong, Sofia?"

"Almost four years, Nicolai," she said. "It doesn't disappear in a moment."

His arms dropped to his sides. "You don't love me? There's someone else?"

"I just need a little time. I've been too long in another world." She slipped into the dressing gown, evading his question. "My attaché case is open on the desk. Why don't you look through the reports while I take my bath?"

"I've ordered a bottle of champagne," he said.

"Good," she said. "I won't be too long."

He watched the bathroom door close behind her just as the doorbell rang. The bellboy placed the champagne in the ice bucket on the small table, then left the room. Nicolai looked from the closed bathroom door to the bottle of champagne. Quickly he snipped off the wire and pulled the cork.

Sofia found the warm water silky with the bubbly gel; she lay back luxuriantly in the tub. Perfume vapors rose to her nostrils, she closed her eyes. The water flowed sensuously across her body. Suddenly a cool draft of air broke the spell; she turned her eyes to the door.

Nicolai was standing there, naked before her, the bottle of champagne in one hand, his red-tipped phallus erect in his other hand held rigid and upright against the mat of black hair covering his belly. He walked to the bathtub and pushed his phallus down to her face and poured champagne over it. His voice was harsh and angry. "You loved champagne and you loved my prick. Let's see if you remember. Now drink both of them!"

"No! No!" she cried out, her hands trying to push his phallus away.

He pulled her face tight against his erection as his orgasm exploded almost instantly. "Bitch! Whore!" he growled.

She was coughing, his semen spilling across her cheeks and dripping down to her chin. He pulled himself from her mouth and stepped into the bathtub with her, then kneeled between her legs, brought her floating to him, her legs embracing his waist until he could shove himself into her. He drove his body into her violently.

Her hands pushed his body from her. "No! Please, no," she whispered.

"You cock-crazy bitch!" he snarled. "What changed you?"

"Please," she was crying. "Can't you feel that I'm pregnant!"

He stared at her. "Pregnant?"

"Yes. Ten weeks. She looked into his eyes. She felt him shrink inside her.

He was silent for a moment, then pushed her away. He stepped

99

out of the tub, still looking down at her. "You're not only a bitch whore," he said contemptuously. "You're stupid. Who is the father, or don't you even know?"

"I know," she said quietly. "Judd Crane."

He silently looked at her in the tub, then he took a bath towel from the rack and wrapped it around himself. "I'm going to dress," he said. "I would like to take your attaché case to the office and photocopy its contents. I'll return everything to you when I pick you up at dinner."

"As you like," she replied dully.

"Li Chuan will join us," he said.

"Yes."

He closed the bathroom door behind him. Suddenly she felt a weariness seep through her. Slowly, standing in the tub, she let the water empty and turned on the shower, the hot and needling spray washing away his ejaculation from her face.

Her legs seemed to turn to rubber and she reached against the wall to support herself. She turned off the shower and stepped from the tub. She wrapped a bath towel around her and went into the other room.

Nicolai was already gone. She looked at the desk. The attaché case had gone with him. She sat on the edge of the bed for a moment, then pulled her purse to herself. She snapped it open and looked down at the vial of cocaine that Judd had given her. Quickly she snorted two toots.

The expected lift never happened. She was too spent, too depressed and weary. She returned the vial to her purse and stretched out on the bed. Her eyes closed, she was soon asleep.

18

♦ A DRAFT OF cool air awakened her. She sat in the bed, sticky with perspiration after a deep sleep. The hum of the air conditioner's motor rattled through the vents. She rose, wrapped a bath towel around herself and closed the window to the terrace. At night, the lights were sparkling along the road that followed the beaches against the bay.

She checked her watch. Eight-thirty. Time for her to dress. Quickly she went into the bathroom and showered again, then got into a light linen suit. The telephone rang just as she completed her makeup.

It was Nicolai. "Awake?" he asked.

"And dressed," she answered.

"Good," he said. "I'll be over in fifteen minutes."

"Shall I wait in the room or would you want to meet in the lobby?"

"The room," he said. "We're having dinner at a restaurant. We have some time. Li Chuan will meet us there at ten o'clock."

"Fine," she said, putting down the telephone.

She looked at herself in the mirror. Makeup was the true miracle. The lines of weariness disappeared. But that was the surface, inside she was still down. Annoyed with herself despite what she saw in the mirror, she picked up her purse.

She opened the inside zippered pocket and took out a silver pillbox and the vial of cocaine. She popped a white and green capsule upper, swallowing it easily without water, then two good snorts of cocaine in each nostril from the small golden spoon that Judd had given her with her initials on the handle.

She felt the rush almost immediately. The combination brought her back to life. She took a deep breath. Now she began to feel more like herself, stronger, and more capable of coping with whatever was going to happen. She returned the vial and pillbox to her purse and turned to the mirror. The face looked even better. The eyes she saw were bright again.

NICOLAI WAITED UNTIL the bellboy opened the bottle of champagne, filled the two glasses and left, closing the door behind him. He handed a glass to Sofia and held up his own to her. "I apologize," he said.

She looked at him. "There's no need to."

"I was stupid," he said, "and insensitive. I should have understood how much you've undergone, too."

"That's unimportant," she said. "Each of us has our own job to do. That's what's important."

He touched his glass to hers. "For you, Sofia. There's never been a woman like you for me."

She sipped at her glass, looking at him over the rim. "Don't look at me like that, don't talk to me like that," she said.

"Damn!" he said. He took a deep breath. "I know I shouldn't be, but I am. Jealous. Jealous of all the time you've been with him and not with me."

"Nicky," she said softly. "You shouldn't feel like that. We were all doing our jobs."

"Is that really all it was for you?" he asked. "You felt nothing for him?"

"I didn't say that," she said. "But you know me better than anyone. At that time I thought I always had to have sex, with or without feeling. Sometimes I thought my body needed it more than food or air. Those years at the Institute where I was so confined, I used my vibrator sometimes three and four times a day. And then when I used it, I always thought of you."

He sipped at his champagne and laughed. "Remember when we first met? I thought you were a nymphomaniac. You never seemed to stop."

She didn't laugh. "When I was young, I used to think that. It was something I couldn't face until the doctors explained to me that my sexual nerves are extraordinarily sensitive. True nymphos never have satisfaction and very rarely reach orgasm. So, Nicky, you see I simply don't qualify. Just talking to you about it, I feel my clitoris twitching and I begin to juice."

"I want to touch you," he murmured.

"Don't, Nicky," she said. "I'm different. I'm not the girl you knew then. I've grown up."

"No," he said emphatically. "I still love you. Even more now than then. And you love me, I know that. That man played numbers with your head with his money, his power, his drugs and his life style. Did he ever say once, just once, that he loved you?"

She didn't answer.

"Did he ever ask you to marry him?"

She shook her head silently.

"He's using you," he said. "Just as he uses everyone else for his own gain, his search for eternal power." He nodded earnestly, looking at her. "He will throw you away as he does a toy that no longer amuses him. Or if you are no longer useful to him."

"He's not like that," she said defensively. "He is considerate and truthful. Even though his truthfulness sometimes seems cruel in its honesty."

"You think you're defending him, but in truth you are defending yourself to convince yourself," Nicolai said. "I'm sure you wouldn't feel that way if you hadn't allowed yourself to become pregnant."

"Maybe," she said thoughtfully. "But what was it? An experiment, that's all. I'm not the first scientist to use my own body as a subject. The old lady was concerned that the treatments might make him sterile."

"So you chose yourself to fuck him to check it out?"

"It was nothing like that. She took sperm from him and placed it into the ovaries of a dozen different women."

"And they all became pregnant?"

"Not all. Ten of them," she said.

"You were one of the lucky ones," he said bitterly.

She was silent.

"What happens now?" he asked.

"Next week will be the tenth week. Each pregnant subject will be aborted."

"You agreed to that?"

"Yes," she said.

He stared at her. "Why you? You were one of the doctors. I'm

103

sure they would have had no problem finding another woman. Why did you choose to involve yourself?"

"Because I was curious about my own body, Nicky," she said. "I have never been pregnant even though I've never used any form of contraception. There is something dynamic about him. I wondered—"

"Now, you admit the truth," he broke in angrily. "You really wanted his baby!"

"Yes," she said flatly, then looked up at him. "What difference does it make anyway? Next week it will be gone."

"You're just as stupid as every other woman," he said sarcastically. "We have been together for many years, why didn't you have a child with me?"

She met his eyes and answered him simply. "You never asked me."

THE ATTACHÉ CASE was open before him. He was turning the pages of her report when she returned to the room. "The old lady is clever," he said. "Eight years and we still don't know if we've discovered the method she uses in her cloning cellular impregnation."

"We know the cellular impregnation method. It's the cloning formula itself, which she always works on alone in her laboratory, that we have not been able to fathom."

"You ever been with her there?" he asked as idly as he could manage.

"No. And I know of no one who ever has," she said. "I'm beginning to think she never had a cloning process. She was hoping that Crane with all his facilities and computers would discover it for her."

He put the papers down and changed the subject abruptly. "Did she tell you that you were going to return to Russia?"

Surprise came into her voice. "No. Why?"

"Because you are supposed to attend Brezhnev."

"She's never said a word about it."

He remained silent for a long moment. "Maybe she thought it better to wait until after your abortion."

"That's possible," she said "What's the problem with the Chairman?"

"I only know rumors," he said. "Cancer, some say; an aneurysm, others say; or cerebral hemorrhages—so far there are only rumors. But I *do* know he moves with difficulty and sometimes he's very slurry with his words. She's had four consultations with him during the last year. Then the word came down that you would be assigned to him."

"But what about the work I'm doing here?"

"It's a matter of priorities," he said. "To us, Brezhnev is more important than Crane."

Sofia nodded thoughtfully. "She's being very clever, Nicky. I know of at least four of her assistants she could assign to Brezhnev, but by sending me she reduces the chance that I might discover her method."

"What makes you think you might have a chance?"

"Everything pertinent to Crane himself and his business affairs is fed into Computer Central in California. While I do not expect that her formula has been fed into the computer, everything she needs in the way of supplies and equipment which has been ordered and purchased is automatically recorded by the computer. If we can retrieve that information we might be a good deal closer to uncovering her method." She shook her head ruefully. "But in order to get that information, we'd have to get the access code to the computer. And the only people that I know who have that are Crane himself, his personal aide, Merlin, and the director of Computer Central."

Nicolai looked at her. "Perhaps there's someone else who can get to it," he offered slowly.

She looked questioningly at him. "I don't understand."

"Li Chuan," he said. "That's why we're meeting him here, Sofia. The man says that he has the access code and can make it available to us."

"It doesn't make sense," she said. "Even if he did have it, I can't believe he'd be so altruistic as to turn it over to us."

"Altruism has nothing to do with it," Nicolai laughed. "Twenty million dollars is more like it."

19

THE SOFT CHIME of the private telephone next to his head echoed above the sound of the television program he had been watching. He picked up the receiver. "Crane."

"Are you awake?" Merlin asked.

"Yes," Judd said. "I've been watching TV."

"I'd like to come over and see you," Merlin said.

"Would eight in the morning be okay?"

"Now would be better."

Judd thought only for a moment. He didn't have to ask Merlin if it was important. The request was evidence enough of that. "How long before you'll get here?" he asked.

"I'm in the office in Boca Raton," Merlin said. "About thirty or forty minutes. There should be no traffic at this hour."

"Get Fast Eddie to drive you and have him bring a change of clothing for me."

"Will do," Merlin said and rang off.

Judd punched the button next to the bed for the nurse and turned off the television set. A moment later, Bridget came into the room.

"Mr. Crane?" she asked.

"Pull these needles out of my arms and help me out of this bed to the shower," he said.

"I can't do that without Dr. Zabiski's order," she answered.

"Then call her," he ordered.

She looked at him hesitantly.

"Now," he said peremptorily.

The door closed behind her. A few moments later the telephone rang.

"The nurse relayed your request, Mr. Crane," the little woman began. "Is it genuinely important?"

"Yes," he replied crisply.

"Very well," she said. "But I'll want to be with you when they withdraw the equipment and to make very certain that you are perfectly well. I'll dress and be in your room in ten minutes. Meanwhile, the nurse will prepare you."

A moment later Bridget came into the room. She was holding a tray with a hypodermic needle covered by a towel. "Lie on your side," she said. "You get this one in your butt."

"What is it?" he asked.

"I'm just the nurse," she parried. "I'm not supposed to discuss what it is, just that the doctor's ordered it."

He turned on his side as she pulled the sheet from him. He felt the cool wetness of the alcohol swab, then the slight prick of the needle.

"Lie still," she said. "This is a long one."

"Shit," he said.

She laughed.

"Sadist," he said. He paused for a second. "I think I'm getting a hard-on. How about sucking it a little?"

She laughed again, withdrawing the needle, then placing a button-shaped Band-Aid on his buttock. "No way," she said. "It's your fault. You were the one in a hurry. I think the shot is to take care of it for you."

He rolled back against the pillows and looked up at her. "Bridget," he smiled. "There's always something taking away the joy of life."

"Rest quiet for a moment," she said. "I'll bring you freshly squeezed orange juice."

"I'd rather have a cherry Coke."

"You'll have orange juice," she said, closing the door behind her.

HE SAT ON the edge of the bed, his legs dangling over the side. Dr. Zabiski finished checking his blood pressure. "Good. One-twenty over eighty-five."

She gestured to a lab nurse who tied a coil around his arm. Quickly, expertly, the nurse drew four test tubes of blood and left him in a portable spirometry machine.

She held a plastic tube to him. "Take a deep breath, then blow out." He did as she asked. "Now, another, this time even deeper." She waited for him to fill his lungs. "Blow out as strong as you can, please," she ordered.

From the corner of his eye, he could see her studying the television screen at the foot of the bed. He pushed until his lungs were wholly deflated. He fell back, gasping for air.

"Good," the little doctor said. "Just one more test, if you will, please." Another assistant rolled what looked like an electrocardiogram machine to the bed. "Lie back," she ordered. "This will be very quick. It's electronic."

The man attached the usual small cups to his legs and chest. He punched the usual buttons and studied the usual tape as it emerged from the machine. Judd raised his eyes to find the doctor reading the same tape on a television screen. After the tape was complete and the assistant had removed the cups and was gone, Dr. Zabiski turned to a handset in her palm. She touched the keys; two banks of television screens on the wall sprang to life at her command.

Symbols flashed across the screens, verticals and horizontals, dancing in unison and parting gracefully in patterns of green and yellow, an ensemble in an abstract ballet. Judd looked at her. "What's all that?"

"Blood analysis," she said. "The whole business, every drop in you, how it's doing everywhere in the body." She paused only for a moment, then nodded. "You're doing well."

"Can I grab a fast shower?"

"No," she replied flatly. "I want you to take things slowly. Bridget will give you a sponge bath, then we'll help you up. I'll want you in a wheelchair for a while before you begin to move around. Remember, you've been in bed almost three weeks and you must get used again to simple things like gravity and standing up. I don't want you falling down unnecessarily."

"You're the doctor."

"So I have to tell you, I'd like to be present at your side during your meeting. I wouldn't like not being there if you had to handle some kind of stress and found yourself—your body—in trouble."

"What could happen?"

"Who knows? We're in terra incognita, a totally unknown land, Mr. Crane. Don't ever forget that."

He looked at her silently for a time. He knew she must have known what was holding back his assent.

"Believe me," she added earnestly. "I have no interest whatsoever in any of your private affairs."

"I know that, Doctor," he said. "But if, as you said, all the tests check out, what could happen that I'd need you right then and there?"

"Possibly nothing," she said. "But I am your doctor and I have a responsibility to you. Maybe I'm being overcautious, but I would rather be that way and end up on the side of error."

He thought for another moment. "Okay," he said. "But I'm beginning to feel like a baby who needs watching every minute."

"Judd, how do you think I feel?" she said softly. "In a strange kind of way, you *are* my baby. Right now, there isn't another mother in the world who could have created a child like you."

"YOU'RE LOOKING GOOD," Merlin said.

"Feel good," Judd replied. He rolled the wheelchair closer to the conference table in the sitting room next to his hospital bedroom.

Fast Eddie smiled. "That Irish nurse you have is prime."

Judd chuckled. "The story of my life. The stuff is always around when I can't get to it."

Merlin looked at Dr. Zabiski sitting in the corner of the room away from the conference table. Judd pointed a finger in her direction. "It's okay. We can talk."

Merlin opened his attaché case and took out a computer printout. He placed it across the table before Judd. "I haven't all the information yet, but I'm convinced our access code has been breached."

Judd looked at him with surprise. "What makes you think that?"

"Little things," Merlin replied. "The printouts keep coming out always perfect. Never a mistake. Usually quite a few errors show up."

"Hunch?" Judd asked.

"Mainly."

"I'll buy it," Judd said. "Change the code."

"I'm glad you agree," Merlin said. "I've already asked Computer Central to do it, but I need your initials to put it into effect and make it official."

"You've got it," Judd said.

Merlin handed him a sheet of paper and a pen. Judd initialed it. There were two carbons. He held one copy for himself, the other copy Merlin put into his attaché, the original was placed in an envelope to be placed in the Computer Central director's safe.

"What else?"

Merlin gestured to the printout in front of Judd. "That's the first printout from the South and Western Savings and Loan Association taken of our accounts since the court approval."

"Yes?"

"Look at page two. Deposits on hand in noninterest-bearing accounts, which includes checking held in individual names. Two hundred million dollars. Look down to supplement two, page two, names and amounts for each account. Eleven names, each held in various amounts, spread among the one hundred and fifteen branches. I've had Security check out the names. Four Cubans, five Colombians, two Peruvians, all reputed to be gentlemen very important in the narcotics trade."

Judd looked down at the printout without comment. After a moment, he looked up to Merlin. "Perhaps we should change the name of the bank to the South and Western Laundry Company."

Merlin didn't smile.

"How much of this money is insured by the FDIC?" Judd pursued.

"At a hundred thousand in each account at every branch, I make it one hundred fifteen million dollars."

"Whoever they are, they are not stupid," Judd said.

"I agree," Merlin said. "We ran a check on individual deposits. Each deposit came in around nine thousand dollars or less. That means, of course, the bank didn't have to report it to the Treasury."

Judd nodded. "Smart. But routine with the trade practice, right?"

"Standard operating procedure. What do we do?" Merlin asked.

"Report it to Treasury," Judd said without hesitation. "They'll take it from there."

"The publicity could blow the bank away," Merlin said. "We could go down four hundred million dollars."

"Then what do you suggest?" Judd asked with a wry smile.

"We could quietly order the accounts closed and return the deposits to the owners."

"That would be compounding the felony," Judd said. "One thing I learned from my father and also from Uncle Paul—never try to improve an unimprovable situation, because sooner or later you get buried in shit. You take the beating you have to and go on as best you can."

Merlin was silent.

"Who was in charge of this situation?" Judd asked.

"McLaren, president of Crane Financial Services."

"And he's said nothing about this?"

"Nothing that we ever heard."

"Nothing in the files?"

"Nothing."

"Fire him," Judd said, his eyes cobalt-blue ice. He remained silent for a long moment before he spoke again. "Is there anything else I should know about?"

"Li Chuan," Merlin said, and resumed at Judd's nod. "He went into the lude business on his own and ran it through our accounts."

"Number two cannon fired," Judd said emotionlessly. "Would you like to go for three?"

Merlin seemed embarrassed. He glanced at Dr. Zabiski still seated in the chair across the room. He hesitated but finally nodded.

The little doctor rose from her chair. "You seem to be doing all right," she said to Judd. "I won't be upset if you'd like me to leave now."

Judd shook his head. "No. You might as well go through the whole silly mess with me."

Merlin glanced from her to Judd. "Sofia," he began. "She's in Havana. So is Li Chuan. And also, Nicolai Borovnik, the number three man in the KGB. We have Security on them but we haven't received any reports from them yet."

Judd looked at the doctor. "Did you know anything about this business of your assistant and the KGB man?" he asked coolly.

The little woman met his eyes squarely. "No. This is completely new to me. But I do know that Borovnik and she have been lovers and that Borovnik at one time tried to divorce his wife to marry her. It was when the divorce was not approved that she volunteered to work for me."

Judd looked at her curiously. "In that case why should she go to all the trouble now to meet him in Havana?" he asked.

"I'm guessing," she said. "But I'd think he wanted to tell her about Brezhnev."

"Leonid himself? The top man of the top men?" Judd was surprised and made no attempt to hide it.

"Yes," she said. "He was to be the next patient assigned to her."

"Then she'll not be returning?" Judd asked dryly.

"She'll come back," the doctor said simply.

"Despite the Chairman?"

"Yes, sir."

"And the Politburo?"

"Yes, sir."

"And the KGB?"

"Yes, sir."

"She can pull that kind of clout?"

"It'll take more than clout. But she'll manage."

"Why, Doctor?"

"There is one very important test that only she can complete."

"Which she can't assign to someone else?"

"That's right."

"What would that be, Doctor?"

"An abortion," Dr. Zabiski said quietly. And added, "Her own."

He stared at her. "You mean that she's one of the—"

"Yes, sir," the doctor answered.

"Why didn't she tell me?"

"She didn't want to."

"Why would she do it?" He saw a tiny light flash in a corner of the doctor's eye. "You know the answer to that, of course?"

"I do."

"Then tell me why, Doctor."

"I cannot, Mr. Crane."

"Even if I ask you nicely, Doctor?"

"Even if you order me, sir."

"Doctor's confidentiality, that it?" Judd said.

"Yes, sir. Thank you for understanding."

"I accept it, but don't understand it."

"I can tell you this: it was at her insistence. She demanded to be one of the volunteers."

Judd took a very deep breath, a faint trace of a grin creasing the corners of his mouth. But, finally, all he could do was to exclaim, "Shit!"

20

◆ THE RESTAURANT WAS in a hacienda located in an ancient residential area at the outskirts of Havana. Its cuisine was comparable to any in Paris or New York, but it was unknown, however, to 99.99 percent of the Cuban people. This was a restaurant only for the elite of Castro's world, as well as their guests. Old-fashioned large tables, with white damask napery, gold and silver cutlery, French Baccarat glassware, English bone china edged in gold set around low flower arrangements. Each table gave a soft golden glow from its small table candles. And, perhaps even more important, each round table was set far from the others. When even more privacy was required, the alcove around the table could be wholly enclosed by dark burgundy velvet drapes.

Sofia was the only woman at an open table of six. Nicky and Li Chuan sat on either side of her. Next to Nicky sat a heavy-set man, Karpov, one of the KGB at the Russian embassy. Across the table from her sat their host, Santos Gómez, a slim tall Cuban in his thirties, wearing the two stars of a major general on the open collar of his field uniform. Between him and Li Chuan was a small Chinese man in a gray business suit, Doy Sing, who was the unofficial representative of the People's Republic of China, which had no official embassy in Cuba.

Dinner had begun at midnight and it was now almost one-thirty in the morning as the waiters brought the coffee, Napoleon cognac and the ever-proffered cigars. Finally, they closed the drapes, to insure the group's privacy.

Li Chuan sipped nothing but his coffee. When he rose he did not have to wait for the group's total attention. "My words may shock you, comrades," he began, "but we are here to talk of power, not theoretical power, but real, effective power. Let me begin by saying power today in this world of ours is not political.

114

Neither communism nor capitalism mean anything. Power is simply money, and the greatest earner of money at this time is energy. Oil and gas. That is the source of the strength of the countries of the Middle East and the OPEC bloc. And energy represents the power of the United States because they have foreseen all this and have gained control of those energy-producing countries.

"Now that other countries have discovered even more sources of energy, the surprise is that the power of the United States grows even more. Let me tell you why. Because one country competes with another, one source of energy pitted against another, they all end up playing against each other to control not only the source of energy but the distribution systems all over the world. Alas, in this game we are the nickel-stakes players. The Yanqui imperialists hold all the cards, they even own the game itself. However, that is only one game. There is another game we can play and beat them at it, if only we have the courage to do so."

His look was a silent challenge to all of them around the table. No one responded to it. He continued with a faint smile that soon faded away. "I am not speaking of confrontation, or battlefields, or the alliances of Third World countries. All that is political chess and does not take into account the realities of money and the power of which I speak. What I am addressing myself to is a cancerous weakness the very riches of the Western world have brought to it. The chronic search for false contentment that narcotics and chemicals bring is what I call to your attention. It began in the sixties, first in America, and has now spread throughout the Western world—which means all of Europe and perhaps other highly productive economies on other continents. We must come face to face, like it or not, with this new fact of enormous financial potential in the world, which cannot, will not, continue to stay much longer where it was once consigned."

He paused for a long time.

The others at the table, as cognizant as he of the situation that had brought them to this place, remained silent and rigidly attentive to his next words. "To put it very simply and quickly," he resumed, after studying their faces for another moment, "once there was a narcotics world controlled by Mafia gangsters.

Through intimidation, corruption and violence, a single source that led through Sicily and France found itself the target of other bold and hungry entrepreneurs from still other countries. The profits they all sought, which I shall come to in a moment, are, to say the very least, staggering. The flood of cash grew so enormous that the trade was no longer of interest only to former dealers in prostitutes and contraband and illegal gambling. Chemical manufacturers, financial market speculators, yes, even distressed political leaders looking for a way out of hopeless domestic turmoil —all kinds of greedy, capitalistic amateurs began to see possibilities in the narcotics trade that could relieve even political pain and agony."

He was silent again for another long moment, then looked at each face around the table before he began again. "And what, I ask you, comrades, *what are we doing about it?*"

Again he looked around the table as if waiting for a response. None came. "If it's morality, comrades, you want to bring up to me, do not bother. We are dealing with hard facts. In our struggle, there is no morality. Only results. Life and death. The strength to achieve our purpose—or a century of political serfdom, knees bent before the great industrial alliance opposed to us, a life of being client-states awaiting the master's pleasure. We have the capability and resources to completely take over this worldwide drug business. And what better time than now have we to bore within and disintegrate the will of the Western world to resist us? What better means to achieve this? What better way for our own countries to reach for the power of which I spoke?"

GENERAL SANTOS GÓMEZ rolled up the window between the chauffeur and his assistant seated in the front seat of the car. He turned on the air conditioner to hide their conversation and looked at Nicky and Sofia beside him. "Li Chuan is a fool," he said. "He talks too much."

Sofia looked at him. She didn't speak. Nicky shook his head, a signal she understood.

"I got him alone long enough to find out what I had to, General," he said.

"Do you think it is important that we acquire the access code he is offering us?" the general asked.

116

"No," Nicky said. "In all probability it would be changed the first time we found a chance to use it."

"I thought that also," the general said. "The man is too concerned about long-range problems, probably because he's greedy and also a fool." He paused a moment. "I'm concerned about Doy Sing though. The Chinese will make a big stink out of it."

Nicky looked out to the night-black street. "Right now we have not many choices," he said. "When Li Chuan's knowledge of their access code gets back to them, it won't take them long to figure out that we're already working on his master plan."

"I'd feel better if I could let Fidel know about it," the general said.

"I would, too," Nicky said. "But if we wait, we might be too late. Doy Sing will surely contact his people the moment he gets to his place. The first people in the market will wind up in a strong position. Even good friends have to consider this."

The general nodded. "You're right." He picked up the telephone next to his seat and pressed a button. An unintelligible voice crackled beside his ear. He spoke one word. "Now."

He put down the telephone and turned to them with a sigh and a grin. "Before the revolution, there was a show in Havana that was a favorite of rich Americans. Even Hemingway has told about it. Of course, come the revolution, it had to be closed legally. But for certain important persons, it's always been open. Perhaps you would like to see it. It's open all night." He reached for a cigar from his pocket. He looked at Sofia. "Of course, it is shockingly pornographic and like nothing else in the world, but it could be very intriguing, Comrade Doctor—or perhaps you would not be interested in viewing it?"

Sofia looked at Nicky, then at the general without answering.

"Of course," the general said, lighting his cigar, "we keep it going to remind ourselves and our friends of decadent capitalism at its worst."

Sofia turned to the general. She had the feeling that he was waiting for her to give her approval. "In that case, Comrade General," she said, "I think it would be profitable for all of us to look at it, if only for research into the nature of bourgeois corruption."

117

"I am sure you will also find it amusing, Doctor," the general said, a look of satisfaction unmistakable on his face.

THE CLUB WAS in a nondescript building near the harbor. The car stopped in the narrow street and they stepped out to a small, unmarked, wooden door guarded by two burly men. They nodded silently to the general and opened the door for the party.

They entered into a foyer, a small chandelier casting little light overhead. A maître d' in a tuxedo bowed to the general and without a word led them through another door to a long corridor leading past a number of closed doors to the last of them. He stepped aside, pushing open this one for them.

The small room was like a private box in a theater. Comfortable sofas were deployed around a low cocktail table. Beyond it, they became aware of a small stage, dim-lit in pink and pale rose lights. They provided the only light in the club. Around them they could see dark shadows in other boxes, but they could not be sure that they were occupied or simply shapes of their own imagining.

Sofia looked down at the cocktail table. Champagne, cognac, Scotch whisky, vodka and rum. There were glasses and a pail of ice cubes. A faint smell of hashish or marijuana floated in the air around them and no one was surprised by a sterling silver cigarette box and dish sparkling with white cocaine, tiny gold spoons and straws lying next to it.

"Champagne?" the general asked.

"Please," Sofia answered.

The general nodded to the maître d'. The man stepped back and two young men and two girls entered the box. They were all naked except for a breechcloth over the genitals. Silently the young men opened the bottles of champagne and filled the glasses before them. The girls offered the silver cigarette box around and then the dish of cocaine.

"Spoon or straw?" the general asked. "For myself, I prefer the straw."

"None for me," Nicky said.

Sofia looked at him, then at the general. "I'll take your suggestion."

Silently one of the girls arranged a number of lines on a mirrorlike plate. She held the straw out to Sofia. Quickly, Sofia snorted a line into each nostril. The cocaine exploded in her brain.

The general laughed at her surprised expression. "Pure," he said. "You don't get this anywhere except here." He took two lines to each of his own nostrils. He turned to Nicky. "You don't know what you're missing."

"It has no significance, General," he said. "The plain fact is that I never was into it. Vodka is enough for me."

Santos Gomez lifted his champagne glass. "A beautiful combination. *Santé.*"

"*Santé,*" they echoed and sipped the champagne.

"The show will begin in a short while," the general said. "But in the meantime, if you like, our attendants will try to amuse you."

"I'm comfortable," Sofia said.

"As you like," the general smiled. He gestured to one of the men, who turned toward him. The general reached across and raised the man's breechcloth. "Fantastic, no? Each of these boys must have a phallus not less than seventeen centimeters long in order to qualify for the job here. How much is that in inches?"

Sofia felt the cocaine heating in her brain. She tried to speak expressionlessly. "I'm bad at numbers, General," she said.

"And you, Comrade, what do you calculate?" the general asked.

Nicky nodded at him. "My only interest is cultural, not mathematical. Comrade General, I'm fascinated by such complete capitalistic decadence."

The general laughed. "But let's not be too dogmatic. It can be amusing." He dipped his straw into the cocaine and took more lines into his nostrils. He pointed to one of the girls. "Give that poor boy a lift so we can see his true size."

The girl knelt before the young man and took hold of his member in her hand, flicked her tongue quickly against the head of his penis. There was no expression on the young man's face, but his phallus began to harden and grow. At just that moment, a soft knock came from the door.

The maître d' entered quickly into the stall and whispered into the ear of the general. The general nodded and rose to his feet.

"I'll be just a moment," he said. "A telephone call. Please don't stop on my account."

The door closed behind him. The girl and the boy carried on as if the general were still there. Nicky had touched Sofia's arm to draw her attention. "It's disgusting," he said in Russian. "Like animals."

Sofia looked at him. "I don't know," she said honestly. "I find emotionally detached sex fascinating."

"You're a whore," he said angrily.

"I'm honest," she said. "At least I tell you what I feel. You can't tell me that you don't find this fascinating and exciting."

"I'm not made of iron."

"Not yet, but it won't be long," she teased. "You're getting hard."

"Bitch," he murmured.

"Why? Because I accept my body for what it is, something you cannot? Perhaps all men are hypocrites at heart," she said very softly, but turned quickly when the door opened with a thrust. Even in the dim light they could read panic in the general's face.

"He's dead!" he exclaimed.

"Who?" Sofia tensed.

"Li Chuan! And the others, too!"

Nicky came to her side calmly. "Your men are very efficient, General," he offered without emotion.

"We didn't kill them," the general said. "My men were not even near them when it happened. They were killed as they came out of the restaurant."

"Anyone see the killers?" Nicky asked.

"No one even heard the shots. The guns had to be fitted with silencers. Their bodies were not discovered until the driver came for them with their car."

"CIA," Nicky said. "We have heard rumors that Li Chuan was working both sides of the street." He shrugged his shoulders. "If it's true, or if they found out he was working with us . . . In any case it doesn't matter. Whoever killed him did us a favor. At least, we don't have to explain it."

"But that means the killers also know that we've been talking to Li Chuan. Maybe they'll be coming after us too," the general said in a worried voice.

Nicky smiled reassuringly. "They don't want us," he said. "They know what side we're on."

Sofia turned to them. "Where do I fit in?"

Nicky shook his head. "I don't think you have anything to worry about. The CIA has no interest in you at all."

"You don't understand," Sofia said. "It's not the CIA I'm thinking about. It's Judd Crane."

Nicky shrugged contemptuously. "He's just one man. And a selfish fool to boot. What can he do?"

"Nicky, you're the fool," she said, getting to her feet. "Li Chuan was thinking about Judd Crane when he talked of power. Judd Crane has power. Power beyond even your comprehension. If it's the CIA who killed Li Chuan, then it's Judd Crane who ordered it."

Nicky stared silently at her.

"I think you'd better order extra bodyguards to take us back to the hotel," she said. "I want to be alive long enough to get on the plane to Mexico City tomorrow morning."

21

◆ JUDD LEANED BACK against his pillow, the breakfast tray across his legs. He sipped at a glass of orange juice. He looked at Bridget placing a note on the chart at the foot of his bed. "I have a hard-on," he said.

She answered noncommittally. "That's normal. It will go after you take a pee."

"Bitch," he said without rancor. "Just once why don't you remember that you're a woman and not just a nurse. Give me a treat, instead of a treatment."

"Mr. Crane," she laughed. "I don't know how to deal with you. Are you a horny teenage boy or a dirty old man?"

"Why not both?" he smiled.

"Unprofessional," she said without expression. "Got to be sure about one's patient."

The telephone rang; he picked it up. "Yes?"

"Merlin." The earpiece crackled audibly against his ear. "How are you this morning, sir?"

"Ready to get the hell out of here," he said. "That doctor said in about an hour or so."

"Good," Merlin said. "We have news from Security."

"Yes?"

"Li Chuan is dead. Security went through his room while he was out to dinner. They discovered a number of items. One of them, the access code to our Computer Central. Also that he intended to sell it for twenty million dollars."

"He was stupid," Judd said. "There's no one in his right mind who'd pay anything like that for it. Any half-assed expert would know that access codes are only made to be changed."

"He wasn't an expert in practical matters," Merlin said. "Security also took a good look at the contents of his travel case. Apparently he had a complete printout of our copy involving South and

122

Western Savings and Loan. So, at least, we know why he dipped into the computer. Now we'll soon find out how he moved the money from our accounts to his own."

"Who killed him?" Judd asked.

"I went into that subject with Security. They live in their own world. But they learned that Sofia's old boyfriend masterminded that with the killers."

He paused for a moment. "What about Sofia?" he asked.

"She's been a busy girl," Merlin said. "I have their tapes hot from the scrambler satellite. I'll play them for you when you come into the office."

Judd laughed. "So you're more of a dirty old man than I figured. What about her assignment to the ailing Comrade Brezhnev?"

"That's true," Merlin said.

"Does that mean she's going directly to Russia from there?"

"No," he said. "She's booked herself Aeromexico to Mexico City. She should be here this evening."

"Okay," Judd said. "Anything else?"

"Nothing that can't wait until you get into the office," Merlin said.

Judd put down the telephone and looked at the nurse at the foot of the bed. "I still have that hard-on, ma'am," he teased.

She held out a pill in a small plastic glass. "Take this with the rest of your orange juice, then a pee and a cold shower. That should take care of it."

He swallowed the pill, glaring at her. "Cold ass," he said, in a mocking, baleful voice.

"Total environment," Dr. Zabiski said.

Judd pulled on his sweater. "What do you mean by that?"

"Just what I said," she said. "If we cannot control the total environment, there's no way we can control your life span. Everything we've done, medically and technologically, has been negated by your life style."

Judd turned from her. "I can't stay in this hospital forever. I'll go nuts."

"I know that," she said.

"And neither would life in a totally environmentally controlled space station be any better."

She nodded. "True."

"Then what do you suggest?"

"Build your own environment. You can afford it." She met his eyes. "In a way you already do that, on your airplane. But that is mobile. I understand you have to travel the world for your business affairs; nevertheless, it means your health objectives take second position to other matters.

"Think about it. Is there anything in this world that you can't bring to you instead of you going out to it? If you built a total environment, everything could be there, communications, technology, food. Even the necessary personal contacts so important to your life style. Everything could come to you, if you demanded it."

He stared at her without comment for a moment. "That would mean building a small city just for myself."

She shrugged her shoulders. "So? You're planning to live forever, aren't you?" she asked. "Why shouldn't you have the place where you do the living exactly as you want it?"

"Crazy," he said.

"Not really," she said. "You have the opportunity, and the money to achieve your ambition—more than any man ever dreamed or could afford. All you need now is the will."

He was silent.

"Think about it," she said. "That island you own off the Georgia coast of the United States is used only as a resort hotel. It would be perfect for what you'd need."

He looked at her. "I'll have to think about it."

"Yes," she said. "Of course."

He took a deep breath. "I don't want to be another Howard Hughes."

"You wouldn't be," she said. "He ran away from the world because he was afraid of it—and afraid of dying. You are afraid of neither: no fear of the world, no fear of death. You could reach out to the world by bringing it to you. To you, death is only a fact of evolution that you want to alter. And to achieve the immortality you desire, you may have to accept that your life will also have to be altered."

124

NICKY WAS ON the telephone when she came in from the bathroom. She had the towel wrapped around her as she walked to the dresser and picked up her brassiere and panties. He put down the telephone and looked at her. "You don't have to rush," he said. "There's been a change of plan."

She looked at him questioningly. "The flight to Mexico is at ten o'clock. The next one is six in the evening."

"You're not going back to Mexico," he said. "We're booked on Aeroflot to Moscow at noon. We want you back there."

"But the abortion," she said. "It's scheduled for tomorrow."

"Not anymore," he said. "They want you to have the baby."

"That's crazy," she said. "We don't know what the child could be. So many things have been tampered with in his bio and chemical systems, the child could turn out monstrous."

"It's a chance we have to take," he said. "As *we* prefer to see it, that child could wind up being his only heir. And with that child, we could control everything he owns: the companies, the money. We'd own one of the most powerful industrial complexes in the Western world."

"But it was nothing but an experiment."

"Not anymore," Nicky said. "It's a fact of life. Power. Remember what that dead Chinese said."

"No," she said. "I'm going back to Mexico as planned."

"No chance, Sofia," he said. "You have your orders."

"And if I choose not to obey them?"

"That's treason," he said. "And you know the penalty for that."

She snapped the brassiere around her and stepped into the lacy bikini. "And who is going to kill me?" she asked casually. "You, Nicky?"

"I have my orders too."

"But you love me," she offered gently. "You always said that."

"That's still true," he said. "It always will be."

"But you love your orders more?" She made no effort to shade her sarcastic tone.

He did not answer.

"Then it's not love for me that you really profess, Nicky," she said. "All it comes to is your ambition, your own desire for power."

He still remained silent.

"Now I understand a number of things, Nicky. I was a bigger fool than I thought," she went on. "You never planned to divorce Ekaterina to marry me. That would upset the applecart. Her father is too high in the council and too close to the Politburo."

He watched her. "Not quite on target, Sofia. That wasn't all of it. On analysis, I decided to use you to get what I wanted because marriage to you was simply not in the cards. They knew all about you and your reputation. Our top people would never accept you."

She stood silent before him and, without a word, pulled her small suitcase from the closet, seemed to change her mind, and slipped into the linen suit he had seen her wear when she had first come there. She placed the valise on the bed and opened it. She looked over the open side of the suitcase between them before snapping it shut. "You'll have to kill me," she said decisively. "I'm going back, Nicky."

He stared at her with dismay. "You can't mean that."

"Neither can I believe that you'd kill me."

He remained rigid in the chair next to the telephone. "Orders. I'm a soldier. I have no choice." A blue-black Beretta pistol came into his hand from his inside jacket pocket. "And neither do you, if you don't return with me."

Her eyes met his briefly, hesitated, then turned down to her valise. He never heard the soft coughing of the silencer as the blast that tore out the side of her valise ripped into his chest, or the second soft cough that sliced his face in half like a melon from chin to head. The force of the silent explosions dropped him from the chair to the floor.

She stood up only long enough to remember the gun in his hand. His blood was splattered around him all the way to the wall and the ceiling. She stared down at him.

"Nicky, poor Nicky," she said softly. "You were stupid. You never knew something Judd Crane taught me. There's always another choice."

22

♦ "FATHER OF THE year," he said. "I never even got laid."

Doc Sawyer laughed. "Don't complain. It was your idea." He fell silent for a moment. "But Zabiski is right. I might as well go the whole route."

"Uncle Paul and the legal department are going to go nuts," Judd said.

"That's what they're for," Sawyer said. "I'm sure that they'll come up with a solution."

Merlin came into the upper deck cabin. "We'll be landing in Mexico City in forty minutes."

"Good," Judd said. He looked up at him. "Any word about her yet?"

"She's on the Aeromexico flight due in about an hour after we come down," he said. "The passenger list shows her still on it."

"Security ready to get her off if there's any trouble?"

"We're doing everything we can," Merlin said. "We were lucky they got into her room the moment she went out. They found him before their own police did and cleaned up everything they could, but we don't know how long we'll be able to pressure them to sit on it."

"We get her off the plane, we're home free," Judd said.

"Security tapes told us that he was going to kill her," Merlin said. "We still don't know how she faked him out."

"I have a hunch," Judd said. "She took my small valise."

Merlin stared at him. "The snub nose thirty-eight with the silencer fitted inside the combination lock?"

Judd nodded. "It can do a lot of things, but it can't walk by itself. It wasn't in my room when I came back from the hospital."

Merlin nodded approvingly. "The lady thinks," he said. "That means she's also dangerous."

Judd laughed. "All ladies worth the trouble are dangerous." He

127

picked up a sheet of paper. "About those other girls?" he began. "The future mothers-to-be. Are we making all the arrangements to place them around the country?"

"Security is working on it now. We should have the plan by tonight." He looked at Judd. "What have you decided about Sofia?"

"I'm thinking on it," Judd said. "I want to talk some more with her."

"You're scheduled to be at the Presidential Palace in Mexico City when she arrives at the airport. We think it's better that you're not around. Besides, the meeting with the commerce secretary about Crane Pharmaceuticals will be at that time. Then you have luncheon with López Portillo before you return to the plane. We're scheduled to depart for Brazil at four P.M. That ought to give you time to think, sir," Merlin said, only half in jest.

JUDD LOOKED DOWN at his wristwatch, then around the luncheon table. Three-thirty, and the President was already an hour late. Judd turned to the finance minister to his right. "Perhaps *el Presidente* has more important matters to attend than just this luncheon. I will not be offended if he should want to cancel."

"There is nothing more important, Mr. Crane," the handsome finance minister said politely in perfect English. "It's only that *el Presidente* never takes his luncheon before four o'clock."

Judd turned to Merlin, then looked back to the finance minister. He rose from the table. "Please give my regrets to *Señor el Presidente* and apologize on my behalf. Alas, I also have a schedule to follow. I have appointments in Brazil tomorrow and my departure is set for four o'clock. That's only a half an hour away. Perhaps our appointment can be rescheduled for the day after tomorrow when I return to the States."

The minister's face expressed a shocked dismay. "But *el Presidente* will be most disappointed, Señor Crane. He has looked forward to meeting with you."

"And I, too," Judd said. "I'm anxious to sit down with him."

"But the business we have discussed . . . I am sure that he's anxious to talk more about it with you."

"There's really nothing we have to talk about," Judd said. "We understand your position. I want you to build the laboratory and

128

factory for thirty million dollars. For that you own fifty percent of Crane Pharmaceuticals Mexico. You offer only five million dollars and want me to invest the remainder, twenty-five million dollars, from my resources. In simple American, that's chicken shit. I am a businessman, Mr. Minister, and I do not intend to become another bank to add to Mexico's loan liability, which is already greater than it can carry reasonably for repayment."

"Your opinion is contrary to the many banks we're doing business with," the minister replied coolly. "Mexico's petroleum fields are the greatest in the world. It's all the collateral we need, no matter how our liabilities look today, sir."

"Possibly, Your Excellency," Judd conceded. "Nevertheless, I am neither an oil shipper nor a refiner. Neither have I any interest in that form of energy. I look only at the things already in hand. This is the end of 1979, and Mexico is already fifty-five billion dollars in debt. At the rate you are borrowing, in the two years remaining of the President's term of office that debt will climb to perhaps eighty billion dollars or more. By that time the world will be awash in oil. They'll stop talking shortage and conservation and demand something be done about the glut in oil. There is no way I can foresee that your debt can be repaid."

"But your scenario means many other countries will find themselves in the same position. It also means that accommodations to the problem will have to be made elsewhere, as well as here."

"True enough," Judd said. "But I don't have to move a finger. None of my banks or financial companies has joined the consortium of lenders on oil production enterprises. The future, as I see it, is no longer dependent on a production or a technological industrial age. It's going to be based on information, communication and medical services.

"The first industry I offer you is medical. The investment I propose is minimal, something you can't do in oil. Within two years, I tell you, the amount I propose for you to come in with, thirty million dollars, will return you two hundred million dollars of business. And that, Mr. Minister, is only in the Central American and northern South American nations. The second industry I plan will be offered only after the solid base we secure in the first is established profitably. That means we will be sure that the first industry we set up will be free of the corruption and thievery that unfortunately has plagued some of your industries. I offer electronic communications and information, all constructed and maintained in Mexico—an enterprise which can blanket and control the Spanish-speaking world. And that market can be worth untold billions of dollars.

"That, Señor Minister, is what I ask you to inform *el Presidente*," Judd concluded.

The minister stared at him. "You speak very bluntly, Señor."

"I know no other way, Señor Minister. Progress can only be built upon the granite of truth, not the timbers of dry rot."

The minister's voice was bitter. "That is the usual North American attitude. Below the Rio Grande we are poor second cousins."

"President Carter came to Mexico City with an olive branch in his hand. He offered greater understanding between our countries. It was simplistic, I suppose, and miracles don't happen between nations, not these days in any case. What he found was invective and studied slights and insults. Tell me, Mr. Minister, what has Castro offered Mexico that makes all of you content to suck his hind tit? Nothing. Except subversion and dissension, attacks on your style of government and your principles of democracy. Why are you people not insulting Fidel, sir?"

The minister was silent.

"Mexico had a profitable sugar-farming industry. Today Mexico imports sugar. It also imports cocoa, coffee, grain. All profitable crops gone in a frenzy of a fever for a product that is buried in the sea and that takes many years to bring up, and that can possibly be replaced by yet another form of energy before it begins to show up profitably on your economic charts."

The handsome finance minister replied in a disappointed voice: "I am sorry to find, Señor Crane, that you have so low an opinion of us Mexicans."

"That's not at all true, Señor Minister," Judd said. "I love the people, their gallant spirit, their generous nature. In my companies, I employ more than one and a half million Mexican workers, both legal and illegal. I find them all competent and industrious. But I do feel sorry for the Mexican people, and especially sorry for the unhappy prospects of their future leaders. Because in two years, when the new government takes its place, they will be so busy scraping the shit from their boots it may not even have the food for the people to lift with their forks."

The minister looked at him. "You believe that?"

"I'm sorry but I do. I believe you will respect my candor and my affection for your country and its people."

"Then what do we do?" the minister asked softly.

Judd met his gaze without blinking. "I am neither Mexican nor am I a politician. I'm an outsider. I don't have answers. I only believe in the greatness of Mexico and I believe that it should be the leader of the Central American world—not the vassal of someone who is himself a vassal, tied and owned completely by people who hold all of you in naked contempt."

The minister broke his silence with a long sigh. "You cannot delay your departure?"

"I'm truly sorry, Mr. Minister."

"But you will return for another meeting?"

"If I am invited, I will be honored, Señor Minister," Judd said.

"I will try my very best for that." The telephone on the table next to him buzzed. He answered and listened for a moment, then spoke into it in Spanish. He listened again for a moment, then covering the mouthpiece with his hand, spoke to Judd.

"The immigration police at the airport are holding a Dr. Sofia Ivancich at the request of the Cuban police. They demand that she remain in their custody until she can be returned, as quickly as possible, to Havana. She says that she is your guest as well as your employee, in transit to your airplane with a correct visa for the United States from her own country."

Judd looked at him. "Where is she now?"

"In the immigration office of the transit lounge."

"Do the Cuban police have any authority there over anything?"

"Not officially," the minister said. "But we have an unofficial understanding."

"But not a legal one?"

"Not a legal one."

Judd looked at him. "Dr. Ivancich is a very important person on our medical research staff. I would appreciate it if you asked your immigration office to conduct her personally to my plane and to tell them I have your word for her safe-conduct."

131

"The Cuban police insist she is charged with serious crimes," the minister said.

"In Cuba," Judd said. "Not in Mexico?"

The minister nodded. "Not in Mexico."

"The transit lounge is still under Mexican jurisdiction, is it not? No Cuban police have any legal power there, sir?"

"That's true. Mexico has sole jurisdiction."

"Dr. Ivancich is working on a special contract between the United States and Yugoslavia. I think her detention could cause needless embarrassment to the government of Mexico if you waive your own sovereign rights to the Cubans. And in addition, sir, I would personally appreciate it very much if you yourself could lend the weight of your office to accommodate my request."

The minister looked at him only briefly before he spoke again into the telephone. A moment later he put it down. "It will be done, Señor Crane. I have already ordered immigration to conduct her, with a full complement of bodyguards."

"Thank you, Señor Minister."

"She should be upon your plane in less than ten minutes."

"Again, sir, I thank you," Judd said.

The minister smiled. "Just one question, Mr. Crane. Were you not a graduate of Harvard Business School?"

Judd nodded. "Yes."

"I, too," the minister smiled more broadly. He held out his hand. "I congratulate you on your ability to muster facts and come up with solutions. I hope one day you'll be playing the game from my position and I will stand in your place."

"I have, sir."

"And, Mr. Crane, did you win there, too?"

"We don't win or lose. We learn to do the best we can. No, Mr. Minister, it's I who must congratulate you."

23

◆ THE LIGHTS OVER Mexico City disappeared in the heavy layer of brown smog that buried it. A moment later the plane was high enough to find the sunny blue above. "Covered in a blanket of shit," Judd said, looking out the window.

"Your orange juice and pill, Mr. Crane." Bridget placed the two glasses on his tray.

"Never forget, do you?" he said dourly.

"That's what you pay me for," she said. She waited until he swallowed the pill and the juice. "Dinner will be at seven-thirty," she said. "Lights at nine."

"I'm no longer in the hospital," he said.

"Doctor's orders," she said. "You stay on this routine for two more weeks."

"How about a fuck?" he teased.

"That's not my department," she teased back. "But you're much better. Soon enough you'll be able to handle problems normally."

"Thanks a lot," he growled. "But don't you wait around. I won't forget how you failed me in my time of need."

He watched her leave his cabin and looked over to Fast Eddie, behind the bar. "They're all cunts," he said.

Fast Eddie flashed all his teeth. "Yeah!"

"Orange shit tastes like any shit," he said. "Give me a cherry Coke."

"Wait a minute, boss," Fast Eddie protested. "Remember the doctor's orders."

"Fuck her," he snapped. "You don't work for her."

"But—?"

"Do what I said."

Quickly, Fast Eddie put the drink together. Judd sipped at it.

"Good," he sighed. He felt himself picked up. "Doctors don't know everything."

Doc Sawyer and Merlin came into his cabin. "Everything okay, gentlemen?" he asked.

"Okay," Merlin said.

"What about Sofia?" he asked.

"She's fine," Doc Sawyer said. Then he noticed the blank expression on Judd's face. He glanced at Merlin. "Did you tell him?"

Merlin shook his head. "I thought you had."

Judd stared at both of them. "What the hell are you talking about?"

Doc Sawyer looked at him. "Someone with a silencer tried to nail her going through the transit lounge. Wasn't a very good shot though, he just hit the soft flesh of her left arm."

"They get the guy?" Judd asked.

"Never even saw him," Merlin said. "Mexican Security never knew she had been nailed. The lady's got guts. She walked through the transit lounge without saying a word. Kept her right hand clamped over the hole in her arm, just as cool as a cucumber, so that no one would notice the blood until she got on the plane."

"Where's she now?" Judd asked.

"Asleep in her cabin," Doc said. "She's lost blood, of course. I gave her two pints of plasma, patched her up and knocked her out. She's okay. She'll sleep about ten to twelve hours."

"Good work, but damn it all!" Judd exclaimed. "I wanted to know what happened in Havana."

"We know pretty well," Merlin said. "The lady remained poised enough to bring back Borovnik's papers. I've gone through them. All those deposits through the South and Western Savings and Loan were part of a Cuban government sanction. The dealers worked through them."

"We really got into something there, didn't we?" Judd said.

Merlin nodded.

"Now what?" Judd asked.

"Our whole fucking government is also in it now," Merlin said. "Besides Treasury, FDIC, IRS, Customs and the FBI, the CIA is swarming all over it."

134

Judd looked at him. "What's the bottom line now for us?"

"Wipeout for S and W Savings. We might have skated through with four hundred million withdrawn, but the way it looks now, with all the agencies in it, looks like we're holding more than six hundred million. The only way we can hold it together is to support it with three hundred million more of our own."

There was no hesitation in Judd's voice. "Do it."

"You could lose the whole bundle anyway," Merlin said.

"It's our name and our money," Judd said, and added, "The money isn't that important. It's our own stupidity I don't like."

They sat silent for a moment. "Anything else?" Judd asked.

"All the girls have completed their medical exams and have checked out beautifully," Doctor Sawyer began. "Legal has all their contracts duly and properly signed, so even the lawyers are content. Security has placed them in different homes in states all over the country. None of the girls knows anything about the others, of course, and none of them has the faintest notion of your own connection with the project. Needless to say, they and their children will be protected for life by an irrevocable trust. That's been set up already. They're all completely satisfied. In six or seven months, we should have a bumper crop of contented mothers and pretty babies such as no one man's come up with since Ibn Saud."

"He had over nine hundred children," Judd said. "At least, he had the fun of making every one of them."

"Ah, well, you can't have everything," Doc Sawyer laughed. "You live in a different world."

Judd was silent for a moment. "There is *one* woman who knows, Doc. Sofia."

Doc Sawyer nodded. "Zabiski and I discussed that. Her abortion will take place as planned. And as far as she'll ever know, so will all the other abortions."

Judd looked out the window. There was a thin orange line as the sun fell into the horizon for the night. He didn't turn to them. "Looks like you've tied everything together."

"We tried," Doc Sawyer said.

"Good." Judd turned to Merlin. "What's happening with Crane Island Resort?"

"Crane Construction has already put together a study team.

Their problem right now is finding the right people to comprehend what we require. But they feel that they'll have that preliminary work done in about two months."

"Then how long until they can build and have it finished?"

"One year to start building, one more year to finish." Merlin looked at him dubiously. "Do you still want to go through with it? I'm guessing we'll be looking at more than forty million dollars, maybe more."

Judd turned to him. "We'll go over the study before we make that decision. We still have the time."

Bridget came into the cabin. "Sorry, gentlemen," she said. "Time's up. My patient has to have his nap before dinner."

"My sweet and attentive bitch," he said. But there was no rancor in his voice. He was beginning to feel tired.

THE SOFT HUM of the jet engines seeped into his stateroom. He opened his eyes slowly. Bridget was standing beside his bed, her white nurse's uniform ghostlike in the darkened room. "Were you standing there long?" he asked.

"Only a few minutes," she said. "You were sleeping so deeply I didn't know whether to awaken you for dinner or not."

"Dinner is a good idea," he said. "Lunch got fucked up. I never ate it."

"Fine," she said. "I'll let the chef know."

He sat up in the bed. "I'll grab a shave and a shower," he said. "When will dinner be ready?"

"Whenever you want it," she said.

"Half an hour okay?"

"Yes."

He watched the door close behind her, then pressed the stateroom light. Looking down he saw the red message light on the telephone blinking. He picked up the receiver.

"Your mother called from San Francisco while you were sleeping, Mr. Crane," the communications officer reported.

"Get her back for me," he said. He put down the telephone and went into the bathroom. The telephone rang while he was still in there. He picked up the wall phone beside the john.

"I have Mrs. Marlowe on the phone for you, sir."

"Thank you," he said. He heard the transfer click. "Barbara."

"It's almost six weeks since I spoke to you," she said. "Where are you?"

"Right now I'm on the john, taking a pee," he said.

"Silly," she laughed. "I mean, where are you?"

"According to the flight plan I should be somewhere over the Amazon but I'm not sure. I just woke up."

"How are you?" she asked. "Are you well?"

"Never felt better," he said.

"What about those treatments?"

"Like a piece of cake," he said. "How are you and Jim?"

"We're good," she said. "I heard that you're going to the inauguration."

"That's right."

"We've had an invitation, too," she said. "I thought it would be nice if we could go together."

"I love the idea," he said. "Let's plan on it."

"We will," she said. She hesitated a moment. "Are you sure you're all right?"

"Yes, Barbara," he said. "I'm superfine. Give my love to Jim and a big kiss for you."

"A big kiss to you, too," she said. "We'll be looking forward to seeing you in Washington. 'Bye, now."

He hung up the phone and stood over the marble bowl. He leaned on it for a moment, then pressed the attendant's button.

Bridget came into his stateroom and stood in the bathroom door. "What's wrong?" she asked.

"Look at it," he said, pointing. "I got such a strong hard-on I can't piss."

"What brought that on?" she asked.

"I spoke to my stepmother on the telephone," he said. "She used to turn me on, I guess she still does."

She looked at him with a half smile. "You incestuous pervert," she laughed. "Get yourself under a cold shower. You won't have any trouble peeing then."

24

◆ "WE'RE TEN MILES off the coast now," the captain's voice came through the cabin speakers.

Judd pressed the intercom. "Put it on the big screen."

The chief steward, Raoul, turned the silvered screen over the long bulkhead wall in Judd's cabin and closed the window shades against the tropical sunlight. Almost immediately a blue sea pressed against a long white strip of sand. It began disappearing into endless miles of green forest.

"The river delta in the center of the screen," the captain said.

Judd pressed the intercom again. "Zoom in close, please."

"We're at forty-four thousand feet," the captain said. "It might be grainy."

"Doesn't matter," Judd said. "That's what I want to see. Then keep a steady course up the river."

"Yes, sir." The captain's voice clicked off.

Judd watched the screen carefully. The image grew larger, filling the screen so that even the muddy color of the vast outpouring of the Amazon became clearly visible. A few moments later the delta was being lost at the bottom of the screen, and the great river began to take over the top of the screen inch by inch until even the screen seemed unable to contain it.

"The factories will be coming up in a minute on the top of the screen, sir," the captain's voice came through.

"Can we come down a bit and circle them?" Judd asked.

"We're cleared for forty-four thousand, sir," the captain said. "They'll raise hell if I change it."

"Fuck 'em!" Judd said. "You take it down to thirty-six. I'll take the responsibility." He turned to Merlin in the seat next to him. "What the hell? This is what we came here for."

Merlin was silent, his eyes glued to the screen.

The first factory was coming on screen. Grayish black plumes

138

of smoke rose from six giant stacks. There were long docks tied to cargo ships and a covered conveyor belt from the side of the factory led directly to the cargo ships. "That's the paper mill," Judd said.

The picture on the screen moved and another factory began to appear. Now the picture became clearer and he could see that the factories were built on the land but anchored in the river to be flush against the land. "This one manufactures wood planking and finishing," Judd said. "It's the waste wood that is sent on down to the paper mill."

"Unbelievable," Merlin said. "Factories like this in the middle of the most primitive jungle on earth."

"D. K. is a genius," Judd said. "It was his idea. He knew that they could not do the actual construction there. So he had the factories built in Japan, towed across the ocean and put in place. Almost overnight they were anchored there and in operation."

A third factory appeared on the screen. Beyond it, the river flowed on relentlessly, although completely covered with logs, thousands, hundreds of thousands of logs, tumbling over and over each other as if in the gaping maws of some gigantic prehistoric monster.

"That would be the lumber mill, stripping and cleaning and sorting," Judd said. He pointed to the top of the screen. A giant concrete dam was beginning to appear. "There's another sign of the genius of Ludwig. Never a need for oil or nuclear energy. Nothing but water. Hydroelectric power, supplied by nature's bounty. Not only did he think of that, he anticipated the needs of nature itself and a future supply of raw material. He developed a reforestation program that tames the forest to give a new crop every twenty years!"

"I don't understand it then," Merlin said. "Why should he want out?"

"Two things, I think," Judd said. "One, the jungle fucked him. He figured a twenty-year turnover for the forests. But the whole jungle moves at racing speed, like nothing man's had to contend with. Ludwig found he needs at least ten thousand men simply to hold back the jungle from overrunning his manufacturing facilities."

"And the other thing?" Merlin asked.

"D. K. himself. The man's over eighty and I think he's beginning to understand that he could be running out of time." Judd was silent for a moment, then looked at Merlin. "Do you think he would want out if he had the gift of immortality?"

Merlin did not answer.

Judd pressed the intercom. "You can resume your course, Captain," he said. "I'm finished for now. Thank you."

"Very good, sir," the captain said. "We'll touch down in Brasília in three hours and thirty-five minutes."

Bridget came into the cabin as Raoul raised the window screens. Sunlight flooded in. "It's that time again," she said, holding the tray in her hand.

He took the pill and swallowed it with the glass of orange juice. "Don't you get bored doing this?" he asked.

"It's my job," she said. She looked down at him. "Dr. Ivancich is awake," she said.

"How is she?" he asked.

"Fine," she said in a cool voice. "She's dressing, but Dr. Sawyer insisted that she keep her arm in a sling."

"I'll drop down to see her," he said.

"You don't have to," she said, still in the same cool voice. "She's planning to come as soon as she puts some makeup on."

Judd looked at her. "Me thinks I hear a tinge of jealousy in your voice."

"Not of her," Bridget said sarcastically. "She's practically old enough to be my mother." She left the cabin with a faint swinging of her hips that he had not noticed before.

He looked toward Merlin. "I have a feeling that Nursey is thawing out a little."

Merlin laughed. "Maybe," he said. "But the kind of figures that I'm into add up and down, not sideways."

Judd smiled. "Anything new on the South and Western bank situation?"

"Every government agency you can think of is in there with both feet. The only thing that might intrigue you is that it seems the biggest partner you have in it is Castro."

"Shit," Judd said wryly. "Why is it that all politicians want to be businessmen?"

140

Merlin got to his feet. "Is it okay if I catch forty winks? I've been awake most of the night."

"You better grab it while you can," Judd said. "I have a feeling that today will not be an easy one."

He watched the door close behind him and called to Fast Eddie standing behind the bar. "Cherry Coke."

"You got it, boss."

Judd was just sipping his drink as Sofia came in. She stood in front of the door for a moment as if she wasn't sure of her welcome. "Come in, Sofia," he said easily, putting down his glass.

She moved to his chair and bent down to his cheek. She kissed him gently. "Thank you," she said.

"You all right, my dear?"

"Yes, sir."

"No pain?"

"No, Judd. It's fine."

He looked into her eyes. "You don't have to apologize for or explain anything, Sofia," he said. "We're friends, aren't we?"

"Yes, yes," she said. "I had hoped so."

He gestured to a chair. He waited until she was seated. "Each of us does what we feel we have to do."

"I was afraid that you might feel that I betrayed you," she said.

"Did you really believe I'd think that?" he asked.

She didn't hesitate. "No."

"Then you didn't," he said.

"It's an old story," she said. "Do you want me to tell you about it?"

He shook his head. "You don't have to. I already know all about it."

"And you're not angry?"

He laughed. "No. I've lived long enough to learn that old loyalties die hard."

She was silent. She looked at the glass before him. "You're not supposed to take that stuff, you know."

"I know," he said. "But that, too, is an old loyalty."

She was quiet.

"And you're not on duty right now, Doctor," he said.

"That's right," she said.

"You look tired, Doctor," he said. "May I offer you a toot?"

"I could use a lift," she said.

He nodded toward Fast Eddie, who came over with the gold vial. Sofia held the vial, but couldn't manage it with the sling on her arm. Fast Eddie held the spoon to her nostrils. She took two dynamite snorts. Fast Eddie went back to the bar.

"That helped," she said. Her eyes met his. "You're a strange man, Judd Crane."

He didn't answer.

"Do you really think you'll live forever?" she went on.

"I didn't say forever," he said. "Immortality was the word I used."

"It's the same thing, isn't it?" she said. "Semantics."

"I never majored in languages. Nevertheless, however you say it, that's what I hope."

"And for your sake, I hope so too." She paused for a moment. "Your new nurse doesn't like me."

"That's not important," he said.

"You're fucking her, of course."

"No, as it happens," he said.

"Don't you want to?"

"Probably," he answered. "But that, too, is not important."

"I'm having an abortion next week," she said.

He nodded. "I know."

Her eyes went into him. "I would like to keep your baby."

His voice went flat. "I don't want that," he said. "We all knew it was nothing but another experiment."

"One out of ten isn't that much of a loss for you," she said.

"It would be one too many," he answered. "It was an experiment and that's the way it will remain, Sofia."

"But what will remain if you die?" she asked.

"I will not die," he said. "And even if I should, nothing will be lost."

She became silent for a moment. "May I have another snort?" she asked.

He gestured at Fast Eddie without answering her. Slowly he sipped his drink and watched her snort two more hits. She turned to look out the window of the plane. "The sky is so very blue," she said.

"It always is at forty-four thousand."

142

She turned back to him. "I'm afraid," she said. "I don't want to die."

"You won't die."

"You don't know them," she said. "They're not like you. In their world, they believe I betrayed them. And they never forget. Sooner or later, they will kill me."

"You can be lost," he said. "In America many have been hidden away from them and never been discovered. Some of their greatest scientists have been forgotten, even by them."

"Maybe," she said. "But not me. My crime was not only betrayal but also murder of a person just one step from the Politburo itself." She took a cigarette from the box on the table and lit it. She pulled the smoke deeply into her lungs. "I was never good at running," she said. "I might as well go back."

He nodded. "Very well."

She looked at him. "Then it doesn't matter that I will die?"

"You won't die," he said. "You're forgetting something very important. They need you."

"For what?" She stared at him.

He smiled. "Brezhnev. Your next patient."

She was silent.

"Do you think they'll dare endanger his life simply because you blew the head off a third-rate asshole son-in-law of a Politburo bureaucrat? Andropov at the KGB is not stupid. If you can prolong Brezhnev's life for even two more years, it gives him that much more time to consolidate his position in order to step into Brezhnev's shoes."

She looked into his eyes. "You believe that?"

"I can guarantee it," he said. "Crane Industries also has important contacts in the Politburo."

25

◆ BRASÍLIA WAS A brand-new city, so new its heart had not yet begun to beat. The streets were wide and clean, the buildings modern, concrete and glass. Even the automobiles and buses, powered by a combination of ethyl and grain alcohol, added no pollution to the clear blue sky above the city.

The conference was held in a large window-walled room, twenty-two stories above the city avenues. They were seated around an oval, burled-oak table in comfortable high-backed chairs covered in soft glove leather the same color as the table.

Judd was placed opposite the chairman of the Brazilian delegation across the widest part of the oval table. On either side of him sat Merlin and Doc Sawyer. The Brazilian chairman, for his part, was also flanked by two men.

They all spoke English, but Judd could hear a faint accent of German in the chairman's voice. "Dr. Schoenbrun," he said. "If I understand correctly, Mr. Ludwig has invested a half billion dollars in this project."

Dr. Schoenbrun nodded.

Judd gazed across the table at him. "And what do you expect from me?"

Dr. Schoenbrun's Germanic accent was getting slightly more pronounced. "In this project, Mr. Crane, we want nothing from you."

Judd masked his surprise by remaining silent, even though several things came to him at once.

"Our negotiations with Mr. Ludwig have been completed," the chairman went on. "The Brazilian government will take over the project completely. Mr. Ludwig has agreed to a fair share of the profits and to a long-term low interest rate. His principal capital return in accordance with various economic factors we'll agree on in good time."

"My congratulations, Dr. Schoenbrun," Judd said. "In my opinion, you have achieved an important contribution to the economy of your country."

"Thank you, Mr. Crane." Dr. Schoenbrun allowed himself a faint smile of pride.

Judd nodded. "Then you must have another proposition in mind for me. Otherwise why did you invite me here?"

"We do, Mr. Crane," Dr. Schoenbrun said. "But first I must apologize to you for misleading you about the real reason. The world has many ears, and we felt it vitally important that we keep our discussion for us alone."

"Agreed," Judd said.

"I speak to you about Crane Pharmaceuticals," Dr. Schoenbrun said. "That industry is one of the weakest sectors in our economy. I must tell you honestly that we have already made various approaches. First to Hoffman-LaRoche, but they decided to be based in Costa Rica. Then to Bayer Chemical Weltgeschaft, but they are only in household products, and the more heavy part of industry they prefer to keep closer to themselves."

Judd looked at him. "Du Pont? Monsanto?"

"They might have been interested," Dr. Schoenbrun answered, "but they were concerned by President Carter's human rights policies. They felt that they would end up with more problems than they could handle."

"Then Crane came up at the bottom of your list?" Judd said dryly.

"Physically, true," Dr. Schoenbrun said candidly. "Actually, not at all. In one area especially, we have always been more close to each other than to any of the others."

"To what do you refer?" Judd asked.

Dr. Schoenbrun looked directly across the table at his eyes. "Nuclear medicine," he said.

After a moment Judd spoke one word: "Germany."

The chairman nodded. "After the war many of the German scientists fled here, as you know. Under the conditions of surrender, Germany was not allowed to develop a nuclear industry for any purpose. Brazil had no such prohibitions. And so Germans, and even more Germans, came here. 'The Silent Industry' we call it. No one speaks of it, but it is there. Today, we have two

145

completely modern facilities already in operation, supplying electric power to Brasília, Rio and São Paulo."

"All manned and staffed by Germans," Judd said.

"Not only by Germans," Dr. Schoenbrun replied quickly. "We have many Americans and French."

Judd looked at him. "You have the bomb?"

"No," Dr. Schoenbrun said. "But of course, we can have it if we want it."

"More nuclear bombs don't excite me," Judd said.

"Nor do they excite me." Schoenbrun looked at him. "We have another installation that might be interesting to you."

"What is that?"

"On the plateau of an extinct volcano in the Andes, four hundred miles north of Ludwig's development, we have built a nuclear generator three hundred meters below the crater. Ludwig had the idea that we could supply all the power for his development. Then he pulled out, and we ran out of money because of the financial crisis. Now it's just lying there, waiting for the jungle to bury it."

"What do you want me to do with it?" Judd asked.

"I thought you could use it to build a nuclear medicine facility. We have three billion dollars in it now. We'll turn it all over to you for one billion. Another two billion will build you the most modern plant in the world. And even more important, it's deeply secret and inaccessible to intruders. That's why it was named Xanadu."

"How would we find the personnel to build it and man it?" Judd asked.

"We have solved that problem. Full staff is already on standby."

Judd thought for a moment. "That might present a possibility for me. When can I see it?"

"At your convenience," Schoenbrun answered.

Judd rose to his feet. "I will get in touch with you." He held out his hand. "Thank you, Dr. Schoenbrun."

"It's creepy," Judd said to Doc Sawyer as Bridget handed him his orange juice and pill. He swallowed it gamely. "All they want is three billion dollars."

"A real bargain," Doc Sawyer said sarcastically.

146

Judd laughed. "It makes Mexico seem like a heaven of integrity by comparison. All these guys want is a corner of the corruption market."

"Then, I take it, you're not going to make a deal with them?"

"Of course I'm making a deal with them. Maybe not exactly what they want, but enough to bait them into a feeling of security about us." He smiled wryly. "In order to negate, sometimes you have to integrate."

Doc Sawyer paused for a moment. "Where do you think all their equipment has come from? All the instructions and signs on the machinery are in English. But it can't have come from the States. Carter would never have allowed it."

"I'll bet my ass, France," Judd answered. Then seeing the incredulity on Doc's face: "Don't be naive. Despite the antiproliferation agreement between France and the United States and the other Western nuclear power countries, when it comes to money, France will find a way."

"Our friends," Doc said sarcastically.

"With friends like that, you don't need enemies." Judd glanced out the window and pressed the intercom for the captain. "Are we anywhere near Rio?" he asked.

"It's approximately two hundred and sixty nautical miles behind us, Mr. Crane," answered the captain.

"Let's go back. Call them for clearance. We'll stay the night," Judd said. He turned to Doc Sawyer. "It's time we had a little fun."

"You're supposed to be in bed by nine-thirty," Doc Sawyer said.

"Just once, Doc," Judd said, "forget you're my doctor. I'm getting bored out of my skull with the hand-job treatments I've been getting. Besides, the girls from Ipanema are really everything the song says. It might even do *you* a little good."

THE SOUND OF laughter awakened Bridget. She looked around the total darkness of her stateroom. The night clock glowed three-thirty. From her window she could see three or four girls leaving two limousines pulled up beside the plane. They giggled as they followed Judd and Doc Sawyer to the elevator.

Bridget turned back to her bed. She stared up in the dark; she heard no sounds. Her room was toward the rear of the plane. She closed her eyes and tried her best to go back to sleep.

Fast Eddie already had twelve long lines of cocaine on the mirrorlike finish of the table. The girls laughed and giggled even louder as they picked up the straws and snorted.

"That's crazy," he said. "I've never done something like this before. Which one do *you* want?"

"All of them," Judd laughed. "Right now, with the kind of hard-on I have, I feel I can fuck all of them into the ground."

Doc Sawyer looked at Judd. "Wait a minute. Don't forget you have to be somewhat careful."

"I'll be careful tomorrow," Judd said. "Right now, I'm a kid in a candy store."

"WHY YOU DON'T come, Judd?" Sylvia gasped. "Your prick is so hard my cunt has been killed with the pain."

Two other girls murmured agreement. "And I too! I never felt one so hard like that!" one said. The other one insisted: "It does not become even just a little soft. It just goes straight always like a steel pipe. All I can feel is the pain. And the divine pleasure!"

Judd looked at the fourth girl. "What about you, kid?"

She hesitated for a moment. "Even when I think I feel blood, the joy is ecstatic!"

He sat up between the girls. "I am sorry," he said. "I truly didn't mean to hurt you. Perhaps I have done too much cocaine."

"Usually too much cocaine makes it soft," Sylvia offered.

"Drugs do different things for different people," he said. He got to his feet and covered himself with a robe. "It is getting late," he said. "Perhaps you would all like to go now. And maybe it will be better the next time for all of us."

Sylvia looked up at him. "But you are still hard," she said. "We feel that we are cheating you."

"You are all beautiful," he said. "And you have not cheated me. I loved being with you."

"Will you see us again soon?" Sylvia asked.

"As soon as I can," he said.

Quickly the girls slipped into their dresses. Judd pressed the button for Fast Eddie. "Take care of them."

Judd kissed each of the girls on the cheek as they left his stateroom. "Now remember, Judd," Sylvia said. "You said soon."

"I'll remember," he said.

He began to walk to his door slowly. From the corner of his eye he saw Fast Eddie lay a thousand-dollar bill on each of the girls. He closed the door and dropped his robe. His erection was even harder and was beginning to hurt intensely. He went into the shower hurriedly and turned on the water, cold as ice.

26

◆ DOC SAWYER CAME into Judd's salon. Fast Eddie was cleaning the bar. "Is Mr. Crane in his stateroom?"

"Yes," Fast Eddie nodded.

"Think he's still awake?"

"I just heard him turn off the shower," Fast Eddie answered.

Doc Sawyer knocked on the stateroom door. "May I come in?" he called.

Judd's voice was muffled. "Yes."

Sawyer opened the door. At first, he could hardly see; the stateroom lights had been dimmed almost completely. Then his eyes adjusted themselves to the faint glow.

Judd was sitting on a chair, his feet against the floor, his body knotted in a crouch over his arms, which were held tightly across his groin. His head was bent far down, the chin resting against his chest.

"The girl," Doc Sawyer began to say, but broke off quickly. "What's wrong?"

Judd looked up at him. "I don't know." His voice was strained, it seemed to emerge from a great distance and not come from him at all. "I think I'm in big trouble."

Doc searched for the wall rheostat. Light filled the room. He saw Judd's face, pale and heavy with the perspiration that comes from pain. The cobalt-blue eyes had turned almost completely black. Quickly, he stepped over to Judd's bent figure. He reached to touch Judd's forehead. Under the dampness, it was cold. "Can you stand up?" he asked, not trying to help him.

"I think so," Judd said.

Slowly, he began to uncoil and to straighten himself. He carefully positioned his hands flat against the chair arms and pushed himself up. His lips were white and grimly pressed together; his nostrils flared as he sought to suck in air; the sweat continued to fall from him in droplets. He was able to raise himself partly, then he had to stop. "I can't make it," he said in a curiously calm voice.

"Don't try then," Sawyer said. "I'll help you." He put his arms under Judd's shoulders. "We'll move you slowly to the bed. Don't panic. You'll be okay."

"I won't panic," Judd replied with a hollow laugh. "Don't you know I'm immortal?"

Doc stretched him on the bed. He called out through the open door to Fast Eddie. "Get the nurse and tell her to bring down my bag and also the first aid kit. Also call Dr. Ivancich to come right down. And have Raoul bring down the portable oxygen tank."

"Got you." Fast Eddie didn't waste time.

Doc knelt beside the bed. "Tell me about the pain. Where is it?"

Judd stared into his eyes. "It started in my prick, then my balls seemed to turn into rocks and the prick got so hard beyond them that they seemed to go inside my asshole. Then the pain began to spread inside me. It stemmed across my groin to each side as if my kidneys and bladder had turned to stone. I wanted to piss but nothing could go through. I felt as if my prick had turned to solid rock, urethra and all."

"Okay," Doc said. "Try to relax. We'll take care of it."

Judd grimaced. "I guess partying wasn't such a good idea after all."

"Maybe," Doc Sawyer said. "But it was a fun idea. Probably you just overdid it, that's all."

"Doc Sawyer." Bridget was standing behind him.

"Set up an intravenous drip," he ordered. "Twenty milligrams Valium, five cc of morphine in a thirty-minute saline solution."

She nodded and went to the emergency medical box. Quickly she assembled the metal stand to hold the bottle, then infused the Valium and morphine into the solution. Finally she attached the tube to the bottle, adjusted the needle to the end and hung the bottle on the stand. "Will you inject, Doctor?"

"Yes," he said. "Hold his arm straight."

She nodded, and a moment later, Doc Sawyer slipped the needle into his vein. Quickly she taped it to Judd's arm. She looked at Doc Sawyer. "The oxygen bottle is here on the caddy."

"Nostril spectacles," he said. "Let's begin with two liters a minute for an hour."

"Yes, sir," she said.

He turned to his bag while she set up the oxygen. He opened it to take out the electronic thermometer. He found the reading low, 97.9. The electronic blood pressure digital numbers flashed their red L.E.D. lights, 102 over 70.

Judd saw the reading. The intravenous drip was already beginning to work. He smiled faintly. "What did you expect, Doc?" he said. "Probably all my blood is stuck in my cock."

"I can check that too if you want," Doc Sawyer laughed. "It probably is big enough to fit."

Judd looked at Bridget. "Only if she does it."

She didn't answer.

"Bet you never saw a prick like this," Judd said. "No matter how much experience you had in that hospital."

"Don't brag," she said in her faint brogue. "I've seen some that make yours look like a baby's."

Sofia came into the room. "Sorry I took so long. I couldn't dress because of the sling. What happened?"

"Acute priapism," Doc Sawyer said.

She looked over his shoulder at Judd. Judd smiled up at her. "Something, isn't it?"

She laughed. "Fantastic. I'm in love."

Judd turned to tease Bridget. "At least some people appreciate me."

Bridget didn't smile. "I would expect she would."

"How are you feeling now?" Doc asked him, to deflect the antagonism between the two women.

"Better," Judd said. "Now I feel I have to urinate."

"Get a bottle, nurse," Doc Sawyer said.

Bridget looked at him. "Ice packs will help."

"You're the expert," Doc Sawyer said. "Okay."

Bridget left the stateroom. Judd looked up at Sofia. "The least you can do is kiss it a little."

"I'd be afraid," she said. "It seems to me you have enough problems already."

Judd turned to Doc Sawyer. The intravenous was really working now. "See," he said, "how the mighty have fallen."

THEY WERE SEATED around the table in Judd's salon when Bridget came from the stateroom, closing the door behind her. "He's sleeping," she said.

"Good," Doc Sawyer said. "Any visible change in his condition?"

"Slight," she answered. "He's been able to pass a little water, but even in his sleep it seems painful."

"I spoke to the urologist in the hospital in Florida. He thought it would be helpful if we could express his prostate gland."

"I've had several patients with the same condition in Devon," she said. "We couldn't do anything until the turgidity was relaxed slightly, so we could induce ejaculation. That in turn reduced the pressure enough to help the patient achieve normal flaccidity."

Doc Sawyer looked across the table at Sofia. "What do you think if we give him a shot of Compazine?"

Sofia nodded. "It should help him relax and at least, if it doesn't work, it can't hurt him."

"How much do we have left with the intravenous?" he asked.

"About fifteen minutes," Bridget answered.

"Okay," Doc Sawyer said. "We'll give him the Compazine as soon as that's completed."

"Do you want him to keep on with oxygen, Doctor?"

"Yes."

"Thank you, Doctor." Bridget returned to Judd's stateroom.

Sofia looked at Sawyer. "She's a strange girl," she said. "What made her specialize in becoming a prick nurse?"

Sawyer smiled. "Maybe she spent her childhood in the back seat of automobiles giving hand-jobs."

Merlin smiled, but Sofia didn't understand any of it. Merlin looked at Doc Sawyer. "What do you want us to do now?" he asked. "Stay here or head for home?"

"Head for home," Doc said. "I'll feel better when we have him under the care of the specialists."

"That creates another problem," Merlin said. "This one concerns Dr. Ivancich."

"Yes?" Sofia asked.

"Security has informed us of a sudden influx of Cubans into our area. Strangers that we haven't yet got a make on. We can only surmise they're looking for you."

"I was afraid of that," Sofia said. "I even mentioned that to Judd."

"I know," Merlin said. "Judd has already asked me to arrange another travel plan for you."

"You've done it?" she asked.

He nodded. "Yes. New identity papers, passport, everything. You'll travel as the wife of one of the security men on this plane right now. From here you'll travel on Varig to Dallas, from Dallas by American Airlines to Washington. We own a private hospital on the outskirts of the city. You'll be registered there under still another name. Judd will see you there next week when he attends the inauguration."

She hesitated for a moment. "I guess I have no choice, do I?"

"Not if you want to stay alive," Merlin said.

She nodded slowly. "I suppose they will arrange the abortion at the same time?"

"That's correct."

She moistened her lips that had gone suddenly dry. "There's no chance that Judd will drop me now, is there?"

"If he wanted to drop you, he would have left you in Mexico," Doc Sawyer answered. "But that's not the way he plays the game."

154

27

♦ "IT'S MICROSURGERY BY laser," the urologist, Dr. Orrin, said quietly. "The technique's adapted from retina transplantation, but as far advanced as the Columbia space shuttle from the Wright Brothers' plane at Kitty Hawk."

Judd looked at him. "It's been tested before?"

"Not in humans, not even in animals," the doctor said. "This has been developed especially for you. But it's been checked and rechecked by the computer. There's no way it can go wrong."

Judd was silent for a moment before he turned to Doc Sawyer. "What do you think?"

"I've thought about it and also spoken to Dr. Zabiski on the telephone to Yugoslavia. We both agree that it's completely feasible and would show no harmful results to our other program."

"I still don't know," Judd said.

Doc Sawyer laughed. "You're strange. You've risked your life with every dangerous experiment we've done. Any one of them might have killed you, but here you hesitate. I'm beginning to think your prick's more important than your life."

Judd turned to the urologist. "What's the alternative choice?"

"Only the old method. We snip the vein that supplies blood to the capillaries in the penis. Then it's over, once and for all, but of course you're impotent for life, and it cannot be reversed," Dr. Orrin replied. "It's your prick and your option."

Judd looked down at the microchip only slightly larger than the head of a pin. "That's all it is?" he asked. "Never has to be changed? No battery to be replaced?"

Dr. Orrin nodded. "That's it. The power is supplied by the electricity of your nervous system. The microchip is made of titanium and is completely organ-tolerable. It replaces the physical functions of that little part of the nerve damaged by the

155

nuclear treatment and, perhaps even more important, it will last forever."

"Then I can perform as if I were normal?"

"Not as if. You will *be* normal, Mr. Crane. We're simply transplanting a manufactured nerve for your own. The erection normal, the orgasm and ejaculation normal, and blood return to flaccidity completely normal," Dr. Orrin said.

"Then how long would it take me to achieve another erection?" he asked.

Dr. Orrin laughed. "That depends on you, Mr. Crane. I can't anticipate the how and whom of your fucking for you."

Judd laughed. "How long does the whole thing take?"

"The physical operation, seven minutes, only because we have to go near the prostate. You should be completely healed and ready for action in twenty-four to thirty-six hours."

Judd looked from Doc Sawyer to the urologist. "Tomorrow morning," he said. He waited until the urologist left the room. "Isn't it ironic that the first part of my body to achieve immortality will be my prick?"

"HARLEM, BABY!" FAST Eddie pointed out the window of the helicopter bringing them into New York from Newark Airport. "Harlem! We're home!"

Judd laughed. He felt good. And it was only three days after his operation. The doctor was right. There was no pain.

"I can see the Empire State Building," Bridget said in an excited voice. "I can't believe it's real and not a film."

"You've never been to New York?" Judd asked.

"Never," she replied.

"Then you'll have time to see it," he said. "We'll be here for two days before we go to Washington for Reagan's inauguration."

"Can I get a couple of days off, too, boss?" Fast Eddie asked. "I'd like to see my old grandpa and look up a few friends."

"You got it," Judd said. He turned to Bridget. "You have the two days too."

"Are you sure you don't need me?" she asked.

"What for?" he smiled. "I'm healed. It's better."

Merlin said from across the aisle, "Don't forget we're due in the office in an hour."

"We'll be there," Judd said. "Fast Eddie will take Bridget to the apartment in the second limo."

New York traffic, as usual, was impossible. Though the office was only thirty blocks from the heliport, the limousine took thirty-five minutes.

It was a quarter to eleven, fifteen minutes before the meeting was scheduled to begin, when Judd walked into his office, the same one that had belonged to his father. He closed the door behind him and looked at the portrait of his father looking down at him. In his mind he heard his father's voice. *"Hello, Son."*

Softly, he spoke a response: "Hello, Father. You see, nothing's been changed. Just as you wished."

"Nothing's been changed," echoed in his mind, yet he thought he could hear his father's voice: *"Yet, everything has changed."*

Judd stood silent, looking up at the portrait.

The echo continued. *"But that's the way it should be, Son. It's a new world out there, your world."*

"It's your world, too, Father," he whispered. "We both made it. Without you it would never have happened."

The echo was gone. Judd walked behind the desk, looked out the windows high over the city, then turned his back to it and sat down. The old-fashioned high-backed leather chair creaked comfortably beneath him. This, too, had belonged to his father. Slowly he picked up the telephone and pressed the secretary's button. "Crane speaking," he said to the machine. "I apologize for not knowing your name."

"No apologies needed, Mr. Crane." The voice was crisply efficient and completely familiar.

"Mother!" He laughed into the phone.

"This is a business office, Mr. Crane, and no familiarity will be tolerated," she said in a straight voice. "But you may call me Barbara, if you wish."

He left the receiver on the desk and crossed the office, opening the door and catching her still holding the telephone. "Barbara!" he exclaimed, lifting her off her feet into his arms.

She was laughing as he kissed her. "Judd."

He led her into the office. "For a moment there," he said, "I felt I was a little boy again."

HE SAT AT the head of the small conference table just as his father had. Barbara sat to his right, Uncle Paul to his left. Merlin was seated next to Barbara, two solemn-looking attorneys below Uncle Paul; a secretary with a stenotype in front of her completed the group.

Judd smiled. "You're beginning to look more like Burl Ives every day," he said. "Why don't you trim your beard and the curls falling from the back of your head instead of looking like an overaged hippie?"

"I like it," Paul said. "And while we're talking about each other, why don't you remember your manners? Your father always had a bottle of Glenmarangie on the table in front of me."

Judd smiled silently and picked up a bottle from the floor and placed it, with an old-fashioned glass, in front of Paul. "No wonder we can't allow you to stay fired. We'd be stuck with the world's largest supply of Glenmarangie. Better now?" he asked.

"Much," Uncle Paul said. He opened the bottle, splashed some whisky in the glass and emptied it. "Now, we can talk business."

"I'm listening," Judd said.

"The South and Western bank business has got us covered in shit," Paul began. "I have it from unimpeachable sources that the House Banking Committee will come down on me real hard as soon as the inauguration is over and Congress convenes. They're already preparing subpoenas for you as well as all the officers, both present and past, to appear at a special hearing."

"Figures," Judd said. "But there's nothing they can do to us. The fact of the matter is that it's we who've brought the government into it."

"Truth is not important in this case," Paul said. "This is politics and politics thrives on headlines. Truth gets buried on the bottom of the last page."

"What do you suggest?"

"We have friends," Paul said. "We use them. Now is the time for people to stand up and be counted."

"Okay," Judd said. "Shoot."

"It will cost a lot of money," Paul said.

"That's what money is for," Judd replied. He paused a moment. "What other good news do you have for me?"

Paul poured another drink. "It's neither good news nor bad," he said. He emptied his glass. "You were correct. Brazil has picked up their nuclear equipment from one of our nuclear friends. We also know that the presidential transition team doesn't give a shit about it. The military feels very comfortable with Brazilians. They feel that Brazil will stand completely behind us against the Soviets."

"That clinches it for me," Judd said. "We'll make the deal with Brazil."

"About Mexico?" Paul asked.

"We'll make that deal also. But another kind. Central America will be set up as a separate market."

"Makes sense," Paul said. "Now just one more item and we can close the meeting."

"Yes?" Judd asked.

"Crane Island for a forty-million-dollar investment is completely crazy," Paul said. "I advise completely and irrevocably against it. Especially since you tell us this is only a way stop until Xanadu is completed. What difference does it make if we wait an extra year or two? You'll never see the money."

"Time is important, not money. Crane Island goes forward." Judd looked around the table. "Any other business?"

"Nothing of major importance," Paul said. "Just to let you know that the Russians have agreed to your suggestion about the Yugoslavian doctor and express their gratitude."

"Then the meeting is ordered closed," Judd said. He rose from his chair and walked around the table to kiss Uncle Paul on the cheek. "Thank you."

"This is a crazy way to end a meeting," Paul said. "Besides I haven't even finished my bottle of whisky yet."

"I'll let you take it home in a doggie bag," Judd said.

28

◆ PAUL TOOK THEM to lunch at his usual poolside table at The Four Seasons restaurant. Barbara and Judd sat on the inside chairs next to the bubbling water softly rising through the limpid green pool. Jim, Barbara's husband, sat beside her and Paul was next to Judd.

Without a word, a waiter placed a double Scotch on the rocks before Paul. "Cheers," he said, taking a sip. Then he asked what they would like to drink.

Paul Kovi and Tom Margittai appeared with a cold bottle of pink champagne, Cristale '75, before they had an opportunity to order a drink. "Madame's favorite," Paul said, as he gently bowed and kissed Barbara's hand.

"You remembered," Barbara smiled. "So thoughtful of you. Thank you."

"We don't see you enough," Tom said. He turned to Judd. "And you either, young man."

"I'm not in town very much," Judd said. "I have to work for a living."

"Of course," Tom said without conviction.

Paul looked at Judd. "I don't know how you do it, but you look younger now than you did when I saw you three years ago. What's your secret?"

Judd laughed. "Early to bed, early to rise—you know the old saying."

The two restaurateurs smiled, and bowing again, walked away as Oreste made a ceremony of opening the champagne. Judd tasted and nodded his approval. Oreste filled the thin tulip glasses. *"Bon appétit,"* he said, and left the table.

Judd raised his glass. "To all of you."

"And to you," Barbara said warmly.

Paul looked at him. "Despite all our problems, the machine

keeps on rolling," he said. "Putting everything together, the Crane Foundation, the trusts, your personal holdings at the end of this current calendar year, will combine to equal more than five hundred billion dollars."

"Those are just numbers," Judd said. "There isn't that much money in the world. If there is, then there is no reason to complain about the investment in Crane Island."

Paul gestured for another double Scotch. "You're probably right," he said. "Despite my normal pessimistic doubts, you always seem to come up right."

"Thank you, Uncle Paul," Judd said. "I never thought I'd hear you say that."

One of the gray uniformed attendants approached them, a telephone in his hand. "Mr. Crane, I have a telephone call for you." At Judd's nod, he plugged the cord into a socket hidden in the tree behind Judd's chair.

Judd checked his pockets. They were empty. "Uncle Paul, take care of him for me."

Paul grumbled, handing the young man a five-dollar bill, "Now I know how you made all that money."

Judd spoke into the telephone. "Crane here."

"Judd," Dr. Zabiski's familiar voice came into his ear. "Merlin told me where I could reach you."

"Where are you?" he asked.

"At the airport. JFK," she said. "It's very important that we meet."

"What terminal are you at?"

"Pan American."

"Wait there," he said. "I'll pick you up in thirty minutes." He rose from the table at once. "You'll have to excuse me from lunch," he said. "Something special has just come up."

They knew better than to ask him what. "Will I see you at dinner?" Barbara inquired.

"I don't know," he said. "I'll call you."

He waved at them and left the table. His chauffeur was already waiting for him in the limousine on Park Avenue. Judd went through the side exit and out the Seagram Building into his car.

"Pan Am at JFK," he said. "Like right now."

THE LIMOUSINE MADE it to the arrival ramp in twenty-three minutes. Judd stepped from the car and ran into the building. She was waiting for him just inside the doors. There were two small valises standing beside her. He kissed her on the cheek, picked up the two valises and led her back to the car. The chauffeur opened the car for them and began to place the bags in the trunk.

"Please, no," she said. "I would prefer them with me."

"Yes, madame." The chauffeur put the valises on the floor before them. He returned to his seat and looked over his shoulder. "Where to, sir?"

"The Fifth Avenue apartment," Judd said.

"We may not have the time," the tiny doctor said. "I am supposed to collect Sofia and bring her with me to Moscow on the Aeroflot flight tonight."

"Then take us to the private plane gate at LaGuardia," he said. He pressed the window button to close off the driver's section, then turned to her. "We can talk," he said. "We're debugged here, no one can hear us."

She took out a cigarette and lit it nervously. "There are many things I have to tell you; I don't know what to say first."

"Then one at a time," he said.

Her tawny eyes softened. "I have cancer," she said. "I have maybe as much as two months. Probably less."

His dark, cobalt-blue eyes searched hers. "That's definite?"

"Quite," she said in a dispassionate, professional tone. "I've known it for some time. Now the clock is running out."

"I'm sorry."

"Don't be," she said. "I've had a good life. I know you thought I was in my late sixties." Her eyes looked again at him. "But actually, I'm seventy-two."

He remained silent.

She dragged at the cigarette again. "Next. My work and research. I don't want it all to fall into the hands of the Russians. I left most of it in my files to make them feel that it's all there." She gestured at the two valises. "The complete work is in these valises. Tapes, microfilm and notebooks. There may be some things missing, but although it's in my own amateurish code, I'm sure that your computers will easily decipher it. All I ask is that you

162

guard it carefully and use it wisely—not solely selfishly but for the benefit of mankind."

He nodded. "Excuse me for just one moment." He picked up the telephone and tapped two numbers. A voice answered. "Crane Aviation."

"This is Judd Crane," he said. "I'll be there in approximately twelve minutes. I want the jet, Falcon Twenty. Clear for Langley Field, Washington. Two passengers going out, three coming back."

"Yes, Mr. Crane," the voice answered.

Judd put down the phone and turned to her. "I'm not calling Sofia in advance. I don't want to take any chances that someone might track into her line."

"I understand," she said. She put out the cigarette. "I don't know how you did it, but the Russians have cleared her completely. I have orders to deliver her personally to Brezhnev."

"What happens to her after he's gone?" he asked.

"I don't know. I only hope that they feel she knows enough about my work to allow her to continue it. I would prefer that she could come back to work with you, but we have no control over that."

"Then afterward, are you returning to Yugoslavia?"

"No," she said. "I will be at Maxim Gorky Hospital in Moscow."

"Then I will not be able to see you?"

"This is so."

He was silent. "Shit." He looked at her. "I'll miss you."

"I'll miss you too, Judd Crane," she said. "I've never known another man like you." She put her hand into his. It was soft, small and frail. "Old ladies fall in love too," she said.

He put her hand to his mouth. "Which keeps them beautiful forever," he said.

THERE WAS ANOTHER limousine waiting for him at Langley Field, as well as two of his security men. One of them took over as chauffeur. After they got into the car, the security men in the front seat, he picked up the telephone and called the clinic. The switchboard connected him to Sofia almost immediately.

He didn't announce his name, nor did he call her by her own. "I am thirty minutes from the clinic," he said. "Don't pack or

163

take anything. Just put on a coat and walk out as if you're going for a stroll. Two streets from the clinic is a shopping center at the corner of Langley and Arlington. There's a big discount drugstore on that corner. Walk inside it and sit at the ice cream fountain, as near as you can to the window so you can see out. Wait there until I come inside to meet you. Got it?"

"Perfectly," she said. The phone clicked off.

Less than a half an hour later he walked into the drugstore. She was sitting at the fountain. He sat down beside her. "Dr. Zabiski is waiting in the car," he said.

"I think I'm being followed," she said.

"Where?"

"There, standing in the doorway of the gift shop opposite. A burly man with a heavy dark coat. I think I've seen him at the clinic several times."

Judd nodded. He moved the small button in his hand toward his ear. "Did you get that?" He paused for a moment. "Good," he said. "Take him out."

He got out of his seat and threw a five-dollar bill on the counter.

The limousine rolled up as they walked toward the exit. It stopped and the passenger door swung open. Judd pushed her before him quickly. She went half-flying into the car, Judd right after, closing the door behind. He pushed her down onto the seat and rose enough to look out the window as the car took off.

He saw the burly man slumped against the store window on the sidewalk. The security man had already disappeared. Then the limousine came out of the parking lot and started speeding back to the airport.

THEY WERE STANDING in the Aeroflot passenger lounge in the Pan Am terminal. The red light flashed the passenger boarding signal.

Judd turned to the little doctor. He was silent for a moment, then he kissed her three times. Once on each cheek, last on her lips. "You've got to be the greatest lady," he said.

"Good luck, Judd Crane," she said. "May all your dreams come true."

164

She turned toward the door and walked through it to the gate. He watched her until she was gone. He turned to Sofia.

She looked up at him, her lips were tremulous; soft tears formed in the corners of her eyes. "I'm sorry. I wanted your baby," she said.

"Better this way," he said.

She shook her head. "I don't know," she said.

He didn't answer.

She took a deep breath. "Will I ever see you again?"

"I hope so," he said.

"Do you really mean that?"

"Yes," he said. "You represent something very special to me. I really hope we see each other again someday."

She threw her arms around him and kissed him. "I love you, Judd Crane," she said. "In my own peculiar way, I really do love you very much." She turned and ran to the door.

He watched her until the door had closed behind her, then walked out from the terminal to his car.

His chauffeur was holding the passenger door open for him. "Mr. Crane," he said, holding out a small folded note to him. "The young lady left this for you."

Judd took the note and sat back in the car. The limousine moved away from the curb and he looked down and opened the note. He read it quickly.

> For Judd—
> Remember.
> Life is for the living.
> Immortality, for history.
> Love, Sofia.

BOOK TWO

The Discovery

1983–1984

1

♦ THE SHAFT OF sunlight reflected by the solar mirrors formed a column beamed into the clear blue sky. "There." Doc Sawyer pointed through the window of the copter. "Crane Island."

Sofia squinted, put on her sunglasses. "It's big," she said. "Bigger than I thought."

Sawyer nodded. "The island is twelve miles long and eight miles at its width near the center. Judd's temporary environment, as he calls it—he does not like to call it a home—is a geodesic dome built entirely of solar mirror energy cells. It is one-third of a mile in diameter, three stories above the ground and two stories below."

Sofia turned to him. "And he plans to live there?"

Sawyer nodded. "Not for long, but it's already nine months that he's remained there. To my knowledge, he's not placed a foot on the mainland."

She lit a cigarette and let the smoke slip out through her nostrils. "Alcatraz," she said reflectively.

Sawyer looked at her questioningly.

"Isn't that the island you Americans placed your prisoners on so that they could not escape? Like Devil's Island was for the French?"

"I hadn't thought of that," he said.

"The idea was Zabiski's, I suppose?" she asked.

"It started that way," he said. "But I don't think even she could have anticipated the extent to which it would be turned into a reality."

Sofia shook her head. "The old lady was crazy. At the end she was completely crazy. I visited her the day she died. She looked up at me. 'He will live forever,' she said. 'I gave him all the knowledge he needs.'

" 'What knowledge, Doctor?' I asked her.

169

" 'All of it,' she said. 'But he must assemble it. It's in bits and pieces. I could not do it. But he has the tools now. Computers. They think a million years in a second. My whole life was not long enough to think that much. Yes, Judd has the tools. He will succeed where I could not. You will see!'

" 'Then why didn't you share your knowledge with the world? Not just him?' I asked. She looked up at me and said 'Because I loved him. And he's the only man I would trust with that knowledge. The world would use it for power and gain. He already has all that he wants. All he needs is time itself.' Then she closed her eyes and slept."

Sawyer looked at her. "Did you speak to her again?"

"No," Sofia answered. "I had to return to my own work. The Premier was leaving on a journey and I had to accompany him. That night I heard she had died."

"Which is why you called Judd that night?" he asked.

A puzzled look crossed her face. "The only person I told that to was the Premier. I haven't spoken to Judd since we said good-bye at the airport in New York. That was more than three years ago and I haven't spoken to him yet."

"Still, someone told him," Sawyer insisted.

"I don't know who," she answered. "But Judd once told me he had important connections inside the Politburo itself."

"That doesn't surprise me," Sawyer said. "Judd has a network of people all over the world."

"I can believe that," she said. A tone sounded and the seat belt and no smoking signs were turned on. She put out her cigarette. "I was in Bangladesh when I got his message."

"You were surprised?"

She nodded. "I thought Andropov and the KGB were the only people who knew where I went after Brezhnev died."

"Do you think they now know you've come here?"

"Probably. I think they know everything I do."

"But they didn't stop you?"

"No," she said. "But they will contact me when they want me —or need me."

The copter pilot's voice came through the cabin speakers. "We are landing on the North Helipad. Fast Eddie will meet you."

Sofia smiled. "Fast Eddie," she said. "I'll be happy to see him."

"THE GULF STREAM is about nine miles east of the island," Fast Eddie said from behind the driver's seat of the air-conditioned Land Rover. "Even in winter, the water's always warm. The small tribe of Seminole Indians who lived there called it 'The Sacred River.'"

"Very interesting," Sofia teased him. "What do you call it?"

Fast Eddie grinned. "Boring."

She glanced around the narrow road. "You don't like it?"

"No."

"And Mr. Crane, what does he think?"

He looked at her. "He doesn't say, so I don't know."

"Has he really stayed there for nine months without leaving?"

"As far as I know," Fast Eddie said. "But I go home one week out of each month."

The car turned into a driveway in front of a small house. Fast Eddie pulled to a stop. He gestured. "Your place. There are twelve guest cottages on the island."

She was silent for a moment. "Suddenly I have a feeling that I could use a snort. It's been a long time."

He looked into her eyes. "I know what you mean," he said, taking the vial off the gold chain. Quickly he removed the cap and handed the vial and the spoon to her.

Her hands trembled slightly, then steadied as she took the hits. Both nostrils, twice. She looked at him. "That helped."

"Good," he said, taking it back.

"I feel frightened," she said.

He was silent.

"Has he changed?" she went on.

"He still dopes." Fast Eddie smiled. "So I guess he hasn't changed completely." He got out of the car and walked around it to open her door. "Come," he said. "I'll show you your place."

The front door opened as they approached it. A black man with a white jacket held it open for them, next to him stood an attractive black lady wearing a gray blouse and skirt under a neat white apron.

"This is Max, your houseman, and his wife, Mae, your cook and maid," Fast Eddie said. He looked at the couple. "Your guest, Dr. Ivancich."

"How do you do?" the couple said almost in unison. "Welcome."

"Thank you," Sofia said. She looked into the hallway. A large living room was on one side of the entrance hall, a dining room on the other. A staircase led to the bedrooms on the floor above.

Fast Eddie turned to her. "They'll take good care of you. Anything you want just ask." He smiled. "The snow is in the center drawer of your dresser."

"You've thought of everything," she said.

"Not me—Mr. Crane," he said quickly. "Dinner will be at nine o'clock. Dress casual. Max will drive you over."

"Will there be other guests?" she asked.

"No," he answered. "Just Mr. Crane and yourself."

"Dr. Sawyer?"

"He's going back to the mainland about six o'clock."

She glanced at her watch. It was three-thirty. She was silent.

"You take it slow, Doctor," Fast Eddie said quietly. "Relax. Take a bath. Easy. Maybe sleep a little. Don't forget you have had a long trip to get here. When you get up, just powder your face, you'll be surprised how much better you'll feel then."

She nodded. "Okay. Thank you."

He gestured to Max. "Please bring in the doctor's valises." Then turned back to Sofia. "Just remember," he smiled. "I'm here."

2

◆ JUDD WAS WEARING a jogging suit and sneakers. A patina of perspiration covered his darkly bronzed face. He gestured Doc Sawyer to a seat as he spoke into the telephone. "Get rid of the fucking bank," he said. "Tell Justice we'll sign the consent decree."

Merlin's voice came through the speaker. "That's two hundred million dollars!" He sounded shocked.

"It's cheap," Judd said. "How much do you think it'll cost me if I have to spend the rest of my life in front of congressional committees answering stupid questions?"

"But we can beat them," Merlin said.

"I don't give a damn," Judd said. "I've wasted four years with it already. Transatlantic wants it, let them have the headaches."

"You're the boss," Merlin said. He laughed suddenly. "You're probably right. Nostradamus said that this would be a bad year for financial institutions."

Judd joined in the laughter. "Just make sure that Nostradamus allows David Rockefeller in on it."

"I've missed you, Judd," Merlin said. "When do you think you'll be getting out of there?"

"Soon," Judd answered. "I promised to try it for a year. Another three months should do it."

"Be good," Merlin said.

"I'll try," Judd said. He put down the telephone and looked across the desk at Doc Sawyer. "I was running when I saw the copter come in. I picked you up on the screen in the office just as you came down the steps. I thought she looked good."

"Thinner, I thought," Sawyer said.

"Couldn't tell from what I could see," Judd said. He picked up a cigarette and rolled it in his fingers. He looked down at the

173

cigarette. "Did Sofia tell you anything about what she was doing in Bangladesh?" he questioned.

"She said nothing about it," Sawyer answered. "Why are you curious?"

Judd threw the cigarette into a wastebasket without lighting it. "I'm guessing, but I think I know," Judd said. "I have a feeling that the old lady gave me only some of her papers. She must have given the rest to Sofia. Our papers start when she began Fountains of Ponce de Leon in 1953 and run to date. There are many notes that refer to papers she had written before that time."

"I read the notes," Sawyer said. "I didn't get that."

"Because we hadn't translated it yet," Judd said. "She had written it in Urdu, the least written language in India. She quoted a swami who was then in that part of India which later became Pakistan, and then Bangladesh. The quote was from several conversations with the Maharishi Raj Naibuhr. 'Man's immortality can only be achieved when his internal peace becomes one with his physical environment.' Probably that was why she wanted me to build this island."

"Do you think that Sofia found the papers?"

Judd smiled. "If she found them in Bangladesh, it was a miracle. The Maharishi has already moved on to greener pastures."

"You mean he's dead?"

Judd laughed. "No. Rich. He's the Maharishi who began a university with over two thousand students in the San Bernadino Mountains. He's also acquired a huge tract of land north of Malibu in California."

"Wait a minute," Sawyer interrupted. "Is that the one they covered on television?"

"That's the man," Judd said. "And believe me, he's as difficult to see in person as the President of the United States or the Premier of Russia."

"And you think that Sofia could get to him?"

"I hope," Judd said. "Maybe something in the papers that the old lady gave her could give her a hold on him. Also, the Maharishi is very big on wives, especially young ones—though that is not public knowledge, even to his adherents."

"He can't be a young man," Sawyer said.

"I think he is in his seventies, although he's said that he's over one thousand years old in his current incarnation."

"Not bad," Sawyer laughed.

"I also have a hunch the old lady treated him, that he was one of her patients."

"Even more interesting," Sawyer offered. "Then what do you think Sofia was doing in Bangladesh?"

"Fucked if I know," Judd answered. "But I'll ask." He glanced at the doctor. "Would you like to stay for dinner?"

Sawyer shook his head. "I'd better get back to Florida. I've got problems up to my ass. I'm a doctor, not a businessman. Crane Medical Research and Pharmaceuticals are running in the red about three million dollars a month. Keep this up for much longer and we'd better have a big infusion of capital, or begin cutting back—perhaps even sell off some of the companies."

"I'm sure you can handle it," Judd said.

"Thanks," Sawyer said. "I'm grateful for your confidence, but I'm not you. My head doesn't work the same way."

"The computers will give you all the information you need. It should be easy."

"To you, not to me," Sawyer answered. "To me, all the computer gives is just information. I still have to make the decision. And how do you pull that out of a printout?"

Judd was silent for a moment. "If you really feel that way, cut the companies until you feel comfortable enough to handle what you can."

"I don't think I have the right to do that. It's your property and you should be the one to take that responsibility."

"I'm one hundred percent behind you," Judd said. "You can dump the whole damn thing if you want and I won't say a word. I really don't care."

"I'm sorry you feel that way," Sawyer said. "You're a very special man, Judd Crane. And you could give many things to the world."

"I feel very old, Lee. I've played all the games, and I'm bored with them."

"You're hardly fifty, Judd," Sawyer said. "If you feel that way now, what makes you think the immortality you seek will make you feel younger and less bored? I think the opposite—you will be even more bored and feeling much older. Life itself is not just surviving, it's sharing and giving."

"I never thought you were that much of a philosopher," Judd commented dryly.

"Neither did I," Sawyer said. "I'm just beginning to feel that way. But I'm a doctor. I don't know what I think anymore or what I'm supposed to be."

Judd looked at him. "You're tired. What you need is a vacation."

Sawyer laughed ironically. "I don't need a vacation, Judd," he said simply. "I need you. Beside me, behind me, sharing with me, inspiring me. Without you I'm not the man I should be."

Judd was silent.

"I'm not alone in that feeling," Sawyer said softly. "Barbara, Merlin, many others, they feel as I—"

Judd interrupted, his voice flat. "Three months more," he said. "I need that much time to decide which way I go. Can you give me that?"

"We've gone this far together, I can go three months more," Sawyer said.

"THERE'S NO WORLD out there," she said. "It's almost as if we were in another universe."

Sawyer stood at the foot of the bed, looking at her propped against the pillows. "It *is* another universe," he said. "Judd's universe."

She watched him silently for a moment, then pushed away the covers and, naked, crossed the room to pick up her silk robe. She slipped into it quickly and walked toward him. "Do you have time to join me in a cup of tea?"

He nodded.

She picked up the telephone. Max answered.

"Yes, Doctor?"

"May we have some tea?"

"Yes, Doctor. Orange Pekoe Ceylon all right?" he asked.

"Perfectly," she said.

"Biscuits or petit fours?"

"Just the tea," she said.

176

"Thank you, Doctor." The telephone clicked off. She turned to Lee. "Shall we go out on the terrace?"

Silently he followed her to the balcony. He watched her close the door. "Do you think the room is wired?" he asked.

"Yes," she said. "Wired and video-scanned."

"Do you know that?" he asked. She shook her head. "Then what makes you think it?" he continued.

"Intuition," she said. "If I were he, I would have done it. Perhaps even this balcony is covered."

He regarded her silently for a moment. "Possibly. I don't know him anymore."

"He's changed?" she asked.

"Yes. And no. I can't put my finger on it. That's why I wanted to talk to you before I went back to the mainland. You're a doctor. I want you to observe him and let me know what you think."

Max knocked on the door of the balcony, brought a tray with a pot of tea, a pot of water, a small pitcher of milk, a plate of lemon slices, a jar of honey, and sugar. He placed it on the round plastic table on the balcony. "Anything else, Doctor?" he asked.

"That's all, thank you," she said. She began to pour the tea as he left, closing the door behind him. She waited until he left the bedroom beyond before she spoke again. She gave him a cup of tea. "You're his doctor," she said. "What makes you think that I could see more than you? You've known him so many more years than I have."

"This is the first I've seen of him since he moved to the island. Our only contact has been by telephone and the computer printout of his weekly physical examination."

"Then he has a doctor in attendance here?"

"No," he said. "There are several nurses who oversee the machines that are wired to him, for that purpose."

"That Irish girl, Bridget, is she still with him?"

"No," he answered. "She left him in New York not long after you'd gone."

"Do you know the nurses?" she asked.

"Not personally," he answered. "Though I've hired them all, of course. Basically, they're more medical and engineering technicians than nurses. They know more about the machines and the computer than they do about medicine."

"Do you have a copy of the latest printout?"

He took a folded sheet of paper from an inside coat pocket and gave it to her. She glanced at it quickly. After a moment she looked up at him.

"Interesting," she said. "All his physical functions have been slowed, heartbeat, blood pressure, body temperature. Lung capacity has increased despite lesser breathing speed. Blood tests and urinalysis normal." She returned the folded printout. "According to this, he's in very good condition. What worries you?"

He looked at her as she sipped the tea. "His head," he said. "Before, he was never bored. Now, nothing interests him."

"Maybe what he needs is a psychiatrist, not me," she said.

"Maybe," he answered. "But you are the only one I can trust." He met her eyes. "Would you help?"

She met his gaze. "I don't know how much help I can be, but I'll try."

Sawyer nodded. "The only thing that I know for sure is that we have to bring him back to this universe. I have a feeling that the kind of immortality he's seeking is only another form of decay."

3

◆ A FEW MINUTES after Sawyer had gone, a soft knock came from the door. "Come in," she called.

The maid entered, a large dress box in her arms. "Mr. Crane sent this for you, Doctor," she said.

Sofia looked at the box. Christian Dior. She turned to the maid. "Would you be kind enough to open it for me?"

"Yes, Doctor." She handed a small envelope to her. "This is also for you."

Sofia opened the envelope. The card inside had his name imprinted on it, the other side was in his handwriting. *I bought this for you, but you were gone before I could give it to you. I hope this time it won't be too late. Judd.*

The box was already open. Sofia took out the dress. It was a long, white silk sheath evening gown, two shoestring straps over the left shoulder and slit on either side from the floor almost to the thighs. "It's beautiful," she said. "But I don't think I can get into it. It's too small."

"Why don't you try it on, Doctor," the maid said. "If it needs just a small adjustment, perhaps Max could do it."

"I don't know," Sofia hesitated.

"It won't hurt you to try," the maid urged.

Sofia hesitated a moment. "Wait for me," she said. She went into the bathroom, placed her robe on a hook and tried to bring the dress down over her arms. "I can't bring it down over my shoulders," she called through the open door.

Mae was standing in the doorway. "That's not the way," she said. "Step into the dress and pull it up."

Sofia followed Mae's instruction. The dress felt as if she had a second skin. She looked at herself in the full-length mirror. It *was* a second skin. Her nipples jutted against the material, her hips and buttocks seemed molded into the dress, almost splitting the material apart. She looked at the maid in the mirror. "It's too tight," she said. "One movement and it will split open."

"It won't," Mae said. "The material gives."

"Even if it does," Sofia said, "I can't wear anything like this. It makes me look completely nude."

"Mr. Crane would like that," Mae said.

Sofia turned to her. "What makes you think that?"

"You don't work for nine months without knowing what your boss likes or doesn't like."

"He's had many girls here?" Sofia asked.

Mae hesitated, not answering.

"You can talk to me," Sofia said. "I'm one of his doctors, even though I am a woman."

"I don't know—" Mae said.

Sofia guessed. "I'm sure Fast Eddie told you something about me."

"Yes."

"Then you can tell me what I have to know," Sofia said. "I'm not simply being curious. Dr. Sawyer asked me to give my opinion and the more I learn about Mr. Crane, the more I can help him."

Mae didn't meet her eyes. She looked down at the tiled bathroom floor. "Mr. Crane has about three girls come over from the mainland each week. They usually stay a night or two and then they go back."

"The same girls all the time?"

"No," Mae said. "Always different. No girl ever comes back again."

Sofia was silent for a moment. "And did he give this style of dress to each one of them?"

Mae nodded.

"Color?"

"Always white, all the same. They come from Paris. Two dozen at a time."

Sofia was silent.

"You won't say anything about what I told you, ma'am?" Mae asked.

"Not to anyone," Sofia said. She slipped the straps from her

180

shoulder and began to move the dress down to the floor, then stepped out of it. She picked it up and handed it to Mae.

"Then you're not going to wear it?" the maid asked.

Sofia looked at her. "You press it," she said. "I'll decide later after I've had a bath and relaxed. I'll call you."

"Thank you, Doctor."

Sofia put on her robe as the maid left the room. She thought for a moment and then opened the middle drawer of the dresser. The vial was exactly where Fast Eddie said it would be. She felt her head clear after the cocaine.

She picked up the card that had come with the dress. She looked down at Judd's handwriting. It was strange. Why should he lie to her? There was no reason to say anything about the dress except that he wanted her to wear it. Sawyer was right. Judd had changed. Before, he could never lie—not to her, not to anyone.

She sat thoughtfully on the side of the bed. Slowly she went through the steps of the treatments that Judd had undergone. There were so many of them. Any one of them could have fucked up his head. She reached for a cigarette and lit it. She let out the smoke slowly. The fact of the matter was that she didn't know. And perhaps no one would ever know. Not even Judd himself.

THE HOUSE WAS a geodesic dome faceted like an enormous diamond, reflecting light into the dark of night. The limousine slowly came to a stop, then Max turned off the motor. Sofia called to him from the back seat. "I don't see the entrance."

"It's there, all right, Doctor," Max said respectfully. "You'll see."

A moment later, the hum of a motor came from underneath the car. Through the driver's window, she saw two giant glass doors slide open; she realized the car was moving slowly toward the open doors. "An electrical driveway?" she asked Max.

"Yes, Doctor," Max answered. "Really a turntable. So automobile emissions don't get into the air filter system."

She watched the glass doors close behind the car and the turntable stop before an inside doorway. Max got out of the car and opened the passenger door for her. She stepped out. The doorway slid open and Fast Eddie came down the three steps to meet her.

He smiled at her. "Rested a little, Doctor?"

"A little," she nodded.

"Good," he said. "I'll take you up to Mr. Crane's apartment."

"What time should Max return for me?" she asked.

"That's no problem," Fast Eddie replied. "We always have cars and drivers on duty."

The entrance hall was a large, white-walled round room. The floor was white marble, the receptionist's desk stood on stainless steel supports, also topped with white marble. The man behind the desk wore a white mess jacket and white slacks. She noted the bulge under his left shoulder that covered his gun. She thought she caught a curious glance in his eyes before he turned to the desk and pressed a button on the panel built into the desk. She heard the door behind her close.

There were three more glass-paneled doors in the room, one on each side of the receptionist, and one behind him. They were all one-way glass so she could not see through them. There were two statues between each of the doors. Almost lifesize, white marble on stainless steel bases, Apollo and Venus, or perhaps Adam and Eve, they stood looking toward each other over the eternity of time.

Fast Eddie guided her to the door on the right. He nodded to the receptionist, who pushed another button and the doors opened to an elevator. Fast Eddie followed her into the elevator and pressed a sensor button. The doors closed and the elevator began to rise. She could look down at the receptionist until he was lost below the floor.

She turned to Fast Eddie. "Do I look peculiar?" she asked. "I thought that the receptionist gave me a strangely curious glance."

"It was your sari," he answered. "He was surprised by all the colors. Usually everyone wears white here."

She looked at him. Even he was wearing a white mess jacket and slacks. "What's the reason?"

"Mr. Crane likes it. It's clean and sanitary. And he also feels that if we all wear the same color and the same style, it prevents ego competition among the personnel."

"And the visitors?" she asked. "Is that why he sent the white dress to me?"

"I didn't know that he sent you anything," he answered.

But she knew that he was not prepared to answer all her questions. She looked through the glass doors at the next floor. There was a receptionist seated there also. "What floor is this?" she asked.

"Communications, business administration offices and the computers." He continued. "The main floor where you entered has the personnel apartments and living quarters. The theaters and recreation rooms are on the first basement level, the second basement level is the clinic, the final basement level is all the power equipment to maintain the building. Mr. Crane's apartment is on the top floor, the third. He has everything there. Bedroom, bathroom, gymnasium, living room, dining room, kitchen, bar and library, and his own private office."

She was silent for a moment. "In a kind of way," she said, "it's very much like the plane, only bigger."

"Something like that," he nodded. He looked at her.

"Care for a toot?"

She met his eyes. "Think I need it?"

"It can't hurt," he said. He held the vial out to her and watched her lift the spoon to her nose. "Take a good one," he urged. "This is a strange world you're entering."

She returned the vial to him, and the doors opened before she could question what he meant.

4

◆ THE SOUND OF a sitar echoed softly through the apartment as they emerged from the elevator. Fast Eddie led her to the library bar. Two small-cushioned couches were separated by a cocktail table. He gestured toward one of the couches and walked to the bar. A few moments later he returned with a large silver tray and placed it on the table before her. She looked down. A kilo can of caviar was surrounded by shaved ice. To one side of the caviar was an open bottle of Cristale, next to an open bottle of Starka vodka frozen in ice; on the other side were all the trimmings—thin toast, onions, white and yellow chopped egg, sour cream, butter. He looked down at her.

"Vodka," she said.

The thin glass was also iced. Quickly he filled it. He placed it on the table before her. "Mr. Crame will be with you in a few moments," he said, and left the room, closing the door behind him.

She looked out the windows before her. A white full moon painted a sparkling path along the ocean. It was beautiful. So beautiful it didn't seem real. She picked up her glass of vodka.

"*Nasdrovya.*" His voice echoed through the speakers.

"*Nasdrovya,*" she replied almost automatically, swallowing her drink. Then she looked around the room. It was still empty. "Do you hear me?" she asked.

"Yes."

"It's been a long time," she said. "I would like to see you."

"I can see you."

"That's not fair," she said. "I can't see you."

"Why didn't you wear the dress I sent?"

"It was too small, I couldn't fit into it," she said. "Perhaps three years ago I might have, but not now."

He was silent.

"Will you be long?" she asked.

"Not long," he said. "There are buttons beside your chair for the television set."

"I don't need it," she said. "The moonlight on the sea is beautiful to look at. I'll wait."

A click came through the speakers and the music of the sitar began playing. She filled her glass once more and sipped it. Suddenly she felt hungry, so she began to help herself to the caviar and toast. She finished four slices of toast and had three more vodkas before he came into the room.

She rose from the couch. Her head felt light. "I think I'm slightly drunk," she said.

He smiled at her and kissed her, then held her elbow. "In that case," he said, "you'd better sit down again."

"What's in that vodka?" she asked, looking up at him.

"Nothing," he answered. "You'll feel better once you have some food."

"You're looking very well," she said. His dark full hair was shot through with gray, his dark cobalt eyes shone in his deeply tanned face. He wore a white silk open-throat shirt, white slacks and moccasins.

"You look well, too," he said.

"I've gained some weight," she said. "More carbohydrates than protein in my diet. But that's because you can't get much variety in Bangladesh. Everything is basically a rice dish." She spread caviar over another slice of toast. "Not quite like this."

He smiled, sitting opposite her. "I imagine."

"May I help you?" she asked.

"No, thank you. Too much salt for me," he answered.

"I'm curious," she asked. "How did you find me in Bangladesh?"

"Simple," he answered. "Your name came up on a hospital order from Bangladesh where you work. All the hospital orders to Crane Pharmaceuticals are put on the computer. All names are then cross-indexed. They get transferred to my personal file if the name is connected."

"I thought you checked with the KGB," she said.

"No. Nothing as complicated as that."

"Why did you want to see me?" she asked.

185

"The files," he said. "Dr. Zabiski had given me only part of them. I have none of her records before 1953."

Sofia was silent for a moment. "I don't understand it. I spoke to her the day before she died and she told me that she had given everything to you."

"Then she left something out," he said. "We still don't have the answer."

"She said that to me, too. What she told me was that she gave you all the tools. She said that you were going to have to find the answers."

"I've gone over everything with all the experts," he said. "Zero."

She took a deep breath. "The old bitch!" she said softly.

"What do you mean?"

"She's had all of us. You, me, even Andropov. She's laughing at us from her grave." She looked at him. "Don't you see it yet? She intended for us to meet again. After all, I'm the only expert left for you to work with."

He looked at her silently.

"You sent for me, didn't you?" she asked. She didn't wait for him to answer. "It's back to square one. We'll have to begin all over again."

"Is that why you went to Bangladesh?" he asked.

"Part of it," she said. "But also because Andropov wanted me out of Russia and Yugoslavia."

"Because Brezhnev died just as Mao had?" he guessed.

Her eyes met his evenly. "I had nothing to do with the death of either of them."

"But does Andropov know that? Mao died. You were his attending physician. Brezhnev died. Again, you were his attending physician. Now, according to our information, Andropov is ill. But he does not call on you for himself as he did for the others. Perhaps he has lost faith in you."

She still met his eyes. "I don't know what he thinks," she said calmly. "He has not taken me into his confidence."

"A long time ago," he said, "Zabiski told me that in their time they all die. That there were no guarantees. That all she could do was help the quality of their lives."

"She told that to me also."

"Yet she led me to believe," he began, but his voice trailed off.

Sofia smiled gently. "Maybe she thought that you could succeed where she could not."

A knock came from the door and Fast Eddie came into the room. "Dinner is served," he said.

THE DINING ROOM was not large. A thick glass table was supported by clear lucite legs shaped like thin rectangular blocks of ice. A single spotlight in the ceiling above the center of the table threw facets of color through the glass. The table was round and could seat six but only two places were set. The place mats were rectangular mirrors and the sterling silver serving plate was matched by the silver cutlery. A white linen napkin was held in a silver ring, the glassware was simple but elegant Baccarat. To the right of each place setting a low white candle was held by a Baccarat candlestick. The chairs were framed in stainless steel, the seats and backs of soft comfortable white cloth.

She was seated across from him. She could see the windows behind him and the moonlight still spilling onto the sea. He turned a rheostat next to his seat and the lights dimmed around the room until the only lights left were those on the table reflecting on their faces.

She smiled. "It looks like a movie set."

He laughed. "It was a set designer who made it. I like the feeling of drama. Usually dining rooms are dull and unexciting, just stalls to ingest food. But there are also other senses that need satisfying."

"I never thought of that," she said. "It's lovely."

"Thank you," he said. "I hope the dinner gives you as much pleasure."

"I'm sure it will," she said.

She heard a door behind her open. Two maids came in, each wearing sheer white shirts and short white miniskirts falling just to the top of their thighs, setting a contrast between the black of their skin and long legs. They looked so much alike as to have been twins: long hair flowing over their shoulders, each wearing a small triangle cap, sparkling eyes and white shining teeth. White lace gloves covered their hands. At the same moment, each maid placed the first course in front of them and left the room.

"Pretty girls," she said.

"Of course," he answered. "Would you expect anything else?"

"American?" she asked.

"No," he answered. "They are from Mauritius. My agent there has sent them under a two-year contract. Six of them."

"They seem very young?"

"Sixteen and seventeen," he said. "They speak French and English and are very anxious to learn and to please."

"And when the contract is over what happens?"

"They go back and we bring in others."

"That's very good for you," she said. "But do the girls get anything?"

"Education, knowledge and a respectable sum for their dowry. They are very pleased."

She smiled. "As they say in America, you have everything organized." She lifted her fork and tasted the shrimp cocktail. "These are delicious."

"Baby shrimp, flown from the Gulf of Mexico this morning," he said. "They're the best."

"Everything you have is the best," she said.

"You're being sarcastic," he said evenly.

"No," she said. "Really, I'm not. I'm just overwhelmed."

He was silent.

"You have to understand," she said. "Yesterday I was in Bangladesh, today I am here. It's another world."

The dinner was very American. Prime rib of beef, medium rare, sliced thin. Mashed potatoes and gravy, peas and salad. The wine was French. Montrachet with the shrimp, Château Margaux with the beef. Dessert was vanilla ice cream topped with a spoonful of crème de menthe.

She looked at him. "I've almost forgotten that people could enjoy food so much." But at the same time she noticed that he had eaten very little; mainly he seemed to be pushing the food around his plate.

"You're welcome," he said, rising. "We'll have coffee and liqueurs in the library." He came around the table and held the back of her chair, looking down at her. "You're still a very pretty lady," he said.

"That, too, I have forgotten," she said. "I was beginning to feel old next to those beautiful children."

"That's something else," he said. "You're a woman. Very real and exciting. They're children playing games."

5

◆ A SILVER COFFEE set stood next to the demitasse cups on the cocktail table as they returned to the library. A smoky bottle of cognac with two snifters was placed between them. Judd looked down at Sofia as she sank into the couch. "Coffee?" he asked.

"Please."

He poured a cup for her. "Cognac?"

"Would you mind if I stayed with the Starka?"

"Not at all," he said, snapping his finger. Fast Eddie came into the room. "The Starka," Judd said.

"And the goodies?" Fast Eddie asked.

Judd looked at her. "We have grass, cocaine, uppers, downers, mind expanders and anything else you can think of."

"I can't think of anything," she said. "The only thing we had in Bangladesh was hashish."

"I'm sure there was opium," he said.

"Yes," she answered. "But that was for dreaming and sleeping. I didn't care much for it."

"We have some opiated grass that can really give you a high. It will expand your consciousness almost like acid, but it will be sweet dreams, no bad trips and, most of all, you will be in control and not fall asleep."

"That sounds interesting," she said. "How long does it last?"

"As long as you want it to," he said. "I told you that you would be in control. You can turn it off the moment you want to."

"Where do you get it?"

"The grass is sensimilla. We have it treated downstairs in our own laboratory."

"You use it?" she asked.

"Sometimes."

"And the others?"

190

"Also sometimes. It depends how I feel."

"Zabiski was always against any kind of drugs. I'm surprised she never forbade your using them. She was afraid it would negate her treatment."

"She told me," Judd answered. "But I have my own ideas. Drugs have been around throughout civilization. I feel there had to be a reason for them."

She was silent for a moment. "Do you feel like taking anything now?"

He shrugged. "I don't know. I know that we both feel slightly uncomfortable with each other. Almost as if we were fencing, not communicating with each other as we used to."

"Isn't that normal?" she asked. "After all, we have been apart a long time. People don't snap back just like that."

"True," he agreed. "But sometimes doping helps."

"I'm not ready for anything just yet," she said. "But I'll take a few snorts. That should keep me up."

Judd nodded to Fast Eddie. "Give the doctor what she wants and give me two XTC pills. Send Amarinth to prepare them for me."

"Yes sir," Fast Eddie said.

She waited for the door to close behind him. "What does that pill do?"

"It's a mood elevator developed in our lab. Something like a super Elavil or Triavil. A gentle high that blows away your inner fears."

"You have everything you want. What is there you still have to fear?" she asked.

He looked at her. "You."

She looked into his eyes. The cobalt-blue seemed suddenly to turn to black. She didn't speak.

"I'm afraid of you," he said slowly. "Your knowledge, your understanding of me. That you have the answer and I do not."

She let out a soft breath. "Don't you know yet that no one has the answer? No one in the world."

He rose from his couch and turned to the window, his back to her. "Sofia," he said. "I can't believe that. You spent too many years with the old lady. You probably know it and don't even recognize it." He turned to her. His voice sounded harsh. "Do you know of a Maharishi Raj Naibuhr?"

"No."

"You didn't go to Bangladesh to search for him?"

"No," she said. "I've never even heard of him."

"Zabiski did," he said. "She has many references to him in her files."

"Maybe she did," she said. "But she never mentioned him to me."

The door opened behind her. Soft feet came to her. Sofia turned. It was another girl, lighter in color than the two at dinner, with long brown hair and green eyes. She nodded smiling at Sofia and then to Judd. In her arms she held a silver tray. She knelt on the floor and placed the tray on the table. She stayed on her knees looking up at Judd. "Mr. Crane," she said in a soft almost singing clear voice. "Shall I prepare you now, sir? Or do you want me to wait?"

"Attend our guest first," Judd said roughly.

The girl bowed her head. Silently she poured Starka in a glass, then held the vial to Sofia.

Sofia looked down at her. "I, too, can wait, child," she said gently.

Judd came back to the couch opposite her. He looked at Sofia. "Frustration," he said. "Every way I turn there's frustration."

Sofia didn't answer.

Judd turned to the girl. "Stand up."

The girl rose to her feet. She was not dressed even as modestly as the girls at dinner. She was wearing a white silk strapless sheath that revealed the nudity of the body beneath it.

"Amarinth is only seventeen," Judd said. "She has one of the most beautiful bodies I have ever seen."

Sofia sipped slowly at her vodka.

"Would you like to see her?" Judd asked.

Sofia met his eyes. They showed no expression. "If you like," she said.

Without taking his eyes from her, he spoke to the girl. "Drop your dress to the floor, Amarinth."

The girl loosened the dress over her breasts. The dress fell easily from her body to the floor and her arms rose in a practiced motion, outstretched above her head, her palms pressed together.

Sofia looked at the girl. Judd was right. The girl was beautiful, like an exquisite ivory figurine.

"Turn around, Amarinth," Judd said. "Let the lady see how really beautiful you are."

Without any self-consciousness, the girl pirouetted, looking over her shoulder toward Sofia. Her tongue licked softly across her faintly smiling lips.

"Amarinth prefers girls," Judd said. "Would you like to keep her for your stay here?"

Sofia tore her eyes from the girl to Judd. "I don't understand you, Judd."

"I know you," he said. "I know the flush that covers your face when your pussy gets wet and you become excited."

"And you think that she has made me excited?"

He looked at her, silently.

Sofia met his gaze. "Of course, she's made me excited. But not her alone. You are here, too, Judd. I could see the excitement in your expression and the sudden bulge in your slacks." She caught her breath suddenly and replaced her glass on the table, her hand trembling slightly. She got to her feet. She raised her hand and opened the snap of the sari on her shoulder. Slowly, she unwound the silk and let it fall to the floor. Beneath it she wore the white dress, clinging to her body, her nipples jutting. She placed one hand across the faint moist spot over her pubis. She looked down at him. "I have been orgasming all the time I have been here, since the moment I heard your voice through the speakers."

He stared at her, still not speaking.

"Is that what you want of me, Judd?" she asked. "To be still sure of the power you have over me?"

He started to shake his head, but she interrupted him.

"You have to be sure of that, Judd, or you're a fool. Don't you know that from the moment we met, I became more your slave than any of the girls you ever bought?"

"You expect me to believe that?" he asked. "That you've never gone with another man?"

"I didn't say that," she said angrily. "You better than anyone else know how much I need sex. But that is something else. I'm not enslaved to sex, but to the whole man. Isn't it enough that I killed Nicky to return to you? Isn't it enough that I came here from across the world at your request?"

He saw the tears beginning to well in her eyes. He took her hand into his own. "I'm sorry," he said.

She shook her head silently.

"Forget the cocaine," he said. "Maybe it would be better if you got some sleep."

"No," she said. "Unless I sleep with you."

"You might not like that," he said. "I sleep with two girls beside me. It's a Chinese custom, Ying and Yang, so your spirit can find balance in your body as you sleep."

"Can we make love first?" she asked.

"Usually I do not," he said. "The girls make love to each other and their energies enter and absorb mine."

"Then what happens?" she asked.

"Usually I awake refreshed."

"And the girls?"

"They sleep away their exhaustion all through the day," he said.

She laughed suddenly. "That sounds crazy."

"Maybe," he said. "But nobody knows, do they?"

"That's true," she said. "But then when do you fuck?"

"Before I go to bed," he said.

She looked at him. "You're not in bed now."

He nodded. He turned to Amarinth. "Prepare the XTC pills for us."

The girl nodded and knelt on the floor beside the cocktail table, then glanced up at him. "Mr. Crane," she asked. "Please, sir, may I prepare one for myself?"

Judd turned to Sofia questioningly.

Sofia looked down at the naked girl. She was beautiful. She knelt down beside the girl and glanced up at Judd. "Let her," she said. "Maybe the two of us will discover a new kind of Ying and Yang for you."

194

6

◆ SHE MUST HAVE been dozing. Suddenly her eyes were open and she sat up on the couch. A faint gray light began to fill the horizon. Amarinth stirred and moved on the floor next to the couch opposite her, then looked across at her. She raised her index finger to her lips to warn Sofia to be silent.

Sofia nodded and looked around the room. Judd was not in the room. She looked down at the girl, then picked up her sari from the floor beside her and began to rise.

Still holding her finger for silence, Amarinth came toward her on silent, naked feet. Softly she touched Sofia's arm, guiding her.

The sari still in her hand, she allowed the girl to lead her. Silently, they went around the corner of the bar and entered another room concealed behind the angle between the window and the bar. Amarinth stopped her, gesturing with her hand.

It was a small, oblique room with the windows pyramidlike at its roof. Beneath the apex of the pyramid, Judd was seated in a lotus position on a round platform about four inches above the floor.

Sofia looked at him. He was motionless, he seemed not even to be breathing, his eyes wide open, yet unaware of the dawn lightening the sky.

Amarinth tugged at her arm and brought her back into the library. She led her across the library to another room and closed the door behind them without a sound. It was a dressing room with mirrored closets around it and, in the center, a round hot tub with scented water bubbling softly. A gleaming, shining, jade-colored tiled bathroom could be seen through the open door. "Come," Amarinth whispered. "We will wash and refresh ourselves in the flowered waters."

Slowly, Sofia followed the girl. "And Judd, will he join us?"

"No," she answered. "The Master is traveling among the stars.

When the sun will close his eyes, he will return to his bed and to his sleep. Ying and Yang will enter into him and express the fluids from his body and relieve his inner tensions and restore his mental balances."

"But we made love with him," Sofia said. "Did it not satisfy him?"

"Very much," Amarinth said. "But that is not the way in which he expresses himself."

She looked at the girl. "Do you mean that he does not achieve orgasm?"

The girl cast down her eyes. "Yes. That is not his way."

Sofia looked at her silently.

"You do not understand," Amarinth said earnestly. "This is the way he gains his strength and conserves his essence."

"Then why does he bother to make love?" Sofia asked. She was beginning to feel as if she was speaking with a child.

"He gathers our essence to mingle with his own," she said.

"Was it this way with all the girls, no matter who they were?"

"Yes," Amarinth said. "He expresses himself only in his sleep. Then he awakes immediately, his strength returned."

Sofia looked at her. "He told me that you prefer girls—is that why?"

Amarinth did not answer.

"Do all the girls feel as you do?"

Amarinth nodded.

"But don't any of you ever want more?" Sofia asked.

"No," Amarinth answered in a small voice. "We are only happy when we serve the Master."

Sofia was silent for a moment. "I would feel better if I could return to my own cottage," she said at last.

Amarinth looked at her. "As you wish." She opened a closet and took out a terry-cloth bathrobe and held it out for Sofia to put on. She slipped into another silk sheath, exactly like the one she had worn before. "Come with me," Amarinth said. "I will show you to your car."

SHE WOKE IN her own bed. The bright sunlight was visible around the corners of the drapes. She pressed the button beside the bed. The drapes slid open and the sun flooded into the room.

196

She glanced at the clock. It was two-thirty in the afternoon. She reached for the telephone.

"Yes, Doctor?" Max asked.

"May I have some orange juice and coffee, please?"

"Of course. Anything to eat?"

"Not just yet."

"You have two messages," he said. "Mr. Crane would like you to return his call when you awake, and Dr. Sawyer would like you to call his office at the Research Center at six o'clock."

"Thank you, Max," she said. "I'll speak with Mr. Crane as soon as I have had some coffee."

"Yes, Doctor," Max said. "Mr. Crane's call number is 1."

The orange juice was sweet and refreshing and the coffee hot and strong. It was good to her taste, not weak like American coffee. She half-finished the cup and dialed Judd.

A woman's voice answered. "Mr. Crane's office."

"Dr. Ivancich returning his call."

"Just one moment, Doctor," the secretary's voice answered. "I will reach him for you."

A moment later there was a click on the telephone and his voice came on. "Did you rest well, Sofia?"

"Very well," she answered.

"Good," he said. "I am arranging for you to read the Zabiski files. It is completely on tape. You have your choice of any language you want as well as the original copies in her own hand."

"I'd prefer the original," she said. "I would also like an English copy as well."

"We'll have it for you. It will be set up on a dual screen processor so that you can read from one to the other as you like. Then we also have the notes for you to review. I have had many specialists study and interpret them."

"That would be very helpful."

"When do you think you could begin?"

"Tomorrow morning if you like," she said. "I would like to be fresh when I begin work."

"That will be arranged. An office will be set up for you."

"Thank you," she said. "There's something else I would like to ask of you."

"What's that?"

"It's been three years since I have examined you. And I am a doctor, if you remember. I would like to give you a physical examination so that I can make a judgment about the progress you've made."

"Would that tell you anything different from what you can make out of her notes?" he asked.

"I don't know yet," she said. "Maybe nothing. But then, on the other hand, something inside you might shed some light on what she was trying to tell me."

"Dr. Sawyer already has all the information you might need about me on the computer."

"That's the computer. With all due respect to Dr. Sawyer, the information would be secondhand to me. I'd feel more comfortable if I could see and understand for myself."

His voice was definite. "I don't think it's necessary."

"Sorry, Judd, but I do."

"No," he said shortly. The telephone clicked off in her hand.

She waited a moment, then called him again. The secretary's voice came on the wire. "Mr. Crane again," she asked.

"I'm sorry, Doctor, but he cannot be reached."

"Can you give him a message for me?"

"Of course, Doctor."

"Tell him that I do not think I could be helpful to him and I would like to make arrangements to return to my own work."

A moment later Judd called her. "You're a bitch," he said.

"Maybe," she said evenly. "But I'm a doctor and I must have my own way."

He was silent.

"You can think about it," she said. "Meanwhile, I'm calling Doc Sawyer to come over and help me."

"Do you think that's all he has to do?"

"That's not for me to judge," she said. "He's your friend. And your doctor. It's up to you to decide."

Judd paused for a moment. "He'll be here tomorrow morning."

"Good," she said. "Then do you think I can see you for an hour sometime this afternoon?"

"What for?"

"It will be helpful if we do a blood workup and urinalysis before we begin the physical. It could save us some time."

"Anything else?" he asked sarcastically.

"I can think of a few more items," she said. "But I'll settle for this."

"Thank you," he said. "Six o'clock all right for you?"

"Perfect," she said.

"Okay. At the same time I'll show you the setup of your office."

"Good. Just one thing more," she said. "That I do not have to wear another one of those white dresses."

"If you promise not to wear a sari."

"I promise," she laughed.

"You're still a bitch," he said.

"I love you anyway," she said and put down the phone.

7

◆ SOFIA TURNED TO Sawyer. "You were right," she said. "Physically he is perfect. Just one small thing bothers me—the electric energies reading by the EEG seems lower than the reading last year."

Sawyer looked at her. "But it's infinitesimal. It could be the time of day it's recorded."

"I had them run it three times at four-hour intervals. It's not the time of the day. The energy output from his brain is consistently lower. Could we possibly persuade him to undergo a scan?"

"I don't think so," Sawyer answered. "He would have to leave the island and return to Boca Raton. He told me he would not leave the island before his first year is over. That's three months from now."

Sofia was silent as she pressed keys on the computer. She matched the EEG reading of last year and superimposed the new readings. She pressed another key and one part of the readings zoomed larger on the screen. "It's the alpha readings. See, they waver over the mean line. I don't understand it."

"We'll transfer it to the computer at Med-Research and see what the neurologists think about it."

"Might help," she said. "But I'd feel more secure with a scan."

"What are you looking for?" Sawyer asked.

"It's more intuition than knowledge," she said. "Remember, you told me that he mentioned his boredom and his sense of growing isolation—I've seen that in his lack of personal interaction with people around him, even under the most physical circumstances."

"Sex?" Sawyer asked.

"Yes. Physically he works at it. But inside, he feels nothing. Even with drugs to get him into it."

200

"Sometimes drugs have the opposite effect, you know, Doctor."

"It's not the drugs," she said. "That's why I said intuition. I'm a woman. I know when a man is fucking and when he's fucking. It's the same act, but it's different."

"It could be the sterility factor," Sawyer said. "It varies with him. One of his experiments was to control his sterility by his mind and to show that he can separate impotence from sterility —that he can even withhold sperm from orgasmic ejaculation. You know he's trying to touch all the bases: medical, physical, technological and metaphysical, yoga, as well as tantric mind control."

"That's good," she said. "The pleasure is in a man's head, not his penis. I want to know what is happening to his brain and I think the scan might give us some clues."

"There's nothing we can do right now," Sawyer said. "We have to wait for him."

She turned off the computer screen. "Anyway, if it's any consolation, physically he hasn't aged one day since the last time I met with him. So something is working, though we don't know what."

Judd came into the room. He glanced briefly at them. "Satisfied?" he asked.

"I guess so," she answered. "There's nothing physically wrong that we can find."

"I could have told you that," he said, without expression.

"Still I'd like to know more about your head," she said. "Both physically and psychologically."

He stared at her. "I don't understand."

"The EEG shows a minuscule drop of brain wave electricity," she answered.

"Shouldn't that be normal?" he asked. "After all, I've slowed up all my physical functions."

"I don't know," she said. She looked up at his eyes. "How do you feel? Do you feel as sharp and keen as you did before? To my mind you don't seem as interested in certain things as you used to be."

"I'm really not interested in those things anymore," he said flatly. "Before, I used to play games. Business, money, people. Now I'm bored with them. I think what I'm doing is more important and more interesting. Anybody can make money if he wants to. I've done it, and I have more of it than anyone, so I don't need to prove myself again. Girls, sex, the same thing. I've done it all. Now it's only necessary for keeping the physical machinery working."

She looked at Sawyer, then back at Judd. "Love?"

"Emotionally?" he asked.

She nodded. "Yes. I think that's important to you, physically as well as mentally."

"Do you think I'm cuckoo?" he asked calmly. "That I don't feel things?"

She met his eyes. "I don't know."

He turned to Sawyer. "What do you think?"

Sawyer held up his hands. "I can't answer. Both of you are over my head."

Judd smiled at her. "I feel different," he said. "I don't think I feel as deeply as you do. But I feel in my own way. Try to understand as I do. I am going to live forever, and if that's true, I have to think all of you are temporary. I mustn't become too attached to any of you, because in twenty years, or one hundred years, or more, you will be gone, and I'll be living with other people, in another time."

"So you suppress your feelings because you are afraid to lose those whom you love? You're afraid of hurting yourself?" She felt the tightness in her throat.

"Maybe," he answered thoughtfully. He took a deep breath. "Perhaps loving is also part of mortality. You die a little bit with everyone you love and lose."

She held back her tears. "If you had children," she said, "you would live on in them."

"But I would not live," he said. "Just as my father does not live. I want to be alive, not a memory."

She turned back to the computer and pressed several keys. Numbers flashed across the screen. She punched two other keys, and the picture turned into a demographic curve. Without turning to him, she spoke over her shoulder. "According to the computer, you have a life expectancy right now of one hundred and thirty years. That means your present physical age of forty-nine is equal to an average man of thirty-one." She turned to him. "Present actuarial tables are L.E. 74. You now have an L.E. of almost twice that."

He looked from the screen to her. "What are you telling me?" he asked.

"At one point, Dr. Zabiski had you up to an approximate L.E. 150. While trying to push it, she almost killed you. Wouldn't you be willing to settle for what you've got now while you're ahead, rather than continue experimenting and possibly destroying yourself?"

"If I'm going to die," he said simply, "it doesn't matter much how long, or when it happens. This moment or another. What I'm searching for is infinity."

"There is no infinity," she said flatly. "Even beyond the stars."

He was thoughtful for a moment, turning from Sawyer to her. "I've had the physical as you requested. Are you ready to begin studying Zabiski's notes tomorrow?"

"Tomorrow morning," she replied.

"Good," he said. "Dinner at nine o'clock tonight?"

"Yes, thank you," she answered.

He turned to Sawyer. "How about you, Lee?"

Sawyer shook his head. "No, thanks. I have to get back. But I'll take a rain check."

"You've got it," Judd said. "But meanwhile, let's all go upstairs and have a drink."

JUDD WAS DRINKING orange juice, Doc Sawyer, Scotch on the rocks, and Sofia, a tiny glass of Starka vodka almost congealed from the freezer. The chime of a telephone sounded next to Judd's chair. He picked it up, listened for a moment, then handed it to Sawyer. "It's your office."

Sawyer held the telephone. "Yes?"

His secretary's voice sounded apologetic. "I'm sorry to disturb you, Doctor, but I felt this was important. We have just received a call from someone in the State Department in Washington asking if Dr. Ivancich was staying with us. I told him she was not."

"Good," Sawyer said. "Besides that's the truth."

"They also asked if I could get in touch with her. I said I couldn't, because I didn't know where she might be. Then they asked for you, and I told them that you're en route and ought to be in the office tomorrow morning."

"Very good," Sawyer said. He put down the telephone. He looked at Judd. "The State Department is looking for Sofia."

"Strange," Judd said. He turned to Sofia. "Do you have any idea why State would be interested in you?"

Sofia shrugged her shoulders. "It's your government, not mine. I know nothing about how it works. Most of the time I don't even know how my own government works."

"Did you pick up your U.S. visa in Bangladesh?" he asked.

"No. I used the unlimited entry visa you obtained for me years ago." She was silent for a moment. "But when I came through immigration at JFK, I listed my visiting address in the States as Crane Medical Center, Boca Raton, Florida."

"That was correct," Judd said. He thought for a moment. "Usually it's immigration that checks up on visitors."

"That's what she said."

"Call her back and find out if she has the name of the person who called. Once we have a name I can have Security run a check. If it is State, there's something going on and I want to know about it."

8

◆ DINNER WAS SET on a small round table in a windowed alcove of the library. Judd turned as she entered the room. "You wore the white dress," he said.

She smiled. "I had it altered."

"You didn't have to," he said. "I would have sent another one."

"I have a sentimental attachment to this one," she said.

He handed her a chilled glass of vodka. He picked up his own glass. *"Santé."*

"Santé." She looked at his hand. "Cherry Coke?"

He laughed. "I have my sentimental attachments, too." He helped her to her chair and sat across the table from her. "I'm not as unemotional as you think."

"I'm sorry," she said. "I didn't mean to hurt your feelings."

"Don't be sorry," he said. "Because I have a dream doesn't mean I'm not human."

"That wouldn't be the thing I'm worried about," she said. "You're human all right, maybe too much so."

"I don't understand you at all," he said.

She smiled. "Don't try. Just blame it on the fact that I'm a woman."

"Okay," he said deliberately. "I thought we'd have a light dinner and go to bed early. We had a heavy day today and tomorrow will be a long one for you."

Dinner consisted of thin slices of breast of chicken with a light consommé gravy, steamed sliced carrots al dente and whole snow peas, and a little salad with a slice of Brie. He drank water and she had a dry Chablis. Neither of them had any coffee.

"Very good," she said, pushing back her chair. "I've had just enough."

"Do you think you can sleep?"

"I'll try," she answered. "If I can't, I'll take a pill."

205

"Disappointed?" He looked at her.

She shrugged. "Not really. I know enough about you now to know that you're not interested in all the details of the subject."

"You're not angry?" he asked.

"No," she said, rising from her chair. "What is it you once told me? An Americanism—'Dif'rent strokes for dif'rent folks.'"

"That's not my line," he said. "That's Fast Eddie!"

She laughed. "It doesn't matter who said it." She looked down at him. "I'm still into it. I love to fuck, I still have to."

"Amarinth—" he began to say.

She interrupted him. "I don't want her. I want you."

"Amarinth is very talented," he said. "She has small soft hands and with one fist she can fill you more and be further inside you than any man."

"No, thank you," she said. "I could do as well with my vibrator. I'd rather settle for my pill."

He sighed and rose from his chair. He kissed her on the cheek and took her hand. "Come," he said. "I'll take you to your car."

THE TELEPHONE CHIME sounded as he entered his bedroom. He pressed a button on the control panel and the wall speakers with built-in microphones clicked open. "Crane here," he spoke in a natural voice.

"I hope I didn't wake you," Merlin said.

"Not at all," Judd answered. "It's only just past eleven o'clock here."

"We closed the bank deal," Merlin said. "Transatlantic will transfer five hundred million tomorrow. They take over the bank operations the next day."

"Justice Department approved?"

"Everything," Merlin answered. "We're sending four hundred million to the foundation. What do you want us to do with your one hundred million?"

"How much are my tax liabilities on it?"

"You don't have any," Merlin replied. "You still have a personal two-hundred-million loss to lay against."

Judd thought for a moment. "Okay. Transfer twenty-five million to Crane Medical as a personal loan and send the balance, seventy-five million, to be divided evenly to my personal accounts in Switzerland and the Bahamas."

Merlin said without expression: "Crane Medical could use more than that, but it's your money."

"That's right," Judd said dryly. "It's my money."

Merlin was silent at his end.

"What else?" Judd asked.

"Mitsubishi Heavy Industries made us an offer of one-and-a-half billion dollars for Crane Engineering and Construction," he said reluctantly.

"What are our current assets?"

"Net: Twice more than their offer. Three billion."

Judd thought for a moment. "Tell them they can have it for two billion."

"I don't want to answer you on that," Merlin said. "I'm beginning to think you're getting rid of everything."

"Maybe I am," Judd said. "Money isn't important to me anymore. I have more than I need."

"But accepting the Mitsubishi offer would result in a billion-dollar loss." Merlin's voice was shocked.

Judd was patient. "If we get the three billion dollars, how much in tax liabilities would we incur?" He could almost see Merlin punching numbers into his computer.

A moment later, Merlin spoke. "Between seven hundred and eight hundred million dollars."

"Then how much net does another billion dollars make? Not enough to go through the pain in the ass that IRS would put us through. And they could keep us tied up for five years for the money. This way, the red ink shows clear, they have no arguments and the net loss to us is only one hundred sixty million to the foundation and forty million to me."

Merlin was silent.

"Don't get down," Judd said gently. "It's time we began getting rid of some of our responsibilities. Maybe then we'll all be able to enjoy life a little more."

Merlin sighed through the speakers. "I don't think your father would have agreed with that."

Judd's voice was flat. "'My father's dead. And I think I've

played his game long enough. I'm still alive and I expect to enjoy life more."

"Okay," said Merlin dejectedly. "I'll pass along your proposal to Mitsubishi."

"Thank you," Judd said. "Good night."

"Good night," Merlin said.

Judd broke the connection and walked across the bedroom to the window. He looked out to the night sea. The moon was climbing into the sky, and its light was beginning to dance on the water. Judd commenced his breathing exercises. He began to feel everything inside his body slowing down.

He felt, rather than heard, little footsteps come into the room. Then they were beside him. Lightly, soft fingers began to undress him. His shirt and slacks seemed to float from his body, tiny hands led him to a round, hard pallet about one-and-a-half feet above the floor. Without seeing the helping hands, he assumed the lotus position, facing the night-painted windows. The room lights were turned down until they matched the night sky. A candle, almost level with his eyes, began to flicker before him.

He stared into the light until its pale glow began to feel heavy on his eyelids. Tiny fingers closed his eyes, but the candlelight remained imprinted within his lids. Soon the footsteps were gone. He was silent, and alone.

His mind wandered through his body. He felt his toes, his feet, then his legs. His testicles and penis were soft and warm, his groin and belly relaxed. His chest moved gently over his lungs, and the easy pumping of his heart echoed in his mind's hearing.

Soon he was far away; his consciousness had gone from him. He felt at one within the consciousness of all the universe. The power within him was the power without. In his mind and with his mind, he soared. And he slept into the endless night of his soul. Another star, another star, another star . . .

9

◆ THE LIGHT ON the table read six-thirty. She pressed the button next to it and the drapes rolled open. The morning sun had already risen above the sea. She picked up the telephone.

"Good morning, Doctor," Max answered.

"Grapefruit, coffee, scrambled eggs with bacon and a big pot of coffee."

"Thank you, Doctor. Immediately."

She hung up the telephone and went to the bathroom. Quickly she showered to wash the sleep from her. She was still feeling sluggish when she came out of the hot and cold shower. She wrapped the bath towel around herself and went into the bedroom. The breakfast table had already been set.

She poured a cup of coffee before she sat down. It was black and strong. She emptied it, took another, sat down and picked up the grapefruit spoon.

The telephone rang. She didn't have to leave her seat to answer it. "Doctor Ivancich," she answered.

"Sofia," Sawyer said. "I hope I didn't wake you."

"I'm already having breakfast."

"I've tried something interesting," he said eagerly. "I've matched the EEGs over the last five years to the scans taken at the same times. We've turned them into mathematics, then reconstructed them. After that, we built them into computer graphics. And they looked so much like the original scans. I did the same process to the EEGs we did yesterday. They're damned interesting, Sofia."

"I wish I could see them," she said quickly.

"You can," he said. "Turn on the television set in your room. It's connected to the central computer. Punch in these numbers— 748,61,011,953. Got it?" He waited until she returned to him.

"I have it, but nothing's on the screen."

"Type in the word below: Computrac."

The screen turned to life. The picture was something very much like a perscan, colors and all. "I've got it," she said. "Now what do I look for?"

"I'm going to superimpose this new stuff over the old scans. Watch the tiny track of blue light on the latest track."

"I see it."

"That's the electric level now. Now look at the same thing on the superimposed tracks. They seem to be moving faster. Also the new scan seems to indicate the total brain is a fraction larger."

"Do you mean to say that his brain could be growing?" She sounded incredulous.

"I'm not sure, but it might show that his brain weight may be increased by as much as two grams. If that's true, that explains the slower impulse rate. He's actually using more of his brain cells, and of necessity more cells have been manufactured to carry the load."

"I'm still trying to comprehend it," Sofia said.

"We have to be cautious," he said. "This is still a computer graphic, not the real thing. But there is one thought that came to me. Do you know if Zabiski injected some of his own brain cells in her cellular therapy combination when she worked on him?"

"I don't know," she said. "That part of the process she kept to herself. She never allowed anyone to watch her."

"It was a thought," Sawyer said, almost to himself. "I would still like to do a scan on him as soon as possible."

"Let's show this to him," she said. "Maybe he'll agree."

"Do you expect to see him later?"

"I guess so," she said. "I'm starting work on the Zabiski tapes this morning. I'll bring this up to him when I see him."

The screen went blank. "Good luck," Sawyer said into her receiver.

"Thank you," she said. "And luck to you, too."

THE SUNLIGHT FILTERED through Judd's eyelids. Without stirring on his hard bed, he opened his eyes. The room seemed blurred; his sight cleared. He turned his head and looked at the girls sitting on the floor beside him.

210

They spoke almost in unison. "Good morning, Master."

"Good morning," he said slowly.

"Have you traveled far?" they asked.

"Very far," he murmured.

"Beautiful," they said. "We are very happy. Thank you, Master." Their naked bodies, golden from the sun rays, gleamed as they ran silently from the room.

He lay quietly on the bed. A moment later he felt his body shiver. He did not move. Again he shivered. He heard the door open. He did not turn his eyes.

Amarinth, in the strapless white dress, looked down at him, her eyes dark and moist. He shivered once more and looked up at her.

"You have traveled very far and you are cold with the ice of your voyage," she said. "Let the fires inside me warm you."

He remained silent. He looked into her eyes, then at her torso inclining to him. He saw her hand clasp his erection, the tips of her fingers circling his testicles. He took a deep breath but he remained silent.

"Your strength is the hard ridge of the palm tree, opening to spill a rivulet of love across my fingers." Her eyes were fixed to the cobalt blue of his own. "Please, Master," she begged, "allow me to serve you."

He didn't speak.

She lifted her dress above her legs to her waist and knelt on the bed, her legs against his sides. Still holding him with her hands, she leaned back on her haunches and guided him inside her. Her buttocks began to roll in orgiastic frenzy. "Master! Master!" she screamed. "Make me a baby! Please, make me a baby!"

Then she looked into his eyes. They were distant and unseeing, behind a film she could not penetrate. "Master," she cried, tears rolling down her cheeks. Slowly she moved from him. He was soft, his erection gone. She slipped to kneel on the bed beside him. Her tears were soft on his hand. "I'm sorry, Master, I'm sorry I could not please you."

He turned to her face and kissed her head. "Do not be sorry, child," he said gently. "You have pleased me. It is I who cannot please you."

He sat up on the bed. "Please draw my bath, child," he said.

"And we will play beautifully together like children in the water."

"But I don't understand, Master. You never come into me."

"It doesn't matter, child," he said. "Death will come only if I allow it to come to me."

"In my land, Master," she said, "we believe that children prolong life."

"That is another land and another country," he said slowly.

THE USUAL GLASS of orange juice was on his desk as he entered his private office. It was eleven o'clock and his dark tanned face was covered with perspiration that even stained his white jogging suit. He sipped at the juice and pressed the button that activated his computerized messages from Computer Central. There were a few: Merlin; Security Control director; Doc Sawyer; his mother, Barbara; Dr. Schoenbrun from Brazil.

He punched in two other numbers. The first call he made was to Schoenbrun. That was the most important on the list. The call was placed instantly over his own Crane satellite. He turned on the screen and Dr. Schoenbrun's face filled the picture. "Dr. Schoenbrun," he said.

The German doctor smiled, satisfied. "I have good news for you, Mr. Crane."

"Good," Judd said. "I can always use good news."

"The nuclear reactor is in place," the doctor said. "Two weeks ahead of schedule."

"My compliments, Doctor," Judd said. "When can I expect completion now?"

"Two months, ten weeks at the latest," Schoenbrun said. "The piping must be completed and the center of the dome welded in place. When that is finished, the bulldozer will cover the installation under thirty feet of earth. Trees and bushes will be planted and in less than a week even the most sophisticated satellite camera will not detect it. It will look exactly like the forest around it."

"Good," Judd said. "And when will we be able to fire the nuclear reactor?"

"Three months or less," Schoenbrun said. "We will have all the checks completed by then."

"No one fires it up except me," Judd said.

"Of course, Mr. Crane," Schoenbrun said smoothly. "You made it possible and only you should have the honor of pressing the start-up button."

Judd was thoughtful for a moment. "The Xanadu Project," he said almost to himself. "It's been three years."

"That's correct, Mr. Crane," Schoenbrun replied. "At first I didn't understand the significance of the name Xanadu. Then I read the poem and I knew. But your dream is greater than Kubla Khan's."

"I want weekly reports from now on."

"Of course, Mr. Crane." Schoenbrun smiled smugly to himself. "No one would ever believe it was here. It is the most powerful nuclear energy plant in the world, buried deep in the ground almost a thousand miles into the Amazon forest."

"Without Ludwig's pioneering work, our own might never have been attempted," Judd said.

"Your genius has made it possible, Mr. Crane. Even I can hardly believe that we have a plant so completely automated that only one man is necessary to operate it."

"Don't underestimate your own genius and work, Dr. Schoenbrun. Perhaps the world will someday appreciate it. As I do," Judd added.

"Thank you, Mr. Crane," Schoenbrun said. He hesitated a moment.

Judd interrupted, for he could anticipate the scientist. "Five million dollars will be transferred to your Swiss account this morning. Another five million dollars comes to you when I press the button that activates the reactor."

"Thank you, Mr. Crane," Schoenbrun said, almost bowing into the screen.

"Good-bye, Dr. Schoenbrun," Judd said.

He pressed the computer key and the connection was severed. He ran the other messages through the computer routinely and called Security Control. The director came on the line. "John?" he began. "Judd Crane."

"Yes, Mr. Crane," the Security director answered. The man was always cautious, "Are we on a scrambler, sir?"

"Yes," Judd answered. "Go ahead."

"Our lady doctor is in the shits again," John said.

"Explain," Judd said.

"She's on four hit lists, sir," John said. "Russia, Yugoslavia, China and the Mafia hired by the Cubans. That makes it four of a kind, four aces, very hard to beat."

"I don't get it, John. Why now? She spent almost three years in Bangladesh, where they could have nailed her anytime they wanted."

"Apparently they feel she's stolen some very top-secret documents and they've just discovered them missing. The documents had something to do with the late Dr. Zabiski's experiments and files, best I can figure."

"They must be the files that Zabiski gave to me," he said.

"Not those. They already know about that bunch. I'd guess you only had part of the file. They allowed Zabiski to give that to you so you'd return Ivancich to her."

Judd was silent. "Where are the rest of the papers?"

"With Ivancich, I should think. Otherwise why would they be so hot after your lady now?" He paused for a moment. "I think we had better beef up the security around Crane Island. It won't take them long to discover where she is."

"Does Sawyer know about this?"

"Not yet," John said. "You're the boss. You get the first message."

"Don't say anything to him just yet," Judd said. "I don't want him to get nervous. But put a heavy blanket around him. I don't want anyone to pull him apart to bleed information from him."

"Yes, sir," John said. "And Crane Island?"

"Four heavy-armored helicopters in the sky over the island twenty-four hours a day. Eight armored speed launches on the water, also around the clock. And twenty of our best sharpshooters deployed on the ground day and night."

"We'll need six hours, sir," John said.

"Two hours. We may not have six hours." Judd signed off.

10

◆ SOFIA'S VOICE WAS angry on the telephone. "That old bitch! She's fucked all of us!"

Judd's voice was expressionless in the receiver next to her ear. "So what else is new?"

"You don't sound excited," she said. "Maybe you don't understand what I said. She never planned that you would get all the answers."

"I'm not stupid," he said. "I knew that. Why do you think I asked you to come here? I thought you'd have some of the answers. Isn't that what you stole from the Russians' files?"

"How did you learn about that?"

"It doesn't matter now," he said. "Half the Eastern world is after your ass. You have no place to hide except with me."

"Is that what State told you?"

"Partly," he said. "Now what about your files?"

"I'll get them," she said. "But it won't be enough. There's still a third file. But I think I know where it is."

"Tell me." His voice was flat. "Whose?"

"The Indian mentioned in your files. She never mentioned him in the Russians' files. It fits. Your file covers everything from the beginning of 1953 onward. The Russians have your files except for any mention of the Indian. Their files go back to 1944, when they captured a German experimental laboratory where she was working."

"She was working with the Germans?" He was surprised.

"Yes," she answered calmly. "What are you so excited about? Didn't you people capture all the German rocket scientists and bring them with you to the States?"

"Okay, okay," he conceded impatiently. "What are you trying to tell me?"

"The Russians got her and some of the other doctors, but some-

215

how the files covering 1941 to 1943 were never found. She told them they had been burned, together with an Indian scientist the Nazis considered non-Aryan. But I think she got him out of there with the files before the Russians came in."

"Then how did she manage to make mention of the Indian in my file?" he asked.

"Look at your original copy. Those notes about the Indian were written with a ball-point pen in her own peculiar kind of shorthand. The rest of the notes are either typed or written with a fountain pen. My guess is that she added them on the plane while coming to meet you. I would also guess that the Indian was not one of the staff doctors. Somehow, he assured the success of her own experiments. That's why she wanted to save him."

"What happened to the others?" he asked.

"The Russian file I have listed many experiments that were buried with the scientists who ran them." She was thoughtful for a moment. "You were right when you said she was a tough lady."

"She *was* a tough lady."

"But she was also a genius. And you were the only one she ever trusted."

"But not enough to go all the way, I guess," he said.

"Maybe she couldn't bring herself to place all the pieces in one file. If she had, the Russians might have gotten hold of it, and she couldn't be sure what use they would make of it. You were the only man in the world she felt she could trust with that power." She paused for a moment. "Now what?"

"Why didn't you try to reach me before?" he asked.

"I did try once. But there wasn't enough time and I couldn't find you. I had to go back. I was still Brezhnev's doctor. After he died I was sent to Bangladesh to work on nutrient experiments at a children's clinic. When I received your message, I left in the middle of the same night. If I had waited till the next day, it would have been all over for me. They would have intercepted your message, and they would have killed me. As useful as I was to them, I still knew too much."

He was silent.

She felt very tired. "I guess it's over now. I might as well go back. You can have the files. You were going to get them anyway, if I died."

"I would prefer to see them while you're alive," he said crisply. "I don't propose to lose you now."

"Do you mean that?"

"I said it, didn't I?" he snapped. "Now lock your office door and don't open it until you hear my voice outside."

THE TELEPHONE CLICKED in her ear. Slowly she put the receiver down and started to rise. A gentle knock came from the door.

She opened her handbag and took out a specially made snub-nosed Magnum and held it out before her in both hands. "Who is it?" she asked.

"Max, Doctor." His voice came muffled through the door. "Mr. Crane asked me to bring you up to his office for lunch, ma'am."

"Come in," she called calmly. "The door's open."

The door opened into the room and she saw him, one hand reaching for something inside his coat pocket. A look of surprise came over his face as he saw the gun in her hands. It was the last thing he ever saw.

The heavy-caliber bullet blew him through the open door, across the corridor, blood pouring from his chest over his white coat. He spun, grasping at the wall opposite him, then slumped slowly to the floor across the elevator doors. The shot echoed down the corridors like an explosion.

She stayed in the office, the gun still held out rigidly in her hands. She heard steps running down the corridor toward her, then the elevator doors opened.

Fast Eddie, holding his big Colt, sprang out of the elevator over the body of Max; he knelt beside it in the corridor as security guards came rushing toward them. Judd, just behind all of them, ran toward the elevator doors.

He sensed rather than saw the door at the corner of the corridor open. "Behind you," he yelled at Fast Eddie.

Fast Eddie wheeled, but Sofia was even faster. She squeezed the trigger of her Magnum the moment Mae appeared in the door, the Uzi machine pistol rising in her already dead hands. Again the shot burst like an explosion down the corridors. Mae tumbled back into the room, the Uzi crashing to the floor.

Fast Eddie looked through the doorway at Mae. He looked back at the others. "She caught it too," he said.

Judd stepped over Max's body and went toward Sofia. He could see the grim pallor on her face, the frozen tension of her body. He held out a hand and took the Magnum from her. "I thought we were supposed to be protecting you," he said softly.

The tension melted from her body, the fear in her eyes disappeared. She let out a deep breath. "I figured this is the only way to go, if you're to live forever, Judd," she said with the faintest trace of a smile.

"They weren't after me," he offered.

"Bullets have a way of altering life expectancy," she said. "One has to be extra-careful."

He looked down at the Magnum. He thumbed the latch and pushed open the cylinder. He turned the barrel up and let the bullets fall into his palm. There were four bullets and two empty cartridges. He examined the bullets. "Cute," he said, looking up at her. "Explosive heads. Everything is special about this gun. Where did you get it?"

"The KGB," she answered. "They have a man who specializes in toys like this."

He nodded. "Had it long?"

"Ten years," she said. "This is the first time I have used it, except in trials."

He dropped the gun and the bullets into the pocket of his jumpsuit. He turned to look at the corridor. It was filled with security men. He gestured to Fast Eddie. "Let's go back to my office," he said, reaching for her hand.

She followed him into the elevator, Fast Eddie entered behind them. Judd covered the button before he pressed it. "Which one of you is the section chief on this watch?"

"I am, Mr. Crane," said a tall, solid man with gray-black hair. "Officer Carlin."

"Clean up this mess, Officer Carlin," he said. "Then send a team over to the cottage. Check out everything there and have Dr. Ivancich's possessions taken to my apartment."

218

"Yes, sir," Carlin replied. "I'm sorry, Mr. Crane. We had no warning. These people had all the proper security passes."

"That's not your fault, Officer Carlin," Judd said. "I'll bring it up with Security Control." He pressed the button and the elevator doors closed.

11

◆ "I'm sorry, Mr. Crane," John said quietly. "I'm afraid you'll have to get off the island. There's no way we can defend it."

Judd looked around his library. Merlin sat next to the security director, John, in front of his desk, Sofia and Doc Sawyer on the couch. Fast Eddie leaned against the bar. Judd turned to the windows and gazed out at the night sky. The sea was dark and ominous; clouds covered the moon.

"I don't know how those two breached our security screen, but they did," John went on. "Nothing was found at the cottage that belonged to them. We have to assume they made contact with their people in Havana. The fingerprints we picked up from the FBI files identified them as among the first batch of refugees Castro shipped to the States over ten years ago." John was apologetic. "How we blew that in our check, I don't know. But we fucked up and there's nothing I can say about it except I'm sorry, sir."

Judd looked at him without expression. "I need three more months here."

"We could have an army here and it wouldn't help, sir. They could put more than a hundred men on the island overnight. The only way I can protect you is by keeping you on the move."

Sofia rose from the couch and looked at Judd.

"Let me go back," she said. "I'm the one they want. Then you'll be able to go on with your affairs without interference."

Judd looked at her. "You're wrong," he said. "If that were true, why did they place their operatives on the island long before anyone even suspected you would come here? I have the distinct feeling they want both of us, either separately or together, but both."

"I happen to agree with Mr. Crane. It's gone beyond just you, Doctor," John offered.

"Even if I bring all the files back with me?" she asked.

"I don't know what there is in those files," John said. "But no matter what you give them, they'll still feel that they have not got all of it."

Sofia turned to Judd. "I'm sorry."

"Don't be," he said. "Don't forget that it was I who invited you here." He turned to Doc Sawyer. "When do you think I can move all the equipment to Xanadu?"

"Xanadu?" he asked. "Is it ready?"

"Not completely," Judd said. "But we could push. Maybe we won't be able to connect everything immediately, but we can get it into place."

Sawyer thought for a moment. "Two weeks to dismantle here, maybe a week to transfer, then maybe two or three to reassemble at Xanadu."

"A month and a half?" Judd asked.

"Thereabouts," Sawyer said.

"Xanadu?" Sofia was puzzled.

"I'll tell you more in time," Judd said. "But I found out early on when we were building the island that Zabiski was not correct in her surmise. She thought only in her own parameters. Crane Island was to be open to the world, pretty much like her own clinic. She thought that three miles off the coast would provide enough protection and privacy. She was wrong. And so was I. At first."

"So you began to construct another complex to replace this?" she asked.

He nodded without speaking, then turned to John. "Do you think we can stay here for six weeks?"

"No." His tone was positive. "You have to be on the move. And no one must know where you're going or how or when you're leaving."

"But the equipment?" Judd asked. "Even if I leave, they'll come in here if they think I'm still on the island."

"We'll let them see you've gone from here," John said. "Then we have to be fast and sneaky. Now they see you, now they don't. You move fast and light."

Judd offered no comment. Merlin showed him his palms. "And what about the business, the companies?"

"We'll have to find a way to keep in touch. Meanwhile we try to unload everything we can except medical and connecting companies."

"You'll be blowing away over four billion dollars," Merlin said.

"What's the difference between four billion dollars and four cents to a dead man?" Judd replied. He turned to John. "Start the ball rolling," he said. "I want to be off the island tomorrow."

"And the first stop?" the security director asked.

"Washington, D.C.," Judd said. "What higher visibility could I achieve than a meeting with the President of the United States at the White House?"

"I would like to do a CAT scan on you," Sawyer said. "I can arrange it in Washington. It will only take ten minutes, and you can have it either on the way to the White House or on your return to the airport."

Judd turned to John. "Do you think we can take the time?"

John nodded. "We can handle it."

"Okay," Judd said. His eyes held Sawyer's. "Have the tests been completed on the chemical cell reconstruction?"

"Yes," Sawyer answered. "The DNA engineering department tells me they're perfect. There's no way you can tell the natural cells from the artificial."

Sofia looked from one to the other. "I'm beginning to feel that I'm out of things here. You're all way ahead of me."

"Not really," Sawyer said. "Moscow has the same kind of project underway."

"I know nothing about it."

"Maybe that's why they had you buried in Bangladesh," Judd said. "But if you stick around, you'll catch up fast."

"There's just one thing to remember," Sawyer went on. "These are only laboratory tests. The cells have never been used clinically on humans. Only on laboratory mice."

"Are you planning to use it on yourself?" Sofia asked Judd.

"At the moment, no," Judd replied. "This is just a backup, if we cannot obtain the real thing."

"Good," she said. "I think you've done enough experimenting on yourself."

Judd glanced at his watch. "It's one A.M. I think we'd all better get some rest. We'll meet again at seven."

222

The men said their good nights; only Sofia and Fast Eddie remained in the library with Judd. Judd looked at her. "Fast Eddie will take you to your room."

She rose from her chair, started toward the door, then turned back to Judd. "What's to happen to the girls?"

"They'll be returned to their home," he said.

"But Amarinth," she said, and held her breath. "She loves you."

Judd met her eyes. "We have no choice. We have enough problems trying to keep ourselves alive. There's no way we can carry excess baggage."

"Excess baggage, Judd?" she challenged him. "She's a human being."

"I know that," Judd said gently. "But I'd rather she was at home and alive than risking her life here. If we get into trouble, she'd be the first to go down. She's an innocent with no defenses."

Sofia took a deep breath. "She'll be hurt. She won't understand. She'll weep."

His eyes went dark blue and without expression as he met her gaze. "I'd weep even more if I were the cause of her death."

12

♦ "HE LOOKS WELL," Barbara said, watching the television screen. "Time stops still for him. I know he's forty-nine but he looks much the same as he did at forty."

Sofia's eyes remained fixed on the screen. "Physically he appears the same, but inside he's different. Psychologically and mentally. He seems to have withdrawn emotionally."

Barbara watched Judd shake hands with the President. When the President waved farewell and went through the doors of the White House, Judd descended from the portico to face the battery of reporters and cameras.

"It was a personal visit with the President," he replied to their questions. "We had no discussions about business."

"You did not ask the President for his opinion about your sale of Crane Engineering and Construction Companies to the Japanese?" one of the reporters asked.

"No," Judd replied. "Nor did the President offer any opinion. These matters are always handled by my legal department and the Justice Department."

"It seems to me," another reporter said, "that you are selling off the assets of your empire, Mr. Crane. The financial community is very concerned about it."

"I don't see why they're concerned," Judd said. "This decision is only one of many others I've been making, and since the companies are wholly owned by me, it does not affect the stock market or any other section of the financial community."

"But your companies are considered among the most profitable in the world," the reporter from the *Wall Street Journal* said. "Why would you want to dispose of them?"

Judd looked at the reporter. "Would it be too much if I told you that I began to feel the responsibility for all those companies had come to weigh too heavily on me? That I haven't enough time for my own life? That only if I retired from these activities would I be able to lead my life according to my own personal inclinations?"

"Do you have any plans for the future?" the reporter asked.

"Many," Judd said. "But first things first. These are the matters at hand. Later I'll sort out my own plans."

"Did you talk about all this with the President?"

"As I said, it was a personal visit. Nothing more." Judd paused for a moment. "That's all I have to say, gentlemen. Thank you." He walked past the group of reporters, stepped inside the waiting limousine, and disappeared behind the blackout windows. The car began to move down the driveway.

Barbara turned off the television set. "So that's it," she said. "He told them nothing."

"He tells nothing to anyone," Sofia said. "Even Merlin and Doc Sawyer."

Barbara went to the small box on the table that contained the cassettes and notebooks. "That's all he wanted you to bring for him?"

Sofia nodded.

Barbara looked into her eyes. "Don't you think you should tell him about the child?"

Sofia shook her head. "I'm afraid of him. I'm afraid of what he'd think if he knew. No one knows what goes on inside his head. He may be living on the edge of sanity."

"Maybe the child will bring him back," Barbara offered.

"I'd be afraid to take the chance by telling him," Sofia said. "Would you?"

Barbara sighed. "Sad. Very sad. He is a beautiful child. He has the same cobalt-blue eyes as his father."

Sofia's eyes misted over. "I wish I could see him. But I know I should not. If I did, I'm not sure I would be able to leave him." She took a deep breath. "Maybe in time. Maybe then Judd will understand."

Barbara nodded. "Where did Judd tell you you were going?"

"He didn't tell me," she answered. "I only know that Security will take me to him."

Barbara looked out the bay window of the breakfast room at the lights strung like a string of pearls across the Golden Gate

Bridge. She turned back to Sofia. "Where is Judd now?" she asked.

"I don't know," Sofia answered. "I know he was going to have a brain scan. He didn't tell me where he would go after that." Sofia thought for a moment. "Xanadu? Did he ever tell you about that?"

"Xanadu?" Barbara repeated. "Isn't that one of the hotels the leisure company is building? I think it's in Brasília."

"Not a hotel," Sofia said. "In the context of his talks with Sawyer, it seemed more like a laboratory. Some of the equipment from Crane Island was supposed to be sent there."

"Then I don't know," Barbara said. "Did you ask him?"

"Yes, but he always said I would learn in time."

"Then you'll have to wait, I guess. I've become used to waiting. Even when he was a boy, if he didn't want to talk he didn't talk, and nothing could pry him open."

The telephone buzzed. A voice came over the interphone. "The doctor's limousine has arrived."

"Thank you," Barbara said. "She'll be right down."

Sofia looked at her hesitantly. "Do you have a photograph of my boy?"

Barbara nodded silently. She opened a small desk drawer. The photograph was in a silver frame. She handed it to Sofia.

Sofia studied it closely. "He's big," she said, half-whispering.

"You have to remember he's almost three," Barbara said. "But he is big for his age. Very bright, too."

"He looks so much like Judd," Sofia whispered.

"You should tell his father."

"He'd never forgive me," Sofia answered. "Especially since I went behind his back to you." She handed the picture to Barbara.

"You can keep it," Barbara said. "I have others."

Sofia shook her head. "I have no privacy. There is nowhere I could hide it that it wouldn't turn up in Judd's hands. Sometime, maybe soon, I'll be able to tell Judd. But not now."

Impulsively, Barbara put her arms around Sofia. She kissed her cheek. For a moment they shared their tears.

Sofia picked up the small container that held the notebooks and cassettes. She did her best to control her voice. "I'll never be able to thank you enough."

Barbara couldn't reply. She watched Sofia leave the room before she placed the photograph on the desk. She stared at it for a long moment, then covered her face with her hands. "God," she whispered. "Please, God. Help them. Help all of us."

Two SECURITY MEN awaited Sofia as she came from the house. They fell into step, one on each side of her as they walked down the front steps. Another man held the door of the limousine. When she entered the car, she observed two more cars escorting the limousine, one before and one behind. Each contained four men.

She sat back in the limousine. The two men who had accompanied her joined her in the back seat on either side. The security man who had held the door closed it quickly and slipped into the front seat beside the chauffeur. All the cars moved smoothly into the street.

"I'm Brad, Doctor," the security man to her right said. "My partner there is Lance. We'll be with you on the plane to Los Angeles."

"That's where we're going? I didn't know that."

"Actually we'll be landing in Ontario. LAX is very busy and has too much traffic." He pulled the jump seat forward and moved to it so he could face her and look through the rear window. "You'll be more comfortable this way."

He gestured to the container. "Are those the files?"

She nodded.

"Leave them in the car when we go to the plane," he said crisply. "They'll be delivered to the office."

"Very well," she said. She saw the sign leading to the Bay Bridge. "We're going to the Oakland Airport?"

"Yes," he said. "We have a plane waiting for us."

Twenty minutes later, the car rolled through the wide wire gate entrance to the private plane section. It swung around several hangars and stopped beside a Lear Jet. She reached for the door.

Brad held her hand. "Wait for a moment, please."

She looked out the car window. Several security men stood near the plane watching them. Two men from the escort cars got out first and spoke to the others. One climbed the ladder into the plane. He disappeared for a moment, then returned to the open hatch and signaled to Brad.

"We can get out now," Brad said, opening the door and stepping out before her.

He helped her from the car and followed her quickly to the ladder and into the plane. He swung up behind her, patted the man still standing in the doorway of the plane. He went down the ladder and Lance came into the plane. The ladder went up and the plane door closed and locked.

She sat in the first seat in the small cabin and looked out the window. Two of the security men from the escort cars got into the rear seat of the limousine. The car began moving away as the jet engine roared to life. A moment later, the plane was turning from the hangar to the runway.

She glanced at her wristwatch. It was ten minutes to ten. The seat belt sign clicked on. She fastened the belt around her. A moment later, the plane was at the head of the runway, picking up speed and climbing into the sky. The lights of San Francisco fell away behind them. She leaned back in her seat; she felt tired. "How long will we be?" she asked.

"About an hour," Brad answered.

"And then where do I go?"

"I don't know," Brad said. "Our orders are to turn you over to another team of security men."

She turned back to the window. She closed her eyes and dozed. She felt a sting on her upper arm. She opened her eyes, startled. She looked up at Brad's face. "What?" she started to ask.

"Don't be afraid," he said gently. "It's only a shot to help you sleep."

Then she was asleep.

13

◆ HER EYES OPENED slowly. Her vision was blurred at first, then rapidly cleared. She looked up at the soft blue of the ceiling, then at the bright sunlight outside the windows. Before she saw the nurse moving toward her, an accustomed odor told her she was in a hospital.

The nurse was a slim Japanese girl in a white uniform with long shining black hair down to her shoulders. The nurse smiled at her from beside the bed. A small round pin glistened on her white cap. "Good morning," she said in a soft, unaccented, American voice. She picked up the telephone on the table next to the bed. "Dr. Walton," she said, "your patient's awake."

She turned to the foot of the bed and pressed a button. The head of the bed rose behind Sofia. "Comfortable?" she asked, then added, "Don't be frightened. You're among friends."

The nurse smiled again. "A cold glass of freshly made pineapple juice will lift you up."

Sofia watched her go to a small alcove. From the refrigerator she took a frosted glass bowl of sliced pineapple chunks. She threw the chunks into a vegetable extractor and a moment later brought Sofia a frost-covered glass.

The cold juice was refreshing. Sofia welcomed the sweet, cool liquid and drained the glass to the bottom. She hadn't known she was so dehydrated. As if she could read Sofia's thoughts, the nurse repeated the whole process without a word and handed Sofia another glass of juice.

Sofia drank it more slowly this time. At the same time she looked around the room. It was not a conventional hospital room: soft blue walls, gentle tropical paintings, lucite table and chairs and a comfortable lounging chair for reading. She looked at the nurse. "The bathroom?"

The nurse opened a door. Sofia could see the tiles in a tropical pattern. She tried to sit up.

"If you feel dizzy," the nurse offered, "let me help you."

Sofia shook her head for a moment. "I think I'll be all right." She sat up, holding the side of the bed for a second. "I'll be fine," she decided.

"You have time for a shower if you like," the nurse said. "Dr. Walton will be in surgery another ten minutes."

Still unsteady on her feet, Sofia turned to the window and looked out as she made her way to the bathroom. Outside, she saw a long white expanse of beach, large palm trees lining the road beside it and white high-rise buildings on the curve of the road. She turned to the nurse. "Where are we?" she asked, only half in jest. "Is this Santa Monica?"

The nurse's speech was American, but the giggle was pure Japanese. "You're a long way from Santa Monica," she said, gesturing toward the window. "Does that look like Santa Monica?"

"I don't know," Sofia answered. "I've never been to Santa Monica."

The nurse smiled, pointing. "That hill sloping out toward the sea is Diamond Head."

"Hawaii?" Surprise echoed in Sofia's voice.

"Honolulu," the Japanese girl said. "Your room is practically in the center of Waikiki Beach."

Sofia stared at the beach for a moment, then turned back to the nurse. "How long have I been here?"

"I've been on duty since seven this morning and you were still asleep." The little nurse laughed. "According to the chart you were admitted at two in the morning."

"I don't remember a thing," Sofia said.

"The night-duty nurse said that you were asleep when you were admitted." The little nurse giggled again. "You must have had the bon voyage party to end all bon voyage parties, Mrs. Evans."

Sofia stared at her without speaking. Mrs. Evans? That was close enough in sound. Ivancich. "I think I need a shower," she said.

"It will pick you up," the nurse agreed. "And meanwhile I'll order some breakfast for you. Scrambled eggs, bacon, toast and coffee, okay?"

"Lots of coffee," Sofia said. "Very strong."

The Japanese giggle sounded again. "We specialize in strong coffee, Mrs. Evans," she said. "It's Kona coffee, the strongest in the world, and it's grown here in Hawaii."

"Will I have time before the doctor comes?"

"Plenty of time," the nurse answered. "Dr. Walton's ten minutes is always closer to a half hour. You'll find fresh bath towels and a lovely silk robe waiting for you in the bathroom."

SHE WAS ON her third cup of coffee when the doctor's knock sounded at the door. The nurse opened it. He was still outside the door as his voice came to Sofia. "You can take a break, Jane," the doctor said in a half-familiar voice. "I'll call you as soon as I have spoken to Mrs. Evans."

The doctor stepped into the room and closed the door behind him. "Had a good night's rest, Mrs. Evans?" he asked with a faint smile.

"Brad?" she asked, surprised.

"Dr. Walton," he answered.

"That was shitty of you," she said. "I'm not a child. I could have been told."

"We thought you'd be more secure if we had you immobilized rather than moving around where even an accidental recognition could bring immediate trouble. The next best thing to being invisible is being a patient on a well-covered stretcher."

"We've not been bothered," she said.

"That's because of our friend," he said. "He's the decoy. There were quite a few agents following him around hoping that he'd lead them to you. Fortunately, he was not the target, you were."

"Are you really a doctor, or a security agent?"

"I'm really a doctor," he smiled. "Moonlighting as a security man."

"Okay, now what happens?"

"I'll try to explain as simply as I can. The U.S. government has a special program administered by the departments of State, Defense and Justice cooperatively. Each for its own reasons often

231

requires an exchange of old identities for new. Welcome to the program, Mrs. Marissa Evans."

She stared at him. "And our friend arranged that?"

"Yes."

"But how? That's a government program."

"He has many friends," Brad said. "And the government agrees with him that you're completely qualified for the program's services."

"Then you are a government agent?" she asked.

"Not really," he replied. "Let us say that this is just another job on which I moonlight."

She remained silent for a moment, then rose and walked toward the window. Without turning to him, she spoke over her shoulder. "Tell me more about this identity that you have planned for me."

"We change you entirely—physically, personality, environmentally. Changing you cosmetically is not enough. A gesture of your hand or the way you walk or talk could give you away to an expert. So we teach you other ways to replace your own habits. And finally, we place you in another environment in which you will make another life, one that will enable you to live safely and securely. Far from the dangers which now confront you."

She still didn't turn to him. "Does that mean I could never go back? Not to anyone or anything I ever cared for?"

"Yes," he said simply.

She turned to him, meeting his eyes levelly. "And what if I do not want to be someone else? What if I like myself the way I am?"

"You're not a prisoner," he said. "You can walk out this door whenever you want. But remember, we guarantee your safety where others you might know endanger it."

She remained silent, watching him.

"And of course you'd be entirely on your own. There is nothing or no one we could send to help you," he said.

"Even our friend?" she asked. "Does he say that, too?"

"I cannot speak for him," he answered. "I can speak only for the program."

She stared into his eyes. "I, too, am a doctor," she said slowly. "All my life I have worked as a doctor, all my life I've tried to push back the frontiers of man's existence. If your program

232

doesn't allow me to work at my dreams, then security means nothing to me. My life means nothing to me."

"Your work will be one of the first things that will have to go. It's a dead giveaway. And I mean, dead."

He paused for a moment. His voice was soft. "I understand you, Doctor. But please, think about the program before you turn it down. There are many other beautiful things in life."

There was definiteness in her voice: "Not for me."

"Okay, it's your decision," he said. "But, at least, let me help you. Perhaps I can give you a little edge."

"How?"

"Looking as you do now, they'd pick you up within three days after you showed up in public. I suggest we perform some slight cosmetic changes. A mini face lift, touch up and a little on your eyes and nose. We'll cap and shorten your front teeth. After that we'll disguise the eyes with brown contact lenses, cut your long blonde hair into soft curls and color it chestnut brown. We'll teach you to use a completely different makeup to complement the darker hair and eyes." He paused for a moment. "It's not perfect, but it's an edge for you. At least, they'll have to look more than once to recognize you. Especially as you become accustomed to your new identity. All the I.D. we'll get for you will help, too. Passport, old credit line at a good bank, store credit cards, driver's license, the works."

"Are you allowed to do that for me even if I don't agree to join the program?"

He hesitated a moment. "Not officially."

"Then why?" she asked.

"I know a little about the work you've done," he answered. "I respect you. You're a real doctor. It would be terrible if all the knowledge you've gained were wasted."

She looked down at her hands. "Thank you, Brad," she said gratefully. "How long will all of this take?"

"Ten days. Maybe less. It depends upon how quickly you heal," he answered.

She took a deep breath. "Okay. When do we start?"

"Tomorrow morning."

14

◆ THERE IS A small beach called Paradise Cove on the Pacific
Coast Highway north of Malibu. On weekends and holidays the
small dirt road leading to the beach is loaded with cars and
vans searching for surf and sun. A small restaurant serves the
more affluent, hence most of the people in it are middle aged.
The greater number of visitors are young and more interested in
surf and sun than food. They bring baskets of food or throng
around the hotdog and pizza stands near the unofficial parking
lot.

It was three o'clock on Saturday, and the sun, beginning to
move into the west, was glaring on the beach and the cooking
bodies. There were not too many surfers because the rollers
came in slowly on the calm sea. To the north, in a small rock
formation leading to a bluff two hundred feet perpendicularly
straight up from the water, gays and lovers found tiny places of
privacy for their own worlds. Occasionally the shrill voice of the
gulls searching for scraps rose above the humming voices of the
bathers and the breaking waves rolling across the beach.

Another sound came from the sky. The rotors of a helicopter.
The nudies grabbed their bikinis, and the topless girls slipped
into bras as they gazed upward at the sky. A muttering of disappointment arose from the beach as the lettering on the copter's
side became evident: CHURCH OF ETERNAL LIFE. Speakers
boomed their message to the beach, as the copter banked toward
the two-hundred-foot-high rock bluff. "THE CHURCH OF
ETERNAL LIFE BIDS YOU PEACE!" And the copter slid beyond the bluff out of sight.

The beach scene returned to normal. The nudies were nude
again, the topless girls turned young breasts up to the sun. An
invisible voice chimed shrilly from one of the rock shelters.

234

"Damn!" the boy's voice complained. "You came all over my face!"

"Shmuck," said a deeper voice. "You shouldn't have turned your head."

"But I thought it was the police copter," the voice whined.

An open-handed slap echoed among the rocks. "Aw, shut up," the other voice answered. Thus the beach began to resume its normal sounds.

What no one on the beach noticed or heard was a blimp floating in the sky, shielded by the hot afternoon sun glaring behind it.

JUDD, FAST EDDIE and John sat in a circle around a fifty-inch television screen. Beneath their feet were the cables leading to the video camera and its telescopic zoom lenses; a directional microphone coordinated the picture beside it.

The video camera operator called to them over his shoulder: "The copter's landing. Shall I cut it in?"

"Go ahead," Judd said. They all studied the screen.

The sound of the rotors roared through the speakers as the copter slipped slowly to a ringed concrete target a hundred feet from the edge of the bluff; very little dust blew up from the downdraft of the blades. The motor was switched off and the rotors slowed to a stop. The sound of young voices singing reached the microphone as the small ladder from the cabin angled to the ground.

Two tall young men dressed in long gray robes appeared first and proceeded down the steps. They turned and knelt, forehead touching the ground, facing the copter door. A moment later the Maharishi himself emerged. Even taller than the two men, his gray hair and beard whipping in the breeze around his regal face, he stood silent, listening to the young voices sing.

"Open up the picture," Judd called. "I want to see the girls."

The picture widened on the big screen. There were fourteen girls, all in violet chiffon saris. All had white blossoms woven into their long hair, and each was holding a basket of flowers. Their soft voices were chanting and the lyric wafted gently in the air. *"Hare Krishna, Hare Krishna."*

The Maharishi, still framed in the copter door, looked down at them, his outstretched arms held over them. His voice was soft and rich. "I bid you peace, my children."

In unison the girls knelt, bending their foreheads to the ground before him. "All peace comes from the Father," they intoned. "All love comes from the Father."

The Maharishi acknowledged the salutation and bade them rise. He began to descend the copter steps. The girls ran before him, strewing flowers from their baskets in his path. The two young men followed him.

"Is she there?" Judd asked John.

"She's there," John said. He called to the cameraman. "Zoom in tight on the middle girl on the right line."

A girl began to fill the screen. She was a pretty girl, but looked just like the others.

"How do you know for sure?" Judd asked. "They all look alike to me."

"Watch," John said.

They watched for a moment as the girl seemed to stumble slightly. One of her flowers fell from her hair and, as she knelt and picked it up to fix it in her hair, she half-turned as if she sought deliberately to face the camera.

"There she is," John said without expression. "I knew she'd be there. Alana is probably the best girl we have."

Judd stood watching her. "Where did you find her?"

"She was in the New York Police Department, street under-cover agent. They wanted her to take a desk job that she didn't want. She likes action. She came to us."

"She's young," Judd said.

"Not as young as she looks," Judd said. "Twenty-five."

"That's young," Judd said. He picked up the telephone to the pilot. "Let's take it back to the base."

John looked at him. "You don't want to look over the retreat and the property?"

"We already have that on tape, haven't we?" Judd asked.

"Yes."

"Then let's look at it in the office. It's got to be more comfortable there than here in this sardine can."

THE OFFICES WERE on the eighteenth floor of a new green, all-glass building on Century Boulevard, near the entrance to the Los Angeles Airport. The conference room was an interior room without windows. In the center of the room was a large table covered completely with a papier-mâché bas-relief map of the Church of Eternal Life and the entire surrounding area.

John gestured with a wooden pointer. "The scale of the map is one inch to the quarter-mile. The red line shows the boundaries of the property, from the bluff against the sea down to the gates closing the private road from the Coast Highway.

"You'll notice two circles of yellow. The larger one indicates the boundary of the bluff where the copter landed. The smaller is the boundary of the open area around the road gates. The yellow lines are our drop targets."

"Why can't we just blow through the gates?" Judd asked.

"Not that easy. There are three tracks of rolled hardened steel bars, twenty feet high, each gate opening in the opposite direction from the next, one to the right, next to the left and so on, finally to the right again. They are all electrified, connected to barbed wire at the top of the stone fence around the property. They are also tied to the police and fire departments of Malibu and Trancas. The Maharishi has made sure that everything is legally correct at the retreat. Needless to say, his relationships with the local authorities are cordial."

"How do you plan to get in then?" Judd asked. "Parachutes?"

"No," John answered. "First, the planes would be heard, second, we'd need at least a two-thousand-foot drop to maneuver the chutes onto the targets. We have to go in low and silent."

"Okay," Judd repeated. "How?"

"Hang gliders."

"Good idea," Judd said.

The pointer touched a peak across the Coast Highway slightly north of the retreat. "There's a plateau at the top of this point that's some eight hundred feet above the bluff," John went on. "I have ten flyers who tell me they can do it."

"But they need the right wind," Judd said. "First they'll drop, but if they don't catch the wind, they won't get up."

"I have two catapults already set up there. We'll catapult straight out, like a plane on an aircraft carrier. They'll get up all right." John nodded, pleased. "The next problem is the Maharishi's security. We're fortunate in one respect. He allows no firearms or other weapons. But all his men are black belts and masters of the martial arts. In addition, he has approximately twelve to fifteen Doberman guard dogs patrolling the grounds at night. But even the dogs are taught not to kill, only to hold and immobilize."

"Those're the pluses," Judd pressed. "What are the minuses?"

"Clear skies," John said. "We could be seen easily. What we need is either fog or a low cloud cover. More than force-four winds from the sea would blow our asses to the ground, far away from the target. Lastly, if we don't silence the dogs and the guards at the very first moment, they'll blow the alarms and we're fucked."

"How do you expect to silence them so quickly?" Judd asked.

John brought out a curious, long-barreled handgun. "This fires twelve darts automatically. Each dart knocks out man or beast on contact. They'll sleep about four hours and wake up with a hangover that will last another two."

Judd looked at the security man. "Suppose everything goes well, then what?"

"You'll be in the car about one hundred yards down the road. We open the gates and you come in like the President himself."

"When do you plan to do this?"

"It's up to the weather," John answered. "The five-day weather forecast isn't great for us. Clear skies all the way. But this is the Pacific. Anything can happen. At most any time."

"Can you give me a one-day advance notice?"

"Probably," John said. "Why?"

Judd looked at him. "It's about ten days since Sofia took her vacation. I thought I'd run over and see her."

"She never went for the program," John said.

"I know," Judd nodded. "She said she doesn't want to be anyone else. She likes being herself."

"You got to hand it to her," John said. "The lady's got balls."

Judd laughed. "That's not all she's got."

"We'll have to rearrange security," John said.

"That's right," Judd said. "But that's the way the game's played."

238

15

◆ A KNOCK CAME at her door. "Mrs. Evans?"

She recognized Judd's voice. "Just one moment," she called, turning to the mirror over the dresser. She touched up her makeup. A little lip gloss; a soft pat of the dark cake of face powder accentuated the dyed coloring of her chestnut-brown, short curled hair. She turned from the mirror to the door and opened it. She allowed herself no facial expression. "Yes?" she asked.

Judd looked at her, then he smiled quizzically.

"Mrs. Evans? I must have made a mistake. Do I know you?"

"Judd!" she laughed. She pulled him into her arms. She pressed herself against him and kissed him. "Now do you know me?"

"Can't miss," he said, smiling. He looked at her approvingly. "My God, you're beautiful," he said. "No matter what they did they couldn't take that away from you. Beautiful."

"Do you really like it?"

"Yes, really. And you were right not to let them cap your teeth. Everything works."

"Don't make me cry," she said, trying to laugh. "I'll lose my contacts, I'm not used to them yet."

He smiled at her. "First you're a woman."

She nodded silently. She knew what he meant.

"Do you feel up to some doctor talk?" he asked. She led him to the table near the window, where they sat. "Some juice?" she asked. "They make fresh pineapple juice. It's very good."

"Fine."

She went to the refrigerator and poured two glasses from a plastic carafe. She held up her glass to him. "It's not Cristale," she smiled. "But cheers, anyway."

"Cheers."

"Okay," she said. "Let me have it."

His face was serious. "Sawyer wants me to stop all the treatments now."

"Did he say why?"

"The scans show a minuscule enlargement of the brain. Less than half a millimeter over the total area, so it's not a growth or tumor that concerns him or the neurologists. The last scan I had was ten months ago. The enlargement has occurred since then."

"Have you had any unusual pressures or headaches?"

"No."

"Any problems of locomotion, orientation, hearing or vision?" she pursued.

"No," he answered.

"Sexual, urinary or digestive problems?"

"No."

She was silent again for a moment. "Do you have any problem sleeping, loss of concentration or physical and mental tiredness?"

"No."

"Weight loss or gain?"

"Always the same," he said, "one-sixty."

"Height loss?"

He laughed. "That's a funny question. Still six-one. Why do you ask?"

"Aging process," she said. "At a certain age the skeleton shrinks."

"I'm not that old yet," he said.

"I agree," she said. "But I'm just asking." Silently, she took another sip of her juice. She looked at his eyes. They were clear and cobalt blue against the bright sun from the window. "Do you feel any slowing down of your thought processes?"

"Quite the contrary," he said. "They seem much faster. Sometimes the thoughts rush so quickly through my head that I consciously have to slow them down to retain them, or the thought seems already the deed."

"Like now?" she asked.

"I don't know what you mean."

"Do you see me as I am now?" she explained. "Or do you see me as I was before my cosmetic changes?"

He looked at her. "You always look the same."

240

"Close your eyes," she said. She waited until his lids were shut. "Describe me," she asked.

"You're five-eight or nine, weight about one-thirty, you have long blonde hair, gray eyes, full breasts about thirty-nine or forty with strong, jutting nipples, waist twenty-six or seven, hips about thirty-eight or nine—"

"That's fine," she said, interrupting him. "Now, open your eyes and describe me."

A surprised look came into his eyes. "You don't look like that at all. You have short brown hair. You have brown eyes." A puzzled sound came into his voice. "Why did I think that?"

"You were describing your memories," she said. "Not what you saw."

He fell silent for a moment. "Is that bad?"

"No," she said. "Quite normal. We all see inside our heads what we remember. It takes a little time to replace memory with reality."

"But I thought my thought processes were faster than before," he said.

"You're probably right," she said. "But your new vision of me is still so fresh in your memory that you reached over it to the older memory. If you closed your eyes again, you would probably see the new reality."

He closed his eyes and sat for a moment. "You were right," he said slowly. He looked at her. "And I thought I was doing something special."

"You sound disappointed," she said.

"I am," he said. "I thought I was far ahead of everyone else."

"You are. And you aren't. Don't forget you're still a human being."

"Will I always be like that?" he asked. "Living in my memories?"

"Probably," she said, then added, "Unless you live forever. Then you'll have to discover a way to lose many of your memories or you may overburden your brain."

He stared at her. "Could that be the reason my brain is enlarging? So that it can store and handle more memory banks?"

She met his eyes. "I don't know. But I should think not. Biologically and anthropologically, the human brain is the result of millions of years of evolution. We have never known of a normal human brain changing as a result of mutation." She fell silent for a moment. "Remember one thing, however. The brain functions within the limitations of the human skull that contains it. And bone does not stretch."

He looked from her face to the wall behind her.

"Also remember," she added, "the size of the brain means nothing in relation to mental powers. The brain of a cow is much larger than a human brain."

He looked into her eyes. "Then what do you suggest?"

"I'll go along with Sawyer," she concluded. "Let's hold up the treatments. At least until we learn more about the cause of this condition."

"Sawyer wants me to go back into the hospital in Boca Raton."

"That makes sense," she said.

"I don't have the time."

She looked at him quizzically. "What difference does time make for a man who plans to live forever?"

He sat there thoughtfully without replying.

"I have a feeling," she went on, "that you know something you haven't shared with Sawyer or me."

He was still silent.

She offered a guess. "Are Xanadu and the DNA chemical cell-engineering project related somehow?"

"Don't be a smart-ass," he said flatly. But he showed no sign of anger. "I told you I'd tell you at the right time."

She shrugged in acceptance. "But you don't plan to go to Boca Raton?"

"That's right," he answered.

"What are you doing then?" she asked.

"I'm planning to have a meeting with the Maharishi," he said.

"The appointment has been made?"

"I didn't say that," he answered. "We're just going to drop in on him."

"I'd like to meet him with you," she said.

"If you do, you might blow your cover," he said.

"What cover?" she asked. "I've already told them I am not interested in their program."

"Sooner or later, then, they'll find you."

242

She looked into his eyes. "I'm not much concerned about that," she said. "My professional curiosity is much more important. Maybe the man has some of the knowledge we're searching for."

"And that's worth your life?"

Her eyes didn't waver. "I myself have no desire to live forever, Judd."

He was expressionless. "I'm beginning to feel that I was selfish in coming to see you."

"Don't feel like that," she said softly. "I love you. And if you hadn't come to see me, I would have gone to you."

16

◆ THE TELEPHONE ON the table between them rang sharply. She picked it up. "Mrs. Evans."

"Dr. Walton," a voice replied. "Is our friend still there?"

"Yes."

"May I speak with him?"

"Of course," she said, then added, "Trouble?"

"I don't know. But Fast Eddie has just come into my office. He thinks they have picked up a tail."

"I'll put him on," she said.

Judd took the telephone. "Yes?" He listened for a moment, then looked over at Sofia. "Go to the window and let me know if you can see a white van about five cars behind the limousine."

Sofia looked down. "Yes," she said. "I can see it."

"Is there any lettering on the side?"

"Island Laundry," she answered.

"Anything else? A telephone number?"

"I don't see one," she said.

"Come back from the window," he told her. "Even though the windows are one-way glass, I don't want to take any chances." He spoke into the telephone. "Island Laundry. Do you have anything on them?"

"Never heard of them," Brad said. "We use Waikiki. Fast Eddie also tells me that two men came into the lobby just as you went up in the elevator, and they are still hanging around there."

"Shit," Judd said.

"Should we hassle them?" Brad asked.

"That'll only give us away," Judd said. He thought for a moment. "We'll pull the old hat trick. Only the hat will be a patient."

"Got it."

"How long do you need to get it together?" Judd asked.

"Give me fifteen minutes," Brad said, clicking off the phone.

Judd looked at her. "I'm sorry."

"What about?"

"Because I blew my own rules. I ordered that no one was to bring you near me for your own protection, and I fucked it up myself."

She looked at him. "Don't feel sorry," she said. "That, too, would have happened sooner or later."

THE LITTLE JAPANESE nurse bent next to Brad as he fixed a nose bandage across Judd's face. He held it gently but tightly. "Put on the tape, Jane," he said.

Deftly the nurse held the roll of surgical tape and covered his nose to his cheekbones until the center of his face was entirely hidden. "Okay, Doctor?" she asked.

Brad checked Judd. "How do you feel?"

"Like my nose is stuffed," he said.

"It's that street shit you been snorting," Fast Eddie laughed. "Told you you'd wind up with a plastic lining."

"Not funny!" Judd said sarcastically. But he was smiling.

Jane turned. "Your turn, Mrs. Evans."

Sofia looked at her. "I thought everything was finished."

"Surgically, yes," the nurse smiled. "But there are still a few touch-ups to finish. Like your hands and arms, for example, or your *décolletage.*"

Sofia looked at her hands. "They look okay to me."

"Hold them up against your face," Brad said. "They're completely white, not at all like the skin tones of your face. They'd be a sure giveaway if anyone was looking for you."

Sofia looked at him silently.

"Jane has a body stain. She's an expert with it. It won't take long," Brad went on.

"Two applications should do it, Mrs. Evans," Jane said. "The first one stays on ten minutes, then you shower and dry off. Then we'll do a second application and dry it into your skin with a hair dryer. The color should stay on your skin for at least two months, even if you shower twenty times a day."

Sofia looked at Judd. "Do we have the time?"

"We don't have much choice," he answered.

245

She nodded to the nurse and started for the bathroom. "Let's begin," she said.

The nurse picked up a large doctor's bag and closed the bathroom door behind her. "Please take off all your clothes, Mrs. Evans," she instructed her. "And then clean off all your makeup."

Quickly Sofia stripped and removed her makeup with a large jar of cold cream. She washed her face with a cloth and dried herself. She turned to the nurse. "Now what?"

"Very good," the girl smiled. "Now step into the shower stall. Put on a shower cap and face me, your eyes tightly shut." She held a spray can in her hand. "The stain may sting slightly but only for a moment. Don't turn your back to me until I tell you."

"Okay." Sofia closed her eyes. She heard the hiss of the spray can, then she felt a faint sting as the spray touched her skin. The stinging crawled slowly down her body to her feet. After a moment the sensation stopped.

She felt the nurse's hand touch her arm. "Still keep your eyes shut," the girl said. "I'll guide you so you can turn around for me."

Sofia felt the girl moving as she turned. "Now stand with your legs slightly apart. You can place the palms of your hands flat against the wall of the shower stall to hold yourself steady."

"I'm fine," Sofia said.

The stinging sensation began again, this time from down her neck, across her shoulders and back, then finally to her legs. She could feel the spray against the back of her legs, then she felt it turn to the inside of her thighs and down to the calves.

She heard the nurse's Japanese giggle. "I'm sorry, Mrs. Evans, but I must ask you to open your buttocks slightly if you can, because your skin there is too white."

"I can't do that standing in this position," Sofia said.

"It's okay if you bend slightly forward," the girl said.

"Damn!" Sofia exclaimed as the spray hit. "This really hurts."

"Many pardons," the girl said. "But most necessary. There is time now, you can relax."

Sofia half-smiled as the girl's embarrassment caused her to revert to Japanese diction. She straightened up, turned back to the nurse and stepped out of the shower stall. She looked at herself in the full-length mirror. "I look yellow!" she exclaimed.

The nurse giggled. "Very Japanese," she agreed. "But do not worry. Next application you'll have normal, dark-white skin."

Judd was alone when she returned from the bathroom ahead of the nurse, who was carrying the black doctor's bag. "I'll be back in a moment, Mrs. Evans," she said. "I'll bring your clothes and help with your makeup if you need me."

"I think I'll be all right," Sofia said. She turned to the makeup mirror on the dresser. She began to apply her lipstick. In the mirror she saw Judd studying her with a strange look. She turned to him. "Anything wrong?"

He shook his head. "Every time I look at you, you look like someone else."

"It's the color," she said. "You're not used to it. It's golden now."

He was silent.

"It reminded me somewhat of Amarinth's color," she said. She loosened her white silk robe slightly. "But darker than hers."

He turned away from her. "Finish your makeup," he said almost harshly. "We're almost ready to go." He picked up the telephone from the table and dialed Brad's office. "Has Valerie Ann arrived yet?" he asked.

Brad's voice crackled through the receiver. "Fast Eddie has just brought her in through the lobby. He wants the two observers to have a good look at her before they go up in the elevators. I'll bring them up to you as soon as they get to my office."

"Who's Valerie Ann?" she asked as he put down the telephone.

"One of the stewardesses on my plane," he said. "You're taking her place. I'm taking no more chances, just in case somebody figures out I've brought an extra girl aboard."

"What will happen to this girl?"

"She'll stay here a few days and then return home on a commercial flight." He walked over to the window. "The van is still there."

"You don't think it's a coincidence?" she asked.

"I know it's not," he said. "While you were in the bathroom we had the license plates checked. They're phony."

A knock came at the door, and the Japanese nurse entered

carrying a small valise and a handbag. She turned to Sofia. "The clothes you wore when you came here are in the valise. Also your handbag."

"Leave it on the bed," Judd said. "She's not using any of it."

"Yes, sir," Jane said. She put the bags on the bed and looked at Sofia. "Can I help you, Mrs. Evans?"

"I think I'm doing okay."

Judd interrupted. "I'd appreciate it if you stayed, miss," he said. "We may have to make a few more changes."

A moment later Brad entered the room, Fast Eddie following him with a light-skinned black girl wearing a stewardess's uniform. The girl's eyes were lively and intelligent, her nose aquiline, and her lips slightly thick and wide. She noticed Judd's nose bandage but remained silent.

"Thank you for hurrying, Valerie Ann," Judd said. "I need to ask an important favor of you."

"You're the boss, Mr. Crane," Valerie Ann said.

Judd gestured. "Valerie Ann, this is Mrs. Evans."

The black girl looked at Sofia. "Mrs. Evans," she said politely.

"Valerie Ann," Sofia answered.

"I'd like you to give her your uniform," Judd said, "so Mrs. Evans can return to the plane with me."

The stewardess looked from Sofia to Judd. "There'll be no problems with the uniform, Mr. Crane," she said, "but she'll never make it as a sister."

"I don't understand," Judd said.

"Black girls are different from white girls," Valerie Ann said. "First, she needs a little more soot on her face, neck and throat where it shows, then her lips need to be made wider and larger. Maybe the most important thing is her walk. Black girls' asses have a bigger *shelf* that makes them move differently. What she needs is some ass falsies. Like Fredericks of Hollywood shows in their ads."

Judd turned to Brad. "Think you can take care of it?"

Brad looked puzzled. "We can take care of the makeup, but the ass is something else."

"I think I can arrange that," the nurse said. She flushed lightly. "Japanese girls usually have low asses. There are several lingerie shops in Little Tokyo that specialize in ass falsies."

"Really?" Judd asked.

Jane flushed even more. "Yes, Mr. Crane. I wear them when I dress up."

"Hurray for the United Nations," Fast Eddie laughed. "What you get is not always what you see. *Vive la différence!*"

17

◆ STILL WEARING THE silk robe that Sofia had given her, Valerie Ann walked to the window and looked down. "They should be coming out any minute now," she said.

Jane came to the window beside her. "Here they come!" she exclaimed.

They could see Fast Eddie opening the door to the limousine. Moving quickly across the sidewalk, Judd entered the car first, then Sofia, Brad beside her. Fast Eddie jumped into the car, pulling the door behind him. A moment later, the car moved out into the traffic.

"They're gone," Jane said.

Valerie Ann turned to her. "What was that all about?"

"I don't know," Jane answered. "But that's nothing unusual around here. Dr. Walton is one of the best plastic surgeons around, and many patients insist that they not be seen."

Valerie Ann went to the table and sat down. "Do you have anything here to drink besides pineapple juice?"

"There's a bottle of white wine in the refrigerator," Jane said.

"Then what are we waiting for?" Valerie Ann asked.

Jane took the bottle from the refrigerator and brought it to the table with the glasses. "Not a very good wine," she said apologetically, turning the plastic cap of the bottle.

"I'm not complaining," Valerie Ann smiled. "Now all we need are some cigarettes and a couple of toots."

Jane filled their glasses, then took a package of cigarettes from one pocket and a half-gram vial from the other. A small spoon was attached to its cap with a chain. She placed them all on the table between them. "That's pharmaceutical, right out of our own dispensary."

"Party time," Valerie Ann laughed.

A few minutes later they were relaxed in the chairs. Jane held the cigarette lighter out to the stewardess. "It's been hectic," she said.

Valerie Ann let out some smoke and sipped at the wine. "Your doctor's cute," she said. "Does he have any prejudice against black girls?"

Jane gave her little Japanese giggle. "Not at all. But it won't help."

"Maybe I can talk him into it," Valerie Ann said.

"Approximately half the nurses in the place would like to. But no chance."

"Very straight?" Valerie Ann asked. "Strictly business?"

The Japanese giggled again. "No business. Straight gay."

"Shit," Valerie Ann said disappointedly. "That's my luck. Every guy I have eyes for turns out to be gay."

"Your boss seems strange," Jane said.

"He is strange," the black girl agreed.

"Did you ever make it with him?"

"No," she answered. "He's ice." She looked at the nurse. "I wonder what he sees in that Mrs. Evans. She's not exactly a kid."

"Maybe he likes older women," Jane giggled.

Valerie Ann smiled at her. "I have this little hook in my nose," she said. "Do you think your boss would spring for a little nose job for me? Just so it doesn't turn out to be a total loss."

Jane laughed.

"Damn it," Valerie Ann said, clapping her forehead. "I just remembered, I promised my sister I would join her this weekend on a retreat at the Church of Eternal Life. Now I'm stuck in Hawaii. Would it be all right if I called her in L.A. and let her know I can't make it?"

"Sure," said Jane. "Just dial direct."

BRAD AND FAST Eddie were seated on the jump seats on either side of console containing the bar, television screen and radio. Set into the top of the console was a telephone and a call director. Brad gestured to Judd and Sofia. "Sit at opposite corners, the rear window, please. I need a clear view."

Brad looked out through the rear window; he leaned over to the driver. "Take the old road to the airport, behind the shopping center.

"Right," the driver replied over his shoulder.

Brad turned back to them. "They're right behind us," he said. He looked down at the call director and pressed a button. A row of narrow red signal lights began to flicker. "They're using a mobile telephone," he said. "Let's see if we can tap into their channel." He pressed the automatic frequency transponder.

Fast Eddie called the driver. "Give me the trumpet case I left on the seat next to you."

The driver held up the black case. Fast Eddie took it, placed it on his lap and began unlocking the snaps.

Brad stared at him. "Don't tell me you're going to play the trumpet at a time like this?"

Fast Eddie grinned back. "Don't you know that music soothes the savage beast?" He opened the case and took out a black cylinder about a foot and a half in length and four inches in diameter. He locked in two arm clamps, one on each side of the cylinder; he fitted a flat rectangular metal box into the opening created for it under the cylinder. "Pretty, isn't it?" he asked.

Without waiting for an answer, he pressed the switch to open the sunroof over the passenger compartment. He raised the cylinder and without standing up through the opening, placed it on the roof and tightly screwed its clamps. Then he looked through a tiny direction finder at the bottom of the metal box. He adjusted the clamps slightly. Finally he turned, smiling to Brad, "Take a look."

Brad looked through the tiny aperture. The white van following them showed exactly in the cross-hairs of a telescopic sight. Brad sat back in his seat. "It's a periscope," he said. "But what the hell do we need it for if we can see it just as clearly through the window."

"It's not just a periscope," Fast Eddie said, a faint hurt in his voice. "Do you think I'd fuck with a toy like that?"

"What the hell is it then?"

"It's a miniaturized version of the Swedish Anti-Tank Weapon that the U.S. Army uses. This little rocket is powered by compressed air and is accurate up to a hundred and fifty yards. It carries enough incendiary explosive to turn that van into a fireball, leaving nothing but dust after it." He looked at Brad sarcastically. "Still think it's a toy?"

Brad stared at him for a moment, then grinned. "You know, Fast Eddie," he said. "I think you're a mean mother."

"I don't like people fucking with us," Fast Eddie said. He took out his gold chain and vial. "Anybody care for a toot?"

"Not my thing," Brad answered, watching the call director.

"I could use one," Sofia said.

"Okay," said Fast Eddie, handing the vial to her. "But be careful, there's a hell of a wind coming down from the sunroof."

Sofia turned her face to the corner, cupping her hands, and snorted. "Good," she said, turning back.

Brad's voice was excited. "I've tapped their channel!" He turned on the speaker.

They heard a man's voice, heavy but crackling clearly through the static. "I'm telling you. There's no extra woman in that car, only the black stewardess that came from the plane."

There was another voice, but the words were unintelligible through a burst of static. The first man's voice came on again. "I don't know why he sent for her. Maybe he wanted her to suck his cock on the way to the plane. How do I know? Maybe he wants her to hold his hand. I told you he's got that big bandage on his nose. Maybe he had himself a plastic lining up there. He's a well-known cokehead."

"Fuck him!" Fast Eddie said angrily. "Let's blast 'em!"

Judd held up his hand. "Let's listen."

"Okay," the man's voice said. "I'm coming in. Over and out."

The red light on the call director went out. Brad looked back through the rear window. The big white van slowed down; they saw it make a U-turn and head back to the city. "They're gone," Judd said with a sigh of relief.

He turned to look out the window. The van was speeding away from them. "I'll take that toot now," he said to Fast Eddie. "And take our toy down. But be careful."

"I'll be careful," Fast Eddie said. "But you'll never make that toot with a spoon with your nose bandaged. "You'll need a straw."

"Screw it," Judd said irritably. He began to take off the bandage.

"Better leave it," Brad said quickly. "They may have some people to check us at the airport."

Judd, seated at the table, remained silent while the plane took off. Sofia glanced through the window as they circled wide around the island, climbing steeply for altitude. It was late in the afternoon; the sun turned everything golden below them, even the white-capped rollers against the beaches. "Beautiful," she said.

He looked at her. He seemed depressed and silent. The bell sounded, the seat belt signal went off. He unlocked his belt and got up. "I'm going to my cabin," he said. "Just tell Raoul when you're ready for dinner."

"What about you?" she asked.

"I'm not hungry," he said, then turned and walked through the lounge to his door. He didn't look back at her as he went into his cabin and closed the door behind him.

Fast Eddie came from behind the bar toward her. She glanced out the window again. "Dusk is falling quickly," she said.

"We're flying into the night," he said. "We'll be landing in San Francisco at nine in the morning."

"Is that where we get off?"

He shook his head. "No, we're going on. But you're getting off because we're changing the cabin crew. The boss figures they'll provide a good cover for you."

He held up a large zippered leather envelope and placed it on the table before her. "Everything inside is for you," he said. "The boss asked me to explain it to you."

He opened the zipper and emptied the contents on the table. She looked down at it. Passport, credit cards, checkbook, driver's license. All in her name. Marissa Evans. Even the photographs on the passport and driver's license were of her. There was also a wallet filled with one-hundred-dollar bills.

"There's five thousand there," Fast Eddie said.

"Fine," she said. "Now what do I do?"

"Simple," he said. "The crew bus drops you in downtown San Francisco. Walk around a few blocks, enough to make sure you're not followed. If you think you are, there's a telephone number on the first page of your passport. Call it and leave your location. Security will pick you up. Don't worry about it, they'll recognize you and call you by name."

"Mrs. Evans?" she asked.

"Yes."

"And if they don't or can't?"

He put a small black .25 caliber automatic on the table. "The bullets have explosive heads. Blow the shit outta them and get the hell away from there. Then call Security again."

"What if I can't get away?" she asked.

"I've seen you in action," he said confidently. "You'll be okay."

She was silent for a moment. "Then what do I do?"

"Go to a department store and buy yourself some clothes and a valise. Pay cash. Dump the stewardess uniform in a covered street trash can and go to the nearest auto rental station and get a good midsize car. Take the freeway to Los Angeles on U.S. 5. Pass all the L.A. exits until you reach the exit to Marina Del Rey. Follow that to the Marina City Club Hotel. There'll be a reservation there for you."

"What if I get lost?" she asked. "I know nothing about Los Angeles."

He laughed. "Ask a policeman."

She smiled. "How much time should the trip take?"

"Following the fifty-five-mile speed limit, seven to eight hours," he answered. "If everything goes according to schedule, you should be on the freeway by noon. Even if you stop for gas and a bite of lunch, you should make it to the hotel between eight-thirty and nine o'clock. Have dinner in your room and wait there. We'll contact you."

She was silent a moment, then returned everything to the leather envelope. She looked up at him. "I think I need some help."

He smiled. "Of course." Then added, "But don't do too much or you'll never get to sleep."

SHE REMEMBERED HIS advice as she stared, wide awake, in the dark of her cabin. Annoyed, she turned on the light beside her bed and sat up. She took a cigarette and lit it, drawing the smoke inside her. "Damn!" she said, blowing out the smoke.

She looked up at the wall clock. Almost three hours into the flight. She had been trying vainly to fall asleep for more than an hour. She dragged again at the cigarette and finally called the lounge on the telephone.

After a moment, a stewardess's voice answered sleepily, "Hello?"

"Is Mr. Crane there by any chance?" she asked.

"No, Mrs. Evans," the girl replied. "He's never come back from his stateroom."

"Thank you," Sofia said, putting down the telephone. She stared at the small door that led directly to the circular staircase into Judd's stateroom. After a moment she rose, wrapped a large bath towel around herself and went up the staircase.

She knocked at his door. "Are you awake?" she whispered.

His voice sounded like a faint echo. "Come in."

She opened the door slowly. It took a moment until her eyes adjusted to the dim red light in the cabin. She could make out Judd seated in the lotus position in the far corner of his bed, his back toward her.

"Lie down," he said, not turning, his voice still a curious echo.

She moved to the bed and stretched out behind him. She watched him, but he was more a shadow than a reality she could see. Gently, she touched his shoulder. "Are you all right?" she asked.

His voice was suddenly harsh. "I want to fuck you."

She was silent.

He stood up quickly beside the bed. She stared at him. In the soft reddish light his erection seemed grotesquely immense and swollen. His voice sounded almost angry. "That is what you want, isn't it?"

She closed her eyes, shaking her head. "No," she whispered. But her voice was smothered as he flung himself upon her. She felt as if she were being torn apart as he entered her. Then, almost instantly, he erupted into an orgasm that triggered a cascading ejaculation. He shouted his agony, then slumped upon her, trying to catch his breath.

After a moment, she touched his face with her fingers. She felt the wet tears on his cheeks. "Judd," she whispered.

His voice was muffled against her shoulder. "Amarinth is dead," his voice, husky with pain, muttered. "You said she would cry. She committed suicide."

She was silent, then slowly she pressed his face to her breast. "I'm so sorry, baby." She wept with him. "Please, baby. Don't hurt."

256

18

◆ SHE AWOKE IN the dark and turned toward him. He was gone. She sat up and turned on the light. The wall clock read 9:30 A.M., Pacific Coast Time. She stepped from the bed to the window and raised the blinds. Sunlight poured in; she blinked her eyes.

She looked down and saw Fast Eddie walking quickly to a helicopter about a hundred yards away. She watched him enter the copter with Judd and the doors close behind them. The rotors began turning at once; a few minutes later, the craft lifted from the ground. She watched out the window until the copter disappeared from sight; then she went down the narrow private staircase to her own cabin.

She felt let down, curiously disappointed. She had become aware of something from him last night, something she had never felt before. Maybe it was only a feeling. She wasn't sure of exactly what it was she felt—whether it was his own feeling he had transmitted to her or her own. She stepped into the shower. It had to be time for her to get started.

Raoul was waiting for her in the lounge. "Good morning, Mrs. Evans."

"Good morning," she said.

"You have time for breakfast if you like," he said.

"Just coffee, thank you," she said. He started away. She called him back. "Did Mr. Crane leave a message for me?"

He shook his head. "I'm sorry, Mrs. Evans. None."

"That's okay." She tried to smile. "I didn't expect one."

"But Fast Eddie left something for you," he said.

She looked at him curiously. He handed her a small white envelope and walked toward the galley. Quickly she opened the envelope. It contained a vial of cocaine with a silver spoon, together with a little note.

She read it quickly. "Just to keep your spirits up, F.E."

She smiled to herself and sat down to await the coffee.

JUDD'S OFFICE IN the executive building in the center of Crane City was very different from the office he had inherited from his father at world headquarters in New York. This one was simple, almost spartan in decor, with modern furniture, mainly white and black plastic and Formica. It was a working office, not for show. Floor-to-ceiling louvers hid the room from the world beyond the windows.

He concealed his surprise when he saw Barbara, Paul Gitlin, Doc Sawyer and Merlin waiting there for him. He glanced at Merlin with faint annoyance. "I hadn't realized I'd called a directors meeting."

"I'm sorry," Merlin said nervously. "I think it's important."

Judd walked behind his desk and sat down. "What's so important?"

Merlin looked at him, then turned to Paul. "Perhaps you can explain to him, Mr. Gitlin."

"Uncle Paul?" Judd asked.

For once, Paul did not have his usual bottle of Scotch on the table before him. "I'll make it simple for you," he began. "You can't dispose of Crane Industries just as you'd like to. Its whole structure is too complicated and too interlocked. There's no way you can unscramble the eggs."

Judd stared at him for a time. "I own it, don't I?" he said.

"Yes," Paul answered. "But you have responsibilities. For example, you have certain bona fide agreements and contracts with the government. These do not allow you to dispose of any companies to parties they do not approve of under their very strict security provisions. For starters, these include Crane Aerospace and Aircraft, Crane Compucrafts, Crane Microcraft and Microconductors, Crane Lasercraft—"

Judd interrupted. "What am I allowed to get rid of?"

"Leisure industries," Paul said dryly. "Hotels, entertainment systems, cable for home or theater, publishing companies, motion picture production."

"You mean mostly the losers," Judd said. "The hardest to sell."

"Not entirely," Paul said. "They wouldn't disapprove of you

258

unloading Crane Land and Development, Crane Financial Services, and the like. I have a long list on both sides I can give you."

Judd fell silent. He glanced around the table from one to the other. "The only thing I'm interested in keeping is the medical and biology engineering group," he said at last.

"No problem about that," Paul smiled. "My hunch is the government would allow you to sell them off anyway."

"Then what do you suggest, counselor?"

"Stay," Paul said. "You've been doing well. Why rock the boat?"

Judd looked steadily at him. "I'm bored with it. I want out."

"You have no choice," Paul said. "It's your baby and you're stuck with it."

Judd was silent. "We couldn't appoint a receiver?"

"Like who?" the lawyer asked. "There's no one who knows Crane Industries as you do. It would turn into a complete disaster."

"Shit," Judd said. "I was planning to settle down in Xanadu."

"That's another dream you had," Paul said. "First it was Crane Island, then almost before you began construction, you changed to Xanadu. You know how much Crane Island cost us. Now Xanadu will go twenty times as much."

"It was my money," Judd said. "I never spent a penny of the foundation's. It's always been my own money."

"I'm not complaining about that," the attorney said. "I simply pointed out that it was a waste, whether it's your money or someone else's. Now I'm saying the same thing about Xanadu."

Judd looked at him coldly. "You have anything else to say?"

Judd saw him drop his eyes to the table. He turned to Merlin. "Sell everything we're allowed to," he ordered.

"That will blow another thirty or fifty billion dollars," Merlin said.

"Net after taxes?"

"No," Merlin answered. "Net, maybe four billion. That's still a lot."

"I'll reimburse the foundation," Judd said. "I'll take all the losses myself."

"That will bring your net worth down to less than half," Merlin said.

"I'll still have more than enough," he retorted. He glanced around the table. "Any more arguments?"

"One question," Paul said, eyes still fixed on the tabletop. "Who runs the show if you take off?"

"Sawyer can take care of the medical corporations," Judd said. "Merlin can handle everything else. Between the two of them, they probably know more about them than I do."

"What if they don't want to do that?"

"They don't have much choice," Judd said, half in jest. "You took care of that. The contracts I've got with them keep them tied to me body and soul."

"There isn't a contract in the world that can force a man to work if he just turns off. What do you plan to do then, sue them?" the lawyer challenged him.

Judd smiled, then looked at the others. "You both plan to quit?"

They were silent.

Judd looked at Paul. "It'll never happen," he said. "They're not just employees, they're friends."

Barbara rose from her chair. "I'm sorry, Judd," she said. "I think what you're doing is wrong. In a kind of way, unfair. You're unloading your own responsibilities onto your friends. I, for one, do not like it, and I don't think your father would have approved of it."

Judd met her eyes. "My father's dead. What he thought when he was alive was important. But not now. It is my life and my decisions that matter now."

She stared at him for a moment, gathered her things, pushed back her chair, and left the room. Judd looked at the others. "Anyone else want to leave?"

There were no answers. He turned to the attorney. "Talk to her," he said. "I don't want her to go away mad."

"Why don't you tell her yourself?" Paul said. "She's your mother, not mine."

He found Barbara seated in the corner of the reception room, a small handkerchief at her eyes. He slipped into the seat beside her. "I'm sorry, Barbara," he said. "I didn't mean to upset you."

She made an effort to control herself. But she still didn't speak. For the first time he realized how frail she had become with time.

"Barbara," he said softly, turning her face to him. "I'm really sorry."

There was hurt mixed with pain in her voice. "I'm really not angry, Judd. I'm really not angry," she said huskily. "It's only that I'm just beginning to realize what a fool you are."

"Because I don't want this business anymore?"

"Not that at all," she said. "It's watching you throw away every chance you have of happiness, just chasing a crazy dream."

"It's not a crazy dream," he said. "I'm getting closer to it each day."

"And you lose more every day," she said. "Not just money. Power. All the things you have, all the people who love you."

He was silent.

She searched his eyes. "You don't even understand what I'm talking about."

"I know what I want," he retorted.

"No, you don't," she said softly. "You've become completely selfish. Your father was selfish about his business, but he found time inside him to love your mother and you and, in time, to love me. But you have no time inside to feel love for anyone."

"I am not my father," he said. "I don't have to feel as he did."

"Perhaps you ought to, Judd," she said softly. "Why don't you give yourself a chance?"

"Don't you think I have?" he answered. "But what did I ever receive in return from others? Nothing for myself. What more could I do for them?"

"Did you ever ask of anyone something for your own self?" she asked quietly. "Like Sofia?"

"All I ever meant to her was another experiment, another discovery," he said.

"You're wrong," she said. "Maybe it started that way, but that's not the way it's turned out. She loves you."

He stared at her without speaking.

"If she didn't love you," she said, "she wouldn't have borne your child and kept him from you." Then her eyes fell away from him, her words hanging in the air.

He forced her eyes to meet his. "Sofia had a son?" he asked harshly.

Barbara didn't answer.

"*My* son?" he demanded. "Why wasn't I told?"

"Because she was afraid of you," she answered. "She didn't want the child used as a weapon."

"I don't believe you," he said angrily. "If it's true, where has she hidden him all this time?"

Barbara looked into his eyes. "With me," she said slowly. "And he *is* your son, Judd, without any doubt. He is very much like you. He even has your eyes. The same cobalt-blue eyes as yours."

His lips tightened. "It's not my child," he said grimly. "It was one of Zabiski's artificial insemination experiments. And they were all failures. Sawyer told me he managed things so they all miscarried. And we arranged an abortion for Sofia."

"I know all about that; she told me. She's also told me that she did not go through with the abortion. Because she was not part of Zabiski's experiments, Zabiski agreed that she would be the control, that you and Sofia would have a normal impregnation."

"She lied to me," Judd said bitterly. "Right up to the moment we met at the airport when she went back to Russia with the old lady. Probably they wanted to keep the child in Russia."

"But she didn't," Barbara said. "How she arranged it, I don't know. But one day she knocked on my door in San Francisco. The next day she was in a private clinic, having a baby, and five days later she was on her way back to Russia."

"And what did you do with the baby?" he asked.

She looked into his eyes. "He was your son," she said evenly. "We did the right thing. We adopted him and we care for him and love him."

"And you've never said anything to me?" he asked bitterly.

"No," she said. "Would you have cared if we had?"

He was silent.

"I don't think so," she said.

"Who else knows?" he asked. "Paul, Sawyer?"

"No one else," she said. "Only Sofia, Jim and I. All the official birth records have been hidden where no one can find them."

"It won't change anything," he said finally, without expression. "As far as I'm concerned he might as well never have been born. I'm still planning my life my own way."

She rose from the couch and looked down. "I feel very sorry for you, Judd," she said softly but firmly, then turned and without looking back left him alone in the reception room.

262

19

"WE'RE THREE WEEKS ahead of schedule," Sawyer said. "The clone culture refrigerating unit is being loaded aboard the plane right now. I'll be with it when the plane takes off from Atlanta."

"I thought you were going to meet me in Boca Raton," Judd said. "And then we'd go down together."

"I'd feel better going down with the cultures myself," Sawyer suggested.

Judd studied him severely. "Okay. I've known you long enough. What's troubling you?"

"That fucking German," Sawyer answered. "He's pushing his nose in where it shouldn't be. All he was supposed to do was complete the nuclear reactor and get the energy plant ready to go. Now I hear he's throwing his weight around the medical laboratories. He's asking questions about the cellular therapy refrigeration units."

"He's supposed to make sure that we have enough energy to operate it," Judd offered.

"Yes," Sawyer countered. "But he's asking a lot more than just that. He wants to know what the units are for. I just don't trust him."

"You're in charge, Doc," Judd said. "Just keep in touch with me."

"I'd feel safer if we had Security go over him again. Maybe there's something we blew. I still can't forget those two that made it to the island."

"Okay," Judd said. "I'll have Security take care of it." He glanced at the window next to his seat. Looking down from thirty thousand feet, he could see nothing but cloud cover. He picked up the telephone next to him and called the flight deck. "What are the weather conditions over the coast around Los Angeles?"

The captain's voice came through the receiver. "Cloud cover all around the area at about nine thousand feet right now, and they expect denser cover and fog to roll into the coast about ten o'clock. Looks like a pea souper. They anticipate they'll have to close LAX by midnight."

"Thank you." He pressed another button on the telephone again. A voice came on. "Security."

"This is Mr. Crane," he said. "I want to speak with the director." A moment later John's voice came on. "Do you have the weather report?" he asked.

"We've got it," John answered. "We are just·waiting to hear from you. I think we may be able to go tonight."

"We'll be touching down at LAX in about forty minutes," he said.

"We'll be ready and waiting for you, sir."

"And pick up Mrs. Evans on the way."

"Will do, sir."

"And one other thing," Judd asked. "Throw another net around Dr. Schoenbrun. We're not happy over the way he's acting."

"We'll get right on it, sir."

"Good," Judd concluded. "See you in half an hour." He glanced across the table at Sawyer. "What connection are you making to Atlanta?"

Sawyer grinned at him. "I'm now the president of Crane Medical, aren't I?"

"That's right," Judd said.

"Presidents don't fly commercial," Sawyer laughed. "CI 2 is waiting for me on the ground."

Judd laughed. "You're learning fast. That's the newest 707 we have."

Sawyer nodded, still laughing. "I had a good teacher."

THE GRAY CLOUDS began to turn to black as the day was coming to its end. The limousine pulled off the road into the field at the top of the mountain plateau that served as the hang glider launching pad. Judd stepped out of the car. He saw John and a man he did not know come toward him.

"Mr. Crane," John said. "This is Mark Davidson, the director of the glider and parachute school."

Davidson was not very tall, but his shoulders were wide and his body stocky and strong. He had a handshake to match. "This looks like the most fun I've had since we jumped in 'Nam."

"I want it to be fun," Judd said earnestly. "I don't want this to turn into a war. You understand there's to be no killing, even in self-defense."

"There won't be any, Mr. Crane," Davidson said. "We know what we have to do. We've completed training with our equipment for the job, sir."

"Good." Judd glanced at the sky. "What do you think?"

Davidson looked at the sky toward the sea. "We have a good chance. If no wind comes up unexpectedly, we should be able to jump off at twenty-two hundred hours."

Judd held out a hand with crossed fingers. "That's for luck."

"Come into the shack," Davidson said. "Let me show you how we've planned it."

Judd turned to John. "What's happened to Mrs. Evans?"

"We have a car picking her up right now, sir," John replied. "She should be here in about half an hour."

"Good." Judd turned to follow Davidson into the operations shack. He paused at the door, turning to see a hang glider head into the wind. Its pilot pointed his feet straight toward the ground, touched down. He bent his knees briefly, then slipping the wings from his arms, he straightened up. Judd looked at Davidson. "Fascinating. Looks like a bird landing."

"That's exactly the technique, sir," Davidson said.

"Like to try it sometime," Judd said.

"I'd love to take you up," Davidson said. "Maybe sometime after this operation is over."

"I don't mean that kind of sometime," Judd said. "What about right now?"

Davidson stared at him. "You can't mean that, sir. You wouldn't have the time to learn the technique, sir."

"How much daylight is there left?" Judd asked.

"Maybe an hour and a half."

"Let's give it a try," Judd said.

Davidson looked at John in consternation. John turned to Judd.

"I'm responsible for your security," he said. "My job is to get you into that compound safely. I can't do that if you're off flying around the sky like a bird, sir."

Judd shrugged, turned without a word to walk around the operations shack to a Quonset hangar. Hang gliders stood against the wall, shining black parachute-silk wings spread like giant bats ready to fall at a signal from the ceiling. He looked out toward the bluff's end where the tracks of the three catapults aimed at the ocean beyond. Near it a group of flyers in black jumpsuits, coffee cups in their hands, sat in a circle. He didn't speak to them.

John came up beside him. "Sometimes the boss can't have all the fun, sir. That's what goes with the responsibilities."

Judd shrugged, then walked back to Davidson. "As you say, when this is over," he said ruefully.

"It'll be an honor, sir. Now let me take you inside and show you how we've planned this operation."

There was a bas-relief map made of papier-mâché covering a large table. Davidson picked up a small pointer. "This hill, the highest on the map, is where we're standing now. This other hill, lower and next to the ocean, is our objective. Between the two hills we cross the Pacific Coast Highway. The distance between the two hills is four thousand two hundred meters. The height of our launching pad is twenty-six hundred meters, the height of the target is two hundred meters. Once we hit the sky we have to manage an average fall of almost two thousand four hundred meters in that distance. It's going to be a hard fall. But I have good men and we can do it."

Judd's eyes were riveted on the map. "How will they be able to see it from the air if the ground is blacked out by fog?"

"We figured that too," Davidson said. He laid a large plexiglass cover over the map. It was opaque and Judd could see nothing through it. Davidson held out goggles to Judd. "Put these on, sir."

Judd fixed the goggles around his eyes. When he looked down at the covered map, his eyes could make out bright red arrows pointing to the objective.

"Infrared night glasses," Davidson said. "We've painted arrows on the roofs of twenty cars we've deployed on the way."

Judd pulled off the goggles and turned to Davidson. "My congratulations," he said. "I'd say you've thought of everything."

"Thank you, sir," Davidson said.

"Except one," Judd said.

Davidson looked puzzled.

"Who's leading this operation?" Judd asked.

"I am, sir," Davidson said. "I'm going off first."

Judd nodded thoughtfully, then smiled. "Then perhaps you better paint your ass red in case any of your men happen to lose their way."

Davidson smiled, then laughed suddenly. "They won't forget my butt," he said. "I'd fucking fire them if they did."

JUDD WALKED OUT to the edge of the hill. Dense fog was rolling in fast. It was heavier near the ocean but beginning to crawl across the highway, turning the headlights of the cars into dim pinpricks of light. He looked at his wristwatch. Twenty-one hundred hours. Davidson came up beside him.

"The way it looks, we'll be right on schedule," he said. "I've got the men suiting up."

Judd nodded, then turned to John. "Where the hell is Mrs. Evans? You said a half hour a long time ago, John."

"Don't worry, sir," John said. "Fast Eddie has two of his best men with him. She'll be here in time."

They went back into the operations shack. John pointed to a big five-pointed star house on the map and then the others in a circle around it. "Alana said the Maharishi lives in the center room of the star house. Each point of the star has a different-colored curtain to the center room and is opened when he gives his audiences. He always sits facing the center room, his back to one of the closed curtains from behind which he appears. It's never the same curtain, each color has a significance of another color plane of life. Tonight's color is red, the color plane of blood. These audiences always take place at exactly ten o'clock."

"That's a break," Judd said. "At least, we'll know where he's going to be."

"There are always two guards behind each curtain," John said. "That means once we take care of the outside we have to handle the guards inside. I'm taking no chances. I've got two cars going in before you, each carrying seven specialists."

Judd nodded. "And where is your girl while all this is going on?"

"She'll be down at the gates, opening them for us."

"There are two men down there," Judd said. "How does she plan to take care of them?"

John smiled. "I told you she was bright. She's going to the gatehouse, stone-cold naked. And I mean she'll seem stoned out of her mind. There's not a single man who won't open his door to see what's going on when it's a body like hers. The minute the door is open she throws two vial glass apples into the guardhouse and they're out of action in two seconds. She needs five seconds more for the gas to evaporate and she presses the button to open the gates. The first two men out of the car are electronics experts. They'll take care of the alarm system, and by that time we're on our way up to the compound. Alana will lead us right to the point of the star behind our man's back."

Judd smiled at him. "She's still stone-cold naked, I hope?"

John didn't smile. "No, sir. We have a jumpsuit ready for her."

A car pulled up outside the operations shack. Fast Eddie came in with Sofia. "What the hell took you so long?" Judd greeted them.

Fast Eddie held out his hands in helplessness. "Women," he said. "I'll never understand them. You know where I finally found her? In the beauty parlor."

Judd looked at her sternly. He didn't utter a word.

Sofia smiled at him. "I discovered a fabulous long-haired wig. Shiny beautiful black hair. Do you like it?"

For a moment he choked, then he found his voice. "You look exactly like a woman in a Marina Del Ray singles bar."

"It is very American," she said.

He nodded. "Yes, very. Now let's get ready. We should be leaving any minute now." He took her by the arm. "Let's get back in the car."

He stood beside the open car door. Davidson came over to him. "It's time, sir. Twenty-two hours."

"Good luck," Judd said.

He watched Davidson walk to the catapult, lock his body into the harness of the batlike hang glider. Davidson placed his feet in position in the catapult. There was a brief whoosh and he disappeared in the fog that hung over the edge of the plateau. After Davidson, one after another, the others went hurtling through the dense air behind him.

When the last glider was lost in the impenetrable fog, Judd got into the car. "Let's go," he said to the others. "We rendezvous in twenty-five minutes."

20

◆ TWO CARS HAD already pulled up in front of the partially opened gates before the limousine rolled up behind them. Judd opened his door and got out of the car. "What's holding us up?" he asked as John came toward him.

"We fucked up," John said flatly. "We never expected the gate openers to be on rotating combinations. The center track opened but the outside track locked after two feet. I've got the electronics experts trying to unscramble it."

"We're losing time," Judd snapped. "Blow it open."

"Do that and we'd have all the cops in California on our ass," one of the experts whispered. John turned back to Judd. "No way we can open the other gates. There's a safety lock on them that goes on the minute the alarm unit has been disconnected."

"We can squeeze through the open two feet," Judd said. "Let's start walking."

"It's three-quarters of a mile to the house," John said. "And we're not sure we've taken out all the guards and their dogs."

"We go in anyway," Judd said.

"Maybe you better wait in the car, Mr. Crane. We'll call you when it's all clear."

"And maybe by that time the Maharishi will be gone. If he's as smart as I think he is, he'll have a safe room and an escape route. Our only shot is to get there as fast as we can. We start running."

John nodded and turned to the men waiting at the gate. He waved his hand. "Go!" he called.

The men pushed through the gate and began racing up the driveway. Fast Eddie and Sofia followed immediately behind Judd. John gestured as they passed the guardhouse. Alana came out, just finishing pulling the zipper closed on her jumpsuit.

"Shit!" she said to John. "I'm sorry. I blew it. I should have figured that one myself."

"It's done," John said. "Now let's make the best of it." He turned to two of the men. "You two stay close to Mr. Crane. I want nothing to happen to him."

They began running up the driveway, Alana leading them. After several yards they could see several of the hang gliders sprawling on the ground. Close to them were two men lying on the ground not far from three Dobermans, stretched out sleeping quietly.

Sofia stared at them and touched Judd's arm. "It's okay," he assured her. "We took care of them with our dope darts. They'll be out for four hours, with nothing bothering them except a headache."

"You should've told me to wear running shoes," Sofia called after him. "High heels aren't meant for running."

"Stop bitching," Judd said. "You can go barefoot."

She kicked off her shoes and was able to keep up with him. They passed other guards and dogs, all stretched out. Beyond them on the ground lay several hang gliders completely smashed.

A few minutes later she was gasping for breath. "I've got to stop," she called. "I can't catch my breath. I've never gone into training for this kind of thing."

"Pop two of these under your nose," Fast Eddie said, putting two white-netted capsules in her hand.

"What the hell would amyl nitrate poppers do for me?" she said. "I'd fall down and have twenty orgasms."

"These aren't poppers," Fast Eddie said. "These are special uppers from our labs. Released oxygen under pressure with a touch of coke." Quickly he snapped one himself. "Yeah!" he said. "I'm Superman."

Sofia followed him. The energy burst through her. Suddenly she wasn't gasping for breath anymore. She felt as if she could run the five thousand meters at the Olympics.

She looked over to Judd, running quickly, easily, with no apparent breathing problem. She wondered if he was doing this naturally or whether he, too, had popped some of the pills. She made a mental note to ask him when they had the time.

As they reached the head of the driveway, several men in black jumpsuits emerged from the darkness. Davidson ran toward them. "You're late," he said to John. "What happened?"

"The gates fucked us," John answered. "How did you make out?"

"Okay," Davidson said. "I think we took them all out. Of course there may be others inside the compound, but we were under orders to wait for you."

"Good," John said. He turned to Alana. "Now which entrance do we go through?"

Alana gestured to the second of the star's spokes. "There's just one thing to keep in mind. The moment we step on the concrete steps around the house, the floodlights all go on."

"Got it," John said. He turned to his men. "I want two men at the entrance of each spoke. Three men at each entrance to the houses at the circumference. Four men at the gates of the kennels. I don't want anyone out of any of the houses. I want them bottled in. Tight."

He turned to Judd. "I take three men with us. We move first. The moment we move, the rest of you take up your positions." He glanced around. "All understand?" No one spoke. He turned back to Judd. "It's your show now, sir."

Judd nodded. "Okay. Let's go."

Even before they began to run toward the house, the floodlights lit, turning night into day.

"Fuck it!" he swore. "What the hell happened?"

Alana pointed toward a large Doberman, who was poised ears up, alert. In the next moment, they heard a slight ping. The dog loped toward the corner of the house, stopped suddenly, raised his leg, pissed happily across a geranium plant, gently lay down and went to sleep.

Alana was at the door first. She opened it. Judd followed her, John and the others just behind. Stepping as softly as they could on the marble floor, she led them to a wide red-beaded curtain. She parted a tiny corner of the curtain.

Judd peered through it, saw the back of the Maharishi. Beyond the Maharishi were seated sixteen to twenty young girls all in the lotus position, eyes fixed adoringly on the guru.

Silently Judd waved his hands to signal the security men to

272

position themselves to take the guru. When they were in place, Judd stepped through the curtain.

He had taken less than two steps when he found himself clasped around his chest from behind by arms like bands of steel, lifting him from the floor.

A voice next to his ear said, "Relax! If you resist, you will not be killed but you may be crippled for life."

Judd struggled only to catch his breath as he was hurled to the floor. Then he heard a faint ping; the arms that had bound him fell away as if their steel had melted.

Another voice, deep and calm, came to him. "Mr. Crane." He saw the figure of the Maharishi turn slowly. "I have been waiting for you for a long time. Perhaps for longer than you thought."

Judd stared at the Maharishi as he rose. He was taller than he had appeared, perhaps because he was standing on a raised platform or possibly because of his ascetic thinness and the drape of the robe that hung from his shoulders to the sandals on his feet.

He turned toward the girls, who began to rise from their seated positions, nervously aware of the sudden intrusion. They seemed eager to flee, though they seemed not to know which way to go. The guru was calm. "Do not be frightened, my children," he urged. "Resume your inner calm. No harm will come to you from these men. They come to me as friends, seeking knowledge."

The girls, reassured, settled on the platform, resuming their lotus positions. The guru turned to Judd. "It would be more conducive for our talk if you would arrange for the departure of your men. The closeness of so many strangers disturbs our calm and meditation. Here we all understand that life stretches from an endless past into infinity."

He stepped down from the low platform and walked toward Judd. His eyes were tawny yellow and piercing. "We have many things to discuss, my son," he said.

"Yes," Judd said.

The guru nodded. "But now I must rest," he said. "I am not as young as I used to be. Without sleep I do not function as well as I should. I think that it will take six hours for your group to leave and to allow the compound to return to normal. I would appreciate it if you could allow me to rest so we could begin our meeting precisely at sunbreak."

Judd was silent, uncertain of the man's intent.

"I give you my word I will not deceive you. We will meet as I promise," the Maharishi went on.

Judd felt something familiar in the presence of the Maharishi. He could not mask his surprise. He stared at the topaz-yellow eyes before him. "I know you," he said tonelessly.

"You are very observant," the guru said. "You knew my sister."

"Zabiski," he exclaimed. "Of course!"

"She was my older sister."

"That explains it," Judd said. "But what—"

"It will all be explained," he said. "My sister was a genius. But we will discuss all this when we meet again at sunbreak. Now, I must rest."

The guru rose to his feet. "I feel more restful with two girls beside me. It balances the Ying and Yang within me."

Judd was silent.

"I have heard that you too have found the same balance. If you so desire, we can offer you the same help."

Judd took a deep breath. "Thank you," he said. "I think not this time. I search only in myself this night."

"As you will," the guru answered. "My friends will show you to your rooms."

THE GUEST ROOMS were in a separate house on the perimeter of the main one. The house was small, as were the guest rooms. A single narrow bed and chair. A small wooden chest with four drawers. The bathroom had only a stall shower and an unpainted wooden closet for clothing. The toilet, without a cover, sat below a window high on the wall. The walls of the room were painted white, without decoration or pictures. It contained neither a telephone nor a radio.

Fast Eddie looked at Judd. "You have more room in the back of your car."

"Don't complain. We'll manage."

"How?" Fast Eddie asked. "I got the eyes for some of those chicks but they ain't no room to squeeze them into these little rooms."

"Maybe if there's a will here, there's a way," Judd laughed. "Maybe one of the chicks will take you to her room."

274

"That'll be the day," Fast Eddie said, disgruntled. "With all those monster bodyguards and crazy dogs. I ain't going to even as much as stick my nose out the door. Especially my prick. I'm small enough as it is."

"Go to bed. We have to be up early tomorrow."

Fast Eddie slid sideways through the door to allow Sofia to enter the room. "What do you think?" she asked Judd at once.

"About what?" he asked.

"Zabiski's brother. Do you believe it?"

"I have no reason not to," he said.

"Strange," she said. "We never heard one thing at all about such a person, but he seems to have heard everything about us."

"What's on your mind?" he asked.

"The only other person that knows that much about us is Andropov."

He stared at her. "Do you think he might be working with the Russians?"

She shrugged her shoulders. "I don't know. I only know that I don't trust anyone anymore. Maybe he's working directly for the Central Committee of the Politburo. They're all old men, even Andropov. And they all would like to extend their lives and their power."

"I don't know what to tell you," Judd said. "Security told me that everybody, FBI and IRS, were trying to get to him."

"I'm afraid," she said.

Fast Eddie hurried into the room. "I scored!" he said.

Judd stared at him.

Fast Eddie looked at him. "You know that stewardess we got on the plane, Valerie Ann?" he asked. "I just met her sister. She's one of the chicks right here and looks a hundred times better than her sister."

He left the room before they could say a word to him. Then Judd looked at Sofia. "That may be the reason the Maharishi was expecting us," he said.

"Perhaps," Sofia said. "But I'm still frightened."

Judd paused a moment. "Nothing's going to happen until morning. I advise that you try to get some sleep."

She stared at him. "Do you mind if I stay with you?"

He pointed to the narrow bed. "In this?"

She nodded. "I don't mind sleeping on the floor."

21

SHE WOKE SUDDENLY on the narrow bed. She rolled, turning around. Judd was seated on the floor, motionless, his legs crossed in the lotus position. His eyes opened toward her. "Good morning," he said.

"Did you sit like that all night?" she asked.

He nodded.

"You didn't have to do that. I'd've made room."

He smiled. "I thought you'd be more comfortable alone on that bed. Besides I'm used to this position." He rose to his feet. "Want to join me in the shower?"

"If there's enough room for both of us, I'd love it."

"Come on then," he said. "We'll find out."

The water from the shower was freezing cold. She gasped for breath. "Jesus!" she exclaimed, shivering.

He pulled her to him. "This better?"

"Much," she said. She looked up at his face. "I don't understand you, Judd."

He smiled. "This is nothing to understand. I feel horny."

She felt his phallus hard against her. "Beautiful," she whispered.

He crooked his arms under her knees and lifted her off her toes. She wrapped her arms around his neck and hung upon his torso. "Oh God!" she exclaimed as she felt him slide deep inside her. "You're so hard!"

He looked into her eyes. "Isn't that the way you like it?" he whispered huskily.

"I love it," she gasped. "I love you. I want to keep you inside me forever." She began shivering orgiastically. "Oh God! I'm coming already!"

His hands grasped her buttocks so tight to his loins she was unable to move against him. "Go slow," he commanded harshly.

"I don't have the control I used to, and I don't want to come too quickly."

She held herself still and reached up to kiss his mouth. "My lover," she whispered. "My beautiful lover."

"Sofia!" His voice was filled with wonder. "I don't know what is happening to me."

She felt the tears coming to her eyes. "Maybe, Judd," she said gently. "Maybe you're falling in love."

He thrust himself into her almost angrily. "No!" he said harshly. "No! I cannot fall in love. I'm not allowed!"

She felt his orgasm begin exploding within her and she began to ride it with her own. She held her lips tightly to him. "Love follows no one's rules," she whispered.

They stayed locked together until their strength gave out and they sank together to the floor of the shower. The ice-cold water kept flooding over them.

THE MAHARISHI'S LIBRARY was walled with bookshelves from floor to ceiling but was without a chair, a couch or desk. Cushions were spread on the rug that covered the floor. His long hair was tied back away from his face, touching the shoulders of his purple cotton caftan. His beard had been neatly brushed. He sat cross-legged on a cushion as he motioned them into the room.

He looked at them as they entered, Fast Eddie following them. He looked up at Judd. "I beg you a thousand pardons," he said softly, "but I would feel more comfortable if just you and the girl would remain in this room."

Judd nodded, looking at Fast Eddie, who hesitated a moment. "Don't worry," Judd said. "I'll be safe here."

Fast Eddie nodded and left the room. The Maharishi pressed a button next to the cushion near him; the door closed and snapped, locked. He looked at Judd. "Thank you."

Judd sat down on a cushion next to the Maharishi. He turned to Sofia as she sat down before he turned to the guru. "The Phoenix is reborn out of the ashes of the Phoenix, just as the Dalai Lama is born at the moment of the Dalai Lama's death."

The Maharishi didn't speak.

Judd met the man's eyes. "You are not the same man I spoke to last night."

The guru nodded slowly. "True. My father warned me that you are a most observant man."

"With respect, I would speak only with your father."

The guru nodded. "My father will be with you in a moment." He pressed another button next to his cushion.

A complete wall of bookcases slid aside to reveal another room. This one was furnished in a more conventional style. Behind an ornate rose and ivory sandalwood desk sat the Maharishi. He, too, was dressed in more conventional clothing, a white suit, shirt and tie, a white silk turban on his head. He rose from his chair and bowed. "Mr. Crane, Dr. Ivancich," he said.

Judd rose to his feet and nodded. "Your son, Maharishi?" he asked. "Or your clone?"

"My son and my clone," the Maharishi said. "He is but one of many of my sons, or clones as you call them." He smiled. "But what, then, are a man's children if they are not clones from his seed?"

"I have come to seek knowledge from you, sir," Judd said. "Not to exchange philosophy."

"They are one and the same thing, my son," the older man said. "I observe that you are much like my sister. She too believed only in science, not in the truth inside man's soul."

"But you allowed her to experiment on you?" Judd guessed shrewdly.

"I was the first," the Maharishi said. "And so the first to learn that science by itself is not enough."

"She entrusted many of her thoughts to you that had never been imparted to anyone else," Judd said politely.

"But still we were always far apart in our belief," he said. "At the end she told me you were to be the heir of all her knowledge." He took out a leather-bound notebook and handed it to Judd. "Here are her notes from nineteen thirty-five until nineteen forty-four."

Judd looked down at the notebook and turned several pages. Some were in ink; most in a scrawled soft pencil. He looked up at the Maharishi. "German?"

"Yes," he said. "They were written secretly at night, in the laboratory of the Nazi prison camp."

"Then she worked for them?"

"We all did," he replied without hesitation. "There was no choice. We worked or were killed."

Silently, Judd gave the notebook to Sofia. He turned to the old man. "What work were they doing there?"

"Studies of longevity. The orders came directly down from the Fuehrer. He, as well as the Third Reich, was to live for one thousand years." He sighed, and turned a little from Judd. "At the end of the summer of '44, we all knew that Germany had lost the war. Panic was everywhere, among prisoners as well as among the guards. Then the orders came down that all the records were to be destroyed. Everyone connected with the experiments was to be killed.

"But my sister resisted. Taking advantage of my dark skin inherited from my father's second wife, who had been Indian, she placed me on the road along which the British Army was proceeding. Putting on peasant woman's clothing, she herself turned to the Russian lines to the north. Inside her clothes she held her Russian mother's identity card. And so we parted. That way at least one of us might survive."

"What experiments had she conducted on you?" Judd asked.

"The same experiments she ran on herself," he said. "It was a form of cellular therapy."

"Like Niehans?" Judd asked. "But where could you find enough of the unborn ewes you'd need for that?"

The old man met his eyes squarely. "There were none."

Judd kept staring at him. For a moment he didn't speak. "Are these the experiments she has written about in this notebook?"

"Yes," the Maharishi nodded.

"But I thought she had discovered some form of self-cloning. Not of using human fetuses."

"That too," the old man said. "But it was only one part of the whole." He took a deep breath. "The human will to survive is stronger than an acceptance of death, stronger even than any sense of morality."

Judd kept looking at him without offering a word.

The old man did not flinch. "Do not feel shock or disgust within you," he offered. "Soon you too will have to make that choice."

"I don't think so," Judd said definitely. "The tremendous advances in DNA genetic engineering make all her methods obsolete. We have already developed a number of human cells in the lab that cannot be distinguished from the original. Even cells that repair themselves if damaged and some that can reproduce themselves if they are beyond repair."

"Are you telling me," the old man said, "that you have discovered the secret of life?"

"Not yet," Judd said. "But maybe someday."

The old man remained silent for a moment; he shook his head dubiously. "I am sad," he said. "The secret of life properly belongs only to the Creator."

"What if it is man himself who is the creator?" Judd said.

The Maharishi looked into his eyes. "Now it is you who are exchanging philosophies."

"Is it any more difficult to think of this than of the methods of your sister?" Judd retorted gently.

"I have said before that I did not always agree with many of my sister's ideas and methods," the old man said again.

"But you did allow her to treat you as she would a guinea pig."

"She also conducted the same tests on herself," the Maharishi insisted. He paused wearily for a moment. "But all that took place many years ago. It is the now to which we must address ourselves."

"Agreed," Judd said.

"There are many things in her notebooks that are difficult to understand and obscure, even in her language. Perhaps with the notes you have already secured these will form a whole. Then perhaps we will be able to comprehend her thoughts and discoveries." He leaned across his desk toward them. "I am an old man," he said. "I would like to help you in that work if I may. My wish is to understand somewhat more of my sister's work and dreams."

Judd turned to Sofia. "Do you think it possible this man can help you learn more than if you proceeded by yourself, Doctor?"

"Yes," Sofia answered. "He is a unique part of a history we could never have known without him."

Judd looked up at the old man. "Would you object to our conducting our work here?" he asked. "We will have to install all the systems necessary for a more complex study. We will have to connect terminals that lead directly into our Computer Central."

"I have no objection," the old man said.

"Then we'll do it." Judd turned to Sofia. "It makes good sense. Besides, you will be safer here than anywhere else near our units."

"And where will you be?" she asked.

"I have other things to do," he said. "But we'll be in constant touch. We will meet as soon as you have completed all your work."

The Maharishi rose. "Thank you, my son, and may peace emerge from your discoveries." He paused, then added, "Now I am weary and I must rest again."

"Thank you, Teacher," Judd said.

The Maharishi smiled faintly. "I see you know some words in Hindi, my son. The word 'guru' means teacher in English." He raised a hand in a sort of benediction. "Peace and truth." He went to the door and was gone.

Judd turned toward the younger man, still seated on the cushion. "Your father is an extraordinary man," he said. "May I inquire how old he is?"

"Of course, Mr. Crane," the younger man said quickly. "He is eternal."

22

◆ AT SIX THOUSAND meters above sea level, white snow covered the top of the Andes, summer or winter. Judd, seated in the copilot's seat of the new Crane VTOL, with its peculiar X-shaped wings, watched the black cross made by its shadow across the glistening white snow from the sinking sun behind it.

"It's beautiful, Mr. Crane," the pilot said.

"Yes, Tim," Judd said. "We don't see snow like this in Florida."

"I mean the plane, Mr. Crane," Tim said. "It handles as if it were born to be an eagle. There's never been a plane like this."

"I know that," Judd said.

"If the Defense Department doesn't take six hundred of these, then they're nuts," the pilot said. "I've flown all of them. From the first Harrier to the last. This puts everything else away."

"They'll take it," Judd said. He looked over the mountainside cresting over the plateau. "We're almost there."

"Five more minutes," the pilot said.

Judd turned toward the rear of the cabin. Fast Eddie sat alone among the six passenger seats. "What do you think of it?" Judd asked.

"If we could bring all that snow into the States," Fast Eddie grinned, "we'd make a billion dollars."

"Always thinking of something to eat," Judd laughed.

"I bet it's bad cold out there," Fast Eddie said.

"Five below zero."

"That's bad cold," Fast Eddie said.

Judd turned to the pilot. "Tell them we're coming in. I want to go into the crater, not land on the plateau."

"Yes, sir, Mr. Crane," the pilot said. He turned to the digital panel of the radio. There was a squawk, then he spoke into it. "Calling Xanadu radio. Calling Xanadu radio."

A voice came through the speaker. "Xanadu radio hears you.

We have you on radar. You are seven thousand, one hundred meters on northeast track. Your coefficient is 21, 21, zero, 93, 21. Acknowledge."

"Acknowledge, Xanadu. We are locking in." He switched on the automatic direction finder. "This is Mr. Crane aboard Crane VTOL Six. Request landing in crater."

"You seem pretty big, Crane VTOL Six," the speaker barked. "I don't think we have enough room down here for you."

Judd spoke through his throat microphone. "Maybe you haven't heard us clearly, controller. I am Judd Crane and you're going to make room for us, and I don't give a damn how you do it."

The voice from the speakers respectfully hushed at once. "Sorry, sir. Just give us a few moments, sir, until we move several of the choppers up to the plateau."

"Thank you, controller," Judd said and switched off his mike. "Asshole," he said.

Ten minutes later the VTOL was descending straight down into the crater as if it were an elevator on cable tracks. Inside they snuggled into their fur-covered, down-lined parkas and waited for the signal to open their doors. A blast of freezing air told them they could disembark. The pilot pressed the button and the staircase opened for them.

Judd came down the staircase first. Doc Sawyer grinned at him beneath his fur parka. "Welcome to Xanadu, the top of the world."

Judd grabbed his hand warmly. Behind Sawyer he could see Dr. Schoenbrun. He reached to take the German's hand. "Welcome, Mr. Crane."

"Let's get out of the cold," Sawyer said, turning away.

They began to follow him. Judd took it all in quickly—men boarding copters being lifted to the plateau, others going up on the covered elevator built into the side of the mountain. Their flight bags told him they were going to board the large C-5s he had seen waiting to take off. Sawyer opened a huge steel door; they stepped into the warmth of the building.

"Two weeks," Sawyer said with no attempt to hide his satisfaction. "We made it in two weeks."

"Yes, Mr. Crane," the German added. "It is all ready for you. In the morning you can press the button and the nuclear generator begins to build up its heat."

"How long will it take to be completely operational?" Judd asked.

"A week," Dr. Schoenbrun said. "As soon as it reaches maximum power, it turns itself off and on automatically. It polices itself by robotics and its life span should be infinity."

"What if it malfunctions?" Judd asked.

"It shouldn't," the German said pedantically. "First, there are no moving parts, it's nothing but pure atomic power. Second, if there is a malfunction, it has capabilities built into it to repair itself. Mr. Crane, I assure you that this is the most perfect perpetual motion machine that man has ever developed."

"I just want to be sure," Judd said. "After all, it's my own life I'm betting on."

"The machine will work," Dr. Schoenbrun said stiffly. "I can't guarantee your life."

"Seven o'clock tomorrow morning," Judd said crisply.

The German doctor looked puzzled. "Mr. Crane?"

"We press the button," Judd said. He turned to Sawyer. "I'm going to my apartment to grab a shower. Okay for dinner at nine tonight?"

Lee nodded. Judd turned to Dr. Schoenbrun. "Doctor?"

"With pleasure, Mr. Crane," he answered with a click of heels.

Lee was seated on a couch sipping a Scotch on the rocks as Judd came into the room from the shower. He waited until Judd had tied the sash around the robe. "Feeling good?" he asked.

"Okay," Judd answered. "Why do you ask?"

"No headaches?"

"None." Judd looked at him. "What are you thinking?"

"I'm curious about the increase in the number of brain cells. What did Sofia think?"

"She said to wait and see. She didn't understand it, either."

"I'd like to run another series. Scans, EEG, the works," Lee said. "I'd feel better if we found the scan showed no further activity."

"What are you afraid of?" Judd asked.

Lee met his eyes. "That you didn't exactly tell me the whole

284

story. I think you did have some of those cloned cells injected into you."

"And if I did?" Judd asked. "I'm okay. I don't feel any bad effects."

"Increasing brain cells can possibly have a bad effect. Wild-growing cells could turn out to be a cancer, or a tumor. We just don't know."

"I'm okay," Judd said, annoyed. "Let's drop it."

"Cheers." Lee sipped his drink. "Being down here for two weeks, I've been out of touch with things. Did you finally meet with the Maharishi?"

"Yes," Judd said.

"Get what you wanted from him?"

"Some," Judd answered. "He had the notes we were looking for. We found out that he was Zabiski's brother. They worked together in a German lab almost until the end of the war. The study was longevity."

Lee was silent.

"The old lady was experimenting on cellular therapy long before anyone. But did you ever wonder what cells she was using?"

Lee nodded. "I have a hunch. Human fetuses."

"What leads you to that conclusion?" Judd pursued.

"Her insistence on artificial impregnation of those girls. After all, just one girl would have been enough to check your ability to produce a normal child. A dozen girls was overdoing it."

"But all those girls miscarried," said Judd.

"That wasn't your fault," Lee said. "I managed that for the girls. My stomach wasn't strong enough for what the old lady wanted to do. Human beings aren't yet ready to replace laboratory animals, no matter what those years working for the Nazis did to the good doctor."

"Did you know that I did have a child?" Judd went on casually.

Lee's surprise was genuine. "No."

"Sofia," Judd said. "I don't know how she managed it, but she didn't go through with the abortion. Then she made her way from Russia to the States to bear the child."

Lee stared at him. "Did you know about it?"

"Not until Barbara told me that day she walked out of the last meeting in San Francisco."

"Have you ever spoken to Sofia about it?"

Judd shook his head. "What was there to talk about? It is no responsibility of mine and I'm not going to change my life."

"But the child," Lee began. "What about it?"

"Barbara has it and that's fine with me."

"Aren't you curious? Not just to see it, but whether it looks like you—"

"Barbara told me all I need to know," Judd broke in. "So he has blue eyes like mine. I really don't care."

Lee rose to his feet for another Scotch. "Your're a strange man, Judd. I guess I'll never understand you. Probably no one ever will."

"That's not important either." Judd smiled. "After dinner do you think we'd have some time to go through the culture labs?"

"If you'd like," Lee said.

"I would like," Judd said. "Very much."

"Meanwhile, before we go down to dinner," Lee asked, "do you mind if I check your heart and blood pressure? Funny things happen at this altitude."

"Go ahead," Judd answered.

Lee picked up a small valise and opened it. "I brought my portable EKG unit." He glanced at Judd. "Have you been doing any dope today?"

"No. I'm clean," Judd answered.

"Lie down on the couch," Sawyer said. He attached the electrodes, carefully read the tape, finally disconnected the wires of the unit and began to check Judd's pressure at both arms and at the calves of his legs.

"You should check it on my cock," Judd said as he got up from the couch.

"No chance. The reading would go off the dial." He grinned at Judd and shook his head admiringly. "You seem fine. Blood pressure 140 over 80, the heart normal, nothing extraordinary anywhere."

"Feel better, Doctor?" Judd teased.

Lee got to his feet. "I'll leave you to get dressed now. See you at dinner."

286

DINNER WAS SIMPLE. Rare filet with mushroom caps, baked potato, julienne green beans and carrots. Afterward, a simple green salad and French Brie. The wine was Bordeaux, Château Mouton Rothschild '76. Then demitasse.

Dr. Schoenbrun's smile revealed his satisfaction. "A good chef is the epitome of civilization."

Judd smiled. "I never really realized you were a philosopher, Doctor."

"Philosophy begins in the stomach, not the head," the German offered.

Judd sipped at his demitasse. "Have you been pleased with your progress, Doctor?"

"Very much, Mr. Crane," Dr. Schoenbrun replied quickly. "By tomorrow the last of the working crew will be gone. Then only the basic technicians will remain. Perhaps no more than seven men are needed for protection purposes. After three months even they will not be required."

"That's very good," Judd said. "I must compliment you, Doctor. I can think of no one who could have accomplished this project so quickly and so well."

The German smiled proudly. "I look forward to the morning."

"I do, too," Judd said. "And, now, if you'll excuse me, I'm going to turn in. I've had a long day."

IT WAS ELEVEN o'clock when Judd joined Sawyer in the elevator that took them down to the laboratory level. They entered the small reception room; a security guard was seated behind a desk opposite the elevator doors.

Sawyer led them into a small changing room, stripped off his clothes and stepped to the shower, gesturing Judd to do the same. Afterward, they put on fresh aseptic linen, surgical caps and long surgical rubber gloves.

Another small antechamber lay between the dressing room and the laboratory. Sawyer closed the door behind them and pressed a button on the wall. A faint odor of ozone came through the ventilator. After a moment, the laboratory door opened by itself.

Two technicians were awaiting them in the lab. Sawyer nodded to them. "This is Mr. Judd Crane," he announced. In their unisex uniforms, Judd could not tell whether they were man or woman. "Mr. Bourne and Ms. Payson," Sawyer introduced. They nodded without shaking hands.

Sawyer led Judd to the bank of plexiglass drawers covering the walls. Each drawer was numbered, using an index system. There were three tables on steel tracks in front of the walls. On top of each table stood a robot arm that could open any drawer at the command of a computer keyboard. Next to the robotic arm, a three-lensed electronic microscope was ready to project the image on a large computer screen.

Sawyer turned to Judd. "At the moment, we're powered by six hundred and twenty-four batteries, working on four-hour relays. When the generator power is turned on, the batteries will cut off automatically. Anything else you would like to take a look at?"

Judd nodded. "Cells from the cortex."

Sawyer gestured to the technicians. Quickly they pressed the keys on the computer. One of the tables began to move along the wall; suddenly it stopped. The robot arm worked its way to the cell bank where it paused only long enough to pull a drawer and place it under the microscope. The technician switched on the large screen.

Simultaneously, all the lights in the lab went off. Judd stared at the screen. It showed a split-screen picture. Index numbers flashed above the top of the screen. One set of numbers was prefixed with the letter "C."

Sawyer spoke to Judd. " 'C' is clone, the other is real."

Judd stared at it for a long moment, then spoke. "I can see no difference between them."

"There isn't any," Sawyer said. "At least, none that we can see. But that is external. We do not know whether they work in exactly the same manner."

"They have to," Judd said. "They are exactly the same."

"Not exactly," Sawyer said.

Judd looked at him questioningly.

"We know what God hath wrought," Sawyer said softly. "What man has, is still conjecture."

23

◆ JUDD CAME DOWN from the Nautilus machine in the gym, his jogging suit soaked with sweat. He took a deep breath as Fast Eddie poured a large glass of orange juice. He drank it in gulps. "God, I needed that," he said. "I was all dried out."

"Have another one for you," Fast Eddie said.

"Hold it for a minute," Judd said, relaxing into a chair.

"There's two things wrong with this place," Fast Eddie said. "First, you can't go outside. You'd freeze your balls off. Second, there's absolutely, positively no pussy around."

Judd laughed.

"Not so funny," Fast Eddie said seriously. "I never figured you'd go for a monk's life. I always figured I'd get along on your leftovers."

"Sorry about that," Judd smiled. "Guess I'm just getting old."

"You're not getting old, Mr. Crane," Fast Eddie insisted. "You're getting bored. Your head's into other things."

"It's only been a week," Judd said.

"Seems much longer." Fast Eddie shook his head doubtfully.

"Anyway, the drought should be over by tomorrow," Judd said. "Sofia is coming down with the Maharishi, and he's bringing a dozen of his girls. He never travels without them."

"I hope they have warmer clothes than what I saw them wearing in California. They'll turn blue before we get them into the house," Fast Eddie said.

"We've got fur wraps on the plane for all of them."

"You think of everything," Fast Eddie said admiringly. "Who all else is coming down?"

"Sawyer and Merlin from Florida. Dr. Schoenbrun, back from Rio. The reactor is due to cut in tomorrow."

"Goin' be a big day."

"I hope so," Judd answered.

"I'm beginning to think that you're goin' a big sweet on Dr. Ivancich," Fast Eddie said slyly.

"It's a working relationship," Judd said, still denying his own feelings.

"A little fuckin' relationship don't hurt neither." Fast Eddie grinned. "Maybe we better have us a couple of toots just to get into training."

"You go ahead. I'm trying to dry out a little. The doctor's planning to check me over again."

Fast Eddie held out the second glass of orange juice. "Then you better have this now. You'll need some help."

"What makes you think that?" Judd asked.

"I know that doctor lady. She's got the real hots for you. She'll fuck your brains out." He laughed as he left the gym.

Judd shook his head in disagreement, but Fast Eddie had already closed the door behind him. Judd sipped at the glass of orange juice and finally turned to the shower.

HIS TELEPHONE WAS ringing as he was drying himself. He picked it up. "Your mother's on the line, sir," the operator said.

Her voice told him she was nervous. "Where are you, Judd?"

"Xanadu," he said. "What's wrong?"

"The baby's been kidnapped," she said, her voice shaking as she forced the words out as fast as she could. "The nurse was bringing him in from the park and two men stepped out of a car, knocked her down, took the baby and left a note in her hand and sped off." Her voice broke.

"Do you have the note?" Judd said calmly.

"Yes," she replied. "Read it, Barbara," he ordered as gently as possible.

"*We know who the child is.*" She read each word with difficulty. "*Also who the father and mother are. No harm will come to him if they agree to our terms.*"

"That is all that's in the note?"

"That's all," she said.

"Remember you told me that no one knew about the baby?" he asked.

She was sobbing into the telephone. "That's what I thought, Judd."

"How long ago did all this happen?" he asked.

"Maybe two hours."

"What time is it in San Francisco now?" he asked.

"Four o'clock in the afternoon," she said. "It took almost two hours to reach you." She began to sob again. "What are we going to do?"

"Have you called John in Security?"

"Not yet."

"Then get on to him immediately. He'll bring some men up there and they'll begin to work on it." He paused for a moment. "If the nurse has any information about the men or what they looked like, make sure that she tells it to the security men."

"What about Sofia? I feel I should let her know."

"I'll take care of it," he said. "Meanwhile, stay calm. They said they want to make a deal with me, so the baby will be all right. I promise you."

"You'll call me the moment you hear anything?" she asked.

"Yes," he said. "And if you hear anything, you call."

She took a deep breath. "I will."

"Now take a tranquilizer and relax," he said calmly. "It will all work out. Bye." He put down the receiver and called Security.

John was on the telephone in a moment. "Have Sofia and the Maharishi left Los Angeles already?"

"Five hours ago," John said.

"My mother will call you any moment now. She'll fill you in on the details. You make sure that everything is checked out. You start talking to your connections at the CIA. Try to find out if there's anything special going on among the Russian agents. Like a kidnapping. Not a spy this time, but a three-year-old boy."

"Got that, sir," John said without emotion.

"Now have you found out anything more about Dr. Schoenbrun? I have a gut feeling he's involved somewhere in this."

"Nothing shows on our records," John said. "Just the usual things. Attended the usual nuclear physics symposiums in the Scandinavian countries, Germany, Japan. Nothing special—they brought together scientists from all over the world, even Russia."

"Do you know whether he ever crossed over to East Berlin?"

"Twice. But only with a busload of tourists."

"Shit." He thought for a moment. "For the hell of it, check

291

Mossad. The Israeli Secret Service are cute bastards—they share information with their allies, if there's something in it for them."

"Good thought, sir. I'll see to it. How do you feel about the security where you are? Think you have enough?"

"We're okay," he answered. "Just find out all you can about that kid." He put down the telephone and called Fast Eddie into his room.

"Yes, boss," Fast Eddie said.

"First, give me that toot, then a cherry Coke," he said.

"Happy days are here again." The black man smiled, quickly putting it all together. "I love your shining eyes."

Judd took his two snorts and sipped at the cherry Coke. He looked over at Fast Eddie. "About how many of the Swedish ATW's do you have?"

Fast Eddie looked at him. "A dozen. You expectin' some trouble?"

He shrugged his shoulders. "Never can tell. You keep them near in a place next to us."

"Okay. Anything else?"

"The sleeve guns, .25 caliber automatic?"

"Two," Fast Eddie answered. "One for each of us."

"Good," Judd said. He took another sip of the cherry Coke. "From now on, the moment any of our guests arrive you stick right next to me."

"Boss, I'll be so near you, they'll think I'm sticking outta your ass."

IT WAS NEAR midnight when the Security telephone rang beside his bed. He reached for it. "Mr Crane, this is John. We have some information for you."

"I'm awake, go ahead," Judd said.

"We don't know about the kidnappers but we tracked two men and a three-year-old boy boarding a Canadian Pacific plane from SFX to Montreal. Then on arrival there, the group boarded a Cuban airliner bound for Havana. We checked with one of our operatives in Havana and they say that the airport there is locked up tight. The rumor is a Russian biggie is also coming in."

"Do you think we can intercept them there?"

"Doubt it. Too risky. But we learned something surprising

from Mossad. Our Dr. Schoenbrun, supposedly in Rio, is in Caracas. Our information is that he has two tickets besides, one for himself, from Caracas to Rio. Stupid son of a bitch, one of the tickets is for an infant under five."

"What about grabbing them in Rio?"

"Haven't got the people," he said. "Even Mossad, which would like to help me, has only two women at the office."

"Then we'll have to handle it ourselves," Judd said. "There's no doubt in my mind, they're going to bring the kid here."

"I can have an army of men at your place by midnight tomorrow," John said.

"That will be too late. Don't worry. We'll handle it."

"I'm sorry, Mr. Crane. We've really fucked this one up."

"You can't win them all, John," Judd said, putting down the phone. He sat for a long time on his bed, thinking. Finally, he called the control tower on the telephone.

"This is Mr. Crane," he said. "I want every copter out of the crater up on the plateau. The only plane I want in the crater is the VTOL. Understand?"

"Yes, Mr. Crane."

"Also any plane asking for landing instructions goes on the plateau. Not one of them in the crater. I mean that goes for *everyone*. Including Dr. Schoenbrun."

"Understood, sir."

"Also, I want to know the moment any plane requests assistance on the radio. I want to know who and how many people are on every flight. Got all that?"

"Yes, sir."

"And beginning at eight in the morning, you check me every hour on the hour whether we pick up any traffic or not. I don't want any plane sneaking in on us. Got that, too?"

"Yes, Mr. Crane. If nothing else comes up, we'll start calling you beginning at eight in the morning. Good-bye, sir."

Judd put down the telephone and switched off his light. Nothing had worked. He didn't sleep. He tossed and turned until the gray light of morning came in through the windows.

24

◆ "WHERE'S THE CHICKS?" Fast Eddie asked, looking up at the television screen and watching the passengers coming down the staircase rolled against the 707, which was parked at the side of the runway on the plateau.

"Give them a chance," Judd said. He, too, was curious. Sofia had already come out of the forward door. She started down the stairway behind the two men assisting the Maharishi. A few moments later three men came out on the landing platform. Finally a few girls appeared. In all there were seven girls descending the staircase.

"They never said anything about the bodyguards," Fast Eddie said.

"He's an old man," Judd said. "Probably he needed their help."

Fast Eddie was silent, still peering at the screen. "The doctor don't look too good. She seems very uptight."

"Probably cold," Judd said. He watched her carefully. Fast Eddie might have a point. Something about the way she was walking was not right.

He turned to Fast Eddie. "You show them to their rooms," he said. "When Sofia is settled in, give a shout."

"Where will you be?" Fast Eddie asked.

"I'm going down to the nuclear generator. Dr. Schoenbrun is down there with Sawyer and Merlin. The generator should be kicking in any minute now. I'd like to see it."

"You told me to stick next to your ass," Fast Eddie said.

"It'll only be for a few minutes," Judd said. "Nothing's going to happen right now."

"Okay, you're the boss." He looked at Judd. "Got your sleeve gun?"

Judd straightened out his arm. The small automatic appeared in his hand. "Okay?" he asked.

"Not bad," Fast Eddie said. "I'll check right back with you."

Judd came out of the elevator doors onto the observation deck, which circled the generator three hundred meters below the crater's surface. Schoenbrun was seated on a high stool, his eyes glued to the instrument panel. Beside him, Merlin and Sawyer stood in rapt fascination.

The German heard the elevator doors open and Judd's step on the steel platform. Without turning his eyes from the instrument panel, he said, "You made it in the nick of time, Mr. Crane. In thirty seconds the generator kicks onto automatic power."

Silently, Judd moved next to him. The second counter digital dial was going down. 25, 24, 23. The circuit lights showing the transfer to automatic power were still on red. He looked down through the glass windows at the generator. The white uniformed technicians were all leaving the generator floor and opening a locked door that would bring them up a staircase to the platform. The counter was going down. Fifteen, fourteen, thirteen, twelve.

Another door on the opposite side of the platform opened and the technicians came through it. Silently, each found a vantage point and stood transfixed as they looked down at the generator. No one spoke. There was no sound of machinery. Only the tiny clicks as the digital counter went down.

Sawyer turned toward Judd and held up his hands, fingers crossed. Merlin caught the gesture and did the same. Judd smiled at them and held his thumb up.

Five, four, three. Each of them sucked in air and held their breath. Two, one, zero. The circuit lights turned from red to green. Suddenly the technicians shouted and began to clap their hands.

Judd joined in the applause, clapping his hands. He smiled at the German. "Congratulations, Dr. Schoenbrun. Congratulations!" He held out his hand.

The German shook his hand, clicking his heels automatically. "I am very pleased," he said, smiling. "My congratulations and thanks to you, Mr. Crane."

Merlin looked puzzled. "But I heard nothing," he said. "No motors, no gears, nothing."

"Be happy, Mr. Merlin," Schoenbrun said, smiling. "If you had heard any noise at all, it probably would have been your last."

"Join me in my office for a drink," Judd said.

"May I stay here for a while, Mr. Crane?" the German said. "I want to look at my baby for a little."

"Of course," Judd said. "Again, my congratulations." He turned to the elevator, Sawyer and Merlin following him.

"Three billion dollars," Merlin said.

"That's cheap," Judd said. "It would have cost twice that much if the nuclear plant had not already been built and paid for, half by Ludwig and half by the government."

"I still don't understand why they stopped halfway," Merlin said.

"Simple," Judd said. "Ludwig cut out because he couldn't see a profit, and the government ran out of money. Brazil was already in debt for eighty billion and no way of borrowing. The banks and the IMF shoved an austerity program down their throat. They were all happy to accept my offer of a billion dollars and cut their losses."

"And you still plan to stay here?" Merlin asked.

"I will stay here," Judd said flatly.

"You tell him that won't work. There's no way he will live forever," Merlin said to Sawyer.

"But I can't say that," said Sawyer. "No one knows whether it will work or not."

"Only time will tell," Judd said.

Fast Eddie came into the office. "They're all settled in," he said to Judd. "I don't get it, though. I thought that the Maharishi didn't allow his guards to carry weapons."

"That's right," Judd said.

"Then there's something wrong," Fast Eddie said. "His men are loaded. Each one of them is packing an Uzi machine automatic."

"Did you talk to Sofia?" Judd asked.

"Couldn't. One of the girls said that she wasn't feeling well and had to lie down right away," Fast Eddie said. "But that didn't make sense to me neither. She looked straight at me and it seemed that she didn't recognize me. I figured she was stoned or something."

296

Judd thought for a moment. "Maybe she is sick. I'll call him and ask if he wants Sawyer to have a look at her." He picked up the telephone as Dr. Schoenbrun came into his office.

The Maharishi came on. "Yes?"

"This is Crane," Judd said. "I understand Sofia is ill. I can have a doctor look in on her."

The Maharishi's voice was reassuring. "I don't think that's necessary," he said. "She's been fighting a cold. I think the flight was a little bit long for her."

"Maybe an antibiotic will help," Judd said. He pressed on the Intertel screen. The face of the Maharishi filled it. Judd turned on the automatic focus. Sofia was seated on the bed behind him, a guard on either side of her.

"I think she'll be all right with a little rest," the Maharishi answered. "We have all the notes transcribed and fed into the computer. We can be ready whenever you say."

"Let's check once Sofia feels better," Judd said. "Give me a call." He put down the phone.

Before he could speak, Schoenbrun did. The German's voice was filled with shock. "Do you know who that man is?"

Judd stared at him. "You tell me."

"He's KGB," Schoenbrun said. "We've known him for a long time but have never been this close to him."

"You said, 'we've known,'" Judd said. "Who's *we?*"

"Mossad," Schoenbrun said. "I am not an agent of theirs, but I've worked with them many times. Even that affair of Eichmann. The KGB tried to get him, but we were ahead of them."

"Fuck it!" Judd swore. "Do you think Sofia is working with the Maharishi?"

"I don't know the girl," Schoenbrun said.

Fast Eddie looked at Judd. "I don't believe she is. I think they got her doped to the ears."

Sawyer walked over to Judd. "Now what do we do?"

"The first thing I do is get you and Merlin out of here," Judd said.

"Like hell!" Merlin said.

"You have no choice," Judd said. "Without you and Sawyer the whole of Crane Industries will go into the shithouse."

Judd called the control tower. "C.I. 2 refueled?"

"Yes, Mr. Crane."

"Get it ready for immediate departure." He put down the phone and looked at them. "Okay, get going."

Sawyer and Merlin stared at him.

"Go ahead!" he snapped. "You both have enough responsibility. I'll work this one out." He turned to Schoenbrun. "You, too, Doctor. This is not your fight."

"The hell it isn't!" Schoenbrun said. "I have relatives who've been trying to get out of Russia for over twenty years."

"But who was it you met in Caracas?" Judd asked.

"My wife and son came in from Switzerland. The boy needed an operation that could not be done here. We had neither the technique nor the equipment."

Judd looked at him.

"Besides," Schoenbrun said, "this is as much my baby as yours. I built that reactor."

Judd turned to Merlin and Sawyer. "Okay. You go now. Once you're in the air, we'll check back with you every two hours."

Silently the two men shook hands with Judd, then left the room. Judd turned to Fast Eddie. "Escort them to the plane. Make sure they board it. I don't want them hiding down some corridor."

25

◆ JUDD TURNED ON the Intertel screen and switched over to the camera scanning the plateau from the control tower. C.I. 2 turned onto the runway. A moment later it was racing into the sky. He watched it for a moment, then noticed another airplane on the runway. He called the control tower. "What plane is that?" he asked.

Before the controller could, Dr. Schoenbrun answered him. "That's mine. It's taking the technicians back to Rio. Now that the reactor is on automatic, I gave them leave to go home."

The controller spoke into Judd's phone. "B-737 for Rio, sir."

"Okay, controller," Judd said. "Any other planes on the field up there?"

"Only two copters and the 707 that just arrived with the last party."

"Where are the plane crews?"

"In the service house on the field, sir."

"Make sure that all planes are completely refueled."

"Yes, sir."

Judd put the telephone down as Fast Eddie came into the office. "They're gone," Fast Eddie said.

"Okay," Judd said, and dialed the personnel director. "This is Mr. Crane. How many personnel do we have here right now?"

"I have it on the computer, sir," the man replied. "Four guards, eight in the housekeeping department, ten in the food department, three in maintenance, four in air control, eight air-crew personnel, three lab technicians, and two in personnel, including myself. Forty-two in all."

"Are the guards armed?"

"No, sir. Their only duties are to record staff and guest movements. They are not security guards."

"I see," Judd said. "Very quietly, place all personnel on evacuation alert."

"Yes, Mr. Crane," the man replied. "I'm Jack Somer, sir," he added. "I'm from Security Central and I am armed if you need my help, sir."

"Just stay at your desk for the moment, Jack," he said. "Thank you. I'll stay in touch with you." He put the phone down and turned to Fast Eddie and Dr. Schoenbrun. "I have a feeling if Sofia is doped, the Maharishi will not get in touch with us until her head has cleared."

They watched him silently. He took a deep breath. "I have a hunch," he said and called Security Central and spoke to John. "We've been suckered all the way," he said. "The Maharishi shoved it up our ass. We've been following a decoy. How many men can you put down on his Malibu retreat right now?"

"Twenty-two, twenty-three men," John said.

"I think the kid is there," Judd said. "That's the only way he could have suckered Sofia into his deal."

"Want us to jump in?" John asked.

"Go in with copters. And blow anybody out of your way," Judd said. "Then let me know immediately whether I'm right or wrong."

"We're on the way," John said.

Judd put down the telephone and looked at them. "We might as well have some lunch while we're waiting."

IT WAS MORE than an hour before the Maharishi called. "Mr. Crane," he said. "Sofia is feeling much better now. Perhaps we can have our meeting?"

"Of course," Judd answered. "Supposing I meet you in your suite, then I will give you the fifty-cent tour of Xanadu. I am sure that you'd be interested in seeing the nuclear generator and the artificial cell-clone laboratory?"

"I would be very interested, Mr. Crane."

"Good," Judd said. "I'll be down in a minute. I will also have Dr. Schoenbrun with me. He has developed this whole installation and can answer any questions you might want answered."

He put down the phone and turned to Fast Eddie. "You go up

300

to the control tower. Set up at least four loaded ATW's and wait for me to call you there."

"I don't like the idea of leaving you," Fast Eddie said.

"You won't be leaving me," Judd said. He turned to Dr. Schoenbrun. "Do you know how to use a gun?"

"Yes," the doctor answered.

"Give him your sleeve gun," Judd said to Fast Eddie. "And show him how to work it."

While Fast Eddie showed the doctor how to use the gun, Judd called the personnel director. "Jack," he said, calling the man by name. "I'm going to meet the Maharishi on his floor, from there we're going to the generator platform, then to the lab. We'll probably wind up in my office. Try to keep us on the screen as much as you can. If you feel that anything might endanger any of the personnel, evacuate them immediately. If there is any danger either to myself or Dr. Schoenbrun, don't do anything. At the moment we're personally not important. Do you understand that?"

"I've got it, sir," Jack said. "I'll keep an eye on you."

Judd turned to Fast Eddie. "Ready?"

Fast Eddie nodded.

"Okay," Judd said. "Let's go."

They went out into the corridor. Judd watched Fast Eddie go up in one of the elevators, and he and the German doctor went down in the other. They came out on the guest floor and walked to the Maharishi's rooms.

One of the Maharishi's bodyguards opened the door. Judd walked into the room, Dr. Schoenbrun following him. The Maharishi gestured and said, "Peace be with you, my son."

Judd smiled. "And to you, my teacher."

Sofia came in from the adjoining room. Judd went to her and embraced her, kissing her cheek. Her face seemed cool. "Are you feeling better, Sofia?"

"Much better," she said wanly. "I think I had the flu or some kind of bug."

"Perhaps you'd be more comfortable in bed," Judd said. "There's no hurry. We can have the meeting tomorrow."

He thought that he caught a hint of fear in her eyes as she

glanced past him toward the Maharishi. "No," she said quickly. "I feel much better now. Really."

Judd nodded. He gestured to Dr. Schoenbrun. "This is Dr. Schoenbrun," he said. "Without him this installation would not have been possible."

Dr. Schoenbrun bowed formally. Shook hands with Sofia, then with the Maharishi. "I am honored," he said.

Judd turned to the Maharishi. "If you're ready, we can follow Dr. Schoenbrun."

"If you don't mind, Mr. Crane," the Maharishi asked, "may we look at the nuclear generator another time? We are more interested in the laboratory. I feel too much movement would overtire Sofia."

Judd covered a smile as Schoenbrun had difficulty covering his disappointment. The generator was his baby. But the German rose to the occasion. "Of course," he said stiffly.

Silently he led them to the floor elevator. The small elevator became crowded when two of the Maharishi's bodyguards joined them.

Judd reached for Sofia's hand. It felt cold and clammy. He guided her through the elevator doors. The guard at the desk by the lab nodded to him. "Mr. Crane."

They went into the dressing room. "The lab is completely isolated," Judd explained. "We have to change our clothing, shower, put on surgical uniforms, rubber gloves, and surgical caps."

The Maharishi glanced at him. "Is there any way we can look into it through a window?"

Dr. Schoenbrun glanced at Judd. Judd nodded. Dr. Schoenbrun answered. "We have a double plate-glass window outside in the corridor."

"I'll call and ask the technicians to show you one of the cell cultures on the screen. You can see that from the window," Judd suggested.

"I think that makes sense," the Maharishi answered.

Silently, they watched the window as the cultures were projected on the screen. Judd looked at the Maharishi, then at Sofia, as he explained that the screen was split to show the real cells next to the artificial cells. The Maharishi peered intently, but it seemed to Judd that Sofia couldn't care less.

"Now we can go to the office," Judd said, "and see what we have discovered from the last batch of your sister's notes."

They walked back to the elevators in silence. At the elevator doors, Judd looked at Sofia. "Sure that you're up to this? We can still go over it tomorrow."

"No!" she said, almost in desperation. "I'm all right. Really, I'm all right."

Judd nodded without comment and let them into the elevator to his office. Once inside the palatial room, he gestured them to a comfortable conversation corner. The Maharishi and Sofia sat next to each other on the couch, the two bodyguards took their place behind them. Schoenbrun sat on a side chair at a right angle to them, and Judd in a straight chair facing them across the coffee table.

"May I offer you tea?" he asked.

The Maharishi answered, "I don't think so. We're comfortable."

"May I go to the bathroom?" Sofia asked.

"Through the door behind you," he said, rising. "I'll show you."

She followed him as he opened the door. "Right in there," he said, palming two oxy-coke poppers into her hand, and then turned back into the office.

He sat down. "What do you think of Xanadu?" he asked conversationally. "As little as you've seen of it, I mean."

"An extraordinary accomplishment," the Maharishi said.

"That's only part of it," Judd said. "When it's all finished, do you know it will be fully automated. I could live completely alone with no personnel. Every one of my needs taken care of, food, rest, exercise, all communications, everything one could want."

"Amazing," the Maharishi said, nodding his head.

Sofia returned from the bathroom. Judd looked up at her. Her eyes were clear and alert now. She sat down next to the Maharishi.

"Now," Judd said, "what have we discovered in those notes?"

The Maharishi turned to Sofia. "I think Sofia might explain it better than I."

Sofia looked at Judd. "Really not much that we hadn't already known or theorized. For the first time we have real knowledge that she had experimented in cellular therapy using the human fetus. Later she began combining the human cells with the cells of various unborn animals, mostly ewes. It appears that the main problem she encountered was that an inordinate number of subjects could not tolerate the cell injections. Many died in anaphylactic shock despite the administration of massive doses of antihistamines and cortisone."

"Then how does that add to our knowledge? We've already gained that information ourselves," Judd said.

"That's why you were being urged to undertake the DNA genetic engineering process to create an artificial human cell clone," Sofia said.

Judd looked at them. "Well, you've seen it. That's already been accomplished. We are at the beginning of immortality. Man can now live forever."

"I am most interested in the formula you developed for this," the Maharishi said politely.

Judd smiled. "It's for myself alone. I have never thought of sharing it with anyone."

"I think you should, my son. You owe it to the world," the Maharishi said unctuously.

Judd laughed aloud. "Fuck 'em. I don't owe anything to anyone."

"I disagree, my son," the old man said. "Your son's life depends on it."

"I have no son," Judd said.

"The son Sofia bore," he said.

"She had the son for herself," Judd said. "I have no responsibility for him."

The Maharishi looked into his eyes. "Let's stop playing games."

Judd stared at him. "I wasn't playing games," he said.

The Maharishi was silent for a moment. "One telephone call and the boy is dead."

Judd reached for a telephone and placed it on the coffee table in front of them. "Be my guest."

Immediately the bodyguards took out their machine pistols. The Maharishi spoke again. "We are also prepared to kill Sofia, and with her, the child she is bearing in her body."

304

Judd stared at her. "Is that true?"

Tears began appearing in her eyes. "Yes."

"You're stupid," he said.

"Please, Judd," she implored. "Please give him the formula. It's not that important."

"It is to me," Judd said coldly.

"Even if they get it, you'll still have it. You will have the immortality you seek," she cried.

He laughed. "No way. Now, you're really being stupid," he said. "Don't you realize that the moment he has the formula, we're all dead. He's not planning to share it either."

The telephone rang, he picked it up. The Maharishi held up his hand. "I want to hear this conversation." Judd nodded, pressed the button, and the voice came over the speakers in the room.

"Mr. Crane?" John asked excitedly.

"Yes, John," Judd said.

"You were right. We have the kid. He's okay. Just crying to go back to his grandmother."

"Take him," Judd said.

"Anything else, sir?"

"No, John. Nothing more for now. Thanks." Judd put down the telephone. He looked at the Maharishi. "You lost one threat."

The old man looked at him. "We still have others." He gestured to his bodyguards. They moved slightly. The explosions of their guns echoed in the room. Schoenbrun slammed back against his chair as the bullets tore into him, then he fell backward with the chair to the floor.

The Maharishi was cold. "That might convince you that we're ready to do as I have said. The next bullets are for Sofia. Unless you give me the formula."

Judd stared at Sofia. She was pale, her lips tightened against fear. He turned to the Maharishi. "I have the formula. But it's very complicated and it's in Computer Central."

"You can transfer it here?" the old man questioned.

"Yes," Judd answered.

The guns turned toward Sofia. "Then do it," the Maharishi ordered.

Judd let out a deep breath. "Okay."

He walked to the computer on his desk. The old man followed

him with one of the bodyguards. The other bodyguard stayed with Sofia. Judd switched on the computer and began to make the connection to Computer Central. A greenish glow filled the screen.

Judd typed in the access code. "DNA HCC ENG. PROJ. FORM."

"What does that mean?" the Maharishi asked.

"DNA Human Cell Clone Engineering Project Formula," Judd said.

"This code is restricted," the words came up on the screen. "Enter your authorization number."

The Maharishi spoke to him. "Can you make a copy here?"

"Yes," answered Judd. He pointed to the tape machine standing against the wall. "Just press the 'on' button at the top, then press the copy button."

The Maharishi turned to his bodyguard. "Turn it on."

As the old man turned away, Judd moved quickly. He pressed the bar. Transmit and erase, forward and back. Then he immediately began typing in his authorization code. "JC1-1-02-102-JC1."

"Acknowledged," the screen showed. A moment later the letters "BEGINNING TRANS. DNA HCC ENG. PROJ. FORM."

The Maharishi called to his bodyguard. "The copier working?"

"Yes, sir," the man said. "I see the words on the screen."

The Maharishi watched the screen over Judd's shoulder. The numbers and letters making up the formula began to appear on the line, then moved slowly to the next line. "How long will this whole thing take?"

"About three and three-quarter hours," Judd said.

"Can you speed it up?" he asked.

"Yes, but it will move so fast that you won't be able to read it. It will just be a blur."

"How long will that take?" the old man said.

"About twelve to fourteen minutes," Judd answered.

"Do it," the old man ordered.

Judd immediately pressed the Speedtrans button. The picture on the screen responded and was transformed into a blur of indistinguishable figures and numbers flying by. He looked over the computer screen at Sofia. The other bodyguard was standing behind her, his automatic pistol at her back.

Her eyes fixed on Judd's dark blue eyes, as she asked, "Is the baby really okay?"

Judd nodded. "Really. You heard John. He's probably on his way to San Francisco and Barbara right now."

She exhaled slowly. "Thank God," she whispered.

Judd was silent. He watched the screen, the blurred lines kept moving. He turned to the Maharishi. "I don't know if you'll be able to understand it."

"Maybe not me," the old man said. "But we have scientists who will."

"Maybe," Judd retorted. He glanced across at the body of the German doctor. "What did that gain for you?"

"That Jew doctor?" the old man said. "We've known about him for a long time. He was due. And maybe it convinced you that we aren't playing games."

Judd was silent. He glanced at the screen. "I suppose you took care of the real Maharishi the same way."

"That was six years ago," he said. "His sister never knew she was communicating with a dead man." He glanced at his watch. "How much longer?"

Judd looked down at the tape meter. "About four minutes."

The Maharishi looked at him. "Call the control tower and ask them to bring our plane to the head of the runway with the door open and the automatic ladder down. Then have them bring a Land Rover to the elevator door with the motor left running and have the driver leave the car."

Judd stared at him for a moment, then called the tower and relayed the order exactly as he had been given it.

"Have the tower call when everything is ready," the old man said.

"Call me when it's all cool," Judd said, and put the phone down. The tape counter began clicking. Suddenly there was a bell and the screen changed to another typeface. "Tape completed. Trans. ended."

Judd turned off the computer. The Maharishi gestured to him. "Take the tape out."

Judd went to the recorder and unlocked the tape reel and took it out. He handed it to the Maharishi. He watched the old man as he opened the tape case and slipped the reel into it.

"Open the door," the Maharishi ordered.

Judd walked to the door and opened it. Three more bodyguards were waiting for them just outside the door.

"Okay, outside," said the old man. "The girl first, then you."

Silently, Judd watched Sofia walk to the door. He looked at her. "I hope God is watching over us," he said in a strong voice. "All that we can do now is keep our cool."

The telephone rang. Judd picked it up. It was Fast Eddie's voice from the tower. "Everything is ready, sir."

"It's ready," Judd repeated, putting down the phone.

"Then you follow the girl," the Maharishi said. "We're all going up in the elevator together."

"We'll need coats if we're going up there," Judd said.

"You won't need coats for long," the Maharishi said flatly.

Silently, they moved into the elevator and up to the plateau. A rush of cold air came blasting over them as the doors opened onto the plateau. The Maharishi gestured to one of his men, who then pushed Judd and Sofia out in front of them. Carefully they followed.

The Land Rover was standing in front of the elevator doors, its motor running as ordered. The 707 stood at the head of the runway a long way down on the plateau, its door open, the automatic ladder hanging to the ground.

Two of the bodyguards pushed past Judd and looked around. "No one in sight," one of them called to the Maharishi.

The old man stepped out. "Both of you. Keep your hands high if you want to live. Start walking slowly in front of us to the car."

They walked slowly, the freezing cold turning them stiff. The bodyguard shoved them roughly. When they were next to the car, the Maharishi quickly jumped into it. Another man jumped behind the wheel. The remaining guards pushed Judd and Sofia to the ground and leaped into the car behind the others.

The Land Rover began moving and Judd rolled over, looking at the two guards, who were lifting their automatic pistols. He thrust himself onto Sofia, raising his sleeve gun, and fired. One of them seemed to slip back clumsily.

The Land Rover was almost a hundred yards from them, and

the other bodyguard aimed his automatic pistol at them. Judd sucked in his breath and tried to mold himself into a protective blanket to shield Sofia.

Then he heard a strange rush of air as the ATW missile seemed to whistle over them. A faint ping was followed by a tremendous explosion. He held Sofia more closely, staring at the Land Rover. It was now a fireball rolling away from them. Then he heard another whistle and another explosion which hit the fireball, breaking it into pieces and flinging them into the air.

Judd pulled Sofia to her feet and began running with her to the elevator. A moment later Fast Eddie was beside them with several men. "Get Sofia into something warm," Judd yelled.

The men began helping her. Fast Eddie turned to look at him. "Are you okay, boss?" he asked.

"Okay," Judd gasped.

"Don't be fooling with me," Fast Eddie smiled. "This is God you been talking to."

THE NEXT MORNING he and Fast Eddie were watching the Maharishi's girls board the airplane. Fast Eddie looked up at the Intertel screen. "Shit," he said. "All that pussy an' I never got none of it."

"*C'est la vie,*" Judd said.

There was a knock at the door. Fast Eddie opened it. "May I come in?" Sofia asked. She held a heavy fur-lined coat on her arm.

Without waiting for an answer, she came into the room to Judd. "I'm sorry," she said.

"Don't be sorry," he answered. "Everything worked out all right."

"No, it didn't," she said.

"I don't understand."

She took out a box of Kleenex from beneath her coat and held it out to him. "This won't work," she said. "Even as it didn't work for Hughes."

"I still don't understand," he said.

"Everything you have here, everything you've done," she said, "it's like Kleenex. It won't work for you. Even if you want to stay here alone, you will not live forever, no matter how hard you try. All you will do is die alone."

He was silent.

She looked into his eyes. "Good-bye, Judd Crane," she said. "I'll tell your children all about you."

He stared at her. "Why are you saying good-bye?"

"Aren't I leaving with the others?"

"I didn't say that," he said. "I had the tapes erased for you, I turned off the power at the lab for you. Then I transferred Xanadu over to a Crane Industries nuclear medicine research facility, to be named for Dr. Schoenbrun. And now you want to leave me?"

"I didn't say that," she said, a faint hint of tears coming to her eyes.

"Then wait," he said simply, reaching for her hand. "Wait. And we'll go home together."